HER BAND OF RAKES

Other books by R. A. Steffan

The Complete Horse Mistress Collection
The Complete Lion Mistress Collection
The Complete Dragon Mistress Collection

Circle of Blood: Books 1-3
Circle of Blood: Books 4-6
(with Jaelynn Woolf)

The Last Vampire: Books 1-3
The Last Vampire: Books 4-6
(with Jaelynn Woolf)

Vampire Bound: Complete Series, Books 1-4

Forsaken Fae: The Complete Series, Books 1-3

Antidote: Love and War, Book 1
Antigen: Love and War, Book 2
Antibody: Love and War, Book 3
Anthelion: Love and War, Book 4
Antagonist: Love and War, Book 5

Diamond Bar Apha Ranch
Diamond Bar Alpha 2: Angel & Vic
(with Jaelynn Woolf)

HER BAND
OF RAKES

R. A. STEFFAN

Her Band of Rakes

ISBN: 978-1-955073-27-1 (paperback)

For information, contact the author at
http://www.rasteffan.com/contact/

Cover by Deranged Doctor Design

First Edition: March 2022

AUTHOR'S NOTE

This book contains descriptions of graphic sex. It is intended for a mature audience.

TABLE OF CONTENTS

ONE

"AT LEAST IN the country, folks won't constantly be whispering and nattering behind your back, Miss. That's worth something, isn't it?"

Cassandra Fenwicke stopped looking out the window of the jouncing coach in favor of meeting Mary's guileless brown-eyed gaze. Her lady's maid was perhaps a decade older than Cassandra, and had only recently come into her aunt and uncle's employ. The departure of her previous maid was only one small aspect of the slow-rolling catastrophe that had unfolded over the last few months. Mary might be plainspoken and unusually blunt for a servant, but Cassandra knew she was lucky to have a maid at all, after the scandal.

The *latest* scandal.

"Have you ever lived in the country, Mary?" she asked.

"Never, Miss."

Cassandra couldn't help the hint of bitterness that crept into her tone. "Believe me when I say, when it comes to gossip, country folk put Londoners to shame. There's very little else to do out here, you see. I daresay my presence will be the talk of Horsham within a fortnight."

Mary wisely did not reply, and Cassandra returned to her listless cataloguing of their surroundings. The Surrey Hills had given way to dense forest as they approached the tiny market town where they would break their journey for the night. Recent heavy rains had turned the roads to mud, slowing the horses and churning splatters of muck onto the sides of the enclosed coach.

At the age of twenty-two, her humiliating exile to a tiny cottage near the Wycliff family seat had come as no surprise to anyone. Indeed, the only surprising thing was that it had taken as long as it had for Cassandra's aunt and uncle to tire of her presence in London, after the shame her actions had brought on them. Most days, Cassandra wished they had never offered to sponsor her Season in the first place. If only they had shuffled her off to the country immediately after the death of her parents, so much unpleasantness could have been avoided.

The shivery, panicked feeling that sometimes tightened her chest when her thoughts turned to the events of *that night* threatened to seize her lungs. She focused intently on the trees sliding past the window, breathing with slow deliberation until the tightness around her ribcage eased.

"Are you all right, Miss?" Mary asked with concern. "You're very pale all of the sudden."

"Yes, fine," she replied in an absent tone, not looking away from the window.

Cassandra's hopes for a decent marriage were, at this point, almost nonexistent. Looking back, she understood that she had been marked for failure long before that fateful night at the Regatta, when she had allowed herself to be lured into the gardens after dark. No... even then, it had been too late for her. She had already been damaged merchandise, good for nothing except further ruining.

If only she'd known.

She took a deep breath, watching the vibrant green of the dappled forest slip past as the coach wheels juddered over muddy ruts. Perhaps the countryside would not be so bad. She'd loved it when she was small, living with her parents on their rural estate before things had started to go wrong. Indeed, she had many fond memories of riding through the woods on her pony, of long walks and quiet evenings on the veranda while the birds and insects chirped a rustic symphony.

If she kept to herself, the locals would eventually move on to other gossip... other scandals. She would become a female hermit, avoiding other people in exchange for them avoiding her. It would take careful budgeting, but if she could save enough of the pittance her aunt and uncle were providing for her upkeep, perhaps she could buy a few paints and take up watercolors again. That would be nice.

And maybe eventually, the townsfolk in Horsham would forget. Perhaps she could make a match with some tradesman or shopkeeper, thereby finding salvation from the loneliness and destitution of permanent spinsterhood.

At any rate, things would work themselves out somehow. She would be all right.

Mary gasped in surprise as the coach gave a violent lurch. Cassandra steadied herself against its side with one hand, her heart racing at the unexpected jolt.

"*Whoa, there!*" cried Leeds, the driver.

"What's happening?" Mary asked, as the coach rocked crazily, slewing to a halt in the mud.

"I don't know," Cassandra said, doing her best to disguise the tremor of fear in her voice. She cleared her throat and called, "Leeds! What is it... what's wrong?"

"Stay inside, Miss Fenwicke!" Leeds replied. "There's men on horseback blocking the road!"

Cassandra ignored him, at least to the extent of craning out of the window to look. She caught a glimpse of dark shapes moving closer before Mary's hand closed around her arm and dragged her back inside, out of sight of the approaching riders.

"What are you doing?" Mary demanded. "Don't let them see you!"

"Don't be ridiculous," Cassandra retorted, trying to ignore the worry churning in her stomach. "Perhaps someone fell from his horse and needs assistance, or —"

"*Stand and deliver!*" The rough voice echoed amongst the trees, carrying the unmistakable tone of command.

"It's bandits!" Mary's hands flew to her face. "Oh, Lor', Miss — its highwaymen!"

Cassandra's galloping heartbeat seemed to have lodged firmly in her throat. She swallowed hard, trying to drive it back down where it belonged.

"Leeds is armed," she said, striving for calm. "He'll chase them off."

"Hands where we can see them, friend," called the commanding voice. "We're after your coin — don't be a fool. Whatever toffs you're ferrying around, they ain't worth your life."

Mary lunged forward in her seat, grabbing Cassandra's hands between hers and holding tight. Outside, two deafening cracks sounded, nearly on top of each other, and Leeds cried out. Cassandra would have cried out as well, but her voice seemed to have disappeared. The coach shifted as a heavy weight slid off of it and landed on the muddy road with a dull thud.

For a dizzying moment, the wheels began to roll again as the restless horses started forward.

"Get those horses under control!" snapped the leader of the bandits.

The coach halted abruptly. Mary shrank back, trying to make herself small, as a man with a mask over the lower half of his face appeared in the window. Cassandra's eyes fell on the muzzle of the pistol that pointed at her. She found herself unable to look away from the dark hole in the centre of the grey cylinder, where death might emerge at any moment in a blast of smoke and lead.

"Hand over your valuables, unless you want to end up like your driver." It was a new voice, higher pitched than the leader's, with a sniveling whine lurking beneath the bravado.

"We have nothing of value." Cassandra hated the quiver she could hear in the words, but she was powerless to stop it. "I have no money or jewelry, sir. Please let me out so I can check on Leeds. Maybe he's only injured —"

Though he was in silhouette from the light outside, Cassandra felt the man with the pistol drag his eyes up and down her body, no doubt taking in her plain dress and lack of adornment.

"Fine coach like this?" he sneered. "And you expect me to believe you're poor as a church mouse? *Get out.*"

Mary gasped and clutched Cassandra's arm. "Don't, Miss! You mustn't leave the coach!"

"*'Oooh, Miss… you mustn't leave the coach,'*" the man mocked in a high falsetto. He steadied the pistol, sighting along it, and Cassandra jerked Mary to the side with sudden, overwhelming certainty as to what was about to happen.

An explosion of sound half-deafened her, and Mary screamed — the cry sounding oddly distant and attenuated. A moment later, Cassandra saw a growing bloom of wet crimson on Mary's arm and screamed, too. The desperate certainty that this could not possibly be real — that it *must* be a dream — gripped her as she tried to support her maid's sagging body in the confined space.

The coach door opened. Rough hands reached for Mary, and Cassandra leaned over her like a lioness protecting its cub.

"*Don't you touch her!*" she snapped, lifting a hand as though to use her fingernails like claws in the absence of any proper weapons.

The brigand grabbed her instead, dragging her snarling and spitting from the vehicle. Mary flopped limply to the floor of the coach as

Cassandra was pulled away. The maid's eyes had rolled back, showing the whites, and her arm still dripped a steady stream of red. Cassandra struggled and howled, trying to break free, until the butt of the pistol crashed into her skull, sending her into darkness.

TWO

FREDERICK ASHBURY, Viscount Rotherdam, was not generally a proponent of lengthy rides through the countryside. However, such journeys were marginally less trying while on horseback than they were in a carriage, and he was hardly going to force his London guests to travel the ten miles from Leatherhead to Hengewick House unescorted.

Aside from the stubborn persistence of highwaymen along the main road running through the nearby market town of Holmwood, the weather had been abominable in recent months. Torrential rains had pounded the area throughout the spring, and though today was a rare sunny day, there was still the danger of flood-damaged bridges and washed-out roads to navigate.

Though Frances Hunter would no doubt inform him that his chivalry was misplaced, Frederick would sooner cut off his right hand than allow her to make that journey alone. With Edmund St. Germain, his man of business, at his side, they'd made the trip to meet her at the inn in Leatherhead. Now, with the sun hanging low in the western sky, they were approaching the end of the return journey.

The horses were laboring in the sloppy mud covering the road, but at least he had no complaints about the company. Edmund was always good for dry and witty conversation, his smile a slash of white teeth against the rich brown of his complexion. Frances — dressed in male attire and riding astride today — was a reliable font of the latest gossip from London. Including, of course, the gossip about *him*.

"Old Treadwell is putting it about that you're planning orgies and satanic sacrifices in the ruins behind the manor," she said. "Apparently, the whole of Horsham is in on it. The town is simply *crawling* with devil worshippers."

"Good God," he replied, appalled. "As if I'd force orgy-goers to debauch themselves in a muddy field. And anyway, orgies are a nightmare to organize. If you lot want that sort of bacchanalia, you can arrange the details yourselves."

Frances let out an exceptionally unladylike bray of laughter, and applied the riding crop to her mount's haunches when the gelding balked at a particularly deep stretch of mud. Her face — too angular to be called pretty and too stubborn to be considered handsome — was shadowed by the brim of a John Bull top hat and framed by roguishly close-cropped chestnut hair.

"I can think of few things that interest me less than an orgy with you bunch of clods," she said, sitting the horse effortlessly as it plunged forward with a lurch. "As you know perfectly well."

"As long as we're not expected to organize the virgin sacrifices as well," Edmund put in. "There are limits, Rotherdam."

Frederick shook his head as he picked his way past a particularly ominous looking puddle.

"Where does Treadwell even come up with these ideas?" he asked.

"Well," Edmund replied patiently, "if you will insist on calling your little get-togethers a Hellfire Club..."

Frederick set his jaw, settling in for a familiar argument. "Don't be foolish. The entire *point* of the name is that we don't believe in any of that nonsense—"

The sound of two pistol shots, so close together that they nearly overlapped, cut him off in mid-complaint, spooking the horses and shattering the serenity of the dappled, late-afternoon forest.

"*What* in the devil's name?" Edmund muttered, his hand going to the butt of the pistol that Frederick had insisted he bring.

"Highwaymen, you said?" Frances, still wrestling her startled mount under control, sounded grim.

She was unarmed, but Frederick drew one of the pair of flintlocks he was carrying for the journey.

"Yes, I did," he said. Reins clasped in one hand, he checked that the weapon was primed and pulled the hammer back to cock it.

The forest had grown deeper over the past few miles, making sounds echo oddly and preventing them from seeing around the next bend in the road. Another shot rang out, followed by the piercing sound of female screams.

"Damn and blast!" Frances cursed, spurring her nervous horse forward.

Frederick exchanged a hard glance with Edmund as they followed suit, overtaking her in the terrible footing so she would be behind them when they rounded the curve. Unlike Frederick, who had seen plenty of action as part of the 1st King's Dragoon Guards against Napoleon's army at Waterloo, Edmund had never been in the military. He could, however, fire a pistol—Frederick had seen to that personally.

Ahead, a fine coach stood half-slewed across the road. Frederick had the brief impression of a mounted man holding the reins of one of the lead coach horses, and another holding a saddled, riderless horse nearby. One man lay unmoving in the mud. Another loomed over a woman, also on the ground. The limp arm of a second woman flopped out of the open coach door.

The three highwaymen—for that was surely what they were—looked up in tandem as Frederick and his companions bore down on them at unsafe speed. The man holding the riderless horse cursed and dropped its reins in favor of scrabbling for his pistol. Frederick clenched his jaw and swerved his mount, in hopes of drawing the man's eye, and consequently, his fire.

The pistol exploded in smoke and sparks. The brigand's shot went wide, though Frederick imagined he felt the heat of its passage near his head. No cries or faltering hoofbeats sounded from his companions behind him, and he let out his breath, charging toward the man with the same reckless disregard that had once distinguished him on the battlefield.

The highwayman's mount tried to skitter away, only to get tangled up with the loose horse. The animal reared in alarm, sending its rider tumbling to the ground with a sharp curse. Frederick pulled his horse to a messy, skidding stop and steadied his aim before shooting the fallen man through the heart.

The bandit who'd been assaulting the unconscious woman backed away in obvious fear, his hand scrabbling for a knife hanging at his belt. Meanwhile, the third brigand was frantically attempting to reload his pistol even as Edmund bore down on him. A dagger blade embedded itself in the flap of Frederick's saddle with a dull *thunk*, and he snarled in irritation, pulling his second pistol free of its holster and shooting the man who'd thrown it.

Another shot, followed by a cry, heralded Edmund's contribution to the brief battle. The third man curled forward in the saddle, wounded — but he managed to yank his horse around and kick it into motion, fleeing the scene.

"Leave him," Frederick called, making a quick assessment of their surroundings before Edmund could decide to go after the survivor and try to finish the job.

Frances had already slid down from her horse and tossed the reins over a hook on the back of the coach. "Edmund — get that coach team under control!" she called, as the wheels creaked into motion.

Edmund gave the escaping brigand a final look and went to take the lead horse's head before the nervous animals decided to bolt. Frances slogged through the muck, checking on the various bodies.

"This one's alive," she said, crouching next to the mud-spattered lady lying on the ground. Next, she moved to peer into the open coach. "Christ. Freddie, get your noble arse down here and help me. This woman's been shot."

Frederick did as he'd been told, bracing himself for the churning nausea he always felt at the sight of a bleeding civilian—especially a female one. His eyes caught on the woman lying on the ground, taking in her spun gold hair and pale, beautiful features, marred by the fresh bloom of a vicious bruise at her temple.

He jerked his attention away, confident that if Frances thought she was the more seriously injured of the two, she'd have said so. Inside the coach lay a plain-faced woman in the conservative dark brown dress and white apron of a servant—the lady's private maid, most likely. Her left arm and side were soaked with blood.

Frances knelt awkwardly on the seat, prodding at the unfortunate woman. She pulled out a folding knife and flipped it open, slicing the long sleeve of the dress away. A bit more poking, and she straightened.

"It's bad," she said. "Though not as bad as it could have been. The ball went straight through her upper arm, but it must have nicked something major. I need to slow this bleeding. Help me lift her onto the seat and then fetch me a stirrup leather from one of the saddles to use as a tourniquet."

Frederick nodded and helped Frances hoist the woman's dead weight onto the cushioned bench. His hands came away bloody, and he firmed his jaw as he went to retrieve a leather strap.

"How are they?" Edmund asked, as Frederick skirted around the unconscious beauty lying on the ground and resisted the urge to waste valuable time checking on her.

"Not good, in the maid's case," he replied. "I'm not sure about the lady yet." He unbuckled one of the straps from the nearest loose horse and pulled it free of its metal bar, sliding the stirrup off and tossing it to the side of the road.

"Where are we going to take them?" Edmund asked. "Holmwood? And, for that matter, can you even drive a coach?"

"Our destination has yet to be determined," Frederick said, thinking that he'd sooner trust Frances' skills than those of the pompous old quack of a doctor who practiced in Holmwood. "And I've at least driven pairs before, if not a four-in-hand. I'll manage."

"Better you than me," Edmund observed.

"Your property is closer, Freddie," Frances called from inside the coach. "Closer is better."

Frederick resisted the urge to sigh, and handed her the stirrup leather before succumbing to the temptation to crouch next to the fallen lady and check her pulse. "Do you have any idea what it's likely to do to these women's reputations if it gets out that they're staying at my manor, unchaperoned?"

A derisive snort, followed by the sound of cloth ripping. "Yes, my dear Rotherdam — I might have some inkling."

"You forget who you're talking to?" Edmund put in.

"Look," Frances said, her voice sounding distracted. "You can have their reputations tarnished, or you can have this one dead of shock and blood loss. Take your pick, *Your Lordship*."

The lady's pulse beat strong and steady beneath Frederick's fingers, though her skin was chilled and she did not stir. "Yes, fine," he said snappishly. "Your point is taken."

"Good," Frances snapped back. "Now get that one in here and put her on the other seat, so we can go."

"Are we leaving the bodies in the road?" Edmund asked, not sounding thrilled by the prospect.

Frederick scooped the lady carefully into his arms, heedless of the mud transferring itself to the knees of his breeches and the sleeves of his tailored coat. "We'll drag the brigands onto the verge — they can rot for all I care," he said, rising and lifting his unconscious burden into the coach. "But let's try to get the driver loaded onto the back."

"Just don't take all day about it," Frances grumbled, perching awkwardly between her two charges.

Frederick gave her a terse nod and climbed up to put the coach brake on, freeing Edmund to help with the corpses without having to worry too much about the team running off. Once they had the road cleared and the unfortunate driver stowed, he peeled off his ruined coat and used it to cover the man's face and upper body, while Edmund made sure his and Frances' horses were firmly tethered to the back of the ungainly vehicle.

Edmund remounted his own horse while Frederick climbed into the driver's seat and took a few moments to sort out the tangle of reins. With a cluck and a snap of the whip, they were off, heading to Hengewick House, his private den of villainy and ill repute.

THREE

THE SOUND OF crashing thunder woke Cassandra with a jolt. She started to haul herself into a sitting position, only to fall back with a groan as pain exploded in her head. Clutching a hand to her temple, she panted rapidly through her nose, trying to remember where she was and how she'd come to be here.

The room was unfamiliar and dark, lit only by a single candle on a nearby table, along with the occasional flash of lightning through the window. Rain pounded against the glass, rattling it in the frame. She was alone, lying on a well-appointed four-poster bed. The fabric of her dress felt stiff and scratchy in places, and her hair was unpleasantly matted in the back.

She was still dressed beneath the covers, right down to her stockings and slippers. It was that rather unexpected fact that finally sparked a connection in her fractured memory. The coach. The highwaymen. Leeds' heavy body, sliding from the driver's box to hit the ground with a wet thump.

Mary, with blood soaking her dress.

With a gasp, Cassandra tried to lunge upright again, with exactly the same result as before. Lying back with a whimper as the flaring pain made her vision waver, she cast her mind back, desperately hoping for any insight into what had befallen her after the pistol butt had impacted her temple.

There was nothing—just a long stretch of blankness broken only be surreal, half-remembered dreams.

The sound of voices beyond the closed door became audible above the crash of the storm outside, growing louder as the speakers approached the room. One of the voices was male, while the other was softer and higher-pitched. Some irrational impulse drove Cassandra to close her eyes tightly, feigning sleep even as her heart raced. The door opened, and the unintelligible murmur of conversation resolved into two speakers.

"Thank you, Sadie," said the male voice—a foppish and effeminate upper class drawl. "If you could, please sit with the lady until she wakes up, and then come get one of us so Miss Hunter may take a look at her head."

"If you're certain, Mr. Fortescue." The second voice was female, very young, and anything but upper class. "I'm only a scullery maid, though—not a proper lady's maid."

"Not to worry, my dear," said the fop. "At the moment, you're the only suitable female in the house who's not either unconscious or busy patching together a gunshot wound. Under the circumstances, I fear you've been thrust into the role of the lady's chaperone by default."

"As you say, sir," said the scullery maid. "In that case, I'll do my very best at chaperoning and come find you once she's awake."

There was a hint of cheekiness in the girl's reply, but Mr. Fortescue did not appear to be offended. "You do that, Sadie. Thank you again."

With that, the door opened and closed once more. Cassandra kept her eyes resolutely closed. There was a bit of rustling as Sadie found a chair and settled in it, followed by quiet—broken only by the pounding rain beyond the window.

As Cassandra registered that she and Mary had apparently been rescued on the road and brought to an unfamiliar country house, the awkwardness of her current situation grew moment by moment. *Pretend to wake up*, she told herself firmly. *Ask about Mary. Find out where you are.*

But somehow, she couldn't make herself move. An irrational fear still gripped her, partly at the idea of one or more unfamiliar men handling her body while she was unconscious, and partly because she didn't want to ask, only to find that Mary had been fatally wounded. *At the moment, you're the only suitable female in the house who's not either unconscious or busy patching together a gunshot wound*, Mr. Fortescue had said.

Mary must still be alive, then. But... a female doctor? Surely that couldn't be right.

"Miss?" The scullery maid's coarse Cockney accent broke into her confused thoughts. "I can tell you're awake. Would you like a glass of water or something?"

Cassandra opened her eyes, caught out. "Where am I?" she tried to ask, only for her voice to catch, bringing on a fit of coughing. Her aching head rang like a bell at the jostling, and she curled onto her side, clutching it gingerly.

The edge of the mattress dipped, and a small, callused hand supported her into a half-upright position before a glass touched her lips. She sipped the cool water gratefully, letting it sooth the dryness in her throat.

"Thank you," she rasped, as the little maid settled her back in the bed. Swallowing a couple of times, she tried again. "Where am I? And how is my maid? She was bleeding..."

"I'm sorry, Miss—I don't know about your maid," Sadie said regretfully. "Mr. Fortescue says that Miss Hunter is tending her."

"What is this place?" Cassandra asked again. "Whose house is it?"

"This is Hengewick House, Miss," said the girl, a bit hesitantly. "It's the country estate of Viscount Rotherdam."

Cassandra blinked rapidly, her stomach sinking. "Viscount... Rotherdam? Are you sure?"

Which, of course, was an utterly ridiculous thing to ask. Of course the girl was sure. She was a maid here, for goodness' sake.

"Yes, Miss," Sadie replied patiently. She seemed to debate for a moment, before adding in a rush, "You don't need to worry, though—truly. Please just lie back and rest for a bit. I'll go and let Mr. Fortescue know you're awake, so he can get Miss Hunter to look at your head once she's done tending to your maid."

Sadie rose and curtsied, flinching a bit when a particularly raucous crack of thunder rattled the walls. She turned and bustled out of the room, closing the door behind her. Cassandra watched her go, not certain how much of her roiling stomach was caused by the sickening ache in her head, and how much by the girl's revelation.

Frederick Ashbury, Viscount Rotherdam. A name that was notorious among London's upper ten thousand. His entire life was a scandal that put Cassandra's own humiliating ruination to shame — the only difference being that he was wealthy, male, and titled. Therefore, while Cassandra was doomed to live in poverty while desperately attempting to scrabble up a husband who could restore some modicum of respectability to her life, Lord Rotherdam was free to revel unapologetically in his scandalous ways.

Whispers in London spoke of a heretical Hellfire Club based at Hengewick House, with pagan rites, unspeakable and unnatural acts perpetrated in the shadows, and the most depraved behavior committed by a group of men without morals, all under the viscount's auspices.

More than one woman had been ruined within these walls. And while Cassandra was already ruined, she could not — *could not* — face the sort of abuse that such men doled out to women trapped in their power. Not again.

The panic started to rise. She pressed her fingers purposely against the swelling bruise at her temple, using the burst of pain to center herself. She had to find Mary, and somehow get both of them out of this house before the unthinkable happened. They were both injured, but that only made it more urgent that they escape. They were vulnerable, and alone, surrounded by the kind of men who cared nothing for a woman's honor.

Ignoring her churning nausea, Cassandra cautiously sat up and swung her legs over the edge of the bed. Vertigo assailed her as she rose to her feet, clutching the bedpost. She breathed through it, waiting until she was sure her legs would hold her. When her knees were steady enough to walk, she crossed silently to the door. No noise could be heard beyond it. The knob turned, the door opening beneath her touch with a creak of hinges.

After looking both ways down the hall to ensure no one was approaching, she slipped out and headed toward a stairwell at the end of the passage. She would scout for an unguarded exit, and then find her injured maid so they could escape.

This plan worked well for the first couple of minutes. The hallways were lit at intervals with candles set in mirrored wall sconces, and while there were signs of life, the sound of voices filtered to her only distantly above the sound of the storm as she made her way down to the first landing. A particularly bright flash of lightning distracted her as she rounded the corner to descend the next flight. She glanced over her shoulder at the window behind her, only to run straight into the broad chest of a man who'd been ascending the stairs just as she was descending.

Strong hands closed around her upper arms, steadying her balance even as her heart thumped in startled terror.

FOUR

"BEGGING YOUR pardon, Miss," the man said in a light tenor, as he set her back on her feet and retreated a step down the stairs, putting a respectable distance between them. "May I direct you somewhere?" He glanced over her shoulder, a furrow forming between his dark brows. "And... do you not have a chaperone to accompany you?"

Cassandra scrambled back a couple of steps as well, until she was looking down at him from a position out of arm's reach. The man was dressed in a sober black jacket and pantaloons — the garb of a servant rather than a noble. That wasn't what caught her attention, however.

He was, quite simply, the most beautiful male specimen she had ever seen. His features brought to mind a marble statue of an angel, sculpted by one of the old masters and animated with the breath of life. As he turned to glance down the stairwell behind him, candlelight illuminated deep russet highlights in his dark hair. It was long and straight — pulled into a tight queue at the nape of his neck to contain it.

"Who are you?" she demanded, clutching the banister as silently she debated her chances of mustering enough authority to order this man to obey her. He was a servant. Might he help her and Mary escape this house, if she demanded it of him?

He gave her a very proper bow. "Robert Barlow, Miss," he said. "I am Lord Rotherdam's valet."

Cassandra really wished that Lord Rotherdam's valet didn't have a velvet voice to match his ethereal beauty. His appearance and manner were putting her at ease, and she couldn't afford to be at ease right now.

"My maid and I need to leave this place as soon as transportation can be arranged," she said, aiming for well-bred haughtiness. "Where is she, and what is her condition?"

Again, that little wrinkle marred his perfect brow for a moment before the valet smoothed his features into an expressionless mask. "Forgive me, Miss. I'm afraid I have not been informed of your maid's condition. I would, however, be pleased to convey you to the room where she is being treated, so you may ask for yourself."

Her plan of surveying the house for possible exits in secret was likely going to be impossible, now that she'd been discovered. She lifted her chin, drawing her tattered self-possession around her like armor. "Please do."

Barlow bowed again, and gestured to the landing she'd just passed. She retraced her steps, standing aside to let him pass so he could lead the way. He headed down the hall toward the opposite wing from the one where she'd woken. His smooth, economical way of moving did not quite succeed in hiding the presence of a noticeable limp.

They grew closer to the muted sound of voices Cassandra had been so intent on avoiding earlier.

Steeling herself, she followed the valet up to a small knot of men gathered outside a closed door. There were four of them, and they all looked up at her approach, falling abruptly silent.

"My lord," Barlow said softly, dipping his chin in respect. "Your guest desires an update on her maid's health."

A self-possessed man with sharp cheekbones, sandy hair, broad shoulders, and very blue eyes stepped forward. "Thank you, Barlow. I will see to it—you are dismissed."

Barlow gave another shallow bow and slipped away like a shadow, though his eyes caught Cassandra's for the space of a heartbeat as he turned to leave.

She drew herself up, meeting the gaze of a man whose reputation made him out to be a monster. "Lord Rotherdam," she said flatly, willing any hint of a tremor from her voice, even as her heart pounded.

"I am relieved to see you up and about, Miss...?" His voice was not so much deep as resonant, and he trailed off in clear invitation for her to introduce herself.

"Cassandra Fenwicke," she said, trying to sound confident and unyielding, rather than terrified.

"Miss Fenwicke," Lord Rotherdam continued smoothly. "Forgive me for allowing you to be left temporarily without a chaperone. I fear we are rather short on female staff in this house."

And we all know why that is, Cassandra thought, but did not dare say aloud.

The other three men were watching the exchange curiously. Like a rabbit before a hound, she did not dare pry her attention from Rotherdam's striking features, but from her peripheral vision, she gained an impression of one very tall man with dark skin, another who was dressed foppishly in a garish waistcoat and plum-colored coat, and a third who appeared wholly unremarkable — the sort of person who could leave a crowded room and be completely forgotten within seconds.

"Mary," Cassandra said. "My maid. How is she? We were assaulted by highwaymen, and the driver of the coach was also shot." She hesitated. "Was he —"

"Killed, I'm very sorry to report." Rotherdam's features drew into a frown. "The coachman, that is. Your maid was shot through the arm. Evidently, she lost a lot of blood, but she's being cared for."

Cassandra swallowed past the lump in her throat as she remembered kindly old Leeds, drawing his pistol against several armed bandits in a doomed attempt to protect them.

"I see." A quaver crept in despite her best effort. She cleared her throat. Between the severity of Mary's wound and the storm outside, it was clear they would not be fleeing to the nearest neighbor's house on foot... assuming there was even a neighbor nearby in the first place. "If you were able to recover the coach and horses intact, might I trouble you for the loan of a driver in the morning?"

Keep calm, she reminded herself. *Act as though you're in control of the situation. Don't behave as a potential victim, lest you become one yet again.*

Rotherdam's expression didn't so much as flicker. "If the roads are passable in the morning, I will see that someone gets you safely to Holmwood. I've no doubt you're eager to be anyplace but here, Miss Fenwicke. Trust me when I say, I am equally eager for you and your maid to be elsewhere."

Cassandra's eyebrows shot up in surprise, since that was not at all the response she might have expected from a notorious rakehell who'd suddenly found himself with an unchaperoned young woman trapped in his house.

Apparently, she wasn't the only one taken aback.

"Good Lord, Freddy," said the fop, whose voice she recognized as her visitor from earlier — Mr. Fortescue. "You might at least *try* to be civil."

Cassandra held up a hand, feeling on slightly firmer footing. "Not at all, sir. It appears the viscount and I are in complete accord. Now, though, I wish to see my maid's condition for myself." She slipped past Rotherdam and rapped on the door, not waiting for a response before opening it and stepping inside.

"Charming as ever, Rotherdam. No wonder you have such a reputation with the ladies," a deep voice said from the hallway. Whatever reply Lord Rotherdam might have made was muffled as she closed the door behind her.

The room was well lit and spacious. A slim figure in mud-spattered boots and rolled-up shirtsleeves straightened from the side of the bed, scowling.

"Thought I told you clods to stay outside unless I called for you." The contralto tone was brusque—not to say rude. Gray eyes flashed in Cassandra's direction and caught in surprise. "Oh. It's you. You probably shouldn't be up, you know. I sent Sadie to take some broth to your room."

Cassandra blinked. The speaker was a woman of perhaps thirty years of age, dressed in male clothing, and sporting a head of rumpled, short-cropped chestnut curls.

"Er, I'm terribly sorry," she said. "But are you a doctor? Sadie—the scullery maid—called you Miss Hunter."

Wide lips quirked in irritation. "No, I'm not a doctor—but I'm the closest you'll get to one in this house. Quickly now, as I'm rather busy at the moment. Any blurriness of vision? Dizziness? Ringing in the ears?"

"Just a very bad headache," Cassandra told her. "I was dizzy for a few moments after I got up, but it passed quickly."

"Lucky girl," Miss Hunter said in a tart tone. "In that case, sit over there, and don't watch what I'm doing if you're at all likely to faint at the sight of blood." One imperious finger pointed at a straight-backed chair in the corner. That finger was, indeed, smeared with red.

Cassandra risked a glance at the pale figure lying on the bed, and looked away quickly upon seeing the piles of crimson-stained cloths and bowls of pink-tinged water. She slunk meekly across to the chair and sat in it, painfully aware that this room — with two other women in it — was the closest she was likely to get to safety in this house... even if one of the women was unconscious, and the other one dressed like a man.

Miss Hunter leaned over Mary's unmoving form once more, her back to Cassandra, doing something complicated with a roll of linen bandages.

"I expect you've realized where you are, and you've been plotting ways to flee into the night," she muttered without looking up. "You needn't bother, for whatever that's worth. The stories about this place are mostly just that. *Stories*."

"Will Mary survive?" Cassandra asked, the words barely a whisper.

Miss Hunter's hands stilled for a moment, before resuming their work with the roll of bandages. "She's lost a large amount of blood. I've managed to stop the bleeding for the most part, but tonight will be critical. If she makes it through to morning, I'll rate her chances more highly. Though I don't know that she'll ever have much use of the arm again."

Cassandra closed her eyes and wrapped her arms around herself, fighting the burn of tears. Her fingers brushed against the stiffened material of her dress, and she recognized the unpleasant texture as that of dried mud. It was in her hair as well.

The thought of both Leeds and Mary dying because Cassandra had been ruined and exiled to the country was unbearable.

"She'll live," Cassandra murmured, willing it to be true. "She has to."

The room fell into silence as Miss Hunter worked steadily over Mary's arm. A clock on the mantelpiece ticked softly, marking the inexorable passage of time.

"Why are you wearing men's clothing?" The words slipped out, hopelessly rude and impossible to call back once they were spoken.

Miss Hunter only snorted, though. "Because no one in this house cares one way or the other whether my legs are encased in breeches or a frock," she replied, rather cryptically.

Before Cassandra could try to come up with a response, a frantic flurry of knocks sounded at the door, and Sadie burst in.

"Miss Frances!" she began, speaking rapidly. "I went to get some broth like you said, but when I got back she wasn't in her room!" Her huge eyes fell on Cassandra, hunched in her chair, and her thin shoulders sagged. "Oh, good, you're here. Sorry, Miss, but you scared me!"

"I apologize, Sadie," Cassandra said. "I shouldn't have gone without telling you. I was worried about my maid." She gestured toward the bed.

Sadie nodded. "Course you were, Miss." She curtsied, suddenly looking very young and self-conscious. "Blast, I shouldn't have barged in like that, just now. Would you like me to bring the broth down here for you?"

Cassandra considered the prospect of trying to eat in the same room as piles of red-soaked bandages and Mary's gray, slack face. "No, thank you. I'm fine. It's kind of you to offer, though."

Miss Hunter glanced at her. "There's nothing you can do for your maid right now. Sadie, take her upstairs and heat some water so she can at least wash the mud off."

Sadie nodded.

"There was luggage on the coach," Miss Hunter continued. "I expect someone will have brought it inside so you can have a change of clothes. If you want to come back here afterward, that's fine. Just be aware that her condition isn't likely to change tonight."

'Unless she dies' went unsaid, but Cassandra heard it all the same.

"I'll be as quick as I can," she promised. "Thank you, Miss Hunter."

The woman waved the words off. "You might as well call me Frances. Everyone else does."

"Then you must call me Cassandra," she replied in kind. "I can't say it's been a pleasure to meet you — not under these current circumstances — but I'm very glad you're here."

Frances gave a decidedly unladylike grunt. "I come to the country for a couple of weeks away from everything, and this is what happens." The words were curt, but Cassandra detected no ill will behind them.

"Then I'm doubly grateful for your efforts," she said. "I'll be back shortly."

With a tentative smile, she rose to unsteady feet and followed Sadie to the door.

❧

After a quick wash that left the water an unappealing muddy brown, along with a change of clothing and the bowl of broth, Cassandra felt marginally more human. Her head still ached, and probably would for days. The purplish lump on her temple was painful and swollen. No doubt it would soon bloom into a hideous splotch of sickly greens and yellows.

Sadie fussed over her, the little maid's obvious good intentions going some way toward making up for her complete lack of skill when it came to dressing a lady. When she was once more presentable, she followed the girl back to Mary's sick room. Frances, now settled in a second chair that had been pulled up to the bedside, gave her a brief nod of acknowledgement.

It was clear that, unlike Cassandra, the odd woman hadn't taken any time for herself since arriving with her injured charges. Her dark jacket, smeared with dried mud, lay draped across the bed's footboard, and her short curls were in disarray.

Sensing that Frances probably wasn't the sort for idle conversation, Cassandra settled herself in the other chair. She intended to keep watch over Mary as well, but before long, the events of the day began to catch up with her. Despite her pounding headache, her eyelids began to droop, and she leaned back until her head rested against the wall behind her. Eventually, she lost the battle to keep her eyes open.

When a knock at the door woke her some hours later, daylight was pouring in the window. Someone had draped a blanket over her during the night. The dull ache radiating from the side of her head brought everything back in a flash, and her gaze darted to the bed. Frances sat watchfully next to her patient, deep bruises of exhaustion darkening the skin beneath her sharp eyes. Mary was still unconscious, but her chest rose and fell in a regular rhythm. Cassandra exhaled in relief.

The knock sounded again.

"Come in already, for God's sake," Frances called testily.

The door creaked open, and the tall black man from the previous night entered. He was dressed as a gentleman, but conservatively so. Cassandra rose instinctively from her chair as he approached, setting the blanket on the seat as she did so.

"Good morning," he said, in the same deep tones that Cassandra had heard earlier, berating Lord Rotherdam for his lack of charm. His accent was London through and through, despite his exotic skin color.

Frances made a sound indicating the quality of the morning was up for debate. "If you say so," she said, and flicked a glance at Cassandra. "May I present Edmund St. Germain, who is far too cheerful for his own good at this ungodly hour.

Edmund, this is..." She trailed off and frowned. "Sorry. I don't actually know your name."

"Miss Cassandra Fenwicke, as I recall," St. Germain said. "A pleasure... though I fear I'm to be the bearer of bad news this morning."

Cassandra saw a flicker of recognition in the other woman's eyes upon hearing St. Germain say her name. She cringed inwardly, but all Frances said was, "Oh, good. More bad news. Just what we needed."

"What news is that?" Cassandra asked warily.

He let out a breath. "The bridge is out between the house and the main road. The stream burst its banks during the storm last night, and it shows no sign of receding anytime soon. I'm afraid it's completely impassable."

FIVE

ST. GERMAIN sounded genuinely regretful, but all Cassandra could focus on was the realization that, if what he said was accurate, she and Mary were truly trapped here.

"You're joking," Frances said with a groan.

"There's no other way off the property?" Cassandra asked, appalled.

"Someone mounted on a decent horse should be able to jump a few fences and ride across country to the nearest bridge that's still passable," he said. "But there's no way to get a coach out."

Cassandra's stomach sank. She might have leapt an aging pony over a few downed logs a decade ago, but she would not be riding cross country over fences on one of her aunt and uncle's coach horses to escape Hengewick House. And even if she were desperate enough to attempt such a reckless thing, she couldn't possibly leave her injured maid behind.

Personal servants seldom married, since their positions demanded all of their time and focus. However, that didn't mean Mary's virtue was any less important than Cassandra's—particularly since Cassandra's virtue was already nonexistent, or nearly so. To leave Mary here, alone and vulnerable, would be monstrous.

Both Sadie and Frances had indicated that perhaps the stories of Lord Rotherdam's infamous country manor were overblown... but the stories themselves were enough to destroy a woman's future. It would only need to get out that Mary had stayed in this house of scandal, particularly if she stayed here *alone*. Her reputation would be tarnished forever.

"How long will it take to repair the bridge?" she asked, dreading the answer.

"That rather depends on how well the weather cooperates, and how quickly the flooding recedes," St. Germain replied, sounding apologetic. "How's your patient this morning, Frances? Because this will also mean there's no chance of getting the doctor from Holmwood in."

Frances scoffed. "He'd probably come here bearing jars of leeches, or wanting to bleed her when she's already half bled out. Good riddance to him, I say."

Cassandra, who had always dreaded doctor visits for exactly that reason, couldn't disagree with the sentiment. "You said last night that you'd feel better about Mary's chances in the morning?"

Frances' expression softened a bit. "Yes. It's a good sign that she's made it this far. The wound is barely seeping now, and as long as it doesn't fester, that means her body can begin to rebalance its humors and strengthen itself."

"That *is* good news," St. Germain said kindly. He turned his full attention on Cassandra, and she was struck by how dark his eyes were — a brown so deep that it almost appeared black. There was understanding visible in that gaze as he regarded her, along with a degree of frankness that was unusual in Cassandra's experience of dealing with gentlemen.

"If I may speak bluntly, Miss Fenwicke," he began, "I'm sure you've heard the stories of this place, and of Lord Rotherdam."

"Yes," Cassandra replied cautiously. "I have."

"Everyone and their dog has heard the stories, Edmund," Frances put in dryly.

St. Germain shot her a quelling look. "What I'm trying to say is this. Despite what you will have heard, you're in no danger here."

Cassandra set her jaw, bracing herself to meet bluntness with bluntness. "That might be the case—though of course, I've only your word for it. However, it's a moot point. By staying here, Mary's reputation may still be ruined."

St. Germain's eyebrow rose. "You're more worried about your maid's good name than your own? That's certainly… admirable."

Frances made an expression like she'd swallowed something sour. "It's not that. Our guest's name has already been dragged through the mud by *le bon ton*," she said, and Cassandra felt a flush of humiliation heat her cheeks at the knowledge that she had, in fact, been recognized. "No doubt she thinks it can't get any worse," Frances finished.

An angry response was on the tip of Cassandra's tongue, but it was cut off by the threat of tears blocking her throat. How dare this eccentric woman speak of Cassandra's ruined virtue while wearing men's clothing and staying openly in Lord Rotherdam's manor?

"Good Lord above, Frances," St. Germain muttered. "Does no one in this house have an ounce of tact?" He shook his head. "The point, Miss Fenwicke, is that Rotherdam only ruins women who ask to be ruined. Right now, no one knows you're here. With luck, no one need *ever* know. We'll hire you a driver who can be trusted to keep his mouth shut, and you can continue on your merry way to wherever you were going in the first place. Tell everyone you were set on by highwaymen and had to shelter in a country home while you recovered. No one needs to know it was this particular country home."

Cassandra blinked, attempting to mentally grasp the rope that had been thrown to her. Could it be that simple? Just... omit the damning details of where, exactly, she and Mary had stayed, and trust Rotherdam and his hangers-on not to speak of it?

She should have asked for an explanation... for further reassurances. But when she opened her mouth, what came out was, "What kind of woman *asks* to be ruined?"

St. Germain exchanged a look with Frances and let out a soft huff. "You're standing in a room with one. Maybe you should ask her."

"Now who's lacking in tact?" Frances muttered, though she didn't sound particularly angry. She met Cassandra's eyes with a decidedly challenging look. "Try being promised to a brute three times your age who beat his last wife to death while she was pregnant. Suddenly, the prospect of being too badly ruined to wed begins to look rosy by comparison."

Cassandra blanched. "So you *asked* Lord Rotherdam...?"

"I begged Freddie to spread it about that I was his latest mistress, yes," Frances said without any indication of shame. "My sadistic old goat of a fiancé couldn't drop me fast enough, once he found out. Neither could my parents. At which point, I was a free woman."

Cassandra gaped at her. "But... how do you live without any support?"

Frances' clothing might be male, but it was of decent quality, and not too old. She had the look of someone with enough food to eat, and a roof over her head. She was a guest at a lord's manor house... or was Rotherdam perhaps supporting her financially?

"I apprenticed myself to a doctor in London who was too much of a drunkard to care that I was a woman, as long as I did my job and kept his practice afloat," Frances said, neatly cutting off Cassandra's wild speculation. "It turns out, if you cure their ills and bandage their hurts, most people in big cities don't actually care if you have tits or not."

Cassandra blushed scarlet at the coarse language, even as her mind raced.

"Please don't scandalize the guests, Frances," St. Germain said, though Cassandra thought she could detect a twinkle of amusement in his dark eyes. "You'll have to forgive her, Miss Fenwicke.

Though in her defense, I doubt she's had a wink of sleep in the last twenty-four hours."

"Indeed, I have not," Frances said in a haughty tone. "So if you could go find Sadie and bring her up here to spell me while I catch a nap on the floor, it would be very much appreciated."

Guilt pricked at Cassandra's conscience, after she'd slept half the night away while Frances tirelessly watched over Mary. "I could—" she began.

Frances held up a hand. "No thank you. You've got a head wound and no medical training."

Cassandra frowned. "And the scullery maid *does* have medical training?"

Frances shook her head. "Perhaps not formally, but she's watched over a lot more injured people than you have, I'm willing to bet. She's helped me before. She knows what to look for and when to wake me if I'm needed. Edmund, why don't you take Miss Fenwicke and get her some breakfast?" She paused. "Assuming we've successfully convinced her that she won't be assaulted in a hallway, or dragged outside to play the centerpiece in a virgin sacrifice."

"It's too muddy outside for virgin sacrifices," St. Germain said, utterly deadpan. "My boots still haven't recovered from slogging through the mud yesterday."

"You're both quite mad," Cassandra told them, looking from one to the other.

"Mad?" St. Germain asked, clearly unoffended. "Us? No, I believe you must be thinking of

Fortescue. No one sane wears waistcoats that garish."

"I like the green and gold one," Frances put in. "But that one with the apricot-colored stripes... definitely not."

Cassandra opened her mouth, aware that she'd lost her grip on this conversation some time ago. Eventually, she managed, "Breakfast would be lovely, thank you."

⚜

Seated in an airy drawing room with a pot of hot chocolate, along with a plate piled high with ginger cakes and brioche, Cassandra attempted to control the nerves that had her stomach full of butterflies.

St. Germain sat across from her, sipping tea. This was the second time in less than a day that she'd been alone with a man to whom she wasn't related. Such a situation would never have arisen in her aunt and uncle's house. Indeed, the last time it *had*...

She ruthlessly shut down that line of thinking, but not before it brought on the first stirrings of panic.

Perhaps something showed in her face, because St. Germain frowned and set his teacup in its saucer. "Would you prefer to dine alone? I can send one of the servants to escort you to your room when you've finished eating—or to your maid's sickroom."

Cassandra took a slow breath and held it, then let it out, her racing heart calming by degrees as she did. St. Germain had been... not the picture of decorum, by any means, but entirely unthreatening. There was a certain aura of serenity surrounding him. Just as she had trusted Barlow, the valet, to conduct her to Mary's side last night, when every rational instinct should have cried out that she was in danger, she wanted to trust St. Germain when he said that no one here would harm her.

"No," she said. "Forgive me. I would much prefer company and conversation to distract me from worry over Mary's injury." She cast around for a conversational topic. "Where is Lord Rotherdam this morning, if I may ask?"

"He's out surveying the damage from the storm, as far as I know," her companion said easily. "Apparently he hasn't had enough of muddy boots yet, unlike the rest of us." He gave a low chuckle. "Though I've no doubt Barlow has had more than enough of dealing with mud."

As the viscount's valet, Barlow would be responsible for cleaning Lord Rotherdam's clothing and keeping his boots polished to a high shine, so she suspected St. Germain was right about that.

"I may owe Mr. Barlow an apology, in that case," she said. "Since I'm indirectly responsible for at least some of his recent travails." It was meant as a joke, but immediately the unwanted thoughts crowded in.

If you hadn't been so stupid, you wouldn't have destroyed your prospects in London.

You wouldn't have angered your aunt and uncle.

You wouldn't have been sent off to the country.

You wouldn't have been in danger.

Mary wouldn't be gravely injured.
Leeds wouldn't be dead.

She glanced down and took a shaky sip of hot chocolate to cover her sudden upset.

St. Germain leaned back in his chair, regarding her.

"Look, do you want to talk about it?" he asked. "I'm sure it's terribly improper of me to ask, but whatever it is, it can't be any worse than Frances' temper or Fortescue's waistcoats."

Her eyes flew to his, shocked that he would ask outright, rather than pretending he hadn't heard Frances telling him she was ruined.

He gave a little tilt of the head that was as effective as a shrug. "I'm no gentleman, despite appearances. This lot" — he gestured at the grand drawing room, indicating *the upper class* in a general sort of way — "it's all about appearances with them."

"Aren't you Lord Rotherdam's friend?" she asked, startled.

He huffed out a breath of amusement. "These days I'm his private secretary. His *man of business*." His tone imbued the words with a faint sense of mockery. "We went to Cambridge together — the viscount, and a no-name son of free Jamaicans. My skin was too dark, and he was too full of heretical ideas. So we ended up as fellow outcasts, drinking too much and debating philosophy into the small hours of the morning. In my spare time, I'm an artist."

Cassandra took that in, her hot chocolate and brioche forgotten.

"Not that being Rotherdam's private secretary leaves much in the way of spare time, considering how much scandal he attracts," St. Germain continued wryly. "But at least the pay is generous."

Cassandra nearly choked on a snort of laughter, scandalized and amused in equal measure — her momentary panic forgotten.

"What sort of artist?" she asked, because that seemed like the safest question.

"A painter," he replied. "I work mostly in oils."

She sat forward. "Really? I'm hoping to return to watercolors once I get settled in Horsham. My parents gave me lessons before… well." She cleared her throat, not willing to complete the thought. "Anyway, I always wanted to try oils, but it's not considered a ladylike pursuit." A bitter little husk of a laugh escaped her throat. "I wasn't even allowed to paint irises or lilies because my tutor thought they were *too sensual*." She frowned. "I've never understood why."

St. Germain stared at her for a moment, and then burst into full-throated laughter. It was a very nice laugh, even if it was probably directed at her.

"Oh, my stars," he said, once he'd regained control. "Too sensual? That really is the back of beyond." He shook his head ruefully. "I'd explain it to you, but Rotherdam would have my hide. Tell you what, though… if you get bored around midday, come to the studio at the end of the hall on the same floor as the room they put you in. No irises, I'm afraid — but I suppose there will still be enough sensuality to go around."

A strange shiver went through her, in tandem with an even stranger realization. No one knew she was here, in the manor that hosted Lord Rotherdam's infamous Hellfire Club. And even if they did, she couldn't possibly be any more compromised than she already was.

She could go to St. Germain's studio and watch him paint something sensual with oils, and there was no one here to disapprove. No one to punish her, or berate her, or consign her to the devil.

"Thank you," she said, a bit distractedly. "I'll... consider your invitation."

He nodded. "You do that. Now, though... *do* you want to talk about it, whatever 'it' is? Because to be utterly frank, no one here cares to judge you, and we're quite difficult to shock."

Unbidden, Cassandra's mind flashed back to what Frances had said to her the previous night. *No one in this house cares one way or the other whether my legs are encased in breeches or a frock.*

Could Frances begging Lord Rotherdam to ruin her so she could escape an unwanted marriage really be any worse than Cassandra's fatal lack of judgment? And would she ever have a better chance to unburden herself than this?

She took a deep breath, the butterflies in her stomach dancing wildly.

"I did something unforgivably stupid," she began. "Worse, I did it twice." She paused. Swallowed. When she continued, her voice was barely a whisper. "But the first time, I will never regret... no matter how many people disapprove of me for it."

SIX

"THERE WAS a man, I assume?" St. Germain asked without judgment. "Or... perhaps two men?"

Cassandra sighed. "Two men, yes. Though separated by several years."

Her companion leaned back in his chair, watching her with interest. "I must say, I'm far more interested in hearing about the one you don't regret."

It had been a long time since Cassandra had truly remembered that fateful night, along with everything that came before, and after. It ached, but in a bittersweet way. She was appalled to find that her memory of Tom's face had grown hazy as time passed.

"There was a soldier," she said softly. "Thomas Jacoby, whose family lived down the road from mine. I was eighteen, and he was twenty. He came home for a visit... and he was no longer the gawky boy I'd grown up with."

"He courted you?" St. Germain prompted.

A sad smile tugged at Cassandra's lips for a moment before disappearing. "He did. And I daresay I encouraged him." It felt oddly liberating to tell the story to someone who might not be shocked by it. She took a deep breath, and let it out slowly. "He snuck onto the grounds one evening, when everyone should have been in bed. I crept out of my room to meet him in the gardens. He was to be deployed to the front against Napoleon's forces, and he wished me to marry him when he returned."

"He didn't go to your parents first?" St. Germain asked.

Cassandra pressed her lips together. "No," she said, after a slight hesitation. "They would not have accepted the match, and I suspect he knew it. They had expectations that I would marry into money, or at least a title. Not wed a penniless soldier born to farmers."

"But you wished to marry him?"

"I was in love with him," she said simply. "I said yes, and he kissed me. Which, unfortunately, was exactly the moment when my father appeared in the garden in a towering rage, having been roused by the butler. Baldwin must have heard us talking and gone to get him — the old goat."

St. Germain winced. "Still, " he said, "if your Thomas had already intended to marry you…"

"That was *my* argument as well," Cassandra said with some heat. "And it should have worked out, with both of us happy — even if my parents were not. But then Tom left to fight that *horrible* war." She drew breath to speak the next words, but they caught in her throat.

The silence stretched for a long moment.

"He didn't come back," St. Germain said quietly, his deep voice subdued.

"No," she said, past the tightness in her throat. "He didn't come back."

Her companion let out a heavy sigh.

"Rotherdam fought in the war, you know," he said slowly. "Barlow, as well. It changed them both."

Cassandra nodded, not surprised. "I noticed Barlow's limp."

St. Germain nodded in reply. "He's a war hero, believe it or not. He saved Rotherdam's platoon by riding through enemy lines for reinforcements during the Battle of Waterloo. Nearly got killed doing it, too—the crazy bastard."

Cassandra blinked, trying without success to picture the mild-mannered, almost unbearably beautiful valet galloping across a field of mud and blood.

"I'm glad he didn't," she said.

"I'm sorry your Thomas did," St. Germain told her.

They sat in silence for a bit, Cassandra picking listlessly at her breakfast.

"At any rate," she continued at length, "that might have been the end of it, had the servants not gossiped. The scandal got out, and while it was perhaps not as bad as it might have been, it still tainted my reputation."

"I see," said St. Germain. "And yet, I somehow doubt this is the scandal that made it all the way to Frances' ears. Would I be correct in assuming that was down to the second man in question?"

Suddenly, the conversation no longer felt liberating. Cassandra's cheeks heated as her pulse picked up, thundering unpleasantly.

"I don't wish to speak of that," she managed.

"Then we won't," St. Germain replied easily, and changed the subject. "Tell me instead about your training in watercolors. I've very little experience with the medium, but John Linnell has been doing some fascinating work painting landscapes with the aid of a camera obscura..."

With relief, Cassandra fell headfirst into the discussion of art techniques, asking questions and answering them until her heartbeat settled and the churning of her stomach quieted.

After breakfast, St. Germain summoned a footman — barely more than a lad — to escort Cassandra back to her room. It wasn't proper, admittedly, but Sadie was doubtless still watching over Mary while Frances slept, and the wide-eyed servant boy was hardly a threat as he self-importantly guided her along hallways and up stairwells.

Despite only having been awake for a short time, Cassandra's exhaustion and aching head drew her to nap for a couple of hours. The sound of distant thunder woke her. Fresh storms were rolling in, it seemed, and she wondered if the weather would further slow the repair of the damaged bridge.

She lay awake, contemplating her predicament. Would it truly be so bad to be trapped here for a few days? If no one could get in, and no one could get out, her presence here with Mary might indeed remain a secret as long as St. Germain was good to his word.

Unless her uncle had sent a letter ahead to someone in Horsham informing them of her imminent arrival, no one there would be expecting her. She'd anticipated arriving to find a cold and empty cottage waiting for her. Her guardians had sent her with only enough money to acquire lodging along the way and purchase a bit of food for the house upon her arrival. Any necessary repairs would no doubt rely on the generosity of neighbors or the local church.

Would her aunt and uncle even notice if Cassandra went missing for a week? She wasn't certain. She would be expected to write a grateful letter to them upon her arrival, thanking them for their generosity in continuing to support her. But the storms and floods would doubtless delay the mail.

Staring at her comfortable guest bedroom nestled inside the huge manor house, it was growing increasingly difficult to muster motivation for a grand escape plan.

Midday had arrived as she lay contemplating her circumstances. Outside, brilliant sunshine played hide-and-go-seek with the approaching storm clouds. Down the hall, St. Germain would be ensconced in his studio, painting something of which Cassandra's long-ago watercolor tutor would surely not approve.

She could go and see... and doing so would not add a single dram of scandal to her already scandalous presence here. No one in the *ton* would say, "*Oh, yes, it's true she spent the night unchaperoned amongst Lord Rotherdam's notorious*

Hellfire Club… but at least she did not observe a man painting in oils."

Speaking of the Hellfire Club—aside from a handful of jests, she'd seen precious little evidence of heretical goings-on since she'd arrived. Admittedly, she'd been asleep or unconscious for much of that time, and the foul weather probably wasn't all that conducive to virgin sacrifices. But even so, she would have expected a Hellfire Club to be more… exciting.

Perhaps she would ask St. Germain.

Decision made, Cassandra rose and put herself to rights as best she could. She was frowning at her unacceptable attempt at a plait when a knock sounded at the door. Despite herself, her breath caught in startlement, but Sadie's high-pitched voice followed a moment later.

"Miss? Are you awake?"

"Come in, Sadie," she called, relieved that she would have an ally in the battle against her hair.

The door opened, and the little scullery maid entered, curtseying. "Thank you, Miss. I'm supposed to tell you that Mary hasn't woken yet, but her breathing and heartbeat are strengthening. Miss Frances says not to bother her unless your head is feeling worse." Sadie's eyes narrowed, focusing on the misbegotten braid Cassandra was attempting to pin into place. "And good Lord… what in perdition's name have you done to your hair?"

Cassandra let the braid fall with a sigh. "I could perhaps use some assistance in the matter," she said with as much dignity as she could muster. Which wasn't much, under the circumstances.

Sadie tutted and bustled over, batting her hands away and unraveling the travesty of a plait. "You should wear your hair *au naturel*," she said, exaggerating a French accent. "It's all the rage in London, and it would suit you. Here..." She grabbed the hairbrush and set to work. "Oh, and Mr. St. Germain said to tell you the invitation to his studio is still open." Sadie's eyes met Cassandra's in the mirror. "You'll go, won't you?"

The words were oddly eager.

"I was considering it, yes," Cassandra told her cautiously.

Sadie's face lit up. "Well, then of course you'll need a chaperone." She finished fussing with Cassandra's hair. "There! Now, we should leave right away. He's already started working."

Cassandra eyed her in the mirror with a hint of suspicion. "You seem very keen."

A bright flush colored the girl's cheeks. "Well..." She cleared her throat. "It's just... he said to come at midday, right? And it's midday now."

Cassandra narrowed her eyes. "What, exactly, is he painting? Do you know?"

The blush grew deeper. "Oh, it's... some kind of Classical Greek whatsit, I think. I'm sure I wouldn't know, Miss."

Cassandra held her gaze for a moment more, wondering what she was about to get herself into, before curiosity won out. "I see." She took a breath, steeling herself. "Very well. I'd hate to keep Mr. St. Germain waiting."

Sadie smiled like the sun coming out and led the way out of the bedroom, down the hall to the studio at the end. She knocked at the door — the same brisk knock she'd used before.

"Mr. St. Germain!" she called cheerfully. "Miss Fenwicke to see you!"

"Well, show her in, then. Don't lurk in the hallway," called a familiar deep voice, muffled by the door.

Sadie was nearly bouncing on her toes as she opened the door and waved Cassandra inside. The room was painted all in white, airy and open with four large windows along the far wall. Her eyes fell first on St. Germain's dark head, bent over an easel with his back to the line of windows. He held a brush in one hand, and a palette balanced in the other.

"Hello," Cassandra greeted, her eyes sliding over the rest of the echoing room as she entered. "Thank you again for inviting me here to... *oh.*"

Words deserted her abruptly as the subject matter of St. Germain's painting came into view. A velvet divan had been placed at right angles to the farthest window, leaving it dramatically lit from one side. And on it, lay Lord Rotherdam's startlingly beautiful valet — naked except for a strategically arranged sheet of red silk, rumpled into artful folds where it draped across his lap and spilled onto the floor.

SEVEN

COLOR ROSE TO Barlow's cheeks, though Cassandra was quite sure it was nothing to compare to her own flaming face. The valet's hand twitched in the direction of the draped cloth, as though to pull it over himself more fully.

"*Tsk!*" St. Germain scolded, halting the movement before it could complete. "Don't you *dare* break pose. You are a terrible artist's model, Barlow. Remind me again why I put up with you?"

Next to Cassandra, Sadie stifled giggles behind her hand. Barlow's hazel eyes narrowed at her.

"I'll have less of that from you, Sadie," he said, falling short in an attempt at severity. His cheeks were still faintly pink.

"Yes, Mr. Barlow. Sorry, Mr. Barlow," Sadie said, not sounding remotely chastened.

"Why do I even bother?" St. Germain muttered, the words barely audible. He returned to a more normal tone, adding, "Stop fidgeting, will you? I'm losing the light as it is, with this blasted storm rolling in."

Cassandra knew that the correct response to all of this would have been to grab Sadie, haul her right back through the door, and not stop until they were both safely back in her borrowed bedroom. Instead, she stood frozen in place, wavering for a long moment as she stared at golden skin etched with lean muscle.

It was, in fact, very much like looking at a classical painting. In this setting, once the initial shock had a few moments to wear off, her attention focused more on the play of light and shadow across skin than the scandalous dearth of clothing.

She had not been wrong before, when she'd thought of him as beautiful.

"What are you calling this one again, Mr. St. Germain?" Sadie asked.

"*Hermes Lamed*," St. Germain replied, dabbing a few brushstrokes against the canvas. "Would you like to see, Miss Fenwicke?"

And Cassandra *did* want to see. She took a steadying breath, willing the heat to fade from her cheeks. "Thank you. I would," she said.

She crossed to stand behind him, and he moved aside so she could get a better look. Rather than the stark white room, the setting in the painting was a storm-blown landscape in the classical style—all dramatic rocks and wind-whipped trees. The figure in the painting, rather than being artfully sprawled across a divan, lay fallen across the flat top of a boulder.

The same rumpled sheet of silk preserved the figure's modesty in art as in life, but in St. Germain's vision, the wind had whipped Barlow's dark waves of hair half across his face. More notably, winged sandals adorned his feet—but one of the wings was twisted. An arrow protruded obscenely from the fallen god's calf, blood dripping from the wound. A caduceus staff lay abandoned on the ground nearby, its base broken.

"Hermes was the messenger of the gods," St. Germain said. "But he was also a psychopomp—a deity responsible for guiding souls to the afterlife."

"Who shot him?" Cassandra asked, fascinated.

But St. Germain only chuckled. "I'm afraid I've no idea. Fortescue thinks it was someone who wanted to prevent an important message being delivered."

"Maybe it was someone who wanted to stop people being taken to the afterlife," Sadie suggested. "Maybe the person's sweetheart died, and they wanted to keep them here instead of going to Heaven or Hell."

Cassandra felt a pang, so soon after the reminder of her poor, dead Thomas.

"The Ancient Greeks didn't really have a Heaven or a Hell," St. Germain pointed out.

"They had Tartarus and Elysium," Barlow said softly, not breaking pose. "Same concept, surely."

Cassandra's eyes were drawn back to him, and she noticed for the first time that the muscles of his left calf were twisted and atrophied in the same place St. Germain had painted the arrow.

"Perhaps Hermes was carrying a message back to Earth from one of the souls he'd led to the afterlife," she murmured. "And the gods struck him down to prevent the message from reaching its recipient in the realm of the living."

The other three considered that for a few moments.

"I like that one," Sadie said.

St. Germain grunted, and returned to his work, filling in the details of Hermes' outstretched hand. "Well, it's moot in the end. There is no afterlife, and people put their own interpretation on every piece of artwork they see."

Cassandra turned to him, genuinely shocked. "No afterlife? You're an atheist?" she asked in disbelief.

St. Germain shot her a glance. "I am. Why? Have I scandalized you?"

"I'm afraid we're all atheists here," Barlow said. "It rather comes with the territory."

"I'm not an atheist!" Sadie protested.

"Forgive me, Sadie," Barlow told her. "I should have said that Lord Rotherdam and the members of his informal club are atheists."

Cassandra blinked at him. "But it's a *Hellfire Club*," she blurted.

St. Germain let out a bark of laughter. "Next time Rotherdam and I have this argument, I'll tell him you said that."

She snapped her mouth shut, taken aback. After a moment, she tried again. "You're not devil-worshippers?"

"We don't believe in the devil any more than we believe in God," St. Germain said dismissively.

"The point of the name is that no one should fear damnation merely because they engage in open discussion about philosophy or art," Barlow put in.

St. Germain paused in mixing his paints. "You're spending too much time with Rotherdam. You're starting to sound like him."

Cassandra thought Barlow's blush deepened for a moment before he cleared his throat and consciously settled back on the divan. "Are you painting or talking, St. Germain?"

The sun chose that moment to disappear behind a heavier bank of clouds, throwing the room into shadow. St. Germain made a noise of discontent and stepped back from the canvas.

"Probably not the former, now that the light isn't cooperating." He gestured to a cabinet in one corner of the room. "Miss Fenwicke, if we haven't already offended your sensibilities to too great an extent, there's sketch paper and charcoal over there. You're welcome to pull up a chair and take advantage of our Hermes if you like."

Her eyes widened, excitement and trepidation flooding her in roughly equal measure. "Really?"

"Why not?" he retorted. "I suppose your tutor never allowed you to attend classes with live models."

"Certainly not," she said, cringing a bit at the thought of her parents' reaction to such a thing.

"Well," St. Germain replied, "consider it your first exposure to a Hellfire Club's ethos. That's a ridiculous restriction, and I can't imagine how many female artists the world has been robbed of, based on a foolish notion of propriety."

Cassandra's eyes darted back to Barlow, and away again. Somehow, the flush of heat that had originally been confined to her face now seemed to have taken up residence lower in her body.

"It really isn't very proper," she managed weakly.

"Is it less proper than when men do it?" Barlow asked, in that soft, disarming voice.

She thought about that for a moment. "Yes," she said. "But... maybe it shouldn't be."

Sadie grinned at her. With a deep, fortifying breath, Cassandra went to retrieve paper, charcoal, and a spare chair, before settling in and allowing her gaze to truly explore Barlow's sleek, uncovered body.

⚜

The unaccustomed warmth pulsing through Cassandra's chest and stomach didn't abate as she alternately stared and sketched in the ever-changing light—but it was joined by a growing fascination at how different these sketches were from the stiff, fully clothed forms of men and women she'd attempted in the past.

She could *see* the way Barlow's joints bent and moved... the way muscle and sinew connected beneath the skin, acting on the limbs like pulleys and cables. She noticed for the first time proportions that she had guessed incorrectly on previous attempts, in the absence of a proper human model.

Time had no meaning, and she had no idea how long she'd been immersed in her work when she became aware of St. Germain watching her. He'd abandoned his painting when the sun disappeared for good behind the clouds. A rumble of distant thunder jerked her attention away from her current sketch. When she glanced toward the windows, it was to find the dark man leaning against the wall with his arms crossed, seemingly as engrossed in her as she had been in drawing Barlow.

She blinked, but before she could decide what the odd tightening sensation in her belly signified, Barlow said, "Do you mind if I move? I'm afraid some of my joints are in danger of rusting solid."

Remorse flooded her. How long had she kept him frozen in place? It must have been more than an hour, easily. "Of course!" she said quickly. "Forgive me. I didn't realize how much time had passed."

A small smile curved the edges of the valet's full lips. Cassandra's fingers itched to commit it to paper. "It's quite all right, Miss Fenwicke. I'm used to it, with St. Germain."

"May I see?" the man in question asked, gesturing at the collection of sketches when she glanced toward him.

Embarrassment washed through her at the idea of letting him critique her work, which was probably amateurish in the extreme. But... he'd invited her to examine his painting. Not to mention inviting her to examine Lord Rotherdam's exceptionally attractive valet in *great detail*.

"If you like," she managed.

"They're really good," Sadie piped up. "They look almost exactly like him!"

For some reason, the praise made her feel more embarrassed, rather than less. St. Germain pushed away from the wall and approached her. He moved as she imagined a tiger would, and unbidden, she wondered what *he* looked like beneath his clothes.

Would he be broader through the shoulders than Barlow? Narrower? What would be the best way to commit his unusual close-cropped kinky hair to paper or canvas?

He stopped and looked down at the topmost sketch in her pile, examining it with a critical eye.

"You've a natural talent," he said after a long moment, and Cassandra let out the breath she'd been holding. With a grunt, he continued, "Your art tutor should be dragged out and flogged for stifling you. That's a very good likeness. It shows a flair of originality and style that's engaging."

Cassandra found herself lost for words, since no one had ever indicated to her that her artwork was anything other than pedestrian.

"Well, now I'm intrigued as well," Barlow said. He rolled into a sitting position on the divan and rose stiffly, wrapping the length of silk around his waist like a skirt. "May I see?"

That prospect was even more nerve-wracking than letting St. Germain see her scribbles. She swallowed and licked her lips.

"Certainly… if you like," she said. "I suppose it's only fair since you're the model."

He limped over to her, favoring his bad leg more heavily than when he'd led her to Mary's room the previous day. Perhaps lying in one position for so long had aggravated it, she thought.

With St. Germain on one side and Barlow on the other, she felt somewhat overwhelmed by the collective maleness looming in her immediate vicinity. Her heart began to pound, and she had to consciously slow her breathing—cursing herself silently for the involuntary reaction of fear.

"Good gracious," Barlow said in clear surprise, as he gazed down at her study in charcoal. "That really is quite good."

"Would you do a picture of me next, Miss?" Sadie asked. "I've never had anyone sketch me before."

Cassandra drew breath to answer, but was interrupted by the door opening.

"Edmund," Lord Rotherdam said, striding in, "I need to speak with you regarding payment for the bridge repair—"

He stopped short, staring at his mostly-naked valet and his man of business leaning over Cassandra's shoulders as she sat frozen in her chair. Disbelief slid across his handsome features, followed quickly by fury.

"Barlow!" he snapped. "St. Germain! What in the name of *sanity* do you think you're doing? Get away from that woman at once!"

EIGHT

CASSANDRA JERKED in place, startled by the anger in Lord Rotherdam's tone. Mortification flooded her an instant later, as she pictured what the scene must look like. Barlow stiffened and immediately backed away from her, nearly tripping over the edge of the silk covering.

"Forgive me, my lord," he murmured, casting his eyes downward—the picture of a perfect servant, except for his state of undress. "I do beg your apologies, Miss Fenwicke."

In an instant, all of the casual familiarity and sense of openness drained from the room. Sadie, Cassandra couldn't help noticing, was watching the exchange with wide eyes. Meanwhile, St. Germain was slower to back down.

"It's *art*, Rotherdam," he said. "You know— that thing you have no eye for? Still—I'm sure you've heard of it."

Rotherdam's demeanor was icy. "All I see is a male employee and a male servant pawing over a female guest in my house."

"They weren't—" Cassandra began, shocked into speech. She paused, and continued in a calmer tone. "Mr. St. Germain invited me to sit in on his work when he discovered I have an interest in painting. He offered me materials so I could do some sketches of my own. Afterward, he gave me a critique, and Mr. Barlow asked to see them as well. It only seemed fair, since the sketches are of him." She paused, before adding defensively, "I have a chaperone."

Rotherdam's piercing blue eyes pinned hers. "Not a very competent one, it seems."

Cassandra shot to her feet, suddenly and irrationally incensed on Sadie's behalf. "How dare you, sir," she said coldly. "I have just been hearing about your passionate defense of the rights of men to discuss art, religion, and philosophy freely, without the constraints imposed by polite society. Clearly the freedoms granted to your *Hellfire Club* do not extend to the fairer sex!"

Barlow was watching her, his eyes growing as wide as Sadie's. St. Germain's brows shot up in evident glee.

"Oh," St. Germain said. "We should go and fetch Frances right now. I feel certain she'd be *fascinated* by this conversation."

Rotherdam gave him a quelling glare. St. Germain appeared... decidedly unquelled.

Cassandra ignored her pounding heart and forced herself to hold the viscount's gaze when he looked back at her.

"And yet," he said, "it will be my name dragged through the mud alongside yours, should the actions of those in my household ever get out."

Cassandra couldn't stop the blood draining from her face, but she raised her chin and retorted, "Why should it get out? And, if it does not, then what do the details matter?"

"Good point," St. Germain said. "You're not planning on spreading gossip around, are you, Rotherdam?"

The viscount scowled at him. "Of course not. Don't be absurd."

"*Of course not,*" St. Germain echoed. He gestured between himself and Barlow. "In which case, you'd better not be accusing either of us of wagging our tongues about what goes on here." Rotherdam drew breath to speak, but St. Germain got in first. "And if the word 'servants' passes your lips, I'll remind you that none of the staff would be here in the first place if they weren't already known to be discreet."

A muscle jumped in the corner of the viscount's jaw. Sadie was biting her lower lip as though she wanted to say something to defend herself, but she wisely held her peace.

Rotherdam's expression grew even stonier. While Cassandra still found it hard to picture the soft-spoken Barlow charging across a battlefield, she could see her reluctant host in that role as clearly as if she'd been there to watch it. Again, that glacial gaze caught hers.

"The attention of these two miscreants was not unwelcome?" he asked.

"It was not," Cassandra said firmly. "So, am I now free to sketch with charcoal in your house if I desire to do so?" She couldn't help the sharpness that crept into her tone.

His eyes narrowed. "I suppose I can hardly object, after my man of business delivered such a rousing soliloquy on the topic of intellectual and artistic freedom."

St. Germain gave him a thin smile. "It was rather good, if I do say so myself."

Rotherdam ignored him. "At any rate, since you are here, Miss Fenwicke, I do have a message for you from Miss Hunter."

Cassandra drew in a sharp breath, fear warring with hope. "About Mary?"

The viscount nodded. "She has shown some improvement, and Miss Hunter believes she may wake in a few hours."

In an instant, Cassandra whirled and shoved the pile of sketches at St. Germain, who took them mostly in self-defense.

"I must go to her at once," she said, already hurrying toward the door. "Sadie!"

"Right behind you, Miss!" said the scullery maid, though she did give Lord Rotherdam a much wider berth than Cassandra had as she barged past.

Cassandra made haste down the hallway and rushed down the stairs to the second floor. Mary's sick room was located in the other wing, right across the length of the great manor house from St. Germain's painting studio.

Sadie kept pace with her the whole way. "D'you think she's awake?" asked the little maid breathlessly.

Cassandra was a bit out of breath herself—and her headache, which had been easing, throbbed in time with her elevated heartbeat. "I don't know," she said. "I hope so."

She hesitated for only a moment before identifying the correct door, and knocked at it softly.

"*Come in*," came the muffled reply.

Cassandra opened the door and entered, trying not to pant like an exhausted racehorse after rushing here. Miss Hunter—*Frances*—looked up from her vigil.

"How is she?" Cassandra demanded, as Sadie sidled in behind her.

To her disappointment, Mary showed no signs of awareness, though the fingers of the hand on her uninjured side twitched weakly against the bedclothes.

"She's been mumbling in her sleep," Frances said. "I believe she will wake soon—though she'll need laudanum for the pain, and that will put her right back into insensibility. With luck, we'll at least be able to get some nourishment into her first."

Cassandra lifted a hand to her heart in relief. "So she will definitely recover?" she asked, just to be sure.

"I'm confident that she will not die of blood loss," Frances said. "Infection is always a possibility, but so far the wound has remained sound. Do you wish to sit with her until she wakes?"

"Yes, absolutely," Cassandra told her, and went to bring the second chair near the bed. Sadie immediately batted her away and moved it for her.

"Oh, good," Frances replied, with obvious relief. "I was hoping you'd say that. Wake me when she starts getting restless, will you?" With that, she grabbed a folded blanket from the end of the bed and shook it out, placing it on the rug by the bed.

"I will," Cassandra promised. After a slight hesitation, she added, "May I ask you a question first, though?"

Frances grunted in a vaguely affirmative manner.

"Are you a member of Lord Rotherdam's Hellfire Club?" Cassandra asked.

"Yes," Frances said simply.

"And you are afforded the same freedoms of speech and action as the men?"

Frances snorted. "There's a limit to how effectively you can train chivalry out of an upper class male. But in general, yes." Her gaze narrowed at whatever expression had found its way onto Cassandra's face. "Oh, God's teeth. What have the idiots done now?"

Cassandra shook her head briskly as though to clear it, and immediately regretted the action as her headache throbbed. She waved the words away. "Oh, nothing, really. St. Germain invited me to watch him paint. He's working on a... classical piece."

She raised an eyebrow. "I assume that's a polite way of saying it's another erotic Achillean ode to male beauty?"

Cassandra flushed scarlet. "It's very... classically Greek."

Frances made a noncommittal noise in the back of her throat. "So he dragged you in to look at a mostly naked man. Barlow? Or Fortescue?"

"Barlow," Cassandra confirmed.

"And did you like it?" Frances asked. "He *is* very pretty, I suppose—if you enjoy that sort of thing."

Cassandra could feel the heat still radiating from her face. "He's very… muse-inspiring."

Frances chuckled.

"Mr. St. Germain offered me the use of some sketching materials, since I'm an amateur artist myself," Cassandra went on. "And I've never had the opportunity to sketch a live model."

"Sounds like a pleasantly scandalous way to pass a few hours, in that case," Frances said. "But…?"

Cassandra sighed. "Lord Rotherdam came in to speak to Mr. St. Germain, and took exception to the scene."

"Well, I did warn you it's difficult to beat the chivalry completely out of his sort." Frances sounded neither surprised, nor particularly bothered by the description of events.

"It's just that… I should like to pursue such opportunities further, as long as I'm obliged to be here anyway," Cassandra tried to explain. "I had hoped to get back to art once I've settled into my new accommodations."

"Then you should do so," Frances said. "I'm sure Barlow and Edmund have no objections."

"She's really good at drawing, too!" Sadie put in, doing nothing to ease Cassandra's self-conscious embarrassment.

"I trust Edmund called Freddie out on his hypocrisy?" Frances asked tartly.

"Words were exchanged," Cassandra replied in a small voice.

Frances huffed in amusement. "Try not to hold it against the man. I don't think he can really help himself — it's too ingrained in the blood. High in the instep — that's Freddie's problem."

Cassandra had to hide her shock at a titleless woman referring to a viscount by his given name — but perhaps in this place, it should not surprise her so.

"Only… give me your word that you will not come back later, cursing him for any resulting slight to your reputation," Frances said, her tone growing serious.

"I have no reputation left to slight," Cassandra replied without hesitation, aware that old bitterness was audible behind her words. "Or, rather, I do — but it can hardly get any worse than it is now."

Frances' lips pressed together unhappily. "Oh, my dear girl. For women, it can *always* get worse. The only way to escape the shame of it, in my admittedly limited experience, is to stop caring altogether."

Cassandra pondered those words for a long time after Frances lay down on the blanket and began to snore softly.

NINE

WHEN MARY finally awoke some hours later, Cassandra felt a little of the invisible weight on her shoulders ease. "Frances!" she called, steadying her poor maid with a hand on her shoulder, as Mary whimpered and tried to curl toward her injured arm.

Frances was awake and upright before Cassandra could blink—though her short hair was mussed, and her eyes underlined with dark circles.

Mary's breathing came in fast, shallow pants, and tears immediately flooded her eyes, spilling over. Cassandra froze, unsure what to do or say that might reassure the poor woman. She must be in terrible pain, and would have no idea where she was or what had happened after the highwayman shot her.

Fortunately, Frances appeared much more competent when it came to bedside manner. She settled on the edge of the bed, placing a gentle hand on Mary's cheek and meeting her eyes frankly.

"You're back with us, my dear," she said kindly. "You've been injured, but you're safe now, and I'll give you something for the pain as soon as I've caught you up with events. Can you tolerate it for a few minutes? It will help if you can take slow, deep breaths."

She gave Mary a moment to take the advice, while Cassandra bit her lip in helpless sympathy.

"What happened?" Mary rasped weakly. "Where—?" The word caught in her throat, and she descended into coughing. Another groan of pain followed.

Frances reached over to the bedside table and retrieved a cup. Lifting Mary's head a few inches, she helped her take a few sips of the contents before easing her back to lie against the pillow.

"My name is Frances Hunter. You and your mistress were attacked by highwaymen on the road, but my companions and I happened to come along at the right moment to interrupt them. Your mistress is fine except for a knock on the head, though I'm very sorry to report that your driver was killed. You were shot in the arm, so we brought you here to recover. The house belongs to a friend of mine, and you're quite safe here."

Mary blinked liquid eyes up at Frances, before her searching gaze moved to take in Cassandra's presence. Cassandra pasted on a watery smile. She took Mary's hand—the one on the uninjured side—and gave it a reassuring squeeze.

"Miss?" Mary whispered, no doubt taking in the bruising on her face.

"It will be all right, Mary," Cassandra managed. "I'm so sorry you were hurt. I've been terribly frightened for you."

"No need for any of that now," Frances said firmly. "Right now, we only have three concerns to address. Food, drink, and pain relief."

"I'm still very thirsty, ma'am," Mary told her, voice meek.

"I don't doubt it," Frances commiserated.

Between them, they got Mary situated against some pillows. Frances patiently fed her spoonfuls of broth with bread soaked in it, more water, and finally a draft of laudanum. When she was once more asleep, Cassandra gave Frances a searching look.

"I cannot thank you enough for your care," she said, meaning every word. "You should get some proper rest now, though. You've barely slept."

"I can watch over her until she wakes up again," Sadie offered. "She's right—you look like you're about to fall over."

Frances gave them a wry look. "Yes, I suppose a few hours in an actual bed wouldn't go amiss. I'll be in the room next door if you need me, Sadie. And you"—she speared Cassandra with a look—"should probably spend a bit of time deciding how you wish to spend your remaining time here. I doubt that damaged bridge is going to be rebuilt overnight."

⚜

Freed of her immediate worry for Mary's life, Cassandra did exactly that. With her chaperone otherwise engaged, she returned to St. Germain's art studio, only to find it deserted.

Unfazed, she began a systematic search of the house until she heard voices raised in spirited discussion. She followed the noise to a generously appointed parlor, where she found the men talking and drinking. Lord Rotherdam was leaning against the mantelpiece, addressing the foppish Mr. Fortescue, who sat in a comfortable chair. The plain-faced man whose name Cassandra had not learned stood behind that chair, leaning his arms on the top of the chair back with the casual familiarity of a close friend. St. Germain was seated on a chesterfield next to the wall, watching the exchange with mild amusement.

Rotherdam's eyes fell on her, and the conversation ceased as the others turned to see what he was looking at.

"Miss Fenwicke," the viscount said cautiously.

"Hello, my dear," Mr. Fortescue greeted, with considerably more warmth. "How fares your maid? Has she awoken yet?"

"She has," Cassandra replied. "She ate and drank, and is resting now after a dose of laudanum. Sadie is watching over her, to allow Miss Hunter some uninterrupted sleep."

"That's excellent news," St. Germain said. Something about the warm sincerity of his tone sparked answering warmth in Cassandra's chest.

"It really is," she said. "I was wondering if there is any update yet regarding the bridge repair?"

Rotherdam looked sour. "Only that it will take time, and is entirely dependent on the weather's cooperation. The flooding was just beginning to subside when this new round of storms sent the waterways over their banks again. I wish I had something different to report."

"Not even a viscount can control the weather," she replied, equally as tart. It was brash of her—probably beyond the bounds of what could be considered a young woman's charming impishness. "And besides," she continued, "I'm certain it would cause Mary terrible pain to attempt to transport her before her wound has had more of a chance to heal."

"You are, of course, both welcome to stay as my guests as long as is necessary to allow your maid sufficient time to heal." It was perfectly civil, but Cassandra would have sworn Rotherdam was forcing the words past clenched teeth.

"Your generosity is very much appreciated," Cassandra told him, sweet as spun sugar. "As is the generosity of your friends—most notably, Miss Hunter. She is a true marvel."

"That she is," St. Germain agreed wholeheartedly.

Cassandra gifted him a heartfelt smile in return, and addressed him next. "Mr. St. Germain—since I am to remain here for the time being, might I impose on you for more opportunities to sketch? I must admit, I'm feeling quite artistically inspired after our earlier session."

Someone made a soft, faintly choked noise. Cassandra thought it might have been the viscount, though a glance at him found his expression absolutely blank.

"It's fine by me," St. Germain replied easily. "I'll be back at it as soon as the light cooperates and Barlow can get away from his duties." He flickered an eyebrow at Rotherdam, their gazes connecting for a bare instant. Cassandra couldn't read whatever passed between them.

"Then I shall find you when the sun returns," Cassandra told him.

Fortescue spoke up. "In the meantime, would you care to join us? I'm sure it's terribly inappropriate of me to ask in the absence of a chaperone, but we were just having the most fascinating conversation about inheritance law."

Cassandra wavered, since this was a subject that was, one might say, close to her heart—after her parents' entailed estate had gone to a distant male cousin upon their deaths, leaving her with nothing. "Indeed?"

"Yes—do come and join in!" Mr. Fortescue said with obvious enthusiasm. "Oh, and you must forgive me—I don't believe you've been properly introduced to my partner." He gestured at the plain-faced man lounging against the back of his chair. "This is Mr. Lawrence Vaughan. Lawrence—Miss Cassandra Fenwicke. There. Now we're all nice and proper."

"Good afternoon," said Mr. Vaughan, with a pleasant smile that leant his unremarkable features a twinkle of warmth.

"A pleasure to meet you," Cassandra said, meaning it for perhaps the first time since she'd awoken to find herself in Hengewick House.

Rotherdam, on the other hand, still looked less than pleased. Cassandra ignored him. St. Germain rose from the chesterfield and offered her a seat there instead. She smiled at him and settled herself on the comfortable upholstery.

"Anyway, as I was saying," Mr. Fortescue began. "I had the most *interesting* discussion with a gentleman in my club last week. Apparently, he is lobbying for a change to settlement laws, in which jointure after widowhood would automatically be set at twenty-five percent of the value of the estate. It will never get anywhere with Parliament, of course…"

Cassandra passed a good two hours immersed in a conversation unlike any she'd ever experienced in her twenty-two years. As a young woman, her mother had educated her regarding matters of law and politics, to the extent that such things might one day impact her directly.

Yet, those discussions had generally been presented as *the way things were* — not as subjects up for debate. Here, among the members of Lord Rotherdam's Hellfire Club, the conversation was all about the ways in which law and society might be changed to make it better. Hesitantly, Cassandra had interjected, at a point where it seemed appropriate, to explain how she had been left destitute and reliant on the charity of relatives when her parents' entailed estate had gone to the nearest male relative, with no provision made for her upkeep.

A spirited discussion of the unfairness of such an arrangement ensued. Lord Rotherdam had put forward the argument that entail prevented estates from being parted out to multiple heirs, generation after generation until there was nothing left of them. The plain-faced Mr. Vaughan had retorted that instead, those intact estates ended up mortgaged to the hilt, unable to be sold, and was that really any better?

It had been, in a word, entrancing.

Afterward, she'd taken dinner in Mary's room with Sadie. Mary was still sleeping soundly, so Cassandra spelled the little scullery maid for a few hours. Frances returned after dark to wake her patient for more broth and medicine. Reassured that all was as well as it could be, Cassandra retired to bed feeling better than she had since this whole horrible mess had started. If not for poor Leeds, whose body lay shrouded in Lord Rotherdam's icehouse until burial could be arranged, she might begin to think that everything would be well again once the bridge was repaired and she was safely to Horsham.

Thoughts of Leeds sobered her, even though she had, in truth, barely known him.

Eventually, she slept. When she woke, it was with an odd determination to make the most of this strange interlude out of time. She felt almost as though nothing that happened in Hengewick House could touch the future. Here, men—and apparently, women—dared to speak of changing the world. They laughed and argued and made art and refused to bow to propriety for propriety's sake.

Outside of Lord Rotherdam's little bubble of safety, society stifled the individual like a heavy woolen cloak in midsummer. Outside, Cassandra was a pariah with no money, no status, and no friends. Here, she was valued for her intellect, her artistic talent—or perhaps merely because she was a person, and the people here believed every person had value.

While checking in on Mary in the morning and sitting with her while she ate a light breakfast, Cassandra noticed that the sun was out. Once Mary was sleeping peacefully again, she made her way to St. Germain's studio with a lighter heart, and a fresh determination to make the most of whatever experiences were on offer.

She found the man himself once more in front of his easel, while the lovely Barlow lay draped across the velvet divan in his familiar pose as *Hermes Lamed*. They both greeted her, and before long she was installed once more with charcoal and paper, sketching a close study of Barlow's scarred leg.

Some time later, St. Germain made a wordless noise of satisfaction.

"Is that inexpressive grunt an indication that I can move without being chastised for it?" Barlow asked mildly.

Cassandra covered an unladylike snicker with a cough.

"Yes, you heathen ingrate," St. Germain told him. "I'm done with you, for this painting, at least. Still a bit of work to do on the background, but that's all."

Barlow rolled onto his back on the divan with a heartfelt moan of relief, and Cassandra swallowed as the sound made something flip oddly in her stomach. To distract herself, she bounced up from her chair and went to look at the almost-finished painting.

"Oh, that's absolutely lovely!" she exclaimed. "Barlow, you really must see it!"

"I will, in a minute or two," said the valet. "Once I can feel all my extremities again."

St. Germain stretched his back, vertebrae popping audibly, and Cassandra's fingers itched to draw him in the same way she'd sketched Barlow these last two days.

"Are you done for the day, then?" she asked.

He considered for a moment. "Yes, I think so. As much as I'd like an excuse to postpone the accounts I need to reconcile this afternoon, my eyes are fatigued and I'd only make a muddle of it if I tried to keep painting."

"You're a horrible man of business," Barlow observed from the divan. "You know that, right?"

It sounded like teasing.

St. Germain scoffed and responded in kind. "Oh, yes? Well, you're a horrible valet as well."

Barlow scoffed right back, though he didn't move from his limp, exhausted sprawl. "Nonsense. I am an *excellent* valet, thank you very much."

St. Germain gave a grunt of acknowledgement. "All right. Yes, fine — you're an excellent valet and the envy of every noble bastard in the *ton*. You win."

"The difference is," Barlow said, "I don't hate my job, and you do."

"It's a good job," St. Germain said immediately. "For God's sake, don't ever repeat this to Rotherdam, but I know I'm lucky to have it."

"He already knows that. And he also knows you hate it." Barlow sounded like this was an argument they'd had more than once.

Cassandra knew it was forward of her, but she was still feeling reckless. "Have you not considered becoming an artist?" she asked. "Professionally, I mean?"

St. Germain hesitated, with an uncertainty that seemed out of character. "I've... considered submitting some of my work to the salons."

"But you haven't," Barlow added.

"It's very competitive," St. Germain said.

"You're a very good artist," Cassandra pointed out.

He was silent for a long moment. "Perhaps someday," he said eventually. "With the right painting."

Privately, Cassandra considered that the painting before her was better than many she'd seen displayed in fine houses or hung in art salons. She did not, however, get the impression that more discussion on the subject would be welcome right now.

So she changed tack, steeling herself to make a request that was both entirely improper and entirely selfish.

A little bubble of safety, outside of time.

"Well, if you need an excuse to rest your eyes before immersing yourself in account books, I have a question, and also a request."

"Hmm. I can hardly resist such an opening, now can I?" St. Germain said, regaining his usual air of teasing confidence. "What's the question?"

Cassandra swallowed and licked her lips nervously, then plowed forward. "When artists study live models, is it usual for them to cover up... certain areas? Like the silk cloth in the painting." She gestured at the folds draped across Hermes' lap.

Color rose to Barlow's cheeks.

St. Germain said, "Ah. I see what you're getting at. No, it's not. The importance of anatomy doesn't cease between the knee and the navel."

Barlow began to look genuinely alarmed.

St. Germain came to his rescue. "However, I should probably add that if your request is about to be for a nude model, Barlow's head might spontaneously combust. I suspect it's because he thinks Rotherdam would kill him in his sleep if he found out about it."

Be bold, Cassandra told herself.

"Actually, I was going to ask if you'd ever modeled before, Mr. St. Germain," she said, amazed to find that her voice emerged steady. "Unless you're also worried that Lord Rotherdam would murder you in the dark of night."

A look of interest kindled in St. Germain's dark brown eyes. "Well now—I'll admit that's not the request I'd expected. And the answer is, no, I have not modeled before." He paused for a moment, considering. "Though I suppose I did say that your lack of artistic education was a travesty."

Barlow sighed. "He might not kill you in your bed, St. Germain, but don't come running to me if he finds out you did this and plants you a facer."

St. Germain didn't reply.

Barlow sighed again. "And... you're going to do it anyway. Right. I suppose you'll need a valet, then. Oh, the irony."

"Will you, though?" Cassandra asked, excitement thrumming through her veins.

"Eh, why not?" St. Germain said after a moment. "What's life, if you don't live dangerously?"

"It's your funeral," Barlow muttered, and rolled upright on the divan with the silk sheet wrapped modestly around his body. "Just don't expect me to be caught in here with you."

"Wouldn't dream of it," St. Germain replied.

The pair disappeared behind a privacy screen set up in one corner of the room. Cassandra returned to her seat and fidgeted, caught halfway between the warmth in her stomach and a growing chill of nervousness lodged in the vicinity of her chest. It seemed like a very long time before Barlow emerged fully dressed, though in reality it had probably been less than fifteen minutes.

He gave her a wan smile. "Do enjoy the rest of your morning, Miss."

"Thank you, Barlow. Good day," she managed, past the dueling sensations fighting a pitched battle inside her.

St. Germain emerged as Barlow left, closing the door behind him. The silk sheet was wrapped low around his hips, revealing a body taller and leaner than Barlow's, seemingly without an ounce of fat. Muscle and sinew moved smoothly beneath skin the color of rich earth after a rain.

Cassandra stared.

St. Germain raised an eyebrow. "How would you like me, Miss Fenwicke?"

Something in his tone made the heat flare, driving back the ice for a moment. Cassandra opened her mouth, but it took a moment before words came out.

"Perhaps... standing? Something different than our Hermes, at any rate." Because of course she was only doing this to further her art. Her *art*.

St. Germain appeared to consider the options for a moment. He approached the side of the divan and faced it, standing in profile to her. The sheet fell away, revealing the sleek muscle of his flank to her wide-eyed gaze. Then he lifted the leg farthest from her and rested his foot on the divan's seat, his knee and hip bent at a ninety-degree angle. He curled his upper body forward, resting his elbow on the raised knee and his chin on his hand.

"How about this?" he asked. "It's good for observing the hip joint's range of motion."

But... Cassandra wasn't looking at his hip joint. Her eyes had flown immediately to the flaccid length nestled in a thatch of tight black curls at the juncture of his thighs. The ice in her chest crackled, expanding to cut off her breath as her mind flew back to the last time she had seen such a sight.

The old, familiar panicked feeling clawed at her from the inside.

Stupid, stupid, stupid, her mind chanted, in the tone of every angry relative who'd ever berated her for her foolish naiveté. *Stupid girl, what were you thinking?*

Abruptly, she couldn't breathe. The charcoal slipped from her fingers to land on the pristine floor. An instant later, her chair clattered to the floor as well, as she scrambled to her feet and stumbled backward until her shoulders hit the nearest wall. The light, airy room around her faded in her wavering vision, to be replaced with the memory of dark, secluded gardens and a very different male figure. With a whimper, Cassandra slid down the wall behind her to land in a heap, hiding her face in both hands and trying to force air past the constriction in her lungs.

90

TEN

EDMUND STOOD frozen for a startled moment as the bright-eyed young woman — the same person who'd debated inheritance law with Fortescue and teased Rotherdam for being unable to control the weather — knocked over her chair in her sudden haste to get away from him. The shock of the sudden change in her demeanor kept his mind from putting the pieces together for a few precious seconds.

When he finally did, he lunged for the silk cloth lying at his feet, cursing under his breath at the same time.

"Damn and blast," he muttered, wrapping the sheet clumsily around his body. Somewhat covered, he backed away to the farthest point in the room from her. "Miss Fenwicke? *Miss Fenwicke.*"

There was no reply. Her complexion had gone pale as milk. She wasn't even looking at him. If anything, she was looking *through* him.

"*Cassandra,*" he tried, but she only hunched further in on herself.

Shock had slowed his wits, but after a moment of indecision, he darted for the door with the silk sheet wrapped around his body like a bloody Greek toga, rather than take the time to dress. Barlow wouldn't have had a chance to get far yet.

"Robert!" he called, catching sight of a drab coat disappearing down the staircase.

There was a pause, and the valet reappeared on the landing, favoring his bad leg heavily.

"Edmund?" he asked in alarm. "Good God, man—why are you running down the hallway half-naked?" He hesitated, his expression darkening. "Don't tell me *I'm* going to have to plant you a facer—because that would be deucedly awkward to explain. What did you do?"

"I stood next to the divan like a statue, you dolt," Edmund snapped. "At which point I discovered that our adventurous damsel's last encounter with an uncovered cock was apparently enough to result in a bout of hysteria when she saw mine. Come back with me—I need you to watch her while I get Frances."

Barlow's eyes widened. "Me?"

"She wasn't frightened of you," Edmund told him impatiently. "Also, you're fully dressed. Now, come on, man! I don't want her left alone."

The valet sighed. "I was wrong earlier," he said, allowing himself to be dragged down the hallway. "Lord Rotherdam's going to kill *both* of us in our sleep."

Edmund gritted his teeth and didn't reply. Thankfully, Miss Fenwicke hadn't fled the scene in his brief absence. When he knocked softly and opened the door, it was to find her still in the same position as when he'd left—curled against the wall, face in hands.

He consciously modulated his voice to something gentle, despite the simmering anger he felt toward the mysterious *second man* who'd mired her in scandal. It was pure speculation, of course, but he would have put money on that nameless bounder being the one who'd put this kind of terror in her eyes.

"Cassandra," he said quietly. "Barlow's here. He's going to stay with you to make certain you're safe while I go find Miss Hunter for you."

She didn't speak or look up. Her shoulders were shaking. The sight made Edmund want to go and beat someone's face into a bloody pulp. It also made him want to gather her up in his arms and hold her close… which would, of course, be the worst possible action he could take.

Barlow slipped inside the room with him, a soft noise of pain slipping free of his throat when he took in her miserable hunch. "There's no need to speak, Miss," he told her in that calming tone that could soothe man and beast alike. "I'm going to sit down over here and keep you company for a few minutes. If it's too much, just point to the door and I'll move outside to the hallway. Or… you could also throw something at me, if that's easier."

Go, he mouthed at Edmund, who nodded and ducked behind the screen to retrieve his clothing.

He took it into the hallway to change, closing the door silently behind him. In the ironic absence of a valet, he contented himself with stockings, breeches, shirt, and an unbuttoned waistcoat. He pulled his boots on and hurried further into the house with his cravat untied and his coat slung over his arm.

Thankfully, Frances was nothing if not predictable—especially when she had a patient to care for. He found her in the maid's room. The injured woman appeared to be asleep. Frances glanced up sharply as he entered, only to raise an eyebrow at his state of dishabille.

"Well," she said. "I'll admit I didn't expect her to move quite *this* fast. Seriously, Edmund?"

He leveled an unamused glare at her. "Come quickly. I need you." His eyes slid to the unconscious maid. "Can you leave her alone?"

Worry replaced the look of mild disapproval on Frances' striking features. "Yes, she'll be sleeping off the laudanum for some time yet. What's happened? Is it Miss Fenwicke? The head wound? That seemed to be doing well enough for the past couple of days."

"No," Edmund said tightly. "Not the head wound."

He described what had happened in low tones as he led her back to the studio at a brisk pace.

"Fucking gutter-mannered toad," Frances cursed, once he'd finished talking. He shot her a sidelong look, but she waved him off. "Not *you*. I meant that syphilitic waste of space, Cecil Pembroke."

Edmund tried and failed to fit that statement into any sort of relevant context. "You mean Baron Malthorpe? Not that I'm arguing with your characterization, but what on earth does *he* have to do with this?"

Her face set in hard lines. "He's the one who dragged her name through the mud. I'd assumed from the gossip that he seduced her. Looks like I may have been wrong about that."

"You still haven't said what, exactly, this scandal was about," Edmund pointed out.

Frances' expression didn't soften. "No. I haven't. I expect if she wants you to know about it, she'll tell you."

I don't wish to speak of that, Cassandra had said, when he'd pressed her over breakfast two days previously.

"Good point," he allowed.

They reached the door, and he knocked on it quietly. A moment later, Barlow opened it and slipped out, closing it again behind him.

"Miss Hunter," he said, with obvious relief. "She still hasn't spoken. You're familiar with soldier's fatigue, yes? Men who, for instance, react violently to the slamming of a door, because it recalls the sound of musket fire on the battlefield?"

"Yes, I am indeed," Frances replied grimly.

Barlow's eyes moved to the door, as though he could see through it to the frightened woman hiding within. "That's how she's reacting right now."

Frances sighed. "Right. Thank you for that, Barlow. It's helpful. Now go away, both of you. And Edmund? You might want to dress yourself properly so that no one else assumes you've just been freshly fucked."

"Probably wise," Barlow agreed. "Perhaps I'd better help you with that."

Edmund dragged a hand down his face, pulling at the skin. "Just... be gentle with her, Frances. And tell her I'm sorry?"

Frances shot him a flat look. "How about I tell her you're an idiot, because none of this is about you. So... once again. *Go. Away.*"

Edmund swallowed his frustration and went, aware of Barlow following at his shoulder like a shadow.

⋙ ♕ ⋘

Cassandra huddled against the wall of the airy studio, trying to control her shaking as the door opened and closed across the room. Footsteps echoed against the marble tile, lighter and more even than the ones that had just left. A slender figure crouched in front of her, a little way beyond arm's reach.

"You know," Frances said, "when I suggested you take some time and decide how you wanted to spend the remainder of your stay here, this wasn't quite what I had in mind."

The sound that escaped Cassandra's throat was caught halfway between a laugh and a sob. She scrubbed at her eyes with the heels of her hands. "I'm such an idiot," she said unsteadily.

Frances made a considering noise. "Well, you *have* been spending rather a lot of time with Edmund. Perhaps idiocy is rubbing off." She stood and held out a hand. "Would you mind? I've spent a lot of time leaning over beds recently, and my lower back would appreciate the divan rather than the floor."

Cassandra took the outstretched hand and allowed herself to be hoisted into a standing position—aware that her own palm was damp with clammy sweat.

"Thank you," she said meekly.

Frances herded her to the divan and sat her at one end before seating herself at the other. "So, you got a look at Edmund's prick and panicked. I assume he wasn't doing anything particularly threatening with it at the time?"

All the blood that had fled Cassandra's face earlier returned now with a vengeance. "He told you?" she asked, mortified.

"He was worried about you," Frances replied.

Cassandra's eyes slid away. "Yes... I suppose it must have been rather disconcerting for him. And, no. He did nothing I did not explicitly request. He was modeling for me, nothing more." She lifted a hand to knead at her temples.

"Head hurting again?" Frances asked.

"Perhaps a little," she allowed. In fact, her entire body felt like she'd just run a mile—aching and shaky.

"Want to talk about it? And by '*it*,' I mean Edmund's prick, of course—not your headache." Frances paused and frowned. "Blast. That still came out sounding wrong."

Cassandra clapped her hand over her mouth to stifle the scandalized noise that wanted to escape. "Yes," she managed. "I'm afraid it rather did." Regaining control, she took a deep breath, steeling herself. "I'm not sure there's much to say. I gather you already know most of it."

"I know what the gossipmongers took such delight in spreading around," Frances told her. "That, I suspect, is not terribly close to what *you* experienced."

Darkness... damp grass soaking through her dress and chilling her knees... a rough hand in her hair, controlling her movements...

It should have brought on the panic again. Instead, she felt oddly numb to the whole loathsome thing. "I suppose not."

Did she want to talk about it? She'd never really had the chance—not beyond her initial, thoroughly doomed attempts to explain herself to her aunt and uncle.

"Tell me what the gossipmongers say about it," she decided.

Frances leaned back against the divan, regarding her frankly. "They say you danced with Baron Malthorpe at Lady Northcotte's Regatta. He took you outside for a walk in the gardens. Some time later, one of the servants informed Lord Northcotte of a disturbance near the center of the hedge maze, and he found you in a... compromising position."

A twisted smile stretched Cassandra's lips even as the unpleasant chill nipped at her insides. The expression felt more like a death rictus. "He claimed that I threw myself at him, desperate for his suit," she said, in an absolutely flat tone.

"For what it's worth, the gossips believe he seduced you," Frances offered. "But it appears both of those things are untrue. He forced you?"

Cassandra wondered if it was possible to live as a frozen statue. In some ways, it seemed preferable to living as the frightened little mouse she'd become. It certainly seemed to make it easier to get the words out.

"Yes. Perhaps I might have been believed, if I hadn't already been caught kissing a soldier when I was younger," she said. "Of course, if I *had* been believed, they probably would have forced him to marry me. As it was, my uncle still tried, but the Baron only laughed in his face and said he had no interest in *damaged goods*."

Frances didn't look particularly shocked by this. "You may not believe it, but you had a lucky escape."

"No. I understand that," Cassandra replied. She swallowed hard against the all-pervasive chill. "What I don't understand is why he would force me to do... what he did. It was so repulsive, and... *nonsensical*."

Frances drew in a deep breath and let it out slowly. "If the gossip is to be believed, he forced you to put your mouth on his member?"

Cassandra shivered, the ice crackling in warning. "Why would a man want that? It was *awful*."

Silence settled over the room for a beat before Frances spoke again.

"There are two answers to that question. The short answer is, because Malthorpe is a swine who takes pleasure in hurting and humiliating those with less power than he has."

Silence reigned for a beat.

"And the long answer?" Cassandra asked, because she had, in fact, figured that part out already.

"That somewhat depends," Frances said. "Has anyone ever discussed the details of sexual congress between men and women with you? Your mother... or your aunt, perhaps?"

"No," Cassandra replied blankly. "Never."

Frances gave a slow nod, a look of resignation settling across her sharp features. "Right," she said with a sigh. "Of *course* they didn't. In that case, I think we need to have a candid discussion— preferably before you spend any more time sketching naked men in the middle of a Hellfire Club."

ELEVEN

AN HOUR LATER, Cassandra stared at Frances, her mind abuzz. "And women do that to men's pricks *voluntarily*?" she asked, in some disbelief.

Frances let out a stifled huff of amusement. "Men's pricks hold very little interest for me, so I am perhaps the wrong person to ask. But some do, yes. When coercion is removed from the equation, it becomes a question of pleasure. Just as another person may enjoy placing their mouth between a woman's legs because it satisfies them to give her pleasure, so someone may fellate a man because his pleasure is pleasing to them."

Cassandra sat with that idea for a long moment. "And it would avoid the possibility of becoming with child."

During this frankly astonishing discussion, several aspects of her rural upbringing had taken on new and startling connotations. How had it never occurred to her that what was necessary to produce calves and lambs and colts might also translate to human beings?

"Indeed," Frances agreed. "A state which, in my humble and solitary opinion, is to be avoided at all costs."

"I do want children someday, though," Cassandra replied wistfully.

"Well," said Frances, "I suppose there's no accounting for taste. Still, I'm confident we can agree that pregnancy is preferable at a time of one's own choosing."

Cassandra gave a delicate shudder at the idea that the baron might have forced her in such a manner as to get her in the family way. "Yes. We can most certainly agree on that."

Frances nodded. "There are means of reducing the risk, of course. I am a huge proponent of lamb's gut quondams, given the sexual habits of some of these idiots I call friends."

A flutter of nervousness sent butterflies swirling in her stomach, but Cassandra steeled herself and asked, "Have you ever? I mean, with—?" Despite her best efforts, the words came out garbled and unsure.

Frances let out a bray of laughter. "With the 'idiots I call friends'? Heavens above, no. I was not being coy when I said pricks hold no interest for me." She leaned forward, elbows on knees. "I only tell you this because you are not currently in a position to ruin me or anyone else," she said bluntly. "And you should understand all the options that are available to you. While it is considered unnatural in the eyes of the church and illegal in the eyes of the state, a woman may desire other women. A man may desire other men. A person might also desire both sexes equally, or desire neither."

Cassandra took in her companion's male attire and forthright, almost masculine manner. "You desire women," she said, testing out the idea.

"Your clothing... is it that you wish to be a man? Or be seen as a man?"

Far from appearing offended, Frances looked almost approving. "A fair question. That is certainly something that arises, and it's yet another thing that our benighted society insists on making into a disorder rather than a simple preference. But, no. Personally, I enjoy the freedom conveyed by some aspects of masculinity—yet I am happy to consider myself a woman in the physical sense. I wouldn't wish to change that, were I miraculously given the means to do so."

"You've given me much to think about," Cassandra said, with considerable understatement. "Would I be right in thinking that this is something else that Lord Rotherdam's Hellfire Club seeks to change?"

Frances raised an eyebrow. "And what would make you think so?" she asked blandly.

"You told me once that no one in this house cared one way or the other whether your legs were encased in breeches or a frock," Cassandra replied. "I wasn't sure what to make of it at the time."

"We protect our own," Frances said. "And we don't judge them. Here, we are all safe to be ourselves without fear of censure. As long as everyone is an adult and freely consenting, one may dally with whomever one chooses, and no harm will come of it."

Cassandra thought of Mr. Vaughan, lounging with his arms crossed on the back of Mr. Fortescue's chair, a roguish smile on his face... and wondered. *My partner*, Mr. Fortescue had introduced him. She thought of St. Germain, a silk sheet wrapped low around his hips. *How would you like me, Miss Fenwicke?*

"I… think I need to speak with Mr. St. Germain and Mr. Barlow," she said, imagining with some trepidation what they must have been thinking after her fit of the vapors.

"Perhaps with everyone clothed this time," Frances suggested.

Cassandra felt familiar heat rising to her cheeks. "Perhaps so," she agreed, before silently adding *for now, at least.*

>~~ ⚜ ~~<

Once more neatly and respectably dressed, Edmund paced up and down the length of Rotherdam's private study. His employer and friend watched him with a faintly wary air from behind the bulwark of his massive oak desk.

"That foul little toad Malthorpe *forced* her, Rotherdam," he growled. "He saw someone in a tenuous situation, and he used her to feed his own twisted, sadistic impulses. Just because she got caught kissing a soldier when she was barely more than a girl—when they were in *love*, damn it—that single minor indiscretion was enough to make her word worthless against his!"

He stopped, focusing his glare on his friend and employer. "Well? Aren't you going to say anything?"

Rotherdam raised an eyebrow. "I was waiting to see if you were finished or not."

"*It's not right*!" Edmund flared, aware on some level that he was focusing his anger outward as a way to keep from focusing it inward.

"The fact that Malthorpe is a filthy-minded cad is hardly news, Edmund," said the viscount. "At the moment, I'm more concerned about how badly I'll want to thump you when you tell me why all of this is coming out now. What in hell's name did you do?"

Edmund scowled at him. "Oh, leave off. We were in the art studio. She asked me to model for her, nothing more."

"Model. For her." Rotherdam echoed flatly, scrubbing a hand down his face. "Nude, I assume?"

The scowl lines etched deeper into Edmund's expression. "She's terrified of men. I think her reaction took her as much by surprise as it did me. That beautiful, vibrant woman... he *ruined* her, and I don't mean in the eyes of *le bon ton*."

"And what precisely do you expect me to do about it, Edmund?" Rotherdam asked.

Edmund waved a hand in a sharp gesture of frustration. "I don't *know*. Can't you... challenge the little toad to duel or something?"

Rotherdam snorted. "Forgive me, but that does rather sound like an overreaction. Not to mention the fact that having me as the one defending Miss Fenwicke's tattered honor would be unlikely to help her situation in the least. Also—"

"Dueling is illegal," Edmund finished, exasperated. "Yes, yes." He sighed. "Perhaps

Vaughan and Fortescue could start a whisper campaign against him in the broadsheets."

"You could ask them," Rotherdam said wryly. "Though as you're aware, their passions run more toward radical politics than gossip rags."

"Malthorpe's probably a Tory," Edmund shot back in an ill-tempered mutter. "That means they ought to hate him on principle."

"You can certainly put your case to them. But one does have to wonder if Miss Fenwicke would appreciate having her dirty laundry aired further."

The calm words made Edmund want to snarl with frustration... probably because Rotherdam was right.

"I need to talk to her," Edmund said, his stomach awash with queasiness as he considered the way he'd left her — curled against the wall, face hidden and shoulders shaking.

"Is that likely to make the situation better?" Rotherdam asked.

"She needs to learn that not all men are monsters!" he shot back.

"Or, alternately, you could *leave it be*," Rotherdam said. "I do concede that at this point, there's little more that can be done to tarnish her reputation — not even being caught staying in my *den of iniquity*, should that fact get out despite our best efforts. However, that doesn't automatically imply that she wishes to be further compromised."

"Not everyone wants to live life as a monk, either," Edmund snapped. "In fact, I think that's only you."

"And, one assumes, the actual monks," Rotherdam retorted, not rising to the barb.

"You're convinced that everything you touch goes to shit, and you're scared to be proven wrong," Edmund said pointedly.

"My life is simpler without those kinds of entanglements," Rotherdam replied. "And other people's lives are simpler without me in them. All of which has little to do with Miss Fenwicke's situation." He let out a sharp exhalation through his nose. "Look, Edmund. I still maintain it would be wiser to let this go. But since we both know you're not going to do that—I trust you not to make the situation worse than it already is. Just... be careful with her. *Please*."

Edmund eyed him for a long moment. "And if I drag Robert into it as well?"

"Oh, for—" Rotherdam cut himself off sharply. The silence fell heavily for a moment before he continued, "Then I don't wish to know about it, Edmund. Barlow saved my regiment from a massacre, and now he blacks my damned boots. What he gets up to in his time off is his own business—not to mention the fact that he's considerably more circumspect than you are when it comes to his dalliances."

"He'd dally with you, if you'd stop holding him at arm's length." Edmund knew it was useless, but he still felt duty-bound to point it out whenever the opportunity arose.

Predictably, Rotherdam narrowed his eyes and straightened his spine. "He is my servant. '*Improper*' doesn't even begin to cover it."

"Your servant, who saved the lives of everyone under your command at Waterloo—nearly at the cost of his own," Edmund pointed out stubbornly. "He worships the ground you walk on."

Rotherdam tried and failed to cover a flinch. "All the more reason for him to steer clear until he gains better sense than he currently possesses."

"I'm never sure which of us you're trying to convince," Edmund told him. "I'll have those accounts ready for your review first thing tomorrow, *my lord*."

With that, he made his escape and went to find Barlow. Rotherdam let him go.

Cassandra spent several hours sitting with Mary. The maid was still weak, but she was beginning to stay awake for longer periods of time. Frances now seemed comfortable leaving her alone for short stretches, but Cassandra was happy to keep Mary company when neither she nor Sadie was available.

The wound—still carefully bandaged—had as yet shown no sign of festering. The biggest fear now was how much damage had been done to the limb itself. A lady's maid needed both arms, and Cassandra was in no financial position to pension a servant who could no longer work. She had a terrible suspicion that her aunt and uncle would scoff at the very idea.

When she had discovered whose house they were staying in, Cassandra had been terrified for Mary's physical safety. Now, she was terrified for her maid's future. Mary, however, did not need to know any of that. She needed to focus all her energy on healing and resting.

And, at the moment, on gossip.

"Are they all terribly wicked?" Mary asked, wide-eyed.

"Not wicked, exactly," Cassandra hedged. "Not that I've seen, at least. Honestly, the place is a bit fascinating."

"That Miss Hunter is a right clever doctor, it's true enough," Mary said. "When I saw she was actually a woman, I wasn't sure what to think — her wearing men's clothing and all."

"She claims she's not a real doctor," Cassandra told her. "But I think she's better at medicine than old Doctor Hartlow ever was. Honestly, I don't know what we would have done if she hadn't been here."

"Do you think they'll get the bridge fixed soon, Miss?" Mary asked.

Privately, Cassandra was of two minds about the bridge. Once it was repaired, she would be back to confronting her dreary future. Until then, there was the Hellfire Club, with its lively discussions and intriguing members... and she still needed to speak with St. Germain and Barlow.

"I don't know," she said. "So far, every time the flooding begins to recede, it rains again and overflows the banks."

A knock on the door heralded Frances' return.

"Hello, you two," she said as she entered. "You're looking better this afternoon, Mary."

A faint tinge of pink colored Mary's cheeks, banishing some of the awful paleness. "I'm feeling a bit more myself, Miss—thank you."

Frances gave her a kind smile and turned her attention to Cassandra. "I've just come from speaking with Edmund. He asked if you would join him and Barlow for a late dinner in his rooms."

Mary's eyes went comically wide. "Miss!" she protested. "In a gentleman's *rooms*? You mustn't!"

Cassandra met her gaze frankly. "Your concern is noted, Mary—but honestly, at this point, what else can be said about me that hasn't been said already? Perhaps it's time I started living on my own terms."

Mary opened her mouth as if to argue, but then closed it.

Frances looked between them. "For the most part, what happens within these walls stays within these walls," she said. "Mary—your job right now is to focus on getting better so that your mistress may once more have a dedicated chaperone."

Mary looked immediately contrite. "Yes, Miss. Sorry, Miss."

"For goodness' sake, don't apologize," Frances said immediately. "That wasn't meant as a rebuke. Here, let me see if that bandage needs changing again."

Mary still looked quite pink as Frances bent to lift her injured arm. Cassandra made her excuses and left them to it, returning to her room to set herself to rights before meeting Barlow and St. Germain for dinner. Too late, it occurred to her that she had no idea where St. Germain's rooms were actually located, having had no cause to visit them before now. In the end, she went to the scullery and asked Sadie, who was elbow-deep in dirty dishes.

Directions in hand, she went upstairs and found the correct door just as the clock in the hallway was striking eight. She knocked, and Barlow appeared in the doorway a moment later. He offered her a pleasant, if slightly hesitant, smile. "Miss Fenwicke. Do come in."

St. Germain rose as she entered. "Miss Fenwicke. Thank you for accepting my invitation on such short notice. I believe I owe you an abject apology."

She met his dark eyes, a sad smile on her lips. "No. I assure you—you really don't. Though it's quite possible I owe you one."

Barlow pulled a chair out for her. "Perhaps we should all sit down, and we can discuss who owes what to whom over dinner."

Her smile grew a bit wider, fondness warming her heart and driving most of the nervousness away. "Yes. That sounds like an excellent plan."

TWELVE

DINNER CONSISTED of roast pheasant and preserves, along with hearty bread and a selection of cheeses. Barlow served all three of them before seating himself at the small table.

"We do seem to be making a habit of sharing awkward and indecorous conversation over meals, Mr. St. Germain," Cassandra said. "I hope you warned Mr. Barlow of that."

"It was understood, Miss," Barlow said serenely. "I trust you are well recovered? Spells such as that one can be deeply unpleasant to weather, as I have personal cause to know."

Cassandra hadn't been sure quite how she would react to the inevitable reference to her... *spell*. But Barlow's words surprised her. Perhaps he had grown up with a sister whose constitution was delicate?

"You do?" she asked, since he seemed to be inviting discussion on the subject.

"It's a common enough affliction among soldiers," he said. "Though most of them are too embarrassed to speak of it."

"Most of them didn't charge enemy lines while bleeding out from a sword wound to the leg," St. Germain muttered.

He's a war hero, believe it or not, St. Germain had told her, the last time they'd shared confidences over food. *He saved Rotherdam's platoon by riding through enemy lines for reinforcements during the Battle of Waterloo. Nearly got killed doing it, too — the crazy bastard.*

"Whatever the case," Barlow continued, "the sound of a fowling piece being fired during a pheasant hunt is enough to send me scurrying for cover — convinced I'm back in the Netherlands, surrounded by French soldiers."

"That's hardly the same thing!" Cassandra said, taken aback.

Barlow's hazel eyes were solemn. "I rather think it is, Miss. I was hurt. I was *terrified*. The sound of a hunter's birdshot convinces some animal part of me that I'm about to be hurt and terrified again. Does that not sound familiar?"

Cassandra stared at him for a long moment before placing her silverware on the table and covering her mouth with one hand.

"*Robert*. You're upsetting her —" St. Germain began.

Cassandra quickly waved him off, trying to put words to her feelings. "No, no. Good heavens... that's exactly it. Only it's still not the same. You have every reason to react to the sound of gunfire. Whereas my reaction to the sight of a male member is, well, *ridiculous!*"

"Under the circumstances, it's *really* not," St. Germain told her.

"Yes, it is!" she insisted, gesturing a bit wildly in the general direction of his lap without quite registering how improper it was. "I mean, it's just a little... *dangly bit of flesh*. It looks like a fat worm poking out of the garden!"

St. Germain blinked, a faintly scandalized expression sliding over his handsome face. Barlow made a choked noise, tried to cover it, and then collapsed into unrestrained laughter, grasping the table edge as though to keep himself upright.

Cassandra stared at them. "Wait—what did I say?"

Barlow dragged himself under control with obvious difficulty—the laughter transforming his normally reserved manner into something a bit wilder... a bit more open. When he'd regained most of his decorum, he scrubbed a hand over his eyes and addressed her in an admirably even tone.

"If I might make an observation, Miss—most men do not appreciate having their manhood described as... a worm. Or as being *dangly*, for that matter."

"Or *small*," St. Germain added under his breath, though some of Barlow's amusement was now mirrored in his gaze as well.

"Oh," Cassandra said. "Well, of the two I've seen so far, yours seemed very... nice?"

Barlow started laughing again.

"This is not precisely the conversation I'd pictured having when I invited you here," St. Germain said. "Just so we're clear."

"No," Barlow said, still sounding choked. "No, this is much better."

Still somewhat bewildered by their reactions, Cassandra attempted to steer things back onto their original course. "At any rate, what I'd hoped to say was that I apologize for putting you in what must have been a very upsetting situation. And… I am abjectly grateful for the kindness you showed me when I was… indisposed."

She picked up her silverware and glanced down at the remains of her roast fowl, as though it was suddenly the most interesting thing in the room.

The silence stretched for a long moment before St. Germain broke it. "I exercised poor judgment. And for that, it is I who must apologize."

Cassandra glanced up sharply. "No, you didn't, though. I've been talking to Frances—"

"Oh, dear," Barlow murmured.

"—and I think perhaps you might naturally have assumed my request was a prelude to…something else," she managed.

St. Germain drew a deep breath and held it, as though considering his words carefully. "I… try not to make assumptions in that sphere. You requested an artist's model, nothing more. There was absolutely nothing untoward or suggestive in your manner. I don't wish to imply that there was."

Cassandra's heart thrummed in her chest, but not with the sort of frantic beat that heralded an attack of irrational fear. This was something… other. It was nerve-wracking, but not entirely unpleasant. In fact, it made her feel very alive, somehow. She screwed up her courage and spoke.

"But what if there had been?"

St. Germain and Barlow exchanged a look she couldn't decipher.

Barlow cleared his throat. "Edmund here has had a word with his lordship, as it happens. Just to ensure that there won't, in fact, be any risk of one of us being murdered in our sleep."

Cassandra remembered the two of them joking about such a thing, just before Barlow had left the art studio. Her heart thudded even faster, though a thread of mortification shot through her. "You discussed me with Lord Rotherdam?"

Barlow looked pained. "This is Lord Rotherdam's house. I am his servant. Edmund is his employee. It does tend to blur the lines of privacy somewhat."

"Rotherdam's got it into his head that you need protecting," St. Germain said bluntly, "and he's taken it upon himself to do so. Now, *me*—I think you could have used protecting on the night when that reprehensible toad of a man hurt you. But as it's now in the past, I think you need control of your own life more than you need a knight in shining armor. In the end, Lord Rotherdam came to see things my way."

Cassandra swallowed. "I *don't* have control of my own life, though. Not in the least. I never have." Her voice shook a bit on the final words.

Barlow held her eyes and leaned forward, slowly sliding his left hand across the table, palm down. He stopped while it was still in neutral territory—but easily within her reach. "In here, Miss—you do."

She gave a small sniffle and tried to settle her emotions.

"I suppose you'd better call me Cassandra, if we're really going to have this conversation openly," she said, unsure where the sudden impetuousness had come from.

"Only if you'll do us the same courtesy," said St. Germain. "He's Robert. I'm Edmund."

Cassandra stared, unblinking, at Barlow's extended hand. After a long moment, she slid her right hand out and tentatively covered it with her own. His skin was warm, the knuckles slightly rough. He turned his palm up enough to tangle their fingers, holding but not restraining.

"Robert," she said, as though trying it out on her tongue. She extended her left hand toward her other companion. "Edmund."

He took it without hesitation, raising it to his lips briefly. "Cassandra," he said, his lips caressing the name. "What is it you wish of us? Tell us, and we'll try to provide it."

It should have felt hopelessly strange, to have both of them here like this. Somehow, it didn't. It wasn't accurate to say that she felt like they came as a set. That was both untrue and somehow demeaning. It was more that... together, they provided the different things that she needed right now to be brave. Edmund was direct to the point of bluntness. Robert was kind in a way that could not be feigned.

"I don't want to be terrified of a dangly bit of"—she cut herself off—"sorry, of a very dignified and not at all wormlike bit of the male anatomy."

Robert let out a soft huff of amusement.

Edmund nodded, apparently unfazed. "All right. Let's discuss that further. What do you think the best way to go about that might be?"

Cassandra let out a shaky breath. "I'm not entirely certain. The circumstances were entirely different, but that didn't seem to help matters. The art studio was bright and well lit, not dark like a garden maze at night. You bear no resemblance whatsoever to the… the…" She struggled to find a descriptor, since the word '*man*' seemed too generous to describe Baron Malthorpe.

"Worm?" Robert suggested, deadpan.

Her startled laugh took her by surprise. "Thank you. Yes… the *worm* who hurt me. And yet it still transported me back to that night."

Thoughtful silence descended.

"Here's a point," Robert said eventually. "I'm still able to fire a pistol or a musket myself, even though it frequently sends me into a spell when someone else fires one."

Edmund let Cassandra's hand slide free as he sat back with a thoughtful expression. "That's a thought, isn't it? Cassandra, what if you were in control? Robert, we could sit you in a chair, hands behind your back. Cassandra could open the fall of your breeches at her leisure; cover you up again if it was too much."

"Too wormlike, you mean?" Robert offered dryly, giving her hand a small squeeze to belie any sting in the quip.

"Too small," Edmund suggested without breaking expression.

"You're both teasing me," Cassandra accused, to deflect from the heat rising in her cheeks.

"Perhaps a bit," Robert allowed. "And it wouldn't have to be me, assuming you even want to try this at all."

"We've already established that my dangly bits are alarming, though," Edmund retorted. "We don't know if yours are or not. Besides, you're more harmless looking in general."

"I gather the French army might disagree with that," Cassandra managed, determined to hold her own in this bizarre conversation.

"Fair point," Edmund allowed. "He's much prettier when he's restrained, though."

To that, she had absolutely no reply. So much for holding her own.

"I should really punch you in the jaw, you know," Robert said, without any real heat. With a final squeeze, he let Cassandra's hand go. She found herself mourning the loss.

"What? It's true," Edmund replied. "Cassandra—is he or is he not a much more attractive man than I am?"

"He's very... classical," Cassandra offered. "Though I find you equally appealing to the eye. I'm actually quite put out that I was unable to take advantage of your kind offer to model."

"I'm sure if you asked him again, he'd say yes again," Robert told her.

"Of course I would. Now, what do you say to taking our Hermes captive so you can examine his dangling parts at your own pace?"

Cassandra felt suddenly quite breathless as she pictured what this was likely to entail. "I think... I would like that, yes," she managed.

The same faint flush of red that she'd noticed rising to Robert's cheekbones on a couple of occasions in the art studio had returned.

"Would you care for dessert first?" he asked, hiding behind the facade of the proper servant.

"I think you'll find you're the dessert, Hermes," Edmund said.

"Perhaps afterward." Cassandra replaced her napkin on the table and rose, feeling too badly on edge to remain seated. "I believe the anticipation would ruin what appear to be perfectly lovely macaroons."

"Well, you heard the lady," Edmund said. He rose as well—pulling his chair out to set it in an open area in the room. "Let's have you, then."

Robert hesitated a moment before pushing his chair away from the table. "I will admit, this escalated rather more quickly than I expected." His tone sounded faintly rueful, and he was still blushing like a maiden.

Cassandra met his eyes, suddenly unsure. "Do you mind, though? I've no wish to force my attention on you if it's unwanted."

"It's not that, Cassandra, I promise you," he said. "I would find it upsetting if I inadvertently brought back bad memories for you, yet again. That's all."

A feeling of warmth burgeoned in her chest; the polar opposite of the chill that took up residence whenever panic was near. "I feel certain that won't be the case," she said. "And if it is, at least it was my choice, for once."

That seemed to reassure him. "As it should be," he told her and rose to his feet, favoring his bad leg, as he always seemed to after he'd been sitting for a while.

He followed Edmund's impatient summons and sat on the chair. With an artist's eye, Edmund moved the various candelabra lighting the room to provide the best possible illumination.

"There," he said. "Now, what can we use...?" Trailing off, he looked around the room before exclaiming, "Ah!" He crossed to the curtains framing the window and freed a length of satin cord being used as a tieback. The heavy drapery on that side fell to hang straight, covering half of the glass.

Cassandra frowned in confusion, only for her eyebrows to climb toward her hairline when Edmund returned to Robert and grasped his wrists, guiding them behind the chairback and wrapping the cord around them several times.

"Are you absolutely certain about this?" she asked, taken thoroughly aback.

"As we discussed," Edmund replied. "Hermes is your prisoner tonight—yours to do with as you will."

Robert must have discerned the depth of her uncertainty. "Believe me, if I had any virtue left, which I really don't, I'm confident Edmund would guard it for me. Honestly—it's fine."

"Virtue is in shockingly short supply in this place, it's true," Edmund agreed. Content with his work, he straightened and retreated to stand next to the wall, arms crossed.

"Well, it is a Hellfire Club, I suppose," Cassandra said faintly.

She contemplated the vision before her, feeling the same nervous heat in her stomach as when she'd first seen Lord Rotherdam's stunning valet laid out on Edmund's divan, draped in nothing but a length of red silk. It was so... *odd*, approaching him and looking down at him, bound and nominally helpless in his chair, awaiting her perusal.

How often had she ever been in a position of power over a man like this? She supposed she'd held sway over male servants, in that they were required to do what she asked—but only within the bounds of her parents' authority, or, later, her aunt and uncle's. She was quite certain she'd never held *this* sort of control before, though.

Sweet heaven—why did he have to be so beautiful? It made her imagine all manner of wicked things, especially after her conversation with Frances.

"The fall of my breeches opens with a row of buttons down either side," Robert said, with all the practicality of a professional valet. "Opening it will reveal my shirttails tucked inside. Lifting the shirttails will reveal, well, *me*."

"Just don't be alarmed if he's a bit less dangly than you expect by the time you get him unwrapped," Edmund advised with clear amusement. "I trust Frances covered that part."

She had indeed, although Cassandra had also experienced that aspect of the male anatomy directly. It had been confusing and unclear in the dark of Lady Northcotte's gardens — not to mention, something she had no desire to recall just now.

"Yes, but thank you for the warning."

"I can do you no harm while tied to a chair," Robert reminded her gently. "And I *would* do you no harm, even if I were not."

"I believe you," she said, and stepped into the space between his knees.

The fastenings of his breeches were exactly as he'd described. How odd that she'd seen such buttons thousands upon thousands of times, but never so much as touched one before. She unbuttoned the row on the right side, snatching her hand back when the material twitched as though a small animal hiding inside had been startled by her touch.

"It's all right," Robert said a bit sheepishly. "It's just me. I'm afraid Edmund was quite accurate in his prediction. Men's pricks tend to have something of a mind of their own. I can try to think of unpleasant things to quiet it — that usually does the trick."

Cassandra shook her head. "I don't want you to think of unpleasant things. In fact, I should say the goal is for *neither* of us to be thinking of unpleasant things."

"Quite right, too," Edmund opined.

Robert met her eyes with an achingly sweet smile. "Then carry on, and I daresay dangling won't be an issue."

With a fortifying breath, Cassandra returned to her work. The front panel of Robert's breeches slid down, revealing, as promised, the pristine white linen of his shirt still covering his member. She tentatively tugged it up, an inch at a time, revealing the fearsome vision of her nightmares, half-hard and nestled in a thatch of wiry, dark hair.

Cassandra stared at Hermes' naked prick, the scene flickering back and forth between Edmund's room and the night of the Regatta. But she was not on her knees, held down by a rough hand in her hair. Instead, she was looming over Robert, whose hands were tied behind his back to ensure that he could not touch her.

She also wasn't alone now, devoid of protection. Edmund stood watchfully a few paces away, to ensure that no one was hurt or forced to do anything they did not want. And this time, her tattered reputation with the *ton* did not hang in the balance. It was already gone. It could not be brought back. If the Duke of Warminster himself were to walk through the door this very instant, she would be no more ruined than she already was.

Her surroundings settled, no longer overlaid with frightening images of the past.

"Are you all right, Cassandra?" Edmund asked.

She stared at the twitching shaft nestled between Robert's thighs.

"Yes," she said. "I believe I am."

"How about you, Hermes?" Edmund asked.

"I'm tied to a chair and being ogled by an exceptionally lovely woman," Robert said mildly. "There are worse fates."

Cassandra dragged her gaze away from Robert's lap and up to his face with surprising difficulty. She blinked, taking in the entire picture laid out before her, rather than merely one piece of it. She had heard the word '*debauched*' used on a few occasions, but her mental image of the concept had always been hazy at best—until now.

Robert Barlow, valet to the Right Honorable Viscount Rotherdam, looked thoroughly debauched. Suddenly, the material of Cassandra's dress and stockings felt very confining, its presence against her skin hard to ignore.

"May I touch it?" she asked Robert, the words sounding breathless to her own ears.

"You may do whatever you like, as I am entirely at your disposal," Robert said. "I'll speak up if something pains me, though it shouldn't unless you are much rougher than I expect you to be."

"I'll be careful," she promised, her attention drawn once more to the stiffening length between his thighs. She crouched before him, wanting a closer view, and tentatively stroked a fingertip along the smooth skin. It was velvety soft, and he drew in a barely audible breath in response. His member stiffened further, bobbing up as though trying to reach out to her.

Emboldened, she let its weight rest in the palm of her hand. It really was a rather extraordinary thing. A smooth head peeked out from the cylinder of looser skin at the tip. Curiously, she enclosed it in her fingers, sliding the skin up and down. Above her, Robert swallowed a low, choked noise. His head fell back, baring the pale length of his throat to her gaze.

THIRTEEN

"IS THAT... good? Or bad?" Cassandra asked uncertainly, stilling her hand on Robert's prick as he groaned.

St. Germain, still standing a short distance away with his arms crossed, chuckled. "It's good," he assured her.

"It's good," Robert confirmed hoarsely.

Cassandra resumed her tentative movements, and he made another low noise, his hips curling up as though chasing the contact. An exceedingly strange sensation of liquid heaviness settled low in Cassandra's belly, making her breath come faster.

"This is one of the ways to give a man pleasure without risking much in the way of consequences," Edmund said. "A nice, steady rhythm, perhaps a bit of experimentation with grip and stroke to see what elicits the greatest reaction. Or you can just ask, assuming the man in question actually knows what he's about."

"Oh, experiment away," Robert said— breathlessly, but not without a hint of gentle humor. "Don't mind me."

Cassandra frowned down at Robert's prick, oddly fascinated by this thing that had seemed so fearful before now. It was wonderfully soft on the outside, especially for being so hard on the inside. It also appeared to hold a shocking amount of power over its owner. She took Edmund's advice and varied her movements, gaze flicking back and forth between her hand and Robert's face.

It was extraordinary. This was how she would want to paint the man, she decided — if only there were some way of capturing his expression of tortured ecstasy for long enough to commit it to canvas. He was no longer Hermes, the fallen Greek god. Now, he was a martyred saint, or perhaps a fallen angel. She wanted to keep him like this forever, just so she could continue to watch his transported expression.

Her thumb encountered slickness at his tip, and he shuddered, thrusting up into the circle of her hand with a breathless noise. She repeated the motion, again and again, trying to elicit that same response.

"Miss," Robert choked out. "I... I'm going to —
"

"Stop," Edmund said.

Cassandra snatched her hand away, unsure if she'd done something wrong.

Robert groaned, slumping against the chair. "For God's *sake*, Edmund."

His prick continued to twitch, even in the absence of her touch. Cassandra watched, transfixed, as a thin dribble of whitish fluid stretched downward from the tip, dripping onto Robert's belly.

"What's wrong?" Cassandra asked, with a hint of trepidation.

"Nothing's wrong," Edmund assured her.

"Matter of opinion, that," Robert muttered with a sigh.

"He was about to spend," Edmund said, ignoring the grousing. "That's what he was trying to tell you, just not very coherently. I didn't know if you'd be prepared to add 'messy' to your list of adjectives, along with 'dangly' and 'wormlike.'"

She looked from him to Robert, slouched in his chair and still half-undone. "That's the part where a man's seed issues from his member?"

"That's the one," Robert said shakily. "If you don't wish to continue, that's fine. Though I would request that someone untie me so I can take myself off somewhere to finish the job in private."

Cassandra's body was clamoring for... *something*, every square inch of skin awake and sensitive. "I should much rather see for myself, if you've no objection."

"Absolutely none at all," Robert said in a heartfelt tone, drawing a chuckle from Edmund.

Breath catching in her throat, Cassandra returned her hand to its previous place and resumed her exploration.

"So good," Robert assured her. "That feels *wonderful*." His hips undulated, following the rhythm of her hand. More moisture beaded at his tip. His movements grew more heated... more desperate. "Yes, Miss. Just like that... *ah*!"

His body went rigid, and the flesh in her hand pulsed. Thin ropes of pearly white seed spilled over her fingers, Robert's belly, and the dark thatch of crinkly hair at his base. It went on for the space of several heartbeats before his body subsided into little twitches, and his muscles finally went limp.

It was the very opposite of dignified — even ridiculous, in a way. And yet, she could scarcely seem to breathe. When she shifted restlessly in place, the apex of her thighs felt slick and damp.

"Congratulations," Edmund said wryly. "Hermes appears to have been thoroughly ravished. Just a moment — I'll get you each a damp cloth to clean up."

Robert made a wordless noise somewhere between appreciation and exhaustion.

"Thank you," Cassandra said, examining the milky fluid coating her fingers with interest in the candlelight. It was already growing unpleasantly sticky.

Edmund appeared, handing her a rag dampened in the washbasin on the corner table. He dropped a second cloth in Robert's lap. "You all right there, Hermes?"

Robert peeled one eyelid open. "What do you think?" He rolled his head into an upright position and met Cassandra's gaze, his own open and unguarded. "Though, what would make it even more perfect is if you would do me the honor of a kiss before I'm freed — but you must promise to say no if you do not want it."

Cassandra watched his beautiful face, her mind flying back to the night Thomas had asked her to marry him. Time had rendered the memory of that kiss less bitter and more sweet, especially of late. She couldn't help thinking that her poor, dead beau would have liked both Robert and Edmund immensely.

She rose from her crouched position and leaned forward, bracing herself with one hand against the chair. Her lips brushed Roberts, tentative, and then with more confidence. It was chaste, especially compared to what she had just done to him — and yet, the brief contact jolted through her body like lightning.

"Thank you," she breathed into the sliver of space separating them.

"I'm quite certain I should be thanking you," Robert replied with an unguarded smile.

Cassandra was aware that a similar smile graced her own lips. She turned it on Edmund, who stood behind the chair, watching them with clear appreciation.

"I think Hermes has earned his freedom from captivity," she said.

"As my lady commands," Edmund teased, reaching down to release Robert's bound hands.

Robert groaned and stretched, then set immediately to cleaning himself up and putting his clothing to rights.

"It's as well that getting stains out of clothing is part of my actual job description," he observed wryly.

Cassandra laughed — she couldn't help it. She still felt sensitive to the lightest touch against her skin and overly warm, but she also felt *light*. Lighter than she had in years, in fact.

"You have the appearance of someone who enjoyed herself," Edmund observed. "I take it the experiment was a success."

"I should say so," she agreed. "Perhaps a man's member is not such a fearsome thing after all. Not when one has control of the situation, at least."

"Indeed not," Edmund agreed. "And will you enjoy yourself further once you return to your room tonight?"

She blinked at him, trying to infer his meaning. "How do you mean?"

Robert finished rearranging his clothing and stood up. "He's asking if you intend to touch yourself once you're alone. I assume Frances mentioned the joys of self-pleasure during your discussion with her? Regardless, feel free to ignore Edmund's impropriety. Or to slap him, if that's more appealing."

"*Oh*," she said. Frances had indeed mentioned it, though Cassandra hadn't paid much heed at the time. Now, though... "I'm not certain."

Well," Edmund said, "on the off chance this will sway your decision, you may imagine me lying naked on that bed and touching myself to thoughts of you." His dark eyes flicked to the neatly made bed on the far side of the room. "Because that is most certainly what I'll be doing, just as soon as I'm alone."

The distracting sensations running through Cassandra's body intensified. "I see," she managed. "I shall keep that in mind."

"Oh, *please* do," Edmund replied.

"And on that entirely inappropriate note, may I escort you back to your room, Cassandra?" Robert asked. "I fear it is growing rather late, and unfortunately my duties begin early."

"Yes, that would be lovely," Cassandra said, thinking that perhaps some privacy would not go amiss. "Edmund, thank you for your kind invitation tonight. The evening has been very" — a ridiculous smile tugged at her lips — "*enlightening*."

Edmund took her hand and raised it to his lips, just as he'd done earlier. "It was my pleasure. Well, mostly Robert's — but mine as well."

Another small puff of laughter escaped her. Impetuously, she stretched up and tugged Edmund down enough to press a kiss to the corner of his mouth. When she pulled away and looked up at him shyly, he was smiling.

"Good night, Cassandra," he said.

"Good night, Edmund," she replied. "Perhaps we might make another attempt at sketching tomorrow."

"I look forward to it," he told her. "Good night, Robert."

Cassandra followed Robert out of Edmund's rooms and back to hers, matching her pace to his hitching gait. When they arrived at her door, he turned to her. "You're all right? Truly?" he asked, looking down at her.

"I truly am," she assured him, placing a hand on his forearm. "Believe me, at this juncture I think I would find it very difficult to be afraid of you. Even your dangly bits."

136

He gave a low laugh and took her hand, lifting it and pressing a kiss to her knuckles as Edmund had done. "Then it appears tonight's mission was a success. I wish you pleasant dreams, Cassandra."

"Pleasant dreams, Hermes," she echoed, and entered her room, closing the door behind her once he'd bowed to her and left.

Poor Sadie's various duties ensured she was not available to act as Cassandra's lady's maid at all hours of the day and night. However, right now she was not at all upset to be left to her own devices. She took down her hair and brushed it out, plaiting it into a simple braid for sleep—one that was only slightly uneven and crooked. After washing her face and hands in the basin, she donned a nightgown and slipped beneath the sheets of the comfortable bed.

Even now, her body still hadn't quieted. Images from the evening played behind her closed eyelids. *'Will you enjoy yourself further once you return to your room tonight?'* Edmund had asked. She thought back to what Frances had said of the sin of self-pleasure—namely, that it was *not* a sin, because it was natural and harmed no one.

'Women touch their breasts,' Frances had explained. *'They cup and rub themselves between their legs in whatever manner feels best. Such things are no one's business but one's own, and it's often much simpler than involving another person.'*

Cassandra had quite enjoyed involving another person, actually. But under the circumstances…

Lying alone in her borrowed bed, she lifted a hand to the swell of her left breast. The skin still felt overly sensitive. She stroked over it, and her nipple hardened into a taut point. A flush of pleasure flowed outward from the contact. She did it again, her fingertip catching on the erect nipple through the muslin of the nightdress. Her breath hitched.

Slowly, she began to explore, her mind adrift with visions of Robert's hips curling off the chair as he thrust into her hand… of Edmund naked on his bed, thinking of her as he pleasured himself. Would he handle his prick the same way she'd handled Robert's? Would he spend in the same manner?

The folds between her thighs were slick with unaccustomed dampness—that private place she was somehow supposed to keep 'pure' for a husband, despite the fact that people acted as though its very existence was inherently dirty and humiliating.

Cassandra would have wagered that Robert and Edmund didn't think it was dirty. Would Robert hold her in his arms and touch her like this, mirroring her actions on him? Would Edmund tease and joke and tell him how to touch her? Would he… join in? What would it be like to lie cradled between them?

Every stroke of her fingertips was building something inside, driving her higher and higher as though she might somehow take flight and never return to earth. The memory of Robert's breathless voice whispered at the edge of her memory. *'Miss, I... I'm going to—'*

He'd defaulted back to addressing her as a superior as he slowly came undone. And *oh*, how she'd liked that. Was this how he'd felt as she'd stroked his hard length. Had he scaled this same peak?

A sensation of exquisite tension flowed outward from the flesh beneath her busy fingers... cresting, cresting, ever higher and as inexorable as the tide. Without warning, it broke over her, scattering carnal pleasure like starlight—taking her breath away as her muscles jerked and twitched. When the sensation ebbed, all of her tension drained away with it, leaving only a faint, throbbing headache left over from her mostly healed injury.

That dull ache was overshadowed by a strange buzz of relaxed wellbeing that made her arms and legs feel heavy with lassitude. At that moment, she couldn't have named a single one of her worries. They were all faraway and unimportant.

She resolved to try the experiment again just as soon as she recovered a bit, to see if it would feel that good every time, or only the first. Yes... perhaps she would make another attempt in a minute or two...

A few seconds later, she was fast asleep.

FOURTEEN

THE ODD, CAREFREE feeling of lightness persisted into the following morning. Sadie appeared as the morning light slanted through the window and gave Cassandra a curious onceover.

"You're looking chipper this morning, Miss," she said. "Did you sleep well?"

Cassandra had slept like the proverbial dead. In fact, she had to wonder why doctors across the country weren't prescribing nightly self-pleasure for their female patients, if it was truly this restorative. She spared a thought for Robert and Edmund, and hoped that such activities had a similar effect for men.

"I slept very well indeed, thank you," she said. "I can only hope that Mary is as much improved this morning as I feel."

"She seems a bit better every day, Miss," Sadie said, fussing around her to help her get dressed and coiffed. "Now, I believe breakfast is being served in the blue drawing room, if you're ready. I am sorry, but I'm afraid my other duties require me to return to the kitchens now. Will that be all right?"

"Yes, of course, Sadie," Cassandra said quickly. "Please, don't feel obligated to wait on me at the expense of your usual duties. While I can't overstate how much I've appreciated your help and company, I imagine I can muddle through on my own if I have to."

Sadie smiled her brilliant smile. "You're very kind, Miss. I enjoy it, though. Never thought I'd get to act as a lady's maid!"

"You've a talent for it," Cassandra told her. "I shall have a word with Frances about your future prospects, if you like."

The young woman gave her a look as though she'd hung the stars in the night sky, and thanked her profusely. Cassandra felt a moment's guilt once she'd gone, as she was forcibly reminded that she did not, in fact, have any standing to improve Sadie's prospects for better employment. She had no standing at all, and it was only the events of the past few days that had made her forget the fact for a few moments.

Just because her views and her person were respected here in this house, it didn't mean they would be respected once she left. The realization sapped much of her earlier enthusiasm for the day. Nevertheless, she made her way to the blue drawing room, where she found Lord Rotherdam and Frances breakfasting together.

"Good morning," she said, with a hint of trepidation.

Rotherdam stood as she entered. "Good morning. Please join us for breakfast, Miss Fenwicke. I trust you slept well?"

Cassandra stood frozen for a moment, somewhat taken aback by the viscount's change in manner since the last time they'd interacted. She'd been braced for anything from a sharp comment about her ongoing lack of a chaperone to a hasty exit.

"You do look *quite* well-rested," Frances said archly. "Good morning, Cassandra."

Breaking herself free of her momentary paralysis, Cassandra crossed to the breakfast table and allowed Lord Rotherdam to seat her. "Thank you. I, er, did sleep rather well, as it happens." She glanced at blue sky visible through the tall windows, and reached for the old English staple of discussing the weather. "At least the rain has finally stopped."

Rotherdam reseated himself at the head of the table as Cassandra served herself a slice of cake and a cup of chocolate.

"Indeed," he said. "You'll be happy to know that work on the bridge is scheduled to start later today, once the water recedes a bit more."

She pasted on a smile to cover the sinking sensation in her stomach. "Oh? Well, I suppose that *is* good news. I'm sure you'll be pleased to have a connection to the outside world once more."

Frances snorted. "Lord Rotherdam and the outside world don't generally get on very well."

Throwing caution to the wind, Cassandra nodded sagely. "It's the orgies, I imagine. Or possibly the virgin sacrifices?"

"Both, I should think," Frances replied, eyes twinkling behind her mock-grave expression. "What do you think, Freddie?"

He blinked at them both, as though unsure for a moment how to respond. After a brief hesitation his handsome features settled into impassivity and he replied, "I'd always assumed it was the satanic rites and witchcraft. It's so terribly difficult to get goat's blood out of black velvet robes."

Frances guffawed, and Cassandra had to cover her mouth with her hand to hold back an unladylike huff of laughter.

"Oh, come now," Frances said. "Surely Barlow has a patent solution for removing goat's blood, after all the practice he must have had at it."

Cassandra felt her face heat and grew very interested in her chocolate, as a memory from last night floated to the fore.

It's as well that getting stains out of clothing is part of my actual job description, Robert had said wryly, looking down at his ruined shirttails.

Rotherdam, too, appeared to regain some of his reserve rather abruptly at the mention of his valet. "Yes, well. I fear I don't involve myself in the details of my valet's affairs to that degree."

Cassandra was entirely unsure whether the double entendre was intentional or merely a figment of her guilt-riddled imagination. Then she was irritated with herself for her guilt. If Robert was to be believed, Edmund had sought Rotherdam's blessing before entering into last night's events… so to speak. While that implied the viscount had some knowledge of the affair, it *also* implied that he hadn't objected — or at least, not enough to forbid his employee and his servant from pursuing it.

"I'm certain that if Mr. Barlow were presented with bloodstained satanic robes, he would do battle against them with valor," she said loyally.

The viscount's expression softened. "Yes. I daresay he would."

It occurred to her that Rotherdam would have more experience than most with the subject of Robert's valor. Curiosity overcame her. "You and he fought in the war together, yes?"

"We did." The reply held a certain hint of caution, but nothing that implied it was a forbidden subject.

"I understand he was injured while doing something quite heroic," she said. "I certainly don't wish to pry if it's a sensitive subject, but I should like to hear more about that."

Frances finished her drink and sat back. "Ugh, war stories. You'll pardon me if I leave you to it. I've heard this one before, and to be perfectly honest, I don't care to think on it too closely."

Cassandra frowned. "Forgive me—I've no wish to drive you away from the breakfast table with my unseemly curiosity. We don't need to speak of it if it's upsetting."

Frances waved a hand dismissively. "No, no. I need to get on anyway. Oh... and be aware that even if the bridge repairs are finished promptly, it will be some time yet before Mary can be moved safely. She's on the mend, there's no question—but her injury was a close-run thing. I won't risk a setback by dumping her in a coach and jostling her across the countryside before she's strong enough."

"No one would dare insist otherwise," Rotherdam said. "Miss Stanhope and Miss Fenwicke will stay as long as necessary to ensure Miss Stanhope's safety."

Cassandra was growing increasingly curious as to the precise content of the conversation between Edmund and the viscount. Whatever it had entailed, it certainly seemed to have altered his attitude in a positive way.

"We're in your debt," she said.

"Oh, dear," Frances said. "Yes — this conversation is becoming tiresome already. Come along to Mary's room when you've finished breakfasting, Cassandra. I'm sure she'd be glad of the company, and you can tell her rousing stories of battle and valor to entertain her."

"I will," Cassandra replied without taking offense. "Thank you, Frances."

Frances gave her a quick, wry smile and excused herself.

Lord Rotherdam's strikingly blue eyes fell on Cassandra and held there. "Frances seems quite fond of you. I wasn't certain how the two of you would get on. She can be a bit…"

"She's an extraordinary woman, and I have her to thank for my maid's life," Cassandra said.

"She is, and I daresay you do," Rotherdam agreed easily. "I am surrounded by extraordinary people."

Cassandra smiled, charmed entirely despite herself. "You are, rather. Perhaps it comes of presiding over a Hellfire Club."

"Not entirely." Rotherdam lifted an eyebrow and sipped at his chocolate. "After all, I met Barlow long before I began indulging my hellish inclinations."

"In the army? My Tom was at Waterloo, as well," Cassandra said, the old ache having dulled somewhat as time passed. "That's where I lost him. We were engaged to be married."

"You have my deepest condolences. So many good men lost their lives that day. What was his full name?"

It hadn't occurred to Cassandra that anyone here might have been acquainted with Tom personally. "His name was Thomas Jacoby."

Rotherdam looked thoughtful. "The name rings a vague bell, but he wasn't one of mine. I am sorry for your loss."

"It's been more than three years," she said. "I do still miss him, though. I think I'd like to hear a story from that day with a happy ending."

"Well," Rotherdam replied, "I can offer a story with a harrowing ending, at least."

☙ ♕ ❧

Frederick studied Miss Fenwicke's expression surreptitiously. Every new facet of his reluctant guest's story seemed destined to make her more appealing, while simultaneously reminding him of why he had no business being within twenty feet of her. And yet, here he was, taking breakfast with her and gathering himself to relay the tale of one of the most significant days of his life.

It was, at least, a tale he was familiar with telling. God knew, he'd told it often enough.

"I was commanding a platoon of heavy cavalry at Waterloo, which I suppose tells you how hard-up they were for officers by that point in the war. It was early afternoon, and the 9th Brigade had just attempted to advance on the French. But the men broke ranks, and the French Army took full advantage, scattering the line and advancing into our territory."

He remembered the frantic shouts of the officers, trying to bully their terrified men into marching on the French, rather than breaking formation and firing wildly across the battlefield.

"My platoon was cut off from the rest of the King's Dragoon Guards. We were pincered on two sides, with open ground at our backs. Barlow attempted to skirt around their lines and ride for reinforcements, but he was seen. Two dozen enemy soldiers closed on him, and he took a serious saber wound to the leg as he was trying to fight his way clear."

Miss Fenwicke's breath caught, and he imagined she was trying to picture kind, soft-spoken Robert Barlow fighting for his platoon's life with pistol and blade. He'd seen it firsthand, and he still found it difficult to reconcile with the gentle valet who buttoned his waistcoat and tied his cravat with careful precision on a daily basis.

"The only saving grace was that the French army was basically reduced to riding elderly farm nags by that point in the war. All of the decent horses on the continent had already been killed, whereas we'd shipped our mounts over with us from England. Barlow managed to open a gap, and he rode hell-bent for leather. He outdistanced his pursuers and reached the rest of our forces, where he alerted the commanding officer to our plight, and promptly collapsed from blood loss."

His rapt audience of one gave an audible gasp.

"I didn't learn of the details until later, of course. Medics hauled him off to the farmhouse we were using for casualties, where one of the surgeons sutured his leg closed and bandaged him up. Meanwhile, we rejoined the rest of the battalion in time for the charge that broke the French infantry lines."

Even now, Frederick occasionally dreamed of the screams of dying horses. But thanks to Barlow, his platoon had survived to fight the battle they'd been ordered to fight. They'd fared better than many, that day.

"And afterward, you hired Robert—Mr. Barlow—as your valet?" Miss Fenwicke asked.

"Yes. It seemed the least I could do." Preferable to sending him back home with a ruined leg and an inadequate pittance of a pension, certainly.

Before that terrible Sunday in June, Frederick had known Robert Barlow only as one private among many—though one with a face of such beauty that he turned heads wherever he went. Only afterward had he truly appreciated the man's selfless nature and purity of spirit. That, combined with his subtle wit and occasional dry, self-deprecating humor, had made his presence in Frederick's life both a blessing and a wicked temptation—one to which he'd vowed never to succumb.

Despite Edmund's accusation of monkhood, Frederick had warmed plenty of beds over the years, with both males and females. But only a monster placed his servant in the position of having to turn down sexual advances from the very person who controlled their livelihood. And for all his many failings, Frederick strove not to be a monster.

"Your valet would seem to be an exceptionally brave and honorable man," Miss Fenwicke said.

Frederick wondered if they'd slept with each other yet, and then cursed himself roundly as a vision of the two together inserted itself firmly into his mind's eye. Blonde hair and russet... tanned skin and creamy pale. He pushed the image firmly away.

"That he is. I was exceptionally lucky to have him then, and the same is true now."

A lovely smile curved Miss Fenwicke's lips. "Extraordinary people, indeed," she murmured. "Though I'm certain you'll be glad to be rid of me, I shall be rather sad to leave your den of iniquity, Lord Rotherdam. The company here is most... agreeable."

Frederick had a fair idea of what awaited her after her departure from Hengewick House, and he couldn't help a twinge of regret on her behalf. He inclined his head. "I'll tell them you said so. I'm not certain *agreeable* is a word most of them are used to hearing in reference to themselves."

Miss Fenwicke's startled laughter transformed her face like the sun coming out.

He stayed until she finished her breakfast, chatting with her about light matters and trying not to curse himself for a fool. Once she left to rejoin her injured maid, he sat back in his chair and stared out the windows until a new presence darkened the doorway.

"Good morning," Edmund said, not without a bit of caution. "Did I see Miss Fenwicke leaving just now?"

Frederick waved him to the table impatiently. "You did. She seemed in quite a good mood this morning."

Edmund sat, still looking rather wary. "Perhaps she found a pleasant diversion to pass the time last night."

The flat stare Frederick gave him spoke louder than words. Edmund only shrugged, and reached for a plate.

"Just be careful with her, Edmund," he said. "And don't get too attached, for God's sake. You know how these things go."

Edmund paused in pouring a cup of chocolate and set the pot down, giving Frederick his full attention. "I know what she's likely to face once she leaves, if that's what you mean," he said.

"A dalliance is just that," Frederick replied, unable to keep the snap of impatience from his voice. "She will move on to something better, and I don't want either of you hurt."

Understanding lit Edmund's gaze, and Frederick set his jaw under that dark-eyed regard.

"She's not Christina, Rotherdam," Edmund said. "In fact, the vast majority of women in the world are nothing like your former fiancé. And the sooner you realize that, the less miserable the rest of your life will be."

"I have no idea what you mean," Frederick retorted, knowing how weak it sounded.

"Of course not," Edmund said with some irony. "However could I have come to such an erroneous conclusion? But you needn't worry yourself, *my lord*. I daresay Robert and I will be able to avoid *that* sort of scandal, at the very least. Miss Fenwicke really isn't the type to jilt a bloke, and we're not the type of blokes to be jilted."

The tight feeling in Frederick's chest and throat might have been justifiable anger. It might equally have been something else.

"Yes, *quite*," he said sharply, and excused himself from the table.

FIFTEEN

CASSANDRA FOLLOWED what was becoming a rather pleasant daily routine, spending time with Mary in the morning before wandering up to Edmund's art studio around midday.

Her maid had been pleasingly awed by Cassandra's recounting of Robert's act of heroism. She was also in a state of excitement after Frances indicated that she might venture from bed soon, as long as her condition continued to improve. The one fly in the ointment was her continuing inability to move her fingers on the injured arm. However, as Frances had reassured her several times, she might yet regain sensation and movement in that hand once the wound knit together more completely.

After delivering a promise to return later in the day with a book to read aloud, Cassandra ventured to the room at the end of the hall on the third floor and knocked on the closed door.

"*Come in!*" came Edmund's familiar voice, muffled through the wood.

Cassandra pushed the door open on its creaking hinges and peered inside. "Hello," she said, taking in the new display of male flesh entangled on the divan. She quickly darted her gaze away, to where Edmund stood at his easel with charcoal in hand. "Er… may I join you today?"

"Hello, Cassandra," Edmund said. "I suppose I should ask these two louts first, if only for the form of the thing. Gentlemen? Miss Fenwicke has been honing her craft with live models during her stay. She's quite talented, and would probably appreciate the chance at some new blood."

The foppish Mr. Fortescue lowered the bunch of grapes he'd been holding poised above Mr. Vaughan's lips. The pair lay tangled together amongst the ubiquitous silk fabric that revealed as much as it concealed.

"Hello, my dear," Fortescue greeted, and Cassandra was certain she could detect a hint of wariness in his tone. "Goodness—I will admit that hadn't expected ladies to be present. I fear we might shock you."

Mr. Vaughan, too, appeared tense, and Cassandra wasn't entirely sure why. At the same time, something about the tableau set butterflies dancing in her stomach. She took a deep breath, steadying herself.

"Forgive me," she said. "I've no wish to intrude if it would make you uncomfortable. I fear my brief exposure to a Hellfire Club has quite played havoc with my sense of propriety."

The tight line of Mr. Vaughan's shoulders relaxed incrementally, and Mr. Fortescue gave her a hesitant nod. "Yes," he allowed. "I suppose it does tend to have that effect on one. Far be it from me to stand in the way of the furthering of the arts.

If you will agree not to be shocked, we will attempt not to be shocking. Lawrence?"

"I've no objection," the plain-faced Mr. Vaughan said cautiously.

"Very well," Edmund said. "Cassandra, you know where the materials are. The light is lovely today, for once."

Indeed, the sun was illuminating the white room with startling clarity after the long days of clouds and storms. Cassandra gave the men an uncertain smile and went to retrieve charcoal and paper.

Edmund marshaled his models back into position, and she sat down to work. The pair on the divan were different from Robert in almost every way. Both had the paleness common to individuals who spent the bulk of their time indoors, in contrast to Robert's golden skin tones. Nor were either of them in much danger of being mistaken for classical Greek statuary.

Cassandra sketched, her brow furrowed in concentration as she studied the slight roundness of Mr. Fortescue's shoulders; the soft paunch of Mr. Vaughan's belly. It was when she came to their faces that she paused, caught by the expressions they both wore as they gazed into each other's eyes.

She had seen that look before—on Tom's face, right after she'd accepted his proposal of marriage. The charcoal almost slipped from her fingers, and she fumbled to hold onto it before quickly turning her face to her work.

Rather than contemplate the impossibility of adequately committing those expressions to paper in shades of gray, she switched to a study of Mr. Fortescue's hand holding the bunch of grapes.

They sketched on; Edmund occasionally trading witty quips with the pair that barely registered in Cassandra's ears, so preoccupied was she. Eventually, he called a halt.

"Oh, good," Mr. Fortescue said. "One would never believe how heavy a few dozen grapes may become over the course of an hour."

Mr. Vaughan snorted softly. "Or how hungry they might make one, when there's no prospect of actually eating them."

He rolled into a sitting position, being very careful to hold the folds of red silk over his middle. His eyes darted to the changing screens at the back of the studio, and Cassandra quickly interpreted the source of his nervousness.

"Thank you both," she said, rising, and lifted a hand to stop them when politeness dictated that they follow suit. "I appreciate the opportunity you've afforded me, but I will leave you to change in peace. I can't wait to see what Edmund has envisioned for his new painting."

She crossed the room to stow her sketches and materials in the cabinet. When she turned to excuse herself, Edmund stopped her with a touch on her shoulder that tingled warmly through the fabric of her dress.

"Perhaps you'll join me for a late nuncheon in half an hour?" he asked. "In the same venue as dinner last night."

She nodded, her breath coming a bit faster as memories of yesterday evening's 'dessert' flitted through her mind. "That sounds lovely, thank you," she replied. "Until then."

With a final smile for the pair on the divan, she let herself out of the studio and paused for a moment in the hallway, her mind awhirl.

>∾ ☗ ∾<

It was still awhirl when she presented herself as requested at Edmund's door. He gestured her inside with a murmured greeting and seated her at the table. A tureen of soup sat in the middle, curls of steam wafting gently from beneath the lid. Once she was served and Edmund had seated himself as well, he gave her his full attention.

"You have questions," he said. "I have answers, but the framework in which they must be given is a complicated one."

Cassandra fiddled with her spoon, straightening it in the placing as she gathered her thoughts.

"Yes," she said, after a pregnant pause. "Frances said, among many other things, that a woman may desire other women, and a man may desire other men. She also said that a person might desire both sexes equally, or desire neither."

'That's right," Edmund said.

"She told me that men's pricks hold no interest for her, which I took to mean that she is a woman who only desires others of her own sex," Cassandra continued. "She said that everyone here was safe to be themselves without fear of censure. That...

seems like it would be appealing to other people in a similar situation?"

Edmund nodded. "Safety for inverts is in short supply in England. But here's the thing, Cassandra. Frances may dally as she likes—and while it holds the potential for censure and even ruin, it is at least not expressly illegal. Whereas a hypothetical man credibly accused of sodomy or attempted sodomy faces the noose."

Cassandra had grown up in a household where one did not discuss such matters in front of young ladies. However, young ladies still had ears and curious minds. She had been old enough when David Thomas Myers was tried and sentenced to death for buggery to suffer burning curiosity as to what his detestable crime actually entailed.

Not that she truly had much more of an idea now, but a few things were clearer, at least.

"I think I understand," she said. "And I don't wish to place anyone in this house in an awkward situation. Even so, it should be known that even if I were inclined to make accusations against anyone in the house for any such thing—which I'm not—they could hardly be considered credible."

Edmund gave her a gentle smile. "I didn't mean to imply that you would; only to explain why I can't give answers relating to other people with the degree of openness I might wish. I can only speak for myself... and I'm not much inclined in that direction personally."

She raised an eyebrow, thinking of Mr. Fortescue and Mr. Vaughan entangled on the couch. "Not even from an aesthetic standpoint?" she asked.

He gave a deep chuckle. "Oh, no—don't misunderstand. It can be quite affecting from an aesthetic standpoint. But I could say the same about a sensual composition of two women, or a man and woman, or a mixed group. I merely mean that aside from a bit of furtive fumbling back in Cambridge, it's not something I tend to seek out."

Cassandra absolutely refused to acknowledge the mental image of Edmund's rich brown skin against Robert's sun-touched gold.

"I understand," she said. "While I might find it interesting to sketch Frances, for instance, I don't think I share her preference for wide hips and creamy bosoms. A pity, really—since the absence of alarming dangly bits might simplify matters."

That startled a real laugh from her host. "It would certainly have been Robert's loss, though... and mine, as well."

Warmth spread through her chest, comfortable, but with a hint of the pleasant, fluttery sensation she was coming to associate with flirtation. The twinkle in Edmund's dark eyes told her he saw the effect he was having, and she found that she did not mind.

He gestured to her bowl. "Don't let the soup get cold," he suggested.

They fell to the simple meal, engaging in a pleasant conversation about the improvement of the weather and Mary's recovery. Cassandra thought this casual exchange should have sufficed to cool the heat gathering in her belly, but it really didn't. When they were both finished with their light repast, Edmund's eyes fell on her with intent.

"Now that the soup is no longer a concern, I suppose we may return to impropriety," he said, with a hint of humor playing around the corners of his full lips. "May I trust that you did, in fact, enjoy yourself last night? Both before and after we parted for the evening, I mean."

The sense of lightness from this morning returned, and Cassandra marveled at it, even as the tips of her ears grew warm. "You may," she said shyly. "And may I trust that you did the same?"

"Oh, indeed," he replied, his gaze growing heated. "Twice."

Cassandra swallowed rather convulsively beneath that burning regard. "I neglected to capitalize on my chance to sketch you earlier," she managed.

His expression softened. "So you did. However, if you wish to see me in my entirety, I should point out that you don't need an excuse. You only need to ask."

Her breath caught. She could just... *ask*. And he would indulge her in whatever manner she chose. No one here would judge her. There would be no repercussions.

The idea was intoxicating.

As though of her own volition, her eyes tracked to the bed across the room.

"Would you... show me what you did last night? After Robert and I left?"

His eyelids lowered to half-mast. "I could be persuaded," he said. "Perhaps we should discuss the details first, though."

She drew herself back from her fantasies, giving consideration to the reality of it instead. "Yes, I... I understand. I'm certain you wish to avoid a repeat of the first time."

"I'm certain you do as well," he retorted.

She gave a small, humorless laugh. "Yes. I can't say I'm eager to relive that unpleasantness yet again."

"Indeed. So, the first question," he said. "My door has a lock. If it's engaged, I fear it might make you feel trapped, should you desire a rapid exit. However, it's still the middle of the day, and although it's unlikely, I cannot give you an absolute guarantee that someone won't ignore good manners and barge in looking for me."

The idea sent a small frisson of... something... down Cassandra's spine, but it was drowned out by the louder clamor of mortification at the idea. She contemplated being locked in the room with Edmund as he... did whatever it was he had done last night.

"The key would still be in the lock, would it not?" she asked.

"Yes, certainly," he agreed. "You would only need to turn it to leave."

She gave a slow nod, picturing how trivial the action would be. "Then locking it seems preferable."

"Very well. I concur." His small, half-hidden smile returned for a moment. "Second question. It was my impression that Robert being mostly clothed last night was helpful to you, but I assure you I was quite thoroughly unclothed last night as I pleasured myself. And unfortunately, that did not go... *well*, the first time we tried it."

Frustration—directed firmly inward—welled in Cassandra's breast. *How much simpler it would be not to have to consider such things.* And yet, failing to do so would be foolish.

"I think it was more the sense of control I felt than the clothes themselves," she said. "And... I should like to be able to move past such things. I *don't* fear you, Edmund. Truly, I don't."

He took her hand in his and bent forward to place a kiss on the knuckles, in a gesture that was fast becoming a source of exceptional comfort to her.

"I know," he said. "And rest assured, I don't take any such reaction as a personal insult. It's to be avoided if possible, and dealt with if not. That's all. You are not to blame for what was done to you by a vicious and dishonorable cad."

And why should those simple words make the back of her eyes burn with tears?

"May I kiss you now?" she blurted, unsure from where the sudden urge had sprung.

Rather than answer directly, Edmund used his light grip on her hand to urge her up and to his side. He was so tall that she barely had to bend to reach his lips, but she appreciated his thoughtfulness nonetheless, as he once more put her in control.

The kiss was light, and he made no attempt to deepen it. His lips were quite different from either Tom's or Robert's—silky soft and pillowy. She wanted to run her fingertips over the interesting curves of his face. The high, rounded cheekbones, the wide, flat nose. There were other things she wanted more, though.

"I believe I would prefer to throw caution to the wind, in order to get an accurate reproduction of your actions last night," she said, pulling back enough to watch his reaction. "Since you'll be on the bed, perhaps we could agree that if my mind decides to play tricks, you could toss a corner of the coverlet across your lap? Then it would be no different than one of your artist's models with their silk coverings."

"Eminently practical," he said. "If you feel distressed, say 'stop.' And if I believe you may be experiencing distress but are unable to say so, I'll cover up as a precaution. Though you should be aware of a short period of time when I may be too distracted to notice."

"I'll try not to hold it against you," she teased, remembering Robert, lost to his own pleasure last night.

He stretched up and tugged her down enough for a second kiss, this one lingering. When they parted, she was breathless. He gave her hand a final squeeze, and she stood back to let him rise. He picked up the chair he'd been sitting in and carried it to the side of the bed where the window was located, placing it to take advantage of the light without throwing a shadow across the top half of the mattress.

"Your throne, my queen," he teased.

Hiding a smile, she gave him a regal nod and lowered herself onto the seat with all the queenly dignity she could muster. He circled to the other side of the bed — again, she thought, to avoid looming over her — and began to untie his cravat.

"I do hope that these kind of... *activities*... are as restorative for men as they seem to be for women," she said, since this seemed like the time to indulge her curiosity.

He gave a little huff of laughter. "Hmm. Is restorative the right word? I fear quite a number of men find it more soporific than anything, though I pride myself in not being among the number who roll over and start snoring immediately afterward."

"Relaxing, then?" she suggested, as his waistcoat came off, followed by his shirt.

"Oh, definitely that," he agreed.

She sat primly, hands folded in her lap, watching as more and more gleaming brown skin appeared. He crossed the room to the mahogany bootjack tucked in one corner, and used it to pull off his tall leather boots. Facing away from her, he unbuttoned the fall of his breeches and slid them slowly down his body.

Cassandra stared in mild fascination at his lean, shapely buttocks, amazed that a body part she would have described as ridiculous and embarrassing could in fact be so beautiful.

"I *will* sketch you," she vowed. "Though not, perhaps, today."

"I look forward to it," he said, sending her an amused smile over his shoulder as he stepped out of the breeches and peeled off his stockings. He straightened, completely bare to her gaze, but still facing away. "Shall I turn around now and come to the bed?"

She took a moment to picture in her mind what it would look like when he did, prodding at the image until she was confident it held no fear for her.

"Yes, please," she told him.

When he turned, the view before her did not match up very well to her mental image. He was already hard, his member bobbing out in front of him. It was, in some ways, an absurd thing, stretching out from his heavy thatch of dark curls like a hound straining at the leash. And yet, it still managed to engender an odd mix of excitement and trepidation in her stomach.

"All right?" he asked, watching her carefully.

She licked her lips. Her surroundings remained unchanged — a familiar bedroom in cheery daylight, rather than a lonely garden maze at night.

"Yes," she said. "I believe so. Please, come lie on the bed. I promise to make no mention of worms, fat or otherwise."

"I'll hold you to that," he said with wry humor.

He approached and settled onto the bed with no evidence of self-consciousness, shifting pillows around so he could rest against the headboard with one leg drawn up. His left hand came up to cushion the back of his head, the movement of his arm stretching skin over muscle, all along his lean torso. Cassandra stared, transfixed, as his other hand slid down to cup the soft sac hanging below his shaft. He rolled the tender flesh, his eyelids drooping as he watched her watching him.

"You've as much as admitted to pleasuring yourself after you left last night," he said, his hand sliding up to circle the hardness of his prick. "Will you tell me what you did?" That secret smile tilted one corner of his generous mouth. "It only seems fair, under the circumstances."

Cassandra's mouth had turned dry as the desert as she watched him, and it took her a moment for the meaning of the words to register. "*Oh*! I... well... I did much as Frances described." She cleared her throat. "I... touched my breasts through my nightdress." Edmund's hand began a lazy slide up and down. "And... between my legs."

For some reason, she couldn't seem to get words to form into any sort of coherent sentences. That same place between her legs was growing heavy and full.

"How did it feel?" Edmund asked. His hand continued to move steadily, with a twist of his wrist at the top of each stroke.

Cassandra's tongue darted out to moisten her lower lip, still tingling from Edmund's kisses earlier. "It felt... strange. Good. Once I started, I didn't want to stop."

"I should think not," he agreed.

"How does it feel for you?" she asked, fascinated.

"Good," he echoed. "Like all the sensation in my body gradually narrows down to a single focus. Nothing else is important. All the cares of the world fall away. There's a heat—a tension—that builds and builds, gathering at the base of my spine like a promise."

"Like a rising tide?" she asked. "Or a wave getting ready to break?"

"Something like that," he agreed, his voice growing deeper. "And what were you thinking about as the tide rose? Did you picture anything in particular?"

She stared at him, utterly unable to look away from the play of dark skin and muscle. "You," she said breathlessly. "You and Robert. I wondered if you were touching yourself the same way I touched him."

Edmund's hand sped up as she spoke. He groaned, his abdominal muscles flexing. His hips curled off the bed, and thin ropes of pearly white erupted from his tip, painting his stomach. Cassandra watched, rapt, the heavy feeling between her legs transforming into a dull throb pulsing in time with her elevated heartbeat. The inside of her thighs felt damp and slippery.

The object of her fascination relaxed against the bed, panting. His head fell back, his eyes sliding closed for a moment before he opened them again to look at her.

"And will you do it again?" he asked hoarsely. "Will you think of this?"

Her hands itched to do it *right now*, here, while he was here watching. She tangled her fingers together so tightly that the knuckles turned white.

"Yes," she whispered.

He let his softening length slide free of his hands, looking every bit as debauched as Robert had the previous night. "I'm pleased to hear it," he said, "In fact, if you'll allow it, I would be more than happy to help you with that."

SIXTEEN

CASSANDRA WAVERED. A lifetime of being told that her body was dirty, that she must never allow her natural effect on men to spill over into action, warred with the desire to let Edmund return her to last night's state of ecstasy.

A man had hurt her, and she'd been blamed for it. Now, a man wanted to please her. She would be blamed for that, too—but only if the knowledge left the bounds of Hengewick House. No one here cared if Edmund touched her inappropriately... or if she touched him inappropriately.

"Yes," she breathed, barely audible. She cleared her throat and spoke in a stronger tone. "Yes, but...only with... not with"—she gestured at his lap—"your member."

He would have been within his rights to laugh in her face. Instead, he gave her an indulgent smile. "You don't wish to risk pregnancy. And I assure you, neither do I. By way of further reassurance, let me just say that so soon after sexual release, there's no danger of my prick doing anything except dangling for at least the next hour or so. Men need time to recover before they can go again—unlike women."

A shivery frisson of excitement prickled fresh gooseflesh across her skin. "Oh," she managed. "That's all right, then."

"You have my word that I will employ only my hands and my mouth," he promised. "May I approach you now?"

His mouth? Cassandra blinked, before realizing that he must mean kissing. "Please," she said.

His smile turned wicked. Lean muscle bunched and slid beneath umber skin as he rolled onto his hands and knees, stalking across the mattress toward her as she imagined a hunting panther might stalk its prey. Her heart fluttered, but the small spike of alarm had more to do with anticipation than any real fear.

He slid off the bed entirely, still on his hands and knees as he crossed the short distance to her chair. Her breath caught at the sight of this powerful, dark-skinned man crawling toward her, his eyes never leaving hers. His hand wrapped around her silk-clad ankle, and she gasped.

"All right?" he asked, pausing.

She nodded, not sure she could have formed even the simplest word. Edmund lifted her foot, pressing a kiss above her anklebone. The sensation was muted through her silk stocking, but it did nothing to slow her galloping heart or dull the aching throb between her legs. He pressed a second kiss a few inches higher on the inside of her calf, and a third, higher still.

Edmund draped her skirt and petticoat over his head, disappearing beneath them as he continued his way upward with slow deliberation. Cassandra squirmed, and was unable to stifle a gasp as his soft lips reached the beribboned garters above her knee and touched bare flesh directly. Her legs fell open to make room for him as he kissed along her inner thigh, the position so crude and unwomanly that it brought the heat of embarrassment to her cheeks.

Strong hands hooked behind her knees and pulled her forward. Cassandra squeaked and grabbed for the sides of the chair to steady herself as her buttocks balanced precariously on the front edge of the seat.

Anticipation and excitement made her feel faint as she awaited the touch of Edmund's fingers... *there*. But when the first touch finally came, it was his lips.

A chill stabbed through her chest. "Stop!" she cried.

Instantly, Edmund pulled away, moving backward until her skirts fell back into place and they were looking at each other directly.

"Cassandra?" he asked carefully.

Her mouth opened and closed a couple of times before words came. "You... you can't want to..." She paused and swallowed convulsively, trying again. "That's what the baron did to me. You can't want to do that." Her body thrummed unhelpfully, distracting her in a most unbecoming manner.

"No," Edmund said slowly. "It's not remotely the same thing he did to you. Malthorpe forced you. No one is forcing me. It would give me pleasure to give you pleasure."

"With your *mouth*?" Cassandra asked in disbelief.

"Yes," Edmund replied. "With my mouth. You smell divine. You taste delicious. It would give me the greatest satisfaction to kiss you there until you cry out my name and fall apart around me."

She couldn't breathe. "What do I taste like?" she whispered.

"Honey and seashells," he said without hesitation, and the ridiculous of it startled a laugh from her.

"That's a very odd-sounding combination," she said. Baron Malthorpe had tasted of stale sweat and smelled like a privy. She determinedly set those memories aside. They had no business here, and she should never have let them into this room in the first place.

"It's you," Edmund said. "And that makes it delicious. May I continue? If you genuinely don't enjoy it, tell me. But please don't assume *I'm* not enjoying it."

After a moment's hesitation, she nodded her permission. She'd thought perhaps he would continue where he'd left off, but instead, he repeated his slow journey of kisses up her other leg. By the time he reached the top, she was squirming again. And this time, he did not stop.

If anything, it felt a bit ticklish at first as his lips brushed the crinkly hair above her bare sex. Then, his tongue delved between her folds, and a full-body shudder wracked her at the sudden pleasure. It was different than using her own fingers—indescribably so. She could not predict how the touches would come, nor exactly where or when.

Edmund teased her mercilessly, spreading her folds apart with his fingers to lap deeper into her body. Her hands clenched at the chair as though it were the only thing keeping her from flying apart in a dozen different directions. There was a strange, birdlike cry echoing through the room—a breathy *ah, ah, ah*, rising in pitch and tenor. It took an embarrassingly long time for Cassandra to realize that it came from her own throat.

Her head lolled against the chair's tall back, eyes sliding closed as Edmund's lips closed around her sensitive bud, his tongue flicking over it rapidly. He sucked and laved, and the pleasure that had been coiling tighter and tighter broke free in a liquid rush. She jerked and shook, strong hands on her thighs preventing her from squirming away.

Edmund's mouth on her gentled until he was barely nuzzling against her curls, and her body was as limp as a used rag. Unthinking, she dragged a hand to the shifting lump beneath her skirts and stroked his head through the fabric. He pressed a closed mouth kiss to the inside of first one thigh, then the other. As he had before, he backed away, letting her skirts fall into place, covering her modestly.

She was reasonably certain she'd left a stain of slickness on the inside of her chemise... unless he'd licked it up. The idea sent another shiver through her.

"So beautiful," he said, sitting naked before her with one knee drawn up, his elbow resting on it. "May I kiss you?"

She blinked. He'd just...

But he'd also said she tasted good. A hint of curiosity threaded through her languor. She nodded and reached a hand out to him. He took it and rose, leaning over her to press his lips to hers.

Cassandra recognized the musky smell from her explorations last night. The taste was... not like honey, though perhaps the comparison to seashells was not as odd as it had first sounded. Something from the sea, at any rate. He pulled back and stroked a loose curl of hair behind her ear.

"Did you enjoy it?" he murmured.

She let out a little huff of breath. "You have to ask? Surely you know that I did."

"Good," he said with a smile.

"Though I fear I shall be quite useless for the rest of the day," she added. "I'm not entirely certain I can even stand up at the moment."

"Would you do me the honor of resting with me in the bed for a short while?" Edmund asked. "Perhaps a nap would be restorative."

It was such a forbidden thing to even contemplate, but... "Yes."

She allowed him to help her up and support her across the short distance to the bed. She lay down, fully dressed, and he lay beside her, fully unclothed. After a moment's hesitation, she turned to face him. He lifted an arm in invitation, and it seemed entirely natural to fit her body to his, her head resting on his shoulder and her hand lying flat over his heart. His skin was warm and smooth, and smelled faintly of sweat. His heart beat a slow, reassuring rhythm beneath her touch. He let out a contented sigh.

Cassandra fell asleep wondering what it would be like to have him here like this, but also to have Robert asleep at her back. She awoke some time later to the sound of an insistent knock at the door and Lord Rotherdam's muffled voice.

"*Edmund? Come here at once! We have a problem.*"

SEVENTEEN

FREDERICK POUNDED on Edmund's door, having a good idea of why said door might be locked in the middle of the day, but no time to be irritated by it.

"Edmund? Come here at once! We have a problem," he called.

"*Just a bloody minute, Your Lordship*," came the muffled reply, the inaccurate title replete with the same irony it generally held whenever any of his friends used it to address him.

He clenched his jaw with impatience as something rather longer than a minute passed, to the accompaniment of rustling and low voices from within the room. When Edmund opened the door, he was dressed, but hastily so, and his expression said there had better be a damned good reason for Frederick's interruption.

Despite himself, Frederick's eyes moved past his man of business to take in the perfunctorily made up bed, and then fell on the flushed but defiant face of Miss Cassandra Fenwicke, seated primly at the small table on the other side of room. Her hair was somewhat askew, and her obvious mortification did nothing to hide the hooded gaze and air of general satisfaction marking her as a woman who'd recently been well fucked.

He cleared his throat and jerked his gaze back to Edmund, cursing the blood that rushed south to fill his prick within the confines of his breeches.

"Well?" Edmund demanded, with obvious impatience.

Frederick found he had to clear his throat a second time before speaking. "We've just had a visitor."

Edmund scowled. "A visitor? How? The bridge is still out."

"It was a lad riding cross country," Frederick told him. "He'd been sent out by the vicar of Horsham."

Miss Fenwicke inhaled sharply, and Edmund glanced back at her.

"The boy had been tasked with asking after a young lady riding in a coach with her maid," Frederick continued grimly. "She was expected in Horsham some days ago, and apparently the vicar became concerned when she failed to arrive."

"You spoke to this lad directly?" Edmund's tone was sharp.

"I did," Frederick bit out. "But not before the footman who opened the door verbally stumbled all over himself in an attempt not to lie."

Edmund scraped a hand down his face. "Wonderful."

Miss Fenwicke appeared frozen in place. "So the vicar of Horsham will know that I am here?" she asked carefully.

"I sent the boy away with a flea in his ear," Frederick told her. "However, if he is quick-witted—and he did appear to be—he will report back that no one at any of the other houses he checked knew anything of you, but a servant at the manor belonging to the notorious Lord Rotherdam was evasive about answering his questions."

Her face, which had been flushed with embarrassment before, grew pale.

"I see," she said.

Something like this had been inevitable — that was the most maddening part. And yet, he was at a loss as to what they could have done differently that wouldn't have risked Miss Stanhope's death from shock and blood loss. Hengewick House had been the closest safe shelter, and Frances Hunter, the best option for saving the maid's life. Then the storms had washed out the bridge, leaving the two women trapped here — and, once again, a lady's reputation would suffer because of her association with his bad name. Suddenly, the fact that Miss Fenwicke's reputation was already tarnished seemed less important than the fact that she would now suffer additional insult because of him.

"How long until the bridge is repaired?" Edmund asked. He sounded tired, in the same way Frederick felt tired. Tired of society and its vicious jackdaws. Tired of the injustice in the world that always seemed to prey on the weakest.

"Five more days if the weather holds, longer if it doesn't, as of the last report," he said.

"Then we have five days to plan a course of action, should any be needed," Edmund said, glancing again at Miss Fenwicke, as though to reassure her.

"Indeed," Frederick agreed. "Although for now, I believe the original plan remains the best—hire a driver who can be paid to keep his own counsel, and send the ladies on to their destination with as little fanfare as possible. Unless the vicar is actively courting scandal, he should be content with their safe arrival after a vague story of mishap and delays."

"One can but hope," Edmund agreed. "And in the meantime, perhaps the servants could be reminded of the need for discretion."

"Yes," he said, and left them to… whatever they had been doing when he interrupted.

✐ ♛ ✐

Upon returning to his suite of rooms in the drafty old manor, Frederick rang for Barlow immediately. His valet slipped into the room mere moments later, silent as a shadow.

"Yes, my lord?" he asked.

Frederick sank into the leather-upholstered chair next to the unlit fireplace with something less than his usual grace, rubbing at the corners of his eyes with one hand.

"Barlow," he began. "We have an issue surrounding your and Edmund's latest conquest." He let his hand drop and looked up.

Barlow's stillness had a careful quality about it. "Indeed, sir?" he asked. "I was given to understand that Mr. St. Germain had already discussed the situation with you."

And this… *this*… was precisely the sort of situation Frederick had hoped to avoid by keeping his damnably desirable valet at arm's length. One did not discuss the personal lives of one's servants with them. As far as the master was concerned, servants weren't supposed to *have* personal lives. Those two spheres were meant to remain separate at all times.

"Not that sort of issue," he said, hating the growl that unintentionally crept into his voice. "Someone from Horsham has been making the rounds, asking after her—and they were suitably motivated in their task to ride cross country through muddy fields so they could ask here, specifically."

There was a slight pause, then, "Ah."

"Quite." He waved Barlow to the other chair.

His valet sat poised on the edge of the seat—back straight, agile hands folded neatly in his lap. The light from the window played across the red highlights in his dark brown hair, its length scraped back and neatly contained in a tight queue at the nape of his neck.

"I suppose that explains the minor commotion in the servants' hall earlier today," he said. "What will you do?"

Frederick sighed and leaned back in his chair. "I don't see that there's anything *to* do beyond what we originally intended—await the repair of the bridge, and send her to her destination."

Barlow's brow furrowed thoughtfully. "Well, sir... I'd hardly say that's the *only* option. Though I will agree it is probably the simplest."

It was Frederick's turn to frown. "What's that supposed to mean?"

"There are other possibilities. Mr. St. Germain could offer to marry her," Barlow said, as though it was obvious. "Or, alternately, you could offer her some sort of employment, thereby freeing her from the hold her guardians have over her."

Frederick blinked at him, taken aback. "Edmund is hardly the marrying type. And I have little doubt that if I attempted to employ the young lady, her relatives would have the Bow Street Runners at my door the moment we returned to London, leveling charges of kidnapping."

"Well, sir—I did say your approach would be the simplest," Barlow replied mildly.

Frederick regarded him with narrowed eyes for several long moments.

"You're soft on her," he said at length, unable to keep the surprise from his tone. "You and Edmund both. Good lord, man—you barely know her. At least, not beyond the biblical sense."

His valet raised an eyebrow at him. "I couldn't possibly comment on Mr. St. Germain's thoughts, my lord. But perhaps someone might inquire as to Miss Fenwicke's opinion on the matter, before any decisions are made?"

Frederick covered a wince. In many ways, Barlow was the epitome of a gentleman's gentleman—but he was occasionally prone to delivering blunt home truths in those cool, placid tones of his. Briefly, he wondered if his valet regretted the fact that his position prevented him from pursuing marriage himself. It was a disconcerting thought.

"Your point is taken," he said. "I will speak to her regarding her wishes; however, I fear Edmund is on his own if he's planning any grand proposals of matrimony."

"I'll be sure to relay that the next time I see him," Barlow agreed. "Was there anything else, sir?"

Surrounded by extraordinary people, and not worthy of a single damned one of them, Frederick thought.

"No," he said. "Thank you, Barlow. That will be all."

EIGHTEEN

BARLOW MADE his way to Cassandra's room, unsure if he would find her there or not. He knocked lightly on the door. A moment later it opened to reveal her freshly washed face; her eyes red-rimmed from crying.

"May I come in?" he asked, his heart aching for her.

She swallowed and gave a silent nod, making space for him to enter before closing the door behind him. With a gesture, she offered him the room's single chair and seated herself on the side of the bed, all formality forgotten.

"Lord Rotherdam told you about his visitor?" she asked, in the tone of someone resigned to an unpleasant fate.

"He did," Robert replied. "We should discuss what you wish to do now."

"I don't think my wishes come into it," Cassandra said. "I will continue to my original destination and hope that Horsham's vicar doesn't wish to pursue the prospect of scandal."

"That is one option, yes," Robert told her.

She met his gaze then, her delicate brows furrowing. "I should think it is the only reasonable option at this point."

Robert took care to choose his words before speaking. "Perhaps not. If there were a way for you to escape your aunt and uncle's control... to live away from their eyes on you... would you take it?"

The dull hopelessness returned to her expression. "Oh. Edmund already spoke to me about becoming a mistress, or an employee, or..." She trailed off, then shook her head sharply. "I will not become some sort of obligation, taken on because of pity. Not to Edmund. Not to Lord Rotherdam."

He gave her a hint of a wry smile. "An obligation like me, you mean?"

She blinked, visibly registering how her words might have sounded to the man Lord Rotherdam had hired as a valet out of a sense of misplaced duty, or possibly guilt. "No!" she said quickly. "No, Robert—that's completely different. You risked your life to save his platoon at Waterloo. I'm an inconvenient spinster who landed on his doorstep with an injured maid and the stench of scandal surrounding me."

Robert closed his eyes for a moment, remembering the long-ago pain and confusion of waking in an unfamiliar farmhouse, crammed in amongst the other casualties from the battle like peas in a pod. He remembered his commanding officer picking his way through the other injured soldiers to reach his pallet; remembered his sense of shock as the mud- and blood-covered viscount dropped to his knees and gathered up Robert's hand, bowing over it and pressing it to his forehead with heartfelt, murmured thanks.

That had been the moment Robert had first fallen in love with Frederick Ashbury, Viscount

Rotherdam — his commanding officer, and the humblest lord he had ever met. When Lord Rotherdam later offered him the post of valet, Robert had swallowed his pride and taken it... unaware that by doing so, he would be trading physical proximity in the gentleman's dressing room for any chance at real intimacy with the man. His master was far too honorable to ever consider tupping a servant — even one that wanted to be tupped.

"It's your choice, Cassandra," he said with the compassion of one who knew what it was like not to fully control one's own destiny. "But I would implore you not to make decisions about your life solely on the basis of the imagined impact on other people."

She gave a lost-sounding little laugh at that. "And yet, that is exactly how I was raised to make such decisions." Her eyes slid down to her hands tangled together in her lap. "At this point, I wish only for a quiet life where I can be left alone and avoid further harm — to myself, and to others. Perhaps I shall paint."

He rose and crouched in front of her, wobbling awkwardly on his bad leg. "No one here will try to take that decision from you," he promised. "But will you make me a promise in return?"

She gave a reluctant nod.

"Think on it a little more first," he told her. "There are other paths besides the one currently laid out before you."

Cassandra tried to smile at him, but it was pained. "I promise," she said, with the air of someone who knew further reflection on the subject would be both short-lived and unproductive.

Saddened and full of misgivings, Robert nodded his acceptance and rose, pressing a kiss to each of her hands before leaving her alone with her thoughts.

⚜

Cassandra's heart hurt with an almost physical pain at the prospect of returning to her drab and solitary existence. She had been telling the truth, though — she still had too much pride to become someone's charity case. Or at least... too much pride to become the charity case of someone outside of her family.

It was too distressing to attempt the charade of maintaining a brave face for Edmund or Robert, so she closeted herself with Mary and Frances instead. Mary, at least, was continuing to improve. Her color had returned, and she frequently grew flustered and red in the cheeks beneath Frances' blunt attention. Cassandra did not think that her maid's feathers had been so easily ruffled before her injury, but perhaps she had merely been too absorbed in her own woes to notice.

Mary had regained a bit of sensation in her little finger and ring finger on the affected hand, but she could barely twitch the muscles into movement, even now. Still, it was progress, even if it was slow. Frances had reluctantly decreed that she would be fit to travel without further endangering her health whenever the bridge repairs were complete. She did not, however, sound happy about it.

That was another problem — Mary would be unable to perform the duties of a lady's maid for some time yet... if ever. Cassandra had silently vowed to keep quiet about it and muddle along however was necessary, rather than risking her uncle sacking Mary and throwing her into the street, destitute and unable to work.

What her relatives didn't know couldn't hurt them. More to the point, what her relatives didn't know couldn't hurt *Mary*... she hoped. No doubt Mary would gain some facility with using only one arm over time, if her other arm never improved.

Both Edmund and Robert made quiet overtures to speak with her as the days passed. Cassandra put them off as politely as she could, relying on their innate chivalry to prevent them from pressing the issue. Oddly, she missed the hours of sketching and painting in pleasant company slightly more than she missed the gentle exploration of carnal pleasure they had shared.

That did not, however, stop her from touching herself, alone in her room at night. Nor did it stop the quiet tears that came after, when she realized she'd been thinking of her two eccentric rakes during the act.

When Lord Rotherdam showed up at Mary's sickroom and requested a private audience with Cassandra, he was not so easy to dodge. Cassandra steeled herself and followed him to a nearby parlor, ignoring Mary's wide-eyed look and Frances' speculative one as she left.

When she was settled on a slightly dusty chesterfield, Rotherdam poured her a glass of sherry and handed it to her, despite the fact that it was barely midday. She took it and sipped, wondering if she drank enough of it whether some of her cares might fade to more manageable levels.

"The bridge repairs will be completed in the morning," he said without preamble. "I do need to speak with you regarding the disposition of your driver's body, though. Did he have family in London?"

Cassandra's heart sank at the reminder of poor Leeds. "Not that I know of. His wife died last year, and they had no children. I never heard him speak of other relatives—if his parents are still alive, they would certainly be quite advanced in years by now."

He nodded. "Then, if it meets with your approval, I will call in a favor with someone nominally respectable who can arrange for his burial in the church grounds at Holmwood."

A sense of relief at the prospect of having someone else to take care of Leeds' final arrangements warred with guilt over not dealing with it herself. The man had given his life in an attempt to protect her and Mary from armed highwaymen, after all.

"Thank you," she said softly.

Rotherdam tried to smile, but it seemed stiff, and did not reach his eyes. "It's nothing. The journey from here to Horsham is slightly more than ten miles. There should be sufficient time for you and your maid to reach your destination before dark tomorrow — if you still wish to go there."

Her heart sank at the prospect of another argument... of declaiming in favor of something she did not truly want.

"It is my aunt and uncle's coach, pulled by my aunt and uncle's horses, and they have decreed that it shall take me to Horsham," she said.

He watched her carefully with his very blue eyes. "That isn't precisely an answer."

"Yes, Lord Rotherdam," she retorted. "It is. You've been entirely generous in your hospitality. More than generous. But Mary and I have imposed on you long enough. No doubt you have orgies and virgin sacrifices to plan, once we're no longer here to delay them." The sad attempt at jollity fell flat, but she plowed onward. "Despite all the care you've shown us, my maid and I are hardly your responsibility. I have a life to look forward to in Horsham. Perhaps it is not as exciting a life as country manor houses and Hellfire Clubs — but it is *my* life, nonetheless."

She rose, intending to excuse herself, and was surprised when Rotherdam stepped close, halting her.

"Very well," he said, looking down at her — his cerulean gaze trapping hers. "But first, I wish to receive assurance from you on one thing, Miss Fenwicke. Can you promise me that you will pursue something that inspires your passions? Whether it be art, or philosophy, or, God forbid, politics — *something* that gives your *quiet life* meaning. I hope I am not the first person to say this to you, but you are more than the sum of a sordid society scandal. You are so much more."

Cassandra's breath caught, her throat thickening with the sudden and completely unexpected threat of tears. Her hand flew to her mouth. Rotherdam reached out, fingertips brushing her cheek, urging her not to look away.

She let her hand fall. "I promise," she managed in a hoarse whisper... and fled the room.

>··· 🐚 ···<

The following morning dawned crisp and blue. She and Mary stood outside Hengewick House as a couple of footmen wrestled her trunk of belongings toward the waiting coach. She dreaded the prospect of bidding farewell to the motley collection of Hellfire Club members gathered around them.

Frances was still fussing over Mary's arm, adjusting the sling and going over directions for treating the slow-healing wound once they reached Horsham. A local lad had been hired to drive them — paid a princely sum, Cassandra gathered, in exchange for keeping his mouth shut about the whole thing.

As the footmen loaded the trunk into place, the clatter of hooves and wheels drew everyone's attention to the long driveway, where a second coach approached, bearing a familiar coat of arms on the door. A terrible, sinking feeling settled in Cassandra's stomach like hot lead. It wasn't possible. Surely her aunt and uncle would not have come down from London on such short notice. Not for her. Not after they'd exiled her to the country for her supposed sins, and all but washed their hands of her.

The coach rattled to a stop, and the door flew open. Cassandra's uncle descended, red-faced and sweating. "*Rotherdam*!" he barked. "Hand over my niece at once!"

NINETEEN

CASSANDRA HELD her breath as Rotherdam's gaze landed on her uncle. A truly unpleasant smile stretched the viscount's full lips.

"That's *Lord* Rotherdam," he said silkily. "Mister…?"

"Wycliff," her uncle snapped. "Henry Wycliff. And I will not stand on ceremony after you kidnapped my niece and exposed her to who-knows-what kind of perverted degradations—"

"Uncle!" Cassandra cried. "It's not like that! We were attacked on the road—Leeds and Mary were shot! Lord Rotherdam and his friends rescued us at great risk to themselves. He brought us here to recover, but then the bridge washed out…"

Her uncle scoffed. "*Great risk*? More like he orchestrated the whole thing himself, so he could get his claws into you, you ungrateful little trollop."

Rotherdam took a menacing step forward, and Cassandra's uncle seemed to realize for the first time that he was spewing vitriol at a viscount while surrounded by a group of the aforementioned viscount's friends.

"That, sir, is actionable slander," Rotherdam said, in a quiet, deadly tone.

Her uncle took a single step back, noticed what he had done, and drew himself to his full—if unimpressive—height. His jowls shook with outrage, his iron-gray muttonchops sticking out like raised hackles. "And this is kidnapping, I say! You are holding a young girl against her will in your… your… *house of ill repute!*"

"I'm twenty-two," Cassandra protested weakly. "And they weren't—" Her eyes sought help from someone, *anyone* in the group.

"*On the contrary.*" Rotherdam bit the words out with vicious precision. "As you may see, should you care to use your eyes, I was putting your niece and her maid on *your coach,* ready to send them on to the destination *you chose,* now that the bridge has been repaired. Which, I might add, only occurred an hour ago."

Cassandra desperately wanted Edmund or Robert to wrap an arm around her shoulders for support, as her breathing grew short and her legs, unsteady. But of course, that would be the absolute worst thing either of them could possibly do right now.

"I know the damned bridge was out!" her uncle snapped. "I've been waiting around this godforsaken hamlet since yesterday afternoon for it to be finished!"

"Then perhaps we might finish loading Miss Fenwicke's belongings, and you may ensure that she and her maid reach Horsham safely." The chill in Rotherdam's tone could have frozen a pot of boiling water. "Assuming that is still what the lady desires, of course."

Momentary panic gripped Cassandra by the throat. He was giving her another choice. She could open her mouth and throw herself and Mary under his protection — even if she still didn't understand why he would offer them such a thing in the first place. But... the thought of looking her uncle in the eye and declaring that she would rather defy his wishes in favor of staying in a Hellfire Club —

She couldn't. She physically *could not* pry her lips apart to form the words.

"The *maid*?" her uncle said in disbelief. "The maid is sacked. What kind of lady's maid lets her mistress parade around in a place like this?"

Mary made a small sound — a tiny, indrawn breath.

"Uncle!" The word should have been a cry of outrage, but it emerged from Cassandra's lips as a pathetic, strangled thing.

Her uncle pushed past Rotherdam and grabbed Cassandra by the arm, dragging her forward. A low noise of rage came from behind her, and she craned around to find Edmund poised as though he might lunge forward and physically assault the man.

"Don't!" she cried breathlessly — aware of how very much worse things might still get if anyone here caused a scene. "*Don't.*"

Her eyes begged him not to act.

He froze, visibly torn. Robert looked stricken, and Rotherdam's hands were clenched tightly into fists at his sides. Frances — supporting a pale-faced Mary with a hand cupped beneath her good elbow, threw Cassandra a grim glance.

"Have the trunk transferred to this coach," her uncle ordered. "And send the other coach up to

Wycliff House in London, unless you wish me to level charges of theft in addition to charges of kidnapping."

Rotherdam's blue eyes slid over her uncle as though he were nothing more than an insect. Then, they landed on her.

"Miss Fenwicke?" he asked, in a grave tone that conveyed, *speak now — this may be your last chance*.

But it was hopeless. Even if she set aside her pride and asked for his help, her uncle would have Bow Street runners pounding down Rotherdam's door the moment he showed his face in London, ready to drag him before a magistrate to face who-knew-what sort of outlandish allegations.

"Leave it," she begged. "*Please*. Just... leave it."

Rotherdam hesitated for a long moment before giving a slow nod. With a sharp gesture, he indicated that the footmen should move the trunk to the coach her uncle had arrived in.

"*Rotherdam*," Edmund hissed — but Robert took him by the upper arm, the grip restraining more than supporting.

"That's more like it," Cassandra's uncle said gruffly, and tugged on her arm again. "Now come on, you silly girl. Get in the coach before the filth of this place rubs off on you more than it already has."

But she set her slippered feet against the rough gravel of the overgrown circle drive, balking long enough to crane around and meet Rotherdam's eyes one final time. "Mary?" she said, in a tone of supplication.

He held her gaze and gave the smallest dip of the chin, his granite expression never shifting. "I'll see to her. You needn't worry on her account, Miss Fenwicke."

Biting her lower lip in anguish, she allowed herself to be tugged and chivvied into the coach—forcing herself not to look back at the group of people she was leaving behind, because it would be too painful. The vehicle rocked on its suspension as her uncle clambered in after her and settled himself next to his wife with a huff.

Her aunt gave Cassandra a head-to-toe onceover, looking like she'd just tasted something sour.

Cassandra swallowed convulsively. "Aunt Lavinia," she said. It emerged hoarse and faint. She cleared her throat. "Hello. You're looking... well?"

A thunderstorm was brewing behind her aunt's expression, but then the coach rocked again as the trunk was loaded onto the back.

It will be all right, Cassandra thought, a bit desperately. *It's no different than before, really.*

Her relatives would see her to Horsham, and then they would go back to London, and she would finally be left in peace. Perhaps, once it was safe, she could send a message to Hengewick House and ask for Mary to be driven down to Horsham to join her there. It would be tricky feeding two people with only Cassandra's pittance of an allowance, but somehow they would make it work. She tried not to think about the promise she'd made Lord Rotherdam earlier. With these new circumstances, there would be no extra money for paints and watercolor paper to pursue her passion for art.

"Well, young lady, what do you have to say for yourself?" Aunt Lavinia's nasal tone was every bit as grating as Cassandra remembered. "You can't even get from London to Horsham without courting yet more scandal! Why am I not surprised?"

"We were attacked by highwaymen along the way," she said weakly.

Uncle Henry gave a loud scoff. "And so you thought it would be a good idea to seek shelter with a perverted atheist afterward? Are you soft in the head, girl?"

"I was unconscious," Cassandra told them. "The bandits *killed* Leeds, Uncle."

"Unconscious?" her uncle repeated, ignoring the part about Leeds. "So the damned man *did* kidnap you. I knew it!"

Cassandra stared at him. "No, he—" she began, only to cut herself off. "Lord Rotherdam has been nothing but kind and considerate. He's provided shelter and care for both of us, and ensured we could continue on our journey. He made every effort to ensure I was chaperoned"— *well, he had at first, anyway*—"and no one in his household ever visited the least impropriety on either one of us."

At least, none that I didn't explicitly ask for, she didn't add.

"That's not what the *ton* will say," Aunt Lavinia said with a sneer.

Cassandra blinked at her. "Does what the *ton* says truly matter so much, if I am living a quiet spinster's life in the country?"

Uncle Henry waved the words away as though they irritated him. "Stupid girl—we didn't come all the way down here just to take you to Horsham."

"You... didn't?" Cassandra asked.

"Obviously not," Aunt Lavinia said. "Why would we do such an addle-pated thing as that? We're here to take you back to London."

Cassandra opened her mouth, but for a long moment, nothing came out.

"*London*?" she managed eventually. Hadn't she just managed to escape from that hellish city full of gossipmongers and backstabbers?

"Yes, *London*," Uncle Henry replied, mocking her high-pitched tone of surprise. "Baron Malthorpe has finally agreed to do the right thing and marry you after that unfortunate business at Lady Northcotte's Regatta. Congratulations, you little wastrel. Thanks to us, you're going to be a baroness."

All the blood drained from Cassandra's face. The invisible band around her ribcage tightened; the familiar feeling of ice crawled into her lungs and froze her breath.

"*What did you just say*?" she whispered hoarsely.

TWENTY

"ARE YOU DEAF, girl?" Aunt Lavinia demanded. "You heard what your uncle just said. *A baroness.* You should be thanking us!"

Avarice shown in her aunt's tiny, colorless eyes, but Cassandra was still mired in the horror of the revelation.

"Why?" she demanded. "*How*?"

Baron Malthorpe had openly laughed in her uncle's face when he'd demanded the nobleman marry her after despoiling her at Lady Northcotte's fateful Regatta. What in heaven's name could have changed his mind?

Uncle Henry waved a pudgy hand. "It was Lavinia's idea. Deuced clever, really. The vicar of Horsham sent us a letter by courier, letting us know what kind of tawdry scandal you'd got yourself into this time. Your aunt thought it might work to force the baron's hand, since he and that scoundrel Rotherdam have so much bad blood between them."

"And it worked, too," Aunt Lavinia said smugly. "Once he heard you were in Rotherdam's clutches, he couldn't declare his intentions fast enough."

Cassandra feared she might be ill. She was certain her complexion had gone sickly gray.

"I will not marry Baron Malthorpe," she stated, imbuing the words with all the strength of conviction she could muster.

"You bloody will," her uncle said, in a tone that promised dire consequences for disobedience.

She raised her chin. "Disown me. Throw me in the street to starve if you must. I can join Mary there. But I will *not* wed that horrible toad."

Her uncle's jaw clenched. "You *will* marry him. You *will* take his title. You *will* cease to be a drain on our resources, and become a source of financial support to this family!"

Panic fluttered at Cassandra's throat. "But… my portion! It isn't nearly large enough to attract a baron, surely."

"He doesn't want your money, girl," her uncle said ruthlessly. "He's got plenty of his own. Apparently, he just wants *you*. God alone knows why."

Icy dread froze her blood, as the coach carried her ever closer to London and her worst nightmare.

Frederick watched the coach disappear around the bend with a deep sense of disquiet. With an angry hiss, Edmund jerked his arm free of Barlow's restraining grip and rounded on him, dark eyes flashing fire.

"What the *hell* was that, Rotherdam?" his man of business demanded. "You should have stopped them from taking her!"

It didn't help that there was an insistent little voice in the back of Frederick's head saying exactly the same thing. However, that inner voice was no more rational than Edmund appeared to be at the moment.

"*Think*," Barlow said—ever the voice of reason. "They're only taking her to Horsham. It's not even a full day's journey from here. Once they leave and return to London, we can contact her discreetly and find out what assistance she needs… if any."

Edmund subsided, though a muscle in his jaw jerked with tension. "I still don't like it."

"None of us like it," Frances put in. She was still supporting Miss Fenwicke's former maid. "But what you seemingly fail to understand, Edmund, is that protesting only would have made her situation worse."

Frederick took in the maid's pasty complexion. "Miss Stanhope. Perhaps you should go inside where you can lie down for a bit. I'm sure this must have been quite a shock, but you have my word I will provide whatever assistance you need after this unfortunate development."

The woman's earthy brown eyes flicked uncertainly from him to Frances.

"He's telling the truth," Frances said dryly. "Don't worry—at least, not about that part. There are plenty of other things to worry about instead."

"What do you mean, Miss Hunter?" Barlow asked.

She raised a sharp eyebrow at him. "Oh, *come now*, Robert. The relatives who banished her to the country just randomly decided to rush down here and check on her? *Really*? Even if the vicar in Horsham sent them a letter about his concerns immediately after his boy showed up here asking about her, such a missive could only have reached them a couple of days ago, at most."

"It's true, your lordship," Miss Stanhope said miserably. "They never gave a whit about her before, except to berate her for tarnishing their reputation."

"That's as may be," Frederick replied, the broad strokes of a plan forming in his mind. "But whatever the case, inserting ourselves into the situation now can only complicate it further. We'll have to be patient."

"*Patient*," Edmund echoed, sounding anything but.

"Yes," Frederick said firmly. He turned to address the servants and the lad he'd hired to drive the coach. "You. See that the horses are put away. We'll need them harnessed and ready to go to London tomorrow morning." The driver started to object, but Frederick cut him off. "Don't worry, I'll make it well worth your while. See the groom about borrowing a horse so you can get back to Holmwood tonight. Or you can stay overnight in the stable—I don't care which, as long as you're ready to travel at this time tomorrow."

"You're scheming something," Frances accused, watching him with a narrow-eyed expression.

"Hardly *scheming*," he said. "Merely setting plans. Come inside, everyone. We need to talk in private."

The others followed him into the house, though Edmund continued to shoot him hard looks. The mood was subdued as Frances excused herself to take Mary Stanhope back to her room. Frederick waited to speak until she returned, ignoring the awkwardness of the silence in the drawing room.

"She's resting now," Frances reported, as she let herself in and closed the door. "So. I assume someone here is going to be riding in the coach when it heads back to London?"

"Indeed," Frederick said. "Someone will need to go to the city and report back when the Wycliffs return from their errand. At that point, it should be safe to contact Miss Fenwicke, as long as it's done with discretion."

"The vicar in Horsham must really have it in for you," Frances observed. "He certainly didn't waste anytime contacting her family with his suspicions."

"Most vicars have it in for me," Frederick shot back. "It's something about the alleged devil worship, presumably."

"Who's going to London, then?" Frances asked. "If you try to send Edmund, he'll just end up assaulting someone. I'd volunteer, but I'm not thrilled with the idea of leaving Mary—er, Miss Stanhope—alone."

"We'll go," said Lawrence Vaughan, exchanging a glance with his lover. The pair had come outside to bid Miss Fenwicke farewell, but had been largely silent during the drama that followed.

Fortescue nodded his agreement. "Yes, we might as well. We can send you a letter as soon as the aunt and uncle return to Wycliff House. It shouldn't be difficult to ascertain."

Frederick dredged up a smile for the pair. "Thank you. I'm sorry to cut your stay in the country short."

"My dear Rotherdam," Fortescue said. "We were promised dark satanic rites, and there hasn't been so much as a single sacrificial goat. If you *will* disappoint your fellow Hellfire Club members in such a way, you must expect the occasional defection."

Fondness warmed Frederick's chest. "Blame the weather," he said. "It's too muddy to be tramping around stone circles. I can't be held accountable for every rainstorm."

"Isn't that exactly the sort of thing the sacrifices are for, though?" Vaughan mused. "Anyway, if it's settled, perhaps we should go pack for our journey in the morning."

"Yes," Fortescue agreed. "Especially if we're expected to rise so obscenely early two days in a row." He sounded deeply put out at the prospect.

"Shameless laggards," Frances accused. Once the pair had taken their leave, she turned to address the three of them who remained. "Now, I'm going to leave you idiots to discuss how you're going to solve this situation permanently. None of you have given a single thought to what happens after you contact her in Horsham, have you?"

"Er," Barlow said.

"In fact, I have," Frederick told her. His gaze fell heavily on Edmund, who scowled at him in evident confusion.

Frances blinked at him. "Well, that's refreshing, at least. Let me know what you decide," she said, and left without another word.

The door closed with a sound of finality, and Frederick turned to his valet and his man of business. "Right. No more beating around the bush. I know you two, and I know you must have discussed this already. Edmund, for God's sake, man—either marry the girl, or set her up properly as a mistress. Otherwise, she's at the mercy of those vapid relatives of hers—and *that*, gentlemen, is no longer acceptable."

TWENTY-ONE

EDMUND GLARED AT him, but Frederick only raised an eyebrow, waiting.

"I already asked," his man of business snarled. "Did you think I hadn't? She turned me down and made me promise never to ask her again."

Frederick blinked, honestly not having expected that. "You asked her to marry you?" The idea hit him oddly, despite the fact that he himself had been the one to suggest it, mere moments ago. "And she *turned you down*?"

What on earth had possessed the woman?

"I offered to set her up as my mistress," Edmund clarified. "It would have been unfair to offer marriage when she barely knows me — at least, not beyond the biblical sense." His expression hardened. "She may be disgraced, but she was still part of the *ton*. She has no idea what it would be like to be tied to the son of Jamaican immigrants, especially one who is little more than a glorified clerk."

"Oh, *Edmund*," Barlow breathed, the words barely audible.

Edmund turned his hard gaze onto the valet. "You know exactly what I mean, Robert." He tipped his chin toward Frederick. "He pays you enough that you could have offered to set her up, even if you're not in a position to marry — not if you still want to black Rotherdam's boots, anyway. But you didn't offer it, because you didn't want her to lower herself by attaching herself to a servant."

Frederick watched them both, thoroughly taken aback. Frances had accused him on several occasions of having no conception of the sorts of challenges faced by *normal people*, as she'd put it. It hadn't occurred to him that Edmund, in particular, might have balked at approaching Miss Fenwicke because he feared dragging her down, or trapping her in a situation that she might find distasteful at some point in the future. He suspected that would not, in fact, have been the case. But even so, it simply wasn't something he'd considered.

"She doesn't want to be my mistress," Edmund concluded, meeting and holding Frederick's gaze. "But she might consent to being yours, knowing what you did to help Frances escape her unwanted betrothal. If you're really so concerned about getting her out from under her family's thumb, maybe you should ask her yourself."

"Edmund," Barlow said softly. "You should know that she only turned down your offer because she felt she would become a burden to you. She told me as much afterward. She still has some pride left, even after everything."

"Good Christ," Frederick said. "The amount of tragic nobility on display in this house is becoming positively sickening. Perhaps *that* is the nature of the conversation you should both have with her, before you suggest she tie herself further to my tainted name."

Barlow gave him a surprised glance from beneath dark lashes, which quickly turned appreciative. Rotherdam tried desperately to ignore the flush of heat he felt in response.

"Yes, my lord," his valet said demurely. "Perhaps we should, indeed, have such a conversation with her before exploring other avenues."

>⟨∾ ♕ ∾⟩<

Cassandra's aunt and uncle's London residence was just as hateful as she remembered. She didn't want to be here, and she most especially didn't want to be here when Baron Malthorpe called on her uncle the afternoon following her return.

It was the first time she'd been in a room with the man since *the incident*, and the only way she was able to maintain her composure was by picturing his limp, pale, stinking prick, and picturing how hard she'd bite it if he ever got it anywhere near her face again.

He hadn't called on her family to court her; that much was obvious. Rather, he greeted her aunt and uncle with open contempt before looking her over like a piece of horseflesh he was contemplating purchasing.

"Passable, I suppose," he said. "More so in the daylight than in the dark, at any rate. I'll acquire a common license from the bishop and arrange for the ceremony to take place in two weeks."

Cassandra lifted her chin and glared at the man, trying to ignore the tremor of terror threatening to rob her of her voice. "I will not marry you. I do not accept your proposal."

His muddy hazel eyes settled on her as though she'd surprised him by having an opinion. "Nobody asked you. If you didn't want to marry then you shouldn't have thrown yourself at me."

Her hands began to shake noticeably. She clenched them into fists at her sides. "You forced me. You *assaulted* me!"

He looked down his crooked nose at her with a sort of cold, emotionless apathy that appalled her. Then his gaze swept back to her uncle. "If you expect me to take Rotherdam's leftovers and make a baroness out of her, you ought teach her better manners before the wedding."

"Of course, Lord Malthorpe," her uncle hurried to reply. "You must forgive her—who knows what horrors and depredations the poor girl suffered at that bounder's hands!"

Outrage joined terror in Cassandra's breast. "Lord Rotherdam was the picture of grace and civility during my stay in his house! Which is more than I can say for any of you!"

A slow smile spread across Malthorpe's soft-chinned visage at her words, as though she'd just revealed a weakness to him and begged him to exploit it. Somehow, *that* was the thing to finally send her panic spinning out of control.

"I have a headache and wish to retire," she managed, pushing the words out from lungs that could barely draw air. With that, she fled, praying that no pursuit would follow.

No one followed her. She slammed her bedroom door shut, closing herself off from the rest of the world and turning the key in the lock. Gray fog swirled around the edges of her vision. She managed to make it to a chair before she succumbed to breathless, choking sobs. The room around her faded into the memory of darkness; the smell of damp grass and stale, musky sweat assaulted her.

She hugged her arms around her torso and wept, longing for the presence of any single person from Hengewick House. She would have fallen into their arms on the instant, whether it was Robert or Edmund, Frances or Sadie, Lawrence Vaughan or Mr. Fortescue, Lord Rotherdam himself, or even the lowest of his servants.

After several minutes of this, her vision cleared and her thundering, stuttering heartbeat steadied. She was once more present in her hated bedroom in this hated, soulless house, rather than a dark garden maze. She took a deep, unsteady breath, and started thinking.

Her mother had at least taken the time to educate her on the practicalities of marriage. Malthorpe had said he would purchase a license. There were two types, but he'd specified a common license—requiring the wedding to take place at his parish church. If there was a church involved, there would also be a curate or a rector presiding. The license might preclude the opportunity for public objection, as there would have been during the normal reading of the banns, but the marriage would still have to be recorded in the parish register to be considered legal.

She could refuse to sign. She could tell the church official that she was being wed against her will. Malthorpe had nothing with which to blackmail her into compliance. He couldn't do any more damage to her reputation. It was long gone, and she had finally buried its desiccated corpse during her stay at Lord Rotherdam's country manor. She could truthfully say that she no longer cared what the baron or anyone else said about her. She wished only to be far away from here.

With this tentative plan of action in place, the last of her panic subsided. This was England. As a woman, she might not have control over many things — but the law guaranteed that she could not be compelled to marry when she did not wish to. It was only the fear of scandal that forced other women into unions they did not want. As long as scandal held no further sway over her, she would be safe.

⌖ 𑁍 ⌖

Days had passed, and Edmund was growing increasingly restless in the absence of any news from London. It was just as well that his employer also counted him as a friend, because he knew his foul temper would have tested the bounds of more conventional employment.

When Frances knocked on Edmund's door and jerked her head toward the nearest drawing room with a terse, "There's a letter," the depth of his relief was startling.

He hurried after her to find Rotherdam, Barlow, and Cassandra's extremely nervous former maid waiting for them. Rotherdam held a sealed letter, which Frances deftly plucked from his hand as she passed.

"Let me see it," she said, cracking the wax seal and unfolding the missive.

She scanned it quickly, while Miss Stanhope did the same over her shoulder. The maid's good hand flew to cover her mouth, and Frances' complexion grew pale.

"What is it?" Edmund demanded, his patience at an end.

Frances lowered the letter. "William says that Mr. Wycliff and his wife arrived in London—along with their niece." Her wide gray eyes fell on Rotherdam. "And the town gossips are aflutter with the news that Cecil Pembroke, Baron Malthorpe, is set to wed Cassandra Fenwicke following a short engagement."

"*No*," Edmund said, his stomach swooping unpleasantly even as rage burned through his blood like vitriol. He met the eyes of first his employer, and then his employer's valet, finding the same stark denial in both shocked gazes.

"Right," Frances said, drawing his attention. She held up the letter. "This is some utter horse shit. So, how are we going to stop it?"

TWENTY-TWO

THE DAYS SLID by in a fog of dread as Cassandra counted down her two weeks of purgatory. On the fourth day, the butler brought up a calling card and presented it to her aunt.

"Francesca Hunter?" Aunt Lavinia muttered. "Never heard of her. What does she want?"

Cassandra's breath caught in her throat. She swallowed her noise of shock before it could escape, covering it with a small cough.

"The young lady claims to be a childhood acquaintance of Miss Fenwicke, up from the country for a visit to London," said Reeves, the stuffy, balding butler.

Cassandra thought quickly. "Francesca? Little *Frances*?" She lifted a hand to her bosom, playing up her excitement. It wasn't difficult under the circumstances—her heart was pounding with it. "Goodness! I haven't seen Frances since we were girls!"

Lavinia shot her a sour look. "Crawling out of the woodwork now that we've secured you a husband with a title, no doubt. I expect you'll find you have all sorts of *friends* now, girl."

"Don't be silly, Aunt," Cassandra said mildly. "Frances is a country mouse if ever there was one. I'd be quite surprised if she'd heard anything about it. I'm sure it's exactly as she says—she is in

London for a visit and wishes to catch up on old times with a childhood friend, nothing more."

Cassandra assured herself that Frances would not have showed up at her relatives' front door in male garb, hoping to heaven it was true. But even so, casting her as a quiet country girl might end up being a stretch. Still, the first order of business was to get her inside, where they might speak.

"Hmm," her aunt said, unconvinced. After a moment, she waved a languid hand. "Very well, show the young lady in." Her pale, deep-set eyes pinned Cassandra. "You may entertain her here in the morning room, under my watchful eye. None of your antics, girl. I'll hear nothing untoward about your husband-to-be."

Cassandra fixed a pleasant smile on her face. It made her jaw ache. "Of course not, Aunt. I'm sure we'll only talk of silly things. I wonder how her family is faring these days?"

It was all she could do to keep her hands from trembling as she waited for Reeves to make his way back to the front door and show Frances in. *The others knew she was here. They'd sent Frances to check on her*. She clutched her needle and embroidery frame until her knuckles turned white.

A small eternity passed, until finally Reeves reappeared in the doorway. "Miss Francesca Hunter," he announced, sounding like he was officiating a funeral rather than standing in an airy morning room.

Cassandra set her embroidery aside and held her breath as the butler stepped back. A chestnut-haired woman in a fashionable light blue dress entered.

Frances was almost unrecognizable. It was all Cassandra could do not to gape at her openly as she offered a demure curtsey.

"Mrs. Wycliff," she said warmly. "Thank you so much for allowing my visit. Your home is absolutely lovely!"

Aunt Lavinia's hackles settled visibly, although she still appeared wary. "You're too kind, young lady. You are up from Warnham, I take it?"

Frances shot Cassandra the most fleeting of questioning glances.

"I told Aunt Lavinia all about our girlhood friendship there," Cassandra said quickly. "Goodness, how long has it been? Five years?"

"Six at least, I should think," Frances replied, playing along. "You're looking radiant, my dear! You *must* tell me all of your news."

Cassandra managed a pained smile. "Only if you do the same. Please, you must come and sit down with me. Reeves, perhaps some refreshment for our guest?"

"Oh, that sounds wonderful," Frances said. "It's rather warm outside today. I confess I'm quite parched."

Reeves bowed stiffly and departed, leaving them alone in the morning room with Cassandra's watchful aunt. Frances lowered herself gracefully onto the settee. She leaned forward, gathering Cassandra's hands in hers as an old friend might. Cassandra returned the grip as though it were a lifeline.

She had to swallow before she could be sure of her voice. "I can't tell you what a pleasant surprise it is to have you visit, Frances. Please — you must let me know how your family is faring."

Frances squeezed her hands in return. "Well, since you ask — I'm afraid we've had some upsetting news recently. Everything is in quite a shambles at the moment. I daresay old Freddie will be making his own trip to London in the coming days, in hopes of sorting everything out."

It took a moment for the name to register — but when it did, Cassandra's heart skipped and stuttered in surprise. She couldn't completely cover the convulsive jerk of her chest and shoulders.

"F-Freddie?" she echoed, faint with shock. "But... he's..."

"Not usually one to stick his nose in?" Frances offered smoothly. "Oh, he's been known to take charge of such matters... when they're important enough."

Her throat closed up.

Frances offered her another smile, more genuine this time. "And especially when his brothers are hounding him nonstop. As you can imagine, they took the news *particularly* hard."

Cassandra was going to cry. She was going to break down in grateful tears right here in front of her aunt.

She couldn't, though. She *mustn't*. Somehow, she swallowed everything down like bitter herbs beneath Frances' understanding gray gaze. Cassandra's visitor settled her shoulders and let her hands slide free after a final, supportive squeeze.

"But enough about our tiresome troubles at home," Frances said brightly. "You must tell me everything! What have you been getting up to, here in London? It must all be *terribly* exciting."

Cassandra drew a steadying breath, aware of Aunt Lavinia's warning glare. "Well, I do have news of some import, as it happens. I'm to be married in ten days."

"Married!" Frances echoed, feigning surprise. "Good heavens, my dear, I had no idea! It sounds as though congratulations are in order."

Cassandra's smile felt like a dead thing on her face. "It was all quite unexpected, really—but under the circumstances, I couldn't say no."

I tried, she attempted to convey with her eyes. *I tried to say no...*

Frances gave a light laugh, at odds with the righteous anger kindling in her expressive eyes. "Yes, well—I've known a few gentlemen like that myself, as it happens. They do make it impossible to refuse."

Utter relief flooded Cassandra's body at the understanding in Frances' tone. It was irrational; her situation had not changed in any material way. But still, she felt lighter knowing that others were aware of her plight and sympathetic to it.

"I do hope we can visit more while you're here in the city," she said softly.

"Oh, yes—we absolutely *must*," Frances replied with enthusiasm. "And dear old Freddie should be up in the next couple of days, as well. Do you promenade on Sundays?"

"Sometimes," Aunt Lavinia said cautiously.

"Then perhaps we could meet in Hyde Park and take the air together," Frances said brightly. "The weather has been *so* perfect now that the rains have subsided, and I've heard *such* wonderful things about Kensington Gardens. I should love to see it in person, especially in such agreeable company."

"That would be wonderful," Cassandra managed in a faint tone. "Aunt Lavinia?"

"We shall see," said her aunt. "Perhaps it can be arranged. I suppose you should be seen walking out more."

"Lovely!" Frances exclaimed. "I shall send a message regarding the particulars once my *dear uncle* arrives."

"I look forward to it," Cassandra said with utter, heartfelt truthfulness. "I'm so glad you visited, Frances."

Sunday came, and Cassandra was practically beside herself with nervousness and anticipation. Apparently, her attempt to portray a dutiful and thoroughly cowed niece, resigned to her upcoming marriage, was working. Aunt Lavinia had declared that they would, in fact, promenade through Hyde Park. She'd badgered Uncle Henry into sending a note to Baron Malthorpe inviting him to join them, but had not even received the courtesy of a reply.

Cassandra could only hope that meant the hateful man wouldn't bother to show up and promenade with his *blushing bride to be*. She shuddered at the very thought of it.

Frances, by contrast, had made good on her promise to contact them with further details. They were to find her at the Cake House on the north side of the Serpentine at three in the afternoon. Cassandra had no idea what to expect of the meeting. Frances had indicated during her earlier visit that Lord Rotherdam would be in London, but she could only imagine the uproar that would ensue if he showed up in public and made a scene.

If the viscount were in London, then surely his indispensable valet would be here as well—though it was highly unlikely that Robert would be taking the air in Hyde Park with his master. And what about Edmund? Was he here as well?

The uncertainty was maddening. Cassandra allowed her aunt's maid to help her dress and arrange her hair, reminding herself that at least she could be confident of Frances' presence. She walked out with her aunt and uncle at a quarter after two, her back straight and her head held high.

As they joined the throngs entering through the gate at Hyde Park Corner, Cassandra became painfully aware of the titters and wide-eyed whispers as she was recognized by some of the people around her. Even now, her reputation preceded her, it seemed. She didn't need to hear the murmurs to know what was being said. *'Finally roped the baron into marriage'*... *'heard she was missing for weeks'*... *'wonder if there was blackmail involved, how else would she have convinced him to change his mind?'*

Once upon a time, she would have cared about what was being said. Perhaps a part of her still did, but now that tiny, humiliated voice was overpowered by a louder one that would happily court a scandal the likes of which these chattering Londoners had never seen, if it meant freeing herself from her current predicament.

I'll refuse to sign the parish register, she reminded herself. *It will be all right. They can't force me to marry — not really.*

They strolled along the path on the north bank of the Serpentine. Uncle Henry seemed oblivious, but Aunt Lavinia's expression had grown increasingly sour in response to the whispers swirling around their little group. She said nothing aloud, however, and before long they approached the old keeper's lodge known as the Cake House, where Frances awaited them as promised.

"Good afternoon, my dear!" she greeted. "And Mrs. Wycliff — how wonderful to see you again!"

Cassandra was honestly impressed by her performance. She would not have pegged the mannish, abrasive medical woman as an actress. As introductions to her uncle were performed, Cassandra scanned their surroundings, but saw no sign of any other familiar faces.

It was difficult not to be disappointed. And yet, Lord Rotherdam's presence — or, heaven forbid, Edmund's — would only have incited a very loud and public argument. Possibly culminating in fisticuffs, in Edmund's case.

Frances chatted lightly with her aunt and uncle for a few moments before declaring her intention to buy Cassandra a syllabub at the Cake House, as fortification for the afternoon's walk.

When she returned, Cassandra thanked her, sipping the frothy confection of curdled milk and sweet wine as she tried to decide what would be safe to say, and how best to say it. Frances, meanwhile, had done an outstanding job of putting Cassandra's prickly relatives at ease. Her hard work paid off when they began to stroll again, and Aunt Lavinia allowed them the courtesy of falling behind a little ways so they could have at least the illusion of a private conversation.

"Did... *Freddie*... arrive in London safely?" Cassandra asked in a quiet voice. The informal nickname felt decidedly odd as it left her lips.

Frances shot her a crooked smile that held something of her normal tart personality. "How funny you should ask right now," she said.

Cassandra startled as she became aware of a male figure who'd materialized silently on her other side as they walked. She stared up at Frederick Ashbury, Viscount Rotherdam with eyes that were surely as wide as dinner plates.

He was turned out in the latest fashion, every stitch of clothing bearing the unmistakable care of one of the best valets in London. The viscount's summer-blue eyes assessed her—no doubt taking in her pallor, along with the dark circles caused by worry and sleeplessness etched beneath her eyes.

"Good afternoon, ladies," he said mildly. "Now, tell me, Miss Fenwicke—just how much scandal are you willing to court if it means getting out of this horrific mess?"

TWENTY-THREE

SHOCK AT ROTHERDAM'S sudden appearance lodged Cassandra's heart firmly in her throat. She swallowed against the obstruction, painfully aware that her earlier vow not to worry any further about her tattered reputation was about to be put to the test in the most public way possible.

She lifted her chin. "Scandal? My dear Lord Rotherdam. As far as I am concerned, the entire *ton* may go straight to the devil, and take their petty judgments with them."

The answering look he gave her showed a hint of approval. He did not smile, however. In fact, he looked more than a little grim. To complicate matters, Aunt Lavinia chose that moment to shoot a furtive glance over her shoulder, checking on her wayward niece. Her aunt's eyes grew comically huge as she recognized the viscount, her mouth opening in horror.

At that point, several things happened in quick succession. Lavinia came to a stumbling halt, dragging Uncle Henry around by the arm. Frances hurried forward to intercept the pair, loudly professing her shock at the same time she physically blocked them from approaching. Lord Rotherdam took Cassandra's hand and drew her to a halt, turning her to face him. Then, he dropped ostentatiously to one knee, looking up at her with a hooded blue gaze. Around them, other people were stopping and staring. A hubbub of confused voices rose as spectators gathered around to indulge their curiosity regarding the strange display.

"Miss Cassandra Fenwicke," Rotherdam began in a voice loud enough to cut through the muttering. "I can no longer stand by, knowing that you are to marry such a cad as Baron Malthorpe in defiance of my love for you. The weeks we shared in my country manor have convinced me that we are destined to be together. Renounce your engagement to Malthorpe and accept my proposal of marriage instead."

Several gasps erupted from the onlookers. Aunt Lavinia shrieked, "*What*?" in a voice like an angry cat that had just been dumped in a washtub. Cassandra stood frozen for the space of a handful of heartbeats. She wasn't sure what she'd expected… but it wasn't this.

Scandal be damned, she reminded herself. It probably wasn't a real proposal, but that didn't mean it wouldn't succeed as a means of driving Malthorpe away. No man wanted to be seen pursuing a jilt who had publicly spurned him.

"Oh, *Lord Rotherdam*," she gushed, playing up the moment like a bad actress on the theater stage. "Had I but known of your feelings for me, before I acted so foolishly! I never dared to dream you returned my heartfelt regard. To think—all of that time spent *together* and *unchaperoned* in your Hellfire Club, and you never said a word! Of course I'll marry you, and not Lord Malthorpe!"

She made certain to speak the last couple of sentences as loudly as possible, despite the alternating chills and sweats that flushed her skin with mortification as the crowd looked on, engrossed. Rotherdam rose to his feet, bringing her hand to his lips for a chivalrous kiss before using the grip to tug her closer to him.

With a feeling of unreality, she fell into his arms and stretched up, hardly believing it when his lips closed over hers. It was nothing—mere playacting, just as this entire scene had been. Unfortunately, her body failed to take note of this very important fact, even as more gasps sounded around them—this time, with a real undercurrent of outrage. With difficulty, she tore her lips away before she did something foolish like moan.

"*Cassandra Fenwicke*!" Aunt Lavinia's cry of fury was shrill enough to set dogs howling across London. "How dare you besmirch this family's good name *yet again*!"

To Cassandra's considerable shock, Uncle Henry took her by the arm, quelling her.

"Now, just a moment, Lavinia." He glared at Rotherdam, avarice warring with dislike in his beady eyes. "Marriage, you say?"

"She's already engaged!" Lavinia bleated.

"To a baron," Henry said speculatively. "But a *viscount*..."

Rotherdam let Cassandra step away, but kept his light grip on her hand. "Indeed. I daresay I can offer a more attractive settlement than a mere baron could manage, good sir. And *viscountess* does have a rather nice ring to it, does it not?"

"Well…" her uncle began uncertainly, while Cassandra tried not to feel like a prime broodmare up for auction.

"Perhaps we might meet tomorrow at noon to discuss the particulars," Rotherdam said, as though he hadn't just scandalized half of the *ton* by proposing marriage to an engaged—and previously ruined—woman that he barely knew.

"Someone must inform the baron, my love," Cassandra put in, since that seemed by far the most important thing in her estimation. "It would not do to leave him in any doubt about my chosen course of action."

"We will do no such thing!" her aunt nearly shrieked—as though word of the afternoon's spectacle wouldn't be buzzing around London's gossips by nightfall.

"We will do no such thing until Lord Rotherdam and I have discussed the matter further," Uncle Henry added, squeezing his wife's arm in warning until she yelped.

"Excellent. Then I will call on you at midday tomorrow to formalize matters," Rotherdam said. "Good day, Mr. and Mrs. Wycliff. Good day, my beloved."

With a final kiss to Cassandra's knuckles, Rotherdam gave a shallow bow and swept away, the gawping crowd opening up a path for him as though they feared devil-worship and moral depravity might be contagious. Cassandra blinked after him, not entirely certain the last few minutes had been real and not a fever dream.

Her aunt looked like imminent apoplexy was a real and valid concern. Her uncle was red-faced in reaction to the very public display, but a speculative expression still clung to his sagging features. Frances had faded to one side as the scene played out, but now she stepped forward again.

"Gosh," she said mildly. "Is London life always this exciting? You don't generally get this sort of thing in Warnham."

Cassandra's eyes widened as she choked on an utterly inappropriate bark of laughter, swallowing it down before it could escape.

Had they done it? Was it really over, except for the lingering unpleasantness?

She wasn't deluded enough to think that the cottage in Horsham and the pittance of an allowance were still in her future. When this new proposal was revealed to be a sham, there was little doubt her aunt and uncle would disown her and throw her out in the street without a penny. She had absolutely no idea what she'd do in that event—and yet, it was still a more appealing prospect than spending another minute in Malthorpe's nauseating presence.

"*You!*" Aunt Lavinia was pointing a shaking finger at Frances. "What kind of friend allows such a scene to occur, and in *public*, no less? This is all your fault! We wouldn't even be here in the park if not for you!"

Frances gave her a nearly convincing look of wide-eyed innocence, as though the accusation cut her to the bone. Cassandra knew a moment's panic at the realization that Frances would leave soon and she would be on her own again—but she had to be strong for a little while longer.

"Now, now, Lavinia," Uncle Henry said, patting and tugging at his wife's arm. "Let's just get away from this crowd and return home where we can talk, eh?"

He kept shooting Cassandra little sidelong looks, as if she were some sort of serpent coiled in his comfortable nest, and he had no idea how she'd ended up there.

Frances caught Cassandra's eye. "I think I should let you have a private conversation with your family, my dear," she said. "It's been a very... *interesting* visit, hasn't it? Perhaps we can speak again sometime soon."

"Er, yes," Cassandra managed faintly. "I certainly hope so."

"Come along, Cassandra," her uncle said, trying for a commanding tone. "We're leaving."

The crowd backed away as she and her relatives turned and headed back toward Hyde Park Corner and the gate. Cassandra had the distinct impression that she had become leprous. Countless eyes stared at her, all with variations of fascinated disgust. She felt their gazes on her skin, like greasy hands touching her through her clothing. For the hundredth time since she'd been torn from Hengewick House and thrust into this nightmare, she longed to fling herself into Robert and Edmund's arms, hiding between them until all of this went away.

That thought inevitably brought memories of falling against Rotherdam's hard-muscled chest...

of his arms closing around her and his lips covering hers. But of course she must not think of that. It had all been playacting, and besides, it was far too confusing. Was there something wrong with her? All around her, girls grew to womanhood without ever kissing handsome soldiers, or fondling men tied to chairs, or watching as other men pleasured themselves and crawled beneath one's skirts to kiss between one's legs.

Was she truly broken inside, to want such things? To *act* on such things? Had Malthorpe somehow sensed that about her? Was that why he had forced her at Lady Northcotte's Regatta?

She shook her head sharply, trying to dislodge the unwanted thoughts. Her vision swam in and out of focus, dizziness from the heat of the afternoon sun combining with the shocking series of events to assail her equilibrium. She concentrated on following meekly along with her relatives, trying not to think about how unpleasant and humiliating the next few days were likely to be.

234

TWENTY-FOUR

AS THE PURPORTED bride-to-be, Cassandra was not invited to join the settlement negotiations when Lord Rotherdam arrived at noon the following day, as promised. She came down anyway.

"This discussion isn't for your ears, girl," Uncle Henry blustered.

Cassandra raised her chin, not backing down. "The negotiation for *my future security* isn't for my ears, Uncle? Why ever not?"

"Of course she must stay," Lord Rotherdam said, in a tone that conveyed he would hear no further argument. "Please, my dearest Cassandra — take a seat."

He held out a chair for her, and she sank into it with a murmur of thanks.

"Most irregular," her uncle muttered. "This entire business is *most irregular*."

"I'm an irregular sort of chap," Rotherdam said, raising an eyebrow. "I'm also willing to double whatever Lord Malthorpe offered as jointure. Cassandra, pray tell, what is your dowry?"

"Three hundred pounds," Cassandra told him, aware that in the world of the peerage, it was the merest pittance.

"Very good," he said, and turned once more to her uncle. "I propose pin money of one thousand pounds annually."

Uncle Henry was still gaping, after hearing Rotherdam's offer to double Lord Malthorpe's offer of annual compensation in the event Cassandra was widowed. Cassandra hadn't yet been told what the original amount had been.

"One thousand a year seems very generous," she said.

Henry seemed to realize at that point that his input was expected. "That seems... adequate," he said cautiously. "But let us revisit the matter of the jointure. After considerable negotiation, Lord Malthorpe offered seven thousand a year. Are you truly proposing to offer fourteen thousand a year?"

"Indeed I am. I can have the contract drawn up by this time tomorrow, if you like," Rotherdam replied. "Now, if we could move on to the provision for any future children..."

Cassandra tried not to choke.

The discussion dragged on for some time, but in the end, Rotherdam rose and shook her uncle's hand — the dislike still clear in his blue eyes. By contrast, her uncle appeared thoroughly dazed.

After offering a promise to return at noon the following day with the settlement contract ready to be signed, Rotherdam bowed over Cassandra's hand. "Until tomorrow, my dear," he said, and took his leave.

Uncle Henry stood staring after him, blinking. "Good lord, you've actually gone and done it, girl. You've made us rich."

Cassandra had some definite opinions on the rights of her aunt and uncle to money negotiated for *her* benefit, and the benefit of her future children. It was moot, however, since Lord Rotherdam would have to be insane to settle anything at all on a woebegone girl who'd been dumped on his doorstep and caused no end of trouble in the time since. He'd done what was necessary to free her from Malthorpe's greasy clutches, and once that task was safely completed, she would break the engagement whenever he asked.

She had been giving some thought to her prospects once her family inevitably disowned her. Those prospects weren't rosy, but if she could travel somewhere her name was not already a matter for gossip, she thought perhaps she might seek out a post as a governess or a lady's companion. She adored children, after all—and it seemed unlikely at this point that she would ever have any of her own.

The thing that pained her most was the prospect of never seeing Edmund or Robert again. It was silly of her—no doubt they'd be charming some rich, respectable widow into their beds before a fortnight had passed. She was not fool enough to believe herself the first they'd dallied with, nor was she fool enough to believe herself the last.

Those were thoughts for tomorrow, though. Not today.

"I'm pleased my propensity for scandal has finally met with your approval, Uncle," she said.

His face darkened. "You've a smart mouth, you little ingrate. I blame your wastrel of a father for not instilling better discipline."

"Then I've no doubt you and Aunt Lavinia will be pleased to see the back of me," Cassandra said. "Which might have happened sooner if you'd simply allowed me to proceed to Horsham with Mary." She paused. "But, of course, then you wouldn't have a nobleman's fortune to lust after. Much less *two* noblemen's fortunes."

Henry's face went red. "How dare you! If anyone knows lust, it is you — not I!"

"And now, as you've said, my evil and lustful ways have made this family *rich*." She sneered at the final word, suddenly and irrationally incensed. "Forgive me, Uncle. I would like to return to my room now."

She turned on her heel and left. Her uncle didn't stop her.

><del>⚜</del>×

By rights, this most recent series of developments should have been cause for silent celebration. In reality, Cassandra spent the next few hours alternately crying and staring listlessly out the window at the bustle of the city below.

The more she thought about things, the more maddening everything felt. Why must she be reliant on the charity of a man who had no desire to marry *anyone*, much less her? Why had she turned down Edmund's offer to become his mistress? What foolish pride had possessed her? How would she ensure that Mary was cared for, when

Cassandra was skeptical of her ability to keep her own body and soul together? Rotherdam had promised to look after Mary, yes — but he could not possibly have meant *for the rest of her life*.

She did not go down for dinner. Instead, she splashed water on her face in an attempt to hide the evidence of tears and rang for a servant. When the maid arrived, Cassandra asked her to inform Aunt Lavinia that she had a headache — true enough after hours of crying. Then she asked for a plate to be brought up to her room.

As soon as the sky outside grew dark, she retired to bed; eager to get through the next few days as quickly as possible. The following morning, she'd barely finished dressing with the fumbling assistance of the housemaid when an impatient knock sounded at her bedroom door, causing the poor girl to drop the hairbrush she'd been holding.

Cassandra gave the maid a reassuring smile and went to open the door, dreading whatever fresh trial lay on the other side. Aunt Lavinia stood in the hallway, her expression livid.

"Lord Malthorpe is downstairs, demanding an explanation," Lavinia said through gritted teeth.

The familiar icy chill settled in Cassandra's lungs. "I don't wish to speak to him. The baron and I have nothing to say to each other."

Lavinia's hand darted out and wrapped around Cassandra's upper arm, her fingernails digging in painfully. "You will come downstairs and explain yourself to the man you *publicly humiliated*." She gave Cassandra a sharp shake. "You will apologize on behalf of this family!"

Cassandra stared at her, aghast. "To the man who assaulted me? I will do no such thing!"

Quick as a snake, Lavinia struck out with her other hand, slapping Cassandra hard across the face. Behind her, the maid gave a little gasp.

"You will—and make your apology a pretty one if you know what's good for you!"

Cassandra lifted a palm to her burning cheek. An entirely inappropriate image that involved hitting Lavinia back with considerably more force flitted through her head. She quashed it, quietly appalled by the impulse.

"Yes, Aunt," she hissed.

Lavinia dragged her out of her room and down the stairs as though she expected Cassandra to make a run for it. Though to be fair, the prospect wasn't entirely unappealing. Lord Malthorpe was waiting with her uncle in the morning room. The inhuman coldness in his muddy hazel eyes made Cassandra's skin crawl.

"My lord," she forced out, curtseying to the horrible toad of a man. "You must forgive me—I'd expected my uncle to send a message explaining the situation yesterday."

"He did not," Malthorpe replied, biting off the words.

"That was a terrible oversight," she said. "Please accept my deepest apologies."

Her stomach churned with bile, but she would do whatever it took to see the end of this farce.

"Your *deepest apologies*," Malthorpe echoed flatly. His tone was one that a tutor might use on a wayward pupil, and it grated on her. "I must discover the perfidy of my betrothed from the gossip rags, and you offer me *your apologies.*"

"Yes," Cassandra replied, her jaw clenched tight around the words. "It was a matter of passion. I am in love with Frederick Ashbury, Lord Rotherdam. I'm certain you are already acquainted with my inability to control my base desires." The words dripped with poison.

Red splotches appeared high on Malthorpe's pudgy cheeks, and sweat beaded his forehead despite the coolness of the early hour. "I stooped to pluck you from the gutter, you vile creature. I deigned to make an honest woman of you, when another man might have ignored your blatant maneuvering for social advancement."

"I never accepted your proposal of marriage," Cassandra told him, certain that her own face was every bit as flushed with anger. "I would rather die than marry you, after what you did to me. You will not have me, and you may go straight to the devil, sir!"

Both her aunt and uncle were staring at her open-mouthed, evidently shocked beyond the capacity for speech. But something dangerous sharpened in Malthorpe's reptilian expression.

"Harlot," he hissed. "You need a husband who will take you in hand and beat the sinfulness from you. I will not allow my wife to behave in such an unseemly manner. You are possessed by an illness of the mind—a weakness of the spirit. But *you will learn.*"

"I will never marry you!" Cassandra shouted, backing up as the baron took a threatening step forward.

"My lord," Uncle Henry said weakly. "Perhaps I was not clear about the generosity of Lord Rotherdam's offer. We have decided…"

Malthorpe lunged forward, grabbing for Cassandra. She shrieked and stumbled back, her hip impacting the edge of a table as the baron's clammy grip closed around her forearm and dragged her stumbling toward him.

"Perhaps you do not understand the nature of a contract," he snarled, his breath rank in Cassandra's face. "Everything is arranged. The license is in order, and it gives me the right to marry you in the parish church at any time within the next ninety days. Therefore, *I choose today.*"

"What?" Cassandra said in disbelief. She jerked against his hold, to no avail. "Let me go! *Uncle!*"

Uncle Henry bristled. "Now, look here! I *say*, sir!"

But Lord Malthorpe was already dragging her in the direction of the front door.

"Stop, I say!" Henry demanded, as Lavinia looked on with wide eyes.

Malthorpe drew a small, pearl-handled pistol from his pocket, and Henry closed his mouth with a sharp clack of teeth.

"Come along, girl," Malthorpe ordered. "Rotherdam thinks he can get his revenge on me by making me look like a fool — but he's the one who'll be humiliated when the gossips learn that yet another woman has publicly spurned him."

Cassandra had no idea what he was talking about. All she could see was the pearl-handled pistol, looming in her vision and bringing back memories of the muzzle of the highwayman's flintlock pointing at her face.

Before she was fully aware of it, she was being marched out of the house and toward an enclosed carriage waiting in the drive. Panic gripped her.

"*Uncle!*" she cried, trying to crane around. But a strong hand dragged her to the carriage door and an arm wrapped around her stomach, tossing her inside. She scrambled up from the floor, but Malthorpe was already inside, slamming the door closed and pointing the little weapon at her.

Cassandra backed into the farthest corner of the carriage, her eyes never leaving the muzzle of the pistol. "Why are you doing this?" she demanded.

"Shut up," Malthorpe snarled. "Stupid woman. You'll do as well as any other when it comes to squeezing out brats for the succession—and if Rotherdam is further disgraced in the process, so much the better. I sent a message to the vicar last night, so he will be waiting for us."

"I won't agree to the ceremony!" Cassandra said. "I'll refuse to sign the register! The marriage won't be legal!"

Malthorpe sneered. "Go ahead and bleat all you like. See how much good it does you. One thing about so-called *men of God*—they're entirely vulnerable to the lure of money. And I have very deep pockets, girl."

The carriage rattled over cobblestones, jolting and swaying through London's uncaring streets.

TWENTY-FIVE

MALTHORPE HELD the pistol trained on Cassandra until the bustle of London gave way to quieter roads—at which point he knocked on the roof of the vehicle and shouted "Whip up those horses, driver! We don't have all day!"

Immediately, a muffled shout of "*Hyah!*" could be heard from the driver's seat, along with the crack of a whip. Cassandra grabbed for a handhold as the carriage jerked and rocked wildly, the horses leaping into a fast canter. With her captor's weapon now resting on his lap, she eyed the carriage doors. But even if she could somehow get one open before Malthorpe reached out a hand and grabbed her, leaping from the vehicle when it was traveling at such speed would be a sure recipe for terrible injury or death.

"Where are you taking me?" she demanded.

"Shut up, you worthless chit," he snapped.

A familiar crossroads appeared through the window, and Cassandra was almost certain that they were following the same southerly route she and Mary had traveled on their ill-fated journey toward Horsham. She realized with some dismay that she had no idea where the baron's family originally hailed from.

How long had his evident feud with Lord Rotherdam existed? Since childhood? Was it possible their families had lived in the same area?

He was clearly *not* taking her to St. George's in Hanover Square for his attempted farce of a wedding. Perhaps they were headed for his family's traditional parish church. And if he intended for the ceremony to take place today, it couldn't be anyplace too terribly far from London. A common license required the ceremony to take place before noon, after all.

None of this did her any real good, unfortunately. Her original plan remained her best. She could not be forced into a marriage against her will. It simply wasn't legal. Additionally, she vowed to scream her fool head off the moment the carriage door opened in whatever town or village was their destination.

Someone would help her. She was certain of it.

This was *England*, for God's sake.

She kept one wary eye on the horrible toad across from her, and the other on their surroundings in hopes of gaining a better sense of her location. The horses cantered on, slowing at intervals for a rest, only to speed up again when Lord Malthorpe yelled fresh abuse at his driver.

The sun was high in the sky when the carriage slowed at the outskirts of a village. A sign marked Old Malden flashed past the vehicle's small window. Cassandra and Mary hadn't passed this way before, Malthorpe's carriage having turned at a crossroads where she and her maid had continued straight.

The place was small and quiet. There didn't appear to be much to it—a few cottages nestled around a village green. The carriage slowed, turning onto a side road, and Cassandra eyed the door. Before she could make the decision to try for it, though, Malthorpe reached across and grabbed her left wrist, his fingers digging in until she gasped.

"Don't," he said dangerously.

She bared her teeth at him and tugged against the unforgiving grip, heedless of the bruises it was likely to leave on her skin. His touch made her flesh crawl, clammy sweat breaking out across her face and neck.

The carriage slowed to a stop. A quaint church lay at the end of the lane—its simple exterior done in the rough stonework of the late medieval period, updated with a newer addition in brick.

"Help me!" Cassandra screamed at the top of her lungs. "Somebody help me!"

Malthorpe backhanded her, the careless blow landing on the same cheek Aunt Lavinia had slapped. She cried out, tasting blood as her teeth cut into the meat of her cheek. The baron opened the carriage door and dragged her out, not releasing his grip on her.

She staggered, dazed—casting her eyes around for anyone nearby. "I need help!" she shouted again. "Somebody… anybody… *please help me*!"

An older man wearing a black cassock over a somber dark suit bustled out of the church, his face a picture of distress. He stopped abruptly when he saw the crest on the side of the carriage, his mouth opening and closing several times in a way that might have been comical under other circumstances.

"M-my lord?" he asked.

Cassandra tried to catch the man's eye. "I've been abducted! I'm here against my will—Lord Malthorpe is attempting to force me to marry him. Please help me!"

The baron gave her a rough shake, drawing an unladylike yelp from her. "Rector. You received my message, yes? This is the woman. As you can see, she suffers from flights of fancy, and is quite mad. I have agreed to marry her in order to save her family from ruin. I assume the modest donation I outlined in my letter will be sufficient to cover the inconvenience?"

It was so completely shameless that Cassandra gaped at him, momentarily speechless. She whirled to the rector. "You're accepting a *bribe* to perform a wedding against my will?"

The elderly churchman flushed red and refused to meet her gaze, replying to the baron as though she weren't even present. "The church roof is in dire need of repair, my lord. Your generosity is"—his brown eyes flickered to Cassandra, only to slide away again an instant later—"most timely."

The baron glanced up at the sky. "It's almost noon. Stop dallying and let's get this done."

"I refuse!" Cassandra said, stamping her foot in frustration—only to realize how that might look to an observer. She gritted her teeth, striving for the most rational demeanor possible. "I am not a madwoman. I've been taken from my family's home against my will. I already have a fiancé! He was to visit my Uncle at noon today to sign the settlement contract!"

"A delusion," Malthorpe said in a condescending tone. "She has an unhealthy fascination with the notorious hellion, Lord Rotherdam. She likes to pretend a scandalous relationship with him that only exists inside her troubled mind. Now come."

The rector's face had grown increasingly pale and troubled during this exchange. He gave the roof of the ancient church a long look before he sighed and nodded, leading the way inside.

"You can't really intend to go through with this!" Cassandra said to his retreating back. "It's illegal! It's… it's *immoral!*"

The rector's stiff shoulders did not relent. The interior of the little church was lovely, with dark wooden pews and ornate scrollwork carved into the structure's support beams. Yet Cassandra balked as though about to enter the maw of a great beast, only to be dragged inside anyway.

Three people awaited them in the narthex—a pair of rough-looking workmen, possibly the church's vergers, along with a fussy little man in an ill-fitting suit.

"Please stop this!" Cassandra called to them. "Somebody help me! I don't want to be here; I don't want this marriage!"

The workmen shuffled in place uncomfortably. The small, clerkly man looked away. None of them intervened.

Malthorpe dragged Cassandra toward the front of the church. "Well? Get on with it, man."

The rector squeezed past them to stand in front of the altar. He closed his eyes for a long moment, as though praying for guidance, and Cassandra held her breath. But then he looked up at the vaulted ceiling. She followed his gaze to find that he wasn't searching for divine intervention, but rather, he was taking in the moldy stains where the roof had leaked—the damage no doubt exacerbated by the recent torrential rains.

He let out a long sigh and reached for a small book. It was marked with a ribbon nestled between the pages, and Cassandra recognized a copy of the Book of Common Prayer. She shook her head slowly back and forth in denial, thinking *this cannot possibly be happening*.

In a solemn voice, the rector began to read the familiar words of the marriage ceremony, while Cassandra pulled and jerked against the baron's painful grip on her wrist. The man droned on about mutual joy and the mystery of the union between Christ and his Church, as though the current situation wasn't an affront against the very deity he professed to serve.

"I require and charge you both, here in the presence of God, that if either of you know any reason why you may not be united in marriage lawfully, and in accordance with God's Word, you do now confess it," he said.

Cassandra perked up. "I can't marry him—I'm promised to another! We... we've had intimate relations!" she improvised. "I might be carrying this other man's child!"

The rector blanched, but Malthorpe spoke over her as though her words meant nothing. "There's no barrier to the marriage. Keep going, man—we don't have all day."

Swallowing audibly, the rector continued, "Cassandra Fenwicke, will you have this man to be your husband; to live together in the covenant of marriage? Will you love him, comfort him, honor and keep him, in sickness and in health; and, forsaking all others, be faithful to him as long as you both shall live?"

"No!" she shouted, appalled. "I absolutely *will not*!"

"She agrees," Malthorpe said through a clenched jaw. "Now *go on*!"

The rector stuttered his way through the rest of the reading, the two nervous-looking witnesses muttering unintelligibly when asked if they would uphold the marriage. Malthorpe dragged her left hand up, squeezing the bruised flesh until she unclenched her fingers with a pained cry. He jammed a plain gold band on her ring finger, and she stared at it as though it were a snake.

"*No*," she said, for what felt like the hundredth time. "I refuse! *I do not consent to this marriage*!"

"Get it written down in the register book and let's be done with the thing," the baron growled, turning and dragging her back down the aisle to the vestry.

The rector hurried along behind. "My lord, she'll have to sign the book or it's not legal."

"She's a gibbering madwoman," Malthorpe snarled. "Does she look like she can sign her name? Have the clerk do it for her."

The small man, who'd been huddled next to the massive tome of the parish registry, straightened in alarm. "My lord! I couldn't possibly!"

The baron sneered at him. "You'll do as you're told, or I'll see you horsewhipped and your entire family ruined."

The man cringed in obvious fear. Cassandra tried to beg him with her eyes, but he wouldn't look at her.

"Mr. Smythe," the rector said urgently, "Just help the... *baroness...* take care of the formalities, and don't make a fuss."

He stumbled a bit over the title, but it wasn't nearly as large a stumble as the one that froze Cassandra's thoughts in her head.

Baroness?

She stared in dismay as the rector, the vergers, the parish clerk, and the baron signed two copies of the marriage lines—one in the register book, and one on a separate piece of paper, which the rector handed to her. She reached out with the hand Malthorpe wasn't strangling in his sweaty hold, taking it and staring at it blankly for a long moment.

Instinct told her to throw it away with every bit of force she could muster. Rationality told her that this might be her only form of proof—her forged signature, written in a hand not her own. She crumpled the paper in her fist and stuffed it in the pocket hole on the right side of her skirt before meeting the rector's worried gaze.

"Your God will judge you for what you've done, if a court doesn't do it first," she told him in a quiet, venomous tone. In a hidden corner of her mind, she wondered what her atheistical Hellfire men would have to say on the subject. Then the burn of tears pressed at the backs of her eyes, and she realized what a terrible, terrible idea it was to let thoughts of her friends and lovers intrude right now.

She blinked the tears away angrily, glaring at the man who thought he could treat her in such a way.

"This means nothing, you swine," she hissed, jerking against Malthorpe's grip even though she could not break it. But inside her chest, the icy steel band around her lungs was tightening, tightening... and she wondered if this would be the time it finally crushed the life from her.

TWENTY-SIX

THE BARON IGNORED Cassandra's hurled insult. "I'll arrange for the donation to be delivered within the fortnight," he told the rector, and left without another word.

The driver was waiting outside with the carriage, and he jumped down to open the door when they emerged from inside the church. Cassandra's breath was coming in labored wheezes past the constriction of panic in her chest as the reality of her current situation truly began to sink in.

Did it matter that the marriage wasn't legal if she was Malthorpe's prisoner, unable to seek outside aid and prove her case in a court of law? And... *dear heaven*, he was taking her to his *house*. She would be completely within his power. The thought was enough to send gray splotches dancing at the edges of her vision.

Once again, she was manhandled into the carriage, too consumed with the need to get air into her lungs to mount any kind of meaningful resistance. When she scrambled inelegantly into the seat, gasping like a fish, it was to find that the pistol was once more resting on the baron's lap as he sneered at her from across the gap between them.

"You'll stay at Elmlake, the family seat," he said. "You can squeeze out an heir and a spare for me, and get the weight of Mother's disapproval off my shoulders. Meanwhile, I shall take great delight in beating Rotherdam at whatever game he's been playing with you." A smile pulled at his thin lips. "Yes, that will be very satisfying indeed."

She stared at him, fighting for comprehension past the low buzzing that seemed to be filling her head. "Why are you doing this?" she rasped. "Why do *any* of this? It's madness!"

His expression snapped back to thinly veiled anger. "It's revenge. Rotherdam stole away my betrothed, so I shall steal away his in return." He eyed her up and down with disdain, the passage of his gaze making fresh gooseflesh prickle across her skin. "Heaven only knows what he sees in you. You're a terribly common little thing."

She shook her head in sheer disbelief. As there was no conceivable way her situation could become worse than it already was, she blurted, "But the entire proposal was a ruse to get me out of marrying *you*! Rotherdam has no interest in me whatsoever!"

"*Balderdash*," Malthorpe said. "You're his lover, aren't you? That's significant—the man's been a virtual monk for years."

"I am most certainly *not*!" Cassandra retorted hotly, aware that feigning insult at the accusation was facile at best, given her involvement with both Rotherdam's valet and his man of business. Again, the sharp pang of longing for their presence pierced her heart and brought tears to her eyes. "How dare you! He took me in after my coach was attacked by highwaymen, and saw that my maid and I were cared for until we could be sent on our way. That's all!"

Malthorpe scoffed. "Yes, and then he publicly humiliated himself by fawning over you in a crowded park before witnesses. Clearly he has no interest in you whatsoever." Irony dripped from the words. "Now stop your bleating and leave me in peace, you little harlot. We'll be at the old manor house within the hour, where I intend to *thoroughly* enjoy my victory."

Cassandra shuddered, fighting nausea as she huddled into the far corner of the carriage. She told herself she was staying quiet and meek so she could think of a plan without arousing either the baron's suspicion or his ire, but her mind was a stubborn blank. The only thoughts on which she could focus circled uselessly in an endless litany of horror.

She could *not* be married to Lord Malthorpe. She could *not* be chattel to the man who'd forced her and ruined her.

In far too short a time, the carriage turned onto the extensive grounds of an estate. There was none of the wildness here that surrounded Hengewick House. No one would imagine stone circles and virgin sacrifices among Elmlake's sterile lawns and gardens.

The carriage pulled up to the main house, an Elizabethan monstrosity sprawling across the carefully trimmed green grass.

"*Whoa, there,*" called the driver, and the carriage rolled to a halt to the accompaniment of snorting and blowing from the exhausted horses.

Without waiting for the servants to arrive, Malthorpe opened the door and pulled Cassandra out, dragging her upright by the arm when she stumbled and fell to one knee on the sharp gravel of the drive.

"Help me," she croaked, when an elderly butler opened the huge double doors for them. "I've been abducted—I don't want to be here!"

The man peered down his beaky nose at her, an expression of some discomfort flitting across his lined features before he hid it and turned his attention to his master.

"My lord. Welcome home. We received your message this morning. Your rooms have been made up, and dinner will be served at five o'clock."

"Why won't anyone *listen to me*?" Cassandra cried.

"Hello, Parsons," Malthorpe said. "This is your new mistress, but as you can see, my baroness suffers from an unfortunate affliction of the mind. Pay her words no heed. Has the attic bedroom been prepared as I asked?"

"Indeed it has, my lord," the butler replied, his gaze sliding across Cassandra's face for the barest of instants before settling on the middle distance.

"Very good," said the baron. "Send Johnson up with laudanum immediately. Oh, and send one of the stable lads up as well, in case I need someone to hold her down."

Fresh panic surged through her. "Laudanum? *No*! Let me go—*let me go*!"

One of the housemaid's daughters in her parents' house had been prescribed laudanum for spells of hysteria when Cassandra was growing up. The drug would steal her will—turn her pliant and listless. *Helpless.*

She screamed and thrashed, desperate to get away even if there was nowhere to run. Distantly, it occurred to her that she was presenting the perfect picture of a madwoman, but the knowledge did nothing to stem her panic. An open-handed slap delivered with devastating force dazed her, sending the world spinning. When it righted, she was dangling over someone's shoulder like a sack of grain, being hauled up a flight of stairs.

She kicked and shrieked and thumped her fists, the blows maddeningly ineffectual. Another flight, Malthorpe cursing and grumbling beneath her feeble onslaught. His hand clamped around her left buttock, and she had never wanted anything *gone* as much as she wanted that hand off her body.

At the top of the stairwell lay a room with an open door. Cassandra had a confused, upside-down view of a plainly decorated bedroom before Malthorpe dumped her onto her feet and gave her a shove. She stumbled toward the fireplace and went down in a crumpled heap. When she looked up, the little pistol was pointed at her again.

Malthorpe jerked the barrel toward a plain wooden chair next to the bed. "Get up and sit in the chair, girl. Johnson will be along with your medicine in a few more minutes, and I daresay you'll be feeling much more accommodating afterward." He gave an ugly little bark of laughter at his own wit.

Cassandra stared up at him—at the weapon trained on her, and the baron's hateful face behind it. Her world narrowed down to an instant of utter clarity. If Johnson arrived with a stableboy to hold her down and pour laudanum down her throat, her life was as good as over. She would be drugged and helpless, reduced to playing the part of the mad wife in the attic for the rest of her short and miserable life.

No one here would lift a finger to save her.

She had no doubt that if Edmund, Robert, or even Rotherdam had known what was happening to her, they would have done their best for her. But it was too late now—in the world's eyes, she was married to this man she despised above all others. At this point, it would take long and drawn-out legal action to unpick the mess.

This was the moment. She would either submit to the threat of Malthorpe's pistol and watch the rest of her life fall away, or she wouldn't.

"Well?" the baron demanded. "Get on your feet, you useless creature, and *do as you're told*."

Cassandra rose slowly to her feet, ignoring the fresh bruises from where she'd fallen. As she climbed to her feet, she grasped the handle of the poker in its stand next to the fireplace, pulling out the heavy length of wrought iron.

"What are you doing?" Malthorpe said, raising the pistol in clear threat. "Put that down, you little whore."

Cassandra shrieked at the top of her lungs and charged at him, swinging the poker with all her might. It impacted the baron's shoulder and he staggered, the pistol flying out of his grip to land near the door. Another, lower swing hit him above the knees, and his legs went out from under him. He fell to the floor with a startled yelp of outrage, clutching at his right thigh.

Cassandra scrambled for the fallen pistol and scooped it up, hurling the fireplace poker toward Malthorpe's head with all the force she could muster. She was out of the room before she saw whether it hit its target or not. Slamming the door shut behind her, she noticed a key protruding from the lock. After twisting it until she heard the click of the lock engaging, she pulled it free and stuffed it in the same pocket hole as the crumpled sheet containing the forged marriage signature.

Her injured cheek throbbed, but the aches and pains of her recent abuse faded beneath the thrumming buzz of blood rushing through her body beneath the force of her pounding heart. She took a precious few instants to examine the weapon in her hand, frantically casting her mind back to her childhood, and an indulgent father with a passion for hunting.

The pistol was different from her papa's hunting rifles, of course—but the firing mechanism looked roughly the same as what she remembered. The frizzen pan was primed, and the hammer half-cocked. She could do this.

Pointing the barrel carefully toward the floor, she raced down the stairs. As she rounded the second flight, a rat-faced man wearing the sober suit of a valet appeared at the bottom, accompanied by a well-muscled lad in simple workman's garb. They froze when they saw her.

She raised the gun, pointing it at the valet, who held a small glass bottle in one hand. "Stop right there," she said, hating the tremor in her voice. "Back away and let me by."

The stable lad gave her a wide-eyed look and started backing up. But Johnson's features hardened.

"You don't know how to use that weapon," he said.

Cassandra held his gaze, unblinking, as she pulled the hammer back to cock the pistol, ready to fire. "I learned to fire a pistol at my father's knee," she lied. "Care to test me?"

In truth, Cassandra had fired a gun once in her life, when she'd begged her father to let her, and he had allowed her to stand in front of him while he guided her through the movements with his own large hands covering hers on the fowling piece.

Nevertheless, it sufficed.

Johnson backed away with a sullen expression, clearing a path for her to get past him.

Once she had, she lifted her chin defiantly. "Your master is locked in the attic bedroom," she said. "He's injured. It could be serious. You'd better go and check on him."

Real alarm colored Johnson's rodent-like features. He turned without another word and hurried up the stairs, where he would find the door locked, the key missing, and his noble employer no doubt livid with frustrated fury.

She didn't have long. There was no way of knowing how much time and effort it would take to kick down the attic door. She met the stable lad's gaze, letting him see her determination... and perhaps, her desperation.

"You. Take me to the stable and saddle a horse for me. *Now*."

His mouth worked for a moment before he said. "We don't have a sidesaddle, my lady."

She stared at him blankly for the space of a breath. Then, "Do I *look* like I care about the *kind of saddle*?"

"N-no, my lady," he said quickly. "Follow me. I'll take you there. Please don't shoot."

"This pistol will be aimed between your shoulder blades the entire time," she warned. "If you cry out for help, I'll shoot you in the back and get the damned horse myself!"

It was something of an empty threat, in reality. Once she fired the flintlock's single shot, her tenuous advantage was gone. But the stable lad didn't appear willing to take the chance. He led her toward the massive front entrance without a word. There, the elderly butler caught sight of them and gasped. A slender footman standing nearby let out an effeminate squeak of fear.

"My lady!" the butler exclaimed. His hands fluttered uselessly by his sides, as though he were unsure what he was supposed to be doing with them.

"Your master is upstairs in the attic," she said. "He's injured. Go attend him now."

She swung the pistol toward his chest, holding it steady. He paled and hurried off, faster than she would have given him credit for, considering his advanced age. Ignoring the terrified footman, she followed the stable hand outside, casting a brief glance at the cloudy English sky she hadn't been certain she'd ever see again.

"This way, my lady," her captive said, leading the way to an airy stable building flanking a generously sized yard.

"No tricks," she warned.

He looked back at her.

"No, my lady." His expression grew troubled. "He's a terrible man. You're right to get as far away as you can."

She lowered the pistol, holding it pointed down and hidden unobtrusively next to her hip as they entered the stable. Several other lads looked up in surprise at her entrance, but her escort shook his head at them.

"The lady is going out for a short hack. Get back to your work," he said.

Cassandra straightened her spine, attempting to convey haughty unconcern as she followed her guide to a row of tie stalls. She didn't let him out of her sight as he pulled out a handsome chestnut mare and retrieved a saddle and bridle.

When the horse was tacked up and ready, the lad turned to her. "She's gentle and fast," he said. "Treat her right, and she'll get you away safe, my lady."

She uncocked the gun and tucked it into the sash of her gown, regarding him steadily. "If you know what a monster the baron is, why do you stay?" she asked.

He gave her a strained smile. "Got nowhere else to go, my lady."

She hesitated. "Did you know why Johnson wanted your help inside the house?"

He shook his head. "No, my lady. He just said to come with him, because the master had some rough work needed doing."

Making a quick decision, she nodded. "All right. In that case, if you want to leave this place, go to Hengewick House and tell Lord Rotherdam that Cassandra Fenwicke sent you." She turned to the mare and hiked up her skirts. "Now, please give me a leg up. Quickly."

The lad flushed scarlet as he bent down and cupped her left knee in his hands. He hoisted her upward as she grabbed the horse's mane and the back of the saddle. She swung her right leg over and settled into place clumsily, several years out of practice.

Gathering up the reins, she fished for the stirrups with both feet, unused to riding astride. Her skirts were bunched around her thighs, and the chafing of the stirrup leathers would probably shred her silk stockings to ribbons before she'd gone three miles.

"Which way to London?" she demanded.

"Turn left at the lane, and right onto the main road," said the lad. "Ride fast, my lady. I fear they may try to come after you."

"Thank you," she told him, meaning it.

The mare tossed her head as Cassandra reined her around, praying that her lack of riding practice wouldn't end up being fatal. The well-bred animal was nothing like the ponies of her girlhood, but she dug her heels in and clung with her knees as the mare leapt into a fast canter.

Left at the lane, and then she let the mare have her head, only pulling up when she reached the turning for the main road. She knew very well that she wouldn't be able to gallop all the way to the city, but for now it felt as though the very hounds of hell were on her heels. She wanted as much distance between herself and Elmlake as she could get, and as quickly as possible.

Her stockings slipped and slid against the saddle leather, and she would have sores where her bare skin rubbed above the ribboned garters. She was also miles from anyone who might offer her help, with no money, no food, and no water.

The immediate sense of relief at escaping her fate gradually gave way to worry, coupled with her growing physical discomfort. She reined in the sweating, blowing mare, letting her slow to a walk to regain her wind for a few minutes. If she could reach a town, perhaps she could pawn the pistol for enough money to buy food and drink, and also send a message to London for help.

She tucked her skirts around her legs as best she could for extra padding against the saddle, and was steeling herself for another gallop when a party of four on horseback rounded a bend some distance ahead of her, riding hard.

Momentary panic flared as she imagined that Lord Malthorpe had sent men after her, and they'd somehow managed to ride around and cut off her escape. Then her eyes were drawn to the tall man on the right... to the dark skin of his face.

A cry of disbelief escaped her. She tugged the nervous mare to a dancing halt, taking in the familiar figures of Lord Rotherdam, Edmund St. Germain, Robert Barlow, and Frances Hunter bearing down on her.

The four figures reined to a stop, milling around her as her mare half-reared in excitement at being unexpectedly hemmed in by strange horses.

"Cassandra!" Edmund cried, leaping from his mount and tossing the reins carelessly to Frances. He caught Cassandra's horse by the bridle, steadying the nervous animal—and then caught Cassandra herself with his other arm, as she slithered gracelessly out of the saddle and stumbled forward to lean against him.

Rotherdam took Robert's horse as the valet dismounted with somewhat more care, limping across to embrace her from behind.

"You're all right?" he asked softly, pressing his face against her hair. Then, more firmly, "You're all right now. We've got you, love."

Cassandra let strong arms take her weight, sagging with relief between her Hermes and her dark-eyed artist.

"You came," she said in a wavering voice.

"Of course we came," Edmund murmured against her temple. "Of *course* we did, Cassandra."

Cassandra buried her face against his starched white collar and burst into tears.

TWENTY-SEVEN

"ARE YOU HURT?" Edmund asked, in a tone that said if she *was* injured, someone would pay.

She shook her head, knowing he'd be able to feel the movement even if he couldn't see it. In fact, she was bruised, winded, and badly chafed—but at the moment, she couldn't feel any of it.

Edmund's shoulders dropped in relief. "Good. Next question—assuming that's a pistol poking me in the hip, *please* tell me it isn't cocked?"

A choked breath of laughter broke through Cassandra's tears. "No, I uncocked it before I got on the horse."

"Can you tell us what happened?" Rotherdam asked. He was still mounted and holding Robert's mare.

She drew breath to speak, but another sob wrenched free as she thought over the details of the past several hours. Robert pressed closer against her back, brushing his lips against her temple and shushing her with murmured words.

After a long moment spent trying to regain her composure, she swallowed hard and pushed against Edmund's chest. Both he and Robert backed off, giving her space. Cassandra forced herself to meet Lord Rotherdam's stormy blue eyes and hold them, knowing her own were puffy and bloodshot from weeping.

"Not here," she said. "There may be riders coming after me."

To his credit, he only nodded. "We need to get off the road, in that case." He paused, assessing their surroundings. "There's an inn at Old Malden —"

"No!" Cassandra said quickly. "Not Old Malden. We came through there earlier."

Again, he didn't question her. "Very well."

"Tolworth," Edmund suggested. "It's a bit farther, but not by much."

Cassandra nodded and mentally braced herself to get back on her horse.

Frances frowned at her. "You're not dressed for riding, much less riding astride. You'll be a mass of bleeding sores by the time we get there."

"Barlow, take your horse for a minute," Rotherdam said.

Robert gave Cassandra's shoulder a final squeeze and did as his master bade. Rotherdam took his own mount's reins in his teeth and shrugged out of his tailored coat — no small feat, given the snug tailoring of the piece. He tossed the coat down to Robert and took up the reins of the valet's horse again.

"Drape that over her saddle with the lining on top," he said.

"Thank you, my lord," Robert murmured, and did as he'd been told. "Here, Cassandra. It's silk-lined, that should help. Edmund, help her mount? Then you'll have to help me as well, I fear."

Cassandra let Edmund give her a leg up, much as the stable lad had done at Elmlake. He and

Robert helped her smooth the borrowed jacket beneath her seat and legs, and Robert quickly adjusted her stirrups a notch shorter so she didn't have to stretch down for the irons. When she was settled, Edmund cupped his hands for Robert's withered leg, hoisting him into the saddle before retrieving his own animal from Frances and mounting.

They set off at a brisk pace in the same direction Cassandra had been traveling originally, her companions keeping a close eye on her to ensure she could maintain the speed. The slick fabric beneath her thighs eased the discomfort of chafing saddle leather, and she merely gave a grim nod whenever one of the others asked if she was all right. She would be *all right* once they were someplace safe and private.

Her tension eased when they turned left at a crossroads. The route to London lay straight ahead, and anyone pursuing her would surely assume that was her destination.

Tolworth was a modest hamlet a couple of miles down the road, built in the shadow of an ancient manor house and surrounded by gently rolling farmland. There was no public house or inn, but one of the locals directed their party to the house of a widow who took in lodgers.

The widow in question was enamored enough by Rotherdam's gold to refrain from asking questions about their unconventional group. Within an hour, the horses were stabled with a neighbor, and Cassandra and Frances were being shown to a comfortable room with a double bed, a desk, and a couple of chairs.

"We'll want a bath drawn later," Frances informed their host. "We'll pay extra if needed, and my companions and I can help haul buckets."

Their hostess, who had been introduced to them only as Widow Nell, was clearly struggling not to react openly to Frances in her male clothing. She managed it, though, and gave an abbreviated curtsey as she bustled out to arrange for a bath and a meal. Once she was gone, Cassandra sat rather abruptly on the edge of the bed and buried her face in her hands.

"Tears later," Frances said briskly. "I'm going to assume you weren't being completely truthful about your lack of injuries. First, though—please take that pistol out of your sash and put it on the table. *Carefully*."

With numb hands, Cassandra pulled out the little weapon and checked that it was still uncocked before placing it on the bedside table. Then she reached into the pockethole in her skirt and withdrew the two items inside, placing them next to the pistol.

"I'm just shaken and a bit bruised," she promised.

Frances poked at the key with a forefinger before plucking the crumpled piece of paper out from under it and scanning the writing.

"Oh, *Cassandra*," she said, placing it carefully back down afterward.

Cassandra didn't like the sadness in her tone, and she frowned. "It's not real. That's not my signature. The parish clerk forged it."

"Right," Frances said with a sigh. "Well, we'll just have to deal with that part when it comes. For now, let me take a look at these bruises of yours."

❧ ♛ ❦

The meal was ready before the water for the bath had heated. The five of them ate together in Widow Nell's homey dining room, having requested privacy for the meal. Frances insisted on food being consumed before Cassandra relayed her story.

The prospect of what was to come managed to spoil her appetite, but she forced down meat and cheese and bread until Frances stopped glaring at her.

They were staying here under false names, not wishing to leave a trail of gossip behind them in case their hostess was less of a gentlewoman than she seemed.

"Now. Tell us what transpired with... *Mr. Pembroke*, please," Rotherdam said, using the baron's given name.

Fighting nausea, Cassandra took a deep breath and nodded, launching into the story of abduction at gunpoint and forced marriage. Rotherdam's expression could have been carved from stone, but Edmund's grew darker and more dangerous as the tale progressed.

"... and then he sent a man to bring up laudanum and drug me, so I hit him with the fireplace poker, stole his pistol, and forced one of the stable lads to saddle a horse for me so I could flee back to London," she finished. She paused, and her brows drew together. "Not that I truly had to force the stable lad. He was honestly very helpful. I told him to present himself at Hengewick House for a better position, and to tell them I'd sent him. I hope that's all right."

"Of course it is, Cassandra," Rotherdam said, surprising her with his use of her first name. The viscount hesitated, straightening his silverware as though it were suddenly the most important thing in the world. "I owe you my deepest apologies. I hadn't imagined that you would get pulled so deeply into the morass of my history with Pembroke."

Cassandra grew very still. "He said you stole away his betrothed?"

The rest of the table was silent.

Rotherdam fiddled with his goblet of wine. "Not... precisely. Pembroke was betrothed to a young woman, yes. Her name was Christina. She wasn't of noble birth, but she'd taken the season by storm the year she came out. I believe he was genuinely smitten with her, but that wasn't enough to overcome his other deficits of character, as you might imagine. When she realized the mistake she'd made, I... assisted her."

"And then he fell in love with her," Edmund added, ignoring his employer's dark look. "But she didn't really want to marry him any more than she'd wanted to marry Mal—" He cut himself off. "*Pembroke*. She jilted Rotherdam at the altar and fled to the continent with her secret lover. That was the last anyone heard of her."

"Yes, *thank you*, Edmund." The viscount's lips were a thin line.

Cassandra looked between them. "So, Pembroke blames you for stealing her from him, but you were just trying to help her get away from him."

"Before everything became more complicated than that, yes."

She forced herself to meet his gaze without blinking. "He's convinced we're lovers."

"Oh, the irony," Edmund said under his breath.

"My actions in Hyde Park were ill-judged," Rotherdam went on.

"Not to mention fairly ridiculous," Frances offered. "But the intentions were good, and it's not as though the rest of us had been able to come up with anything better."

Cassandra sighed. "My signature in the parish register is forged, as is the one on the marriage lines. So, something can be done through the courts, surely?"

"With your testimony, combined with some examples of your signature from existing documents, it should be possible, yes," Rotherdam said.

Edmund stiffened in his chair. "That's *it*? Just bring in the solicitors and pretend that toad-faced bastard didn't kidnap and brutalize her?"

The viscount's granite expression grew dangerous. "Hardly. This childish feud has grown into a criminal attack. I will visit *Mr. Pembroke* first thing in the morning to see honor fulfilled."

"Not alone, you won't." Robert's words were so soft Cassandra had to strain to hear them. The valet was looking down at his half-eaten meal, not up at his master. It was the first time she could recall him confronting Rotherdam on, well, *anything*.

The viscount looked at him sharply, but Edmund cut in before he could reply. "He's right. We're both coming with you. Frances can take Cassandra to Hengewick House and look after her there."

"No," Cassandra whispered. Everyone turned to look at her, and she cleared her throat. "This is my fight as much as it's yours. More so, even. We'll go together, or not at all."

The look Rotherdam gave her was assessing, perhaps even challenging. She lifted her chin and returned it.

"You don't have to see that swine again, Cassandra," Edmund said. "Not unless it's in a courtroom."

Cassandra didn't look away from Rotherdam as she spoke. "Oh, I think I do."

"Well, you're not riding again without proper attire," Frances said. "And that *doesn't* mean a borrowed jacket across the saddle."

Rotherdam wasn't looking away, either. "I'll hire a cart."

"Thank you," she said, not entirely certain why she felt such a strong need to be included in whatever confrontation he had planned. She only knew that she wouldn't be able to meet her own eyes in the mirror until she'd stood up to Malthorpe on more even terms and said what needed to be said.

~~~ ❦ ~~~

By the time the bath was ready, Cassandra's exhaustion was beginning to catch up with her. She could scarcely credit everything that had happened in the course of a single day.

Frances insisted on checking not only her bruises, but also the damage caused by riding astride without the proper clothing. Cassandra blushed furiously throughout the examination, but dutifully accepted the herbal concoction her companion pushed on her and promised to apply it as soon as she finished bathing.

The copper tub wasn't large, but the heat of the water was welcome as a distraction from her circling thoughts. The sting of it against her scrapes and sores eased after a few moments, at which point she sank back, letting her tense muscles begin to unwind. As she soaped the washrag and ran it lazily across her skin, she remembered how it had felt to lean on Edmund and Robert's strength as they embraced her between them.

Idly, she imagined Robert's careful touch replacing her own with the washcloth, as Edmund poured warm water over her hair and lathered it with sweet-smelling shampoo. A frisson of pleasure cascaded down her spine. In her waking dream, she imagined opening her eyes to find Lord

Rotherdam standing in the doorway, watching them with avid eyes.

She gasped, shocked at herself—appalled to find that her nipples had hardened into taut peaks despite the steamy warmth of the room. Putting such fancies firmly out of her mind, she finished washing as efficiently as she could, being careful of her various hurts.

A heavy length of toweling hung by the bath, along with a dressing gown loaned to her by their hostess. When she was dry, with Frances' healing cream covering the worst of her injuries, she tied the dressing gown around her waist and hurried back to the room she was to share with Frances.

It was still early in the evening, but all she wanted now was sleep.

"Get some rest," Frances greeted when she entered. "You could certainly use it."

Cassandra climbed into bed in her chemise. "How is Mary faring?" she asked. "I didn't dare ask when you visited me at my uncle's house."

"Worried," Frances replied simply. "I think she would have asked to come along today, only she doesn't know how to ride a horse."

Warmth bloomed in her chest at the thought that her maid would care so much, even though Cassandra had ultimately been unable to protect her. "And her arm?"

Frances smiled. "Still improving, I'm pleased to say. She was able to lift an empty teacup and return it to its saucer when I left for London."

"I'm glad," Cassandra said with real relief. "I can't thank you enough for everything you've done, Frances. All of you, of course—but I'm quite certain you saved Mary's life with your medical skills."

Frances shrugged, though a faint smile still graced her sharp features. "It's what I do. I'm glad I could make a difference. Now. *Sleep*. I have a feeling tomorrow is going to be another trying day for everyone involved."

Cassandra nodded and settled beneath the covers, making sure to stay well to one side of the mattress so Frances would have room when she eventually came to bed. Sleep arrived easily, but unfortunately, so did nightmares. After the third time she jerked awake with a cry, the slimy feeling of Malthorpe's touch on her skin, Frances perched on the edge of the mattress and frowned down at her in the candlelight.

"It's late," she said. "I think our hostess is fast asleep in her own bed by now. Would you rather have Robert or Edmund in here than me?"

Cassandra gazed up at her with pathetic gratefulness. "Is that a terrible thing to admit?"

Frances' expression softened. "No. No, it's not. Honestly, I'm relieved nothing happened to you today to make you shy away from their presence. Stay right here. I won't be long."

Cassandra smiled in thanks and sat up, pulling her knees to her chest beneath the covers and hugging them tight. Unfamiliar shadows danced in the corners of the rented room. She stared at the candle flame, her thoughts far away, until the softest of knocks sounded against the door, and it creaked open.

She looked up, relief melting her tension as Robert and Edmund entered silently.

"Frances said you were having nightmares," Robert said in his quiet voice.

She nodded wordlessly and scooted to the center of the bed, stretching out her arms toward them. It almost felt like another dream when they approached and climbed in with her, pressing close to fit. They were each clothed in linen shirts, breeches, and stockings, while she wore only her thin muslin chemise. She could feel the heat of their bodies leaching the chill from her skin, and let out a slow sigh of contentment.

"You're safe now," Edmund murmured, tugging her a bit tighter against him. "We won't let anything happen to you."

She nuzzled into his shoulder, covering Robert's arm with her own where it circled her waist. "What will Lord Rotherdam do in the morning?"

Edmund's chest rose and fell. "He's going to challenge that perverted little toad to a duel. Which he should have done years ago, if you ask me."

Silence fell over the room for a long moment before Robert spoke.

"Men die in duels." His velvet voice held a hint of a rasp, and Cassandra knew that he was as worried for his master's safety as she was.

"As long as it's Malthorpe that meets his end on the field of honor, then so be it," Edmund said with an air of finality. "If I had enough social stature that he wouldn't laugh in my face, I'd call the sorry bastard out myself."

Cassandra buried her face against his shoulder again, but she could feel the faint tremor in Robert's arms as he pressed against her back.

TWENTY-EIGHT

THE PHAETON Rotherdam had hired rolled down the same roads Cassandra had galloped during her mad flight from Malthorpe's estate the previous day. The viscount himself drove the conveyance, while Robert, Edmund, and Frances rode behind them.

Cassandra didn't know for certain if the baron had sent men out to scour the area after her escape, much less whether they might still be abroad the following day. With the exception of Frances, every member of their party was armed. Rotherdam had personally cleaned and reloaded Cassandra's stolen pistol before returning it to her with great solemnity. She had absolutely no intention of drawing it except as a last resort, but she appreciated the gesture nonetheless. Foolish though it probably was, its presence tucked in her sash was a comfort.

Edmund had made a final attempt to talk her out of coming with them before they'd left that morning, but she'd stood firm. Robert, by contrast, said nothing, but the paleness of his features proclaimed the depths of his misgivings. She remembered the story he'd told her about his violent reaction to the unexpected discharge of firearms after what he'd gone through in the war.

He'd been speaking of hunting. She couldn't imagine how much worse it must be for him, knowing that people he cared about might become targets.

They turned onto the lane leading through the extensive grounds of Elmlake. Cassandra felt clammy sweat prickling beneath her gown at the prospect of being in this horrible place again, but she would not back down. Gravel crunched beneath the phaeton's oversized wheels, and before she was ready for it, the massive house came into view.

Footmen scurried out to meet them, the apparatus of nobility running as seamlessly as clockwork despite the events of the previous day. At least, until one of the footmen looked up and let out a gasp, shrinking back as he recognized her. After a blank moment, she remembered him as the boy who'd been standing in the entryway with the butler, Parsons, when she'd made her dramatic exit.

A groom hurried out to deal with the horses, and to her considerable relief, she recognized her cooperative stable lad from the day before.

"My lady," he said, lifting a hand to tip his cap as he reached for the horse's bridle. His expression was worried, and his look said clearly that she should have stayed far away from Elmlake's foreboding walls.

"Hello again," she managed. "I do hope you'll take me up on the offer I extended yesterday. This is Lord Rotherdam. Lord Rotherdam, this is the man I told you about."

The viscount spared the stable lad a single nod of acknowledgment before his attention fixed on the front door of the manor. The others were already dismounting, hooking their horses' reins to the back of the phaeton. Edmund reached up a hand and assisted Cassandra down from the high cart.

Malthorpe's butler appeared — his rheumy old eyes going comically wide as he took in Cassandra's presence. Rotherdam swung out of the cart and rounded on him. Whatever expression showed on his face in his face caused Parsons to take a single, hasty step back before he caught himself.

"S-sir," he said. "May I ask who's calling?"

"You may not," Rotherdam said succinctly. "Convey us to your master without delay. I would have words with him."

Parsons' jowls flapped ineffectually for a moment, as the demands of protocol warred with the conspicuous presence of multiple weapons wielded by multiple very angry-looking people.

"This is highly irregular, sir," he managed eventually.

"Will you leave your *new mistress* standing on the step, Parsons?" Cassandra said, unable to keep vitriol from dripping off the words. "Surely Lord Malthorpe is eager to see me."

"I—" Parsons looked rapidly back and forth between her and the others. Then he seemed to deflate, his haughty stature crumpling in on itself. "Forgive me. Right this way, my lady."

He led the way toward the back of the first floor. "If you would all wait in the drawing room—"

"No." Rotherdam cut him off. "Convey us to your master—*now*." Each word dropped like a brick, and Parsons blanched.

"Most irregular," he rasped, his hands visibly shaking. He clenched them behind his back.

Cassandra had seen the second floor landing only as an upside-down blur as she was carried over someone's shoulder, but the butler led them down a hallway to the north wing. He stopped before a closed door and raised a tentative hand to knock.

"M-my lord?" he called.

Rotherdam moved the old man aside with an uncompromising hand on his shoulder and shoved the door open without ceremony, barging into the baron's study like a hunting dog with its prey in sight.

"*What* the devil!" Malthorpe staggered to his feet, red-faced. Across from him, an older gentleman with muttonchops also rose in surprise.

"I say," said the second man, whose face Cassandra vaguely recognized from London society. "This is a private meeting!"

She scarcely had time to concern herself with that, however. Rotherdam stalked across the room until he was face-to-face with her nemesis. Without missing a beat, he pulled a pair of tan leather driving gloves from his breeches and smacked them across Malthorpe's cheek with a vicious snap of hide against flesh.

"You pus-soaked pail of two-day-old dog shit," Rotherdam snarled. "You rancid, piss-bathing *goat fucker*. How *dare* you drag an innocent woman into your schoolyard squabble with me?"

Malthorpe's face was blotchy with rage as he regarded Rotherdam, and his expression was one of utter loathing. "*Parsons*." His voice was a hiss. "Get more men and bring them here to turf these *lawless bandits* out of my house. All except for *my wife*. I intend to have words with her."

A cold shudder went up Cassandra's spine as the butler's footsteps hurried away. Her hands clenched into fists.

"*Try it.* I won't aim for your arm, next time," she ground out.

"Lord Malthorpe," the man with the muttonchops said. "What precisely is the meaning of this unpleasantness? Is *this* your missing wife?"

Her eyes flew to him. "I am *not* this man's wife," she spat.

"She is, as I have explained, deranged," Malthorpe said, his eyes locked on Rotherdam's even as he directed the words toward his guest. "This infamous rake has taken advantage of her feeble mind, corrupting her and drawing her into his foul web of devil worship and hedonism."

Cassandra's jaw dropped. She drew breath to say '*How dare you*,' but Rotherdam got in first.

"I call you out, Malthorpe. Name your second, and choose your weapon."

"Don't be ridiculous," Malthorpe snarled... but a bloodthirsty light was beginning to kindle behind his mud-colored eyes.

Rotherdam leaned in another inch. "You have impugned the lady's honor, kidnapped her, forced her into an illegal marriage by forging her signature, and physically assaulted her on multiple occasions. *You will be called to account.*" His gaze snapped to the older man standing nearby. "Lord Donnebrooke. You are witness to my challenge."

"*Lies,*" Malthorpe snapped. "This is all lies. Your reputation precedes you, Rotherdam. Everyone in London knows exactly what sort of a cad you are."

Lord Donnebrooke cleared his throat. "Nonetheless… these are serious allegations, Lord Malthorpe. Honor demands—"

Whatever honor demanded was cut off by the sound of heavy boots pounding along the corridor outside.

"My lord!" Johnson, the valet, slid to a stop just inside the doorway, taking in the scene with a look of confusion. His eyes landed on Cassandra, and his rodent-like features hardened into anger. A motley collection of male servants gathered behind him, peering inside with varying expressions of curiosity and disquiet.

"Remove these people from my property," the baron said, enunciating each word as if it had personally offended him. "*Now.*"

"Just a moment!" Donnebrooke sounded appalled. "Your honor has been challenged by an equal, Lord Malthorpe. You are bound by the gentleman's code to reply!"

Malthorpe's face twisted at the word *equal*, but Rotherdam wasn't done with him yet.

"We both know you can barely tell which end of a sword is which," he said silkily. "But wouldn't you just love a chance to put a bullet through my heart and get away clean afterward?"

Fingers brushed Cassandra's and she gripped them without thought, Robert's hand held tight in hers. The bloodthirst in Malthorpe's expression bloomed into deep, boundless hatred. He leaned forward until his lips were inches from Rotherdam's ear.

"That's my *wife* you've been fawning over, you godless heathen," he said. "But then, you never could keep a woman of your own—could you, *Freddie*?"

Robert twitched, but Rotherdam only smiled coldly. "No more than you could, *Cecil*."

An equally unsettling smile stretched Malthorpe's thin lips. Silence settled heavily for a beat. The group of servants hovered just outside the room, awaiting further orders and probably wishing they'd brought weapons with them.

"Very well, then," said the baron. "You shall have what you seem to want so badly. My valet Johnson will act as my second. We will duel with pistols at noon. There is a clearing east of the crossroads at the end of the lane. Be there, and then we shall see which of us will finally be rid of the other."

Donnebrooke huffed. "Well, now—what a thing this is. I suppose you'll no longer be needing the loan of my men, Lord Malthorpe, now that your wayward bride has turned up on her own."

"Actually, Lord Donnebrooke," Rotherdam said. "I would appreciate your presence as an objective observer, to ensure that both parties acquit themselves with honor. I am aware of your reputation as a duelist in your younger days."

Donnebrooke gave a short cough. "Ah. Yes. I suppose there should be someone there to observe. Honor must be satisfied, and all that."

"Thank you." Rotherdam lifted his chin, still locked in silent contest with Malthorpe. "Then I shall see you both at noon." His blue gaze narrowed dangerously. "*Don't be late.*"

With that, he broke away, turning toward the door. Cassandra let Robert's hand slide from hers as they turned to follow, her heart beating like a drum with some unholy combination of terror and bloodlust—not so terribly different than the hatred she'd seen in Malthorpe's eyes. For the first time in her life, she wanted to see a person *dead*.

"Wait!" called the baron. "Where do you think you're going with *my wife*, you oaf? The girl stays here."

Edmund, who had by some miracle managed to remain silent through all of this, drew his pistol and cocked it with an ominous click. "No," he said. "She doesn't."

Robert and Lord Rotherdam had hands on the butts of their pistols as well, and the knot of servants at the door gave ground uneasily. Edmund put his free hand on the small of Cassandra's back and urged her to follow Rotherdam, who walked through the pack of men like Moses parting the Red Sea. Robert and Frances followed them, and they headed warily toward the main floor and the open air outside.

No one stopped them.

Cassandra accepted Rotherdam's hand up as she climbed into the phaeton, aware that her own was shaking. The others mounted their horses, and they were off.

Her skin felt too hot and too tight as they trotted down the lane toward the crossroads. She wanted to swoon, yet somehow she also wanted to be the one gazing along the length of a gun barrel at Malthorpe's hated, sneering face on the field of honor. She wanted Edmund between her legs again, with her hand on Robert's prick and Rotherdam's lips devouring hers.

She wanted to hug Mary and shout at her uncle and never, ever see London again.

She wanted this to be over.

"We'll set up in the clearing and wait for them to arrive," Rotherdam called to the others. "It's only a couple of hours until noon."

It felt like a couple of years. Frances volunteered to keep watch at the crossroads for the approach of Malthorpe's party, perhaps sensing that the rest of them needed to be alone. Oddly, it was Robert who seemed closest to losing his composure—when Cassandra really felt that ought to be *her* job.

"Stop pacing, Robert," Edmund told him. "You're getting on my last nerve."

Rotherdam, who appeared more relaxed than he had a right to be, reached out a long arm and hooked Robert by the shoulder, bringing him to an abrupt halt. The valet's face was chalk white, and he wouldn't make eye contact with his master.

"I'm sorry, Barlow," Rotherdam said softly. "But the man truly is useless with a sword. It would have been dishonorable to press him on the choice of weapons."

At that, Cassandra understood. Pistols at twenty paces — and with the discharge of the twin shots, Robert's mind would be thrust back to mud and blood and dying soldiers. If Rotherdam fell…

"You shouldn't be here, Robert," said the viscount, still in that soft voice. "There's still time. Ride back to Hengewick House and wait for us there."

"No." Robert's voice shook audibly. "No, I'm not leaving you, my lord. Just… please don't die."

Cassandra's stomach twisted, a heavy lump rising in her throat. In that moment, she vowed to bridge whatever gap separated the viscount from this man. Robert loved his master with the sort of selfless devotion that would keep him glued to Rotherdam's side through war, and peace, and through painful phantasms of the mind. Edmund's hand came to rest on her shoulder, his thumb stroking her skin through the muslin of her dress. She looked up at him, seeing perfect understanding in his face.

Conversation lulled, the sun climbing the sky overhead until hoof beats drew their attention and Frances rode into view.

"They're here," she said. "It's time."

TWENTY-NINE

THREE RIDERS approached, entering the clearing and pulling their mounts to a halt. Malthorpe had chosen his valet Johnson to act as his second for the duel. The rat-faced little man wore a grim expression, and carried an ornate wooden box beneath one arm.

Lord Donnebrooke huffed as he eased his bulk out of the saddle and led his horse to the nearest tree to tie it out of the way.

"Lord Rotherdam. Lord Malthorpe," he said, once the others had done the same. "A challenge has been issued, and a man's honor impugned. But even now, blood need not be shed. If this matter can be settled with words, honor can still be satisfied."

"No," Rotherdam said, in a tone devoid of inflection. "It really can't."

"Then it is the duty of the seconds to negotiate the particulars of the duel," Lord Donnebrooke said.

Cassandra huddled between Robert and Frances, watching with a pounding heart as Edmund moved to the phaeton and retrieved a similar wooden box to the one Johnson was carrying. It was proof, if any were needed, that Rotherdam had been intent on calling Malthorpe out, even before he and the others had found Cassandra fleeing the baron's manor.

Both boxes would contain dueling pistols, Cassandra knew. Her father had owned such a set when she was growing up. The pair of weapons held within would be identical, putting the duelists on an even footing.

"Right," Edmund said, meeting Johnson midway between the two parties. "I propose the French method—simultaneous shots at fifteen paces. We draw straws to determine which set of pistols is used first, and first choice of weapon goes to the man who doesn't own that set."

Johnson's eyes slid to his master and away again. "Eighteen paces."

Edmund snorted softly. "Fine. Whatever you say."

Johnson cleared his throat. "The duel concludes with first blood."

"The duel concludes when one of them can no longer continue," Edmund shot back. "At which point, he can either concede, or his second can take his place." He smiled a truly disconcerting smile— white teeth a slash against dark skin. "And to be exceedingly clear, in the case of your master, conceding means agreeing to go before a magistrate and confess to forging an unwilling woman's signature in a parish marriage registry."

Johnson blanched—the expression of a man who knew his master would throw him onto the dueling field as cannon fodder long before he ever conceded to such a demand. "I don't think—"

"Or we can always say 'to the death,' instead," Edmund continued. "If that's simpler."

Again, Johnson threw his master a helpless look. Malthorpe glared at him, his face red with anger.

"Yes, fine," Johnson choked out. "Until one is disabled and concedes, with the seconds stepping in as necessary."

Edmund's smile grew cruel. "We're agreed, then. Lord Donnebrooke. Would you do the honor of collecting a long and a short straw for drawing lots? We'll say the long straw is for Lord Rotherdam's pistol set, and the short straw is Lord Malthorpe's. Your master is welcome to pick the straw."

Beside Cassandra, Robert was practically vibrating with tension. Frances muttered something under her breath about male foolishness. Cassandra wished with all her heart that she could somehow close her eyes, and have all of this be over when she opened them, with Edmund and Rotherdam safe.

Would Malthorpe *ever* concede, if it meant admitting to his wrongdoings? She couldn't picture it, even under the most extreme duress.

I want him dead, she thought again — knowing she should be horrified at herself, but somehow unable to muster the feeling.

Malthorpe drew the long straw from Donnebrooke's closed fist, and scowled. "How am I expected to trust that this villain hasn't sabotaged one of the pistols?"

Donnebrooke gave him a look laced with mild disdain. "You have the first choice of weapon, Lord Malthorpe. What benefit would he gain from sabotaging a weapon he might have to use himself?"

Malthorpe grumbled something inaudible before saying in a louder voice, "I demand the opportunity to examine the weapon first."

"Certainly," Edmund said, holding out the open box with the two fine pistols on display. "Take your time, *my lord*."

Malthorpe chose one and retreated to check it was properly loaded and in working order. Rotherdam took the other.

"Are you satisfied, Lord Malthorpe?" Donnebrooke asked.

"If you're too afraid to use another man's pistol, you can always concede now," Rotherdam taunted.

Malthorpe's jaw clenched. "Trying to wiggle out of this like the worm you are, Rotherdam?"

"Not at all," Rotherdam replied. "Eighteen paces, I believe it was?"

"That's right," Edmund confirmed. "Stand back to back, you two. Pace off the distance to my count, and then halt. Turn when I say 'turn,' and fire when I say 'fire.'"

As she had done earlier, Cassandra took Robert's shaking hand in hers and squeezed hard. The uncertainty of the next few moments felt like an icy-hot brand pressed into the space beneath her ribcage. On her other side, Frances let out a sharp little huff. Her spine was very straight beneath her tailored male clothing.

The two duelists turned back to back, their matching pistols held with the barrels pointed upward. They strode off eighteen paces as Edmund counted aloud in a clear, strong voice.

"*Halt,*" he ordered. "*Turn.*"

Robert's fingers squeezed Cassandra's until her knuckles ground together, the slight pain a welcome distraction from her sick feeling of fear.

Rotherdam and Malthorpe swung around in unison, raising their pistols to sight down the barrels. With an absolutely emotionless expression, Rotherdam lowered his weapon until the muzzle pointed not at his opponent's heart, but between his legs.

Malthorpe's eyes widened, his face going milk-white. Without waiting for Edmund's command, he squeezed the trigger, and the deafening sound of the single shot rang out. Beside her, Robert jerked as though he'd been the one in the bullet's path, his breathing going heavy and ragged. Cassandra's heart stuttered and skipped in shock.

On the field, Rotherdam remained standing tall. His eyes narrowed, and a slow, icy smile crept over his handsome features as Malthorpe lowered the spent pistol and Donnebrooke stuttered with outrage.

"A perfect capstone to your worthless life, Cecil," Rotherdam said, and squeezed the trigger.

Malthorpe cried out and collapsed to the ground, clutching at his groin as crimson blood pulsed between his fingers. He writhed like a landed fish, heaving great, wracking breaths that sounded like sobs.

"Goddamn you!" he cursed, his voice cracking. "Goddamn you, I'll... I'll..." Another sob of pain wracked him. "Johnson! Kill him, you worthless cur! Kill him now!"

Cassandra stood paralyzed. So did Johnson, for the space of a heartbeat. Then, the valet dove for the wooden box containing Malthorpe's dueling pistols and came up with one in his hands, pointing it at Rotherdam, who was now weaponless.

"Stop this at once!" Donnebrooke bellowed. Everyone ignored him.

Quick as a flash, Edmund had his own pistol in hand and aimed at Johnson. "*Don't*," he said, cocking the weapon with an ominous click.

Johnson glanced wildly between him and Rotherdam, his pistol wavering back and forth between the two targets as Malthorpe continued to gasp and curse, writhing helplessly on the ground. The valet looked like a trapped rat, and Cassandra had a horrible, overwhelming premonition that he would pull the trigger rather than risk Malthorpe's wrath.

Without thinking, she wrenched her hand free of Robert's frozen grip and pulled her tiny stolen pistol free of her sash, rushing toward Johnson as she pointed the barrel directly at his head. "Pull that trigger and you'll die in the next second!" she cried, aware of the waver in her voice, but unable to quell it.

Johnson's terrified gaze whipped to her, but his weapon remained aimed in Rotherdam's direction.

A larger form slipped past Cassandra, moving fast but with an uneven gait. Robert descended on Malthorpe's valet with a feral snarl, grabbing the man by the hair and jamming the muzzle of his pistol beneath Johnson's chin.

"Put. It. *Down*." His normally velvet voice was a hoarse growl.

Johnson let out a single, pathetic squeak of terror and dropped the gun. Cassandra cautiously darted in and picked it up from the ground before backing away. She had been close enough to see the look on Robert's face, and she wasn't at all certain he was aware that he was in an English clearing and not a blood-covered field in the Netherlands.

"Robert?" she said uncertainly.

"I say, sir!" Donnebrooke blustered. "You are not involved in this duel!"

Rotherdam approached, moving slowly to put himself in Robert's field of vision. "*Private Barlow*," he said sharply. Then, in a softer tone, "Stand down."

Robert gasped in a breath of air, a harsh shudder going through him. His eyes flew to Rotherdam and after a frozen moment, he stepped back—lowering his weapon and letting Johnson go. The baron's valet collapsed to the ground and curled his arms around his knees. A dazed expression passed over Robert's handsome features, and he blinked several times.

The viscount closed the final distance and took Robert by the arm. Edmund joined them, eyeing Johnson warily.

"You're all right?" Edmund asked Rotherdam, taking Robert's other arm. "He didn't get you?"

"No, I'm fine," Rotherdam said.

Donnebrooke joined them as well, and they all turned to look at Malthorpe. The baron had subsided into raspy breathing, his hands still pressed weakly over his wound.

"Someone should get this man medical attention, I suppose," Donnebrooke said. "Shocking behavior for a baron—to fire before the word was given."

Frances grunted and went to crouch next to Malthorpe, who blinked up at her, grey-faced.

"You'd better let me see that," she said, without much enthusiasm. "If we don't get the bleeding stopped, things may not go well for you."

Cassandra carefully placed Johnson's pistol back in its wooden box. Drawn by some strange compulsion, she walked over and gazed down at the injured man on the ground. Rotherdam might not have actually shot off Malthorpe's prick, but he'd come damnably close. The baron sneered up at the two women bending over him, his lip curling back to reveal yellow, uneven teeth.

"A *woman*?" His voice was hoarse and weak. "A bitch dressed up in men's clothing? Keep your filthy hands away from my person."

Frances shrugged. "As you like. Far be it from me to impose where I'm not wanted. Enjoy the next few days, *my lord*. Or the next few hours, at any rate." With that, she got up and walked away.

Cassandra remained, staring at the man who'd haunted her nightmares and ruined her life. He was breathing in shallow pants as his eyes grew glassy.

"Tell Lord Donnebrooke that you had my signature forged in the parish register," she said. "I want to hear you admit it before witnesses."

Hatred flared behind the baron's pain-filled eyes. "Go to the devil, you worthless whore. You're mine, and I'll take great pleasure in ensuring the rest of your life is filled with misery beyond your wildest imagining."

"Hmm. Quite a speech," she told him. "In that case, I suppose I'll see you in the magistrate's court." Her gaze dipped to the sickening pool of crimson clotting in the fabric of his breeches. "Or possibly not."

Then she, too, turned and left.

"I believe a hunting accident would be the best story," Donnebrooke was saying to the others. "The man isn't well-liked. I doubt anyone will question it." He looked up at Cassandra's approach, his expression growing troubled. "Ah. Lady Malthorpe. Someone will need to ride back and arrange for a cart to transport Lord Malthorpe to his manor. May I escort you there?"

Her eyebrows flew toward her hairline. "You most certainly may not. And don't *ever* address me by that title again, my lord."

Donnebrooke appeared taken aback, as though he couldn't imagine why she would respond in such a way. She wondered if he'd even been listening when she'd denied the legitimacy of the marriage, repeatedly and vehemently.

Frances appeared and shoved a saddlebag into the old man's hands. "Bandages and the like, assuming anyone can be bothered to use them. I certainly can't be."

Donnebrooke stared at her in such a way as to make it painfully obvious that he'd only just realized she was a woman. Frances ignored his bug-eyed expression and turned to Rotherdam.

"Time to leave, I think," she said. "This isn't a populous area, but the hunting accident story won't hold up if someone wanders across the current scene. Are we going back to Widow Nell's for the night?"

Rotherdam looked between Robert—pale and dazed under his grip—and Cassandra, with her filthy dress, bruised face, and stolen pistol.

"No," he said. "It's farther away, but we're going straight to Hengewick House."

Something settled inside Cassandra's chest, like an unbalanced weight finally coming to rest.

Home, she thought—aware of how irrational that was, but not caring in the slightest. *Oh, thank heavens. We're finally going home.*

THIRTY

FREDERICK ASHBURY, the Right Honorable Viscount Rotherdam, straightened from emptying his stomach contents into a chamber pot. Bracing one hand on the bed frame in the familiar environs of his suite in Hengewick House, he wiped the other across his lips and took a moment to let the room stop spinning.

Brandy was definitely called for. If nothing else, it would wash the taste of bile from his mouth.

He was alone, at least for the moment... away from the gazes of his friends and the woman whose honor he'd arguably defended. That was by design. He'd seen—and caused—more death than anyone should ever have to during his time in the army. But the sight of bleeding civilians had always sickened him, even when he hadn't been the one to pull the trigger.

Cecil Pembroke was a predator... a stain on humanity whose continued existence dragged down the collective virtue of the human race to a notable degree. Frederick had not a single regret when it came to the duel and its outcome. His stomach, however, had its own opinion on the day's events.

He poured brandy from the decanter on the mantle with a shaking hand, and threw back the glass in a single gulp. It burned more than usual going down, with his throat already raw from vomiting.

A light knock sounded at the door. Upon their arrival at his manor house, Frederick had sent Frances, Edmund, and Barlow away with Miss Fenwicke, to make certain she was all right. And, additionally, to give himself a few moments of privacy to pull his composure together. The tenor of the knock on his bedroom door was unmistakable; he would know it anywhere. Unbidden, his mind replayed the memory of his valet jamming a pistol beneath the chin of the man who had threatened him, snarling like a wild beast protecting its offspring.

"Come in," he called, his voice rougher than usual.

Barlow entered. He was still pale, and his striking hazel eyes were haunted. "My lord," he murmured, by way of greeting. He paused just inside the doorway. "Forgive me, but are you certain you're well?"

Of course, he would have smelled the reek of vomit the moment he'd walked in.

"As much as you are, I imagine," Fredrick told him, and silently cursed himself for bringing attention to his valet's earlier lapse of control.

But Barlow only dipped his chin— acknowledgement, coupled with an obvious desire not to discuss his extreme reaction to the sound of pistol fire.

"May I help you change for dinner, my lord?" he asked, carefully formal.

Dinner was just about the last thing Frederick could stomach right now, but he said, "Yes, of course. Thank you, Barlow."

Barlow padded silently around the room, readying Frederick's attire and avoiding eye contact. His limp seemed more pronounced than usual, and the pallor of his normally golden skin was conspicuous.

"How is Miss Fenwicke?" Frederick asked, in lieu of directing his concern toward his valet.

"Miss Fenwicke is magnificent," Barlow replied. "She is also — to all intents and purposes, at least — a baroness." He draped a fresh shirt over the back of a chair and turned to Frederick, still not looking at him directly.

Frederick thought of Cassandra overpowering her captor with a stolen flintlock to escape Elmlake, and could not disagree about the first part. As to the second...

"It's not a legal marriage," he said. "And even if I have to throw half my fortune at solicitors to deal with the matter, I *will* see her free of it."

"I know, my lord," Barlow said quietly. His deft fingers reached for Frederick's cravat... and they were shaking.

Frederick didn't mention it, or otherwise call attention to the lapse. After a moment's fumbling, Barlow freed the pristine white neck cloth and slid it from around his collar. In the next step of the familiar dance, he moved behind Frederick and grasped the lapels of his coat, sliding the snugly tailored fabric over his shoulders and down. Frederick freed his arms and turned to say something more on the subject of Miss Fenwicke, only to stop cold, the words dying on his lips.

Barlow stood frozen in place, staring at Frederick's coat in his hands. Frederick followed his gaze and saw a perfect bullet hole torn through the fabric of the side panel, a few inches below the right armscye. He blinked, flashing back to the climactic moment of the duel. As he had stood poised on the field with his right arm raised to fire, the fabric of his unbuttoned jacket would have hung loose and to the side.

Malthorpe's shot had passed within a handsbreadth of Frederick's ribcage. He hadn't even felt the tug as it tore through the cloth, so focused had he been on his aim.

Barlow made a muffled choking noise and swayed alarmingly in place. Frederick lunged forward and caught him just as his bad leg buckled, managing to swing the other man around a step so that his backside hit the conveniently placed chair rather than the floor. His valet's hands still clutched the heavy material of the coat as though it were a lifeline in stormy seas. Barlow's lips parted. They were bloodless, and his breath came in ragged gasps.

Frederick eased the coat from his death grip, kneeling on the floor in front of the chair and setting the ruined item aside in favor of gathering Barlow's hands in his.

"Robert," he said. "Please breathe."

Frederick was surprised to find that he felt nothing at all about the revelation of his close call. Barlow was feeling the emotion for both of them, it seemed—and Frederick wasn't sure how to approach the idea that his valet cared more for his life than he did.

Barlow curled forward over their tangled hands until his forehead rested against Frederick's knuckles. His skin was icy cold. Frederick didn't flatter himself to think this reaction was solely about his brush with mortality. He should have insisted the Barlow leave before the duel began, damn it all. Barlow's heroism at Waterloo had saved Frederick's platoon, but it had also broken something inside him, and this was the shape of the wound.

"I asked you not to die," Barlow said wretchedly. "I *begged* you..."

At a loss, Frederick guided one of Barlow's hands to his chest, pressing it over his shirt and waistcoat to feel the beating heart beneath. "I didn't. I didn't die, Robert. I'm right here."

Barlow looked up and drew in a shuddering breath. "You could have."

"But I didn't."

The valet swallowed convulsively. "He would have drugged Cassandra. Raped her. *Kept* her. I know that. But she'd already rescued herself, my lord. Everything after that was just meaningless revenge."

Frederick hesitated. "Maybe so. But some men can't be taught, and they can't be changed. They can only be removed from the field of play."

He let Barlow's touch slip away and stood up. The skin over his heart tingled where his valet's palm had pressed, even through two layers of fabric. He went and poured Barlow a brandy, returning to press it into the man's shaking hand.

"Drink this," he said. "That's an order, Private Barlow."

Robert tipped the glass up and swallowed, coughing a bit at the burn. Some of the color returned to his lips, and he huddled over the empty tumbler, cradling the cut crystal in both hands.

"Better?" Frederick asked.

"Not even remotely, my lord," Barlow said. "Please promise me you'll never do anything like that again?"

"I've no plans to," Frederick assured him, honesty compelling him to add, "but honor is honor. Even if I've little care for my own, other people's honor still has value."

"Not at the cost of a life," Barlow whispered, looking up at him with pleading eyes. "Not at the cost of *your* life."

At a loss, Frederick stared down at Robert Barlow's strikingly beautiful face for a long moment before he said, "How about this—I give you my solemn vow that I will never again risk my life over a situation that can be addressed by any other means."

Barlow's eyes slid closed, and after a short hesitation, he nodded. When he opened them again, they sparked with a fire more suited to a battlefield than a bedroom. Frederick couldn't look away.

I'll hold you to that, my lord," his valet said, in a tone that brooked no argument.

THIRTY-ONE

CASSANDRA LAY entangled with Robert on the velvet divan in Edmund's art studio, a draped length of blue satin acting as a half-hearted nod to modesty. Rays from the late summer sun slanted in through the large windows and warmed her skin, a welcome reminder that she was safe in Hengewick House, far away from the icy terror of Elmlake.

"Chin up, Robert," Edmund chided from behind his canvas. "You're supposed to be abducting a goddess to the underworld, not contemplating a recipe for boot blacking."

Robert sighed and lifted his chin in an attempt look suitably godlike. Cassandra didn't dare risk Edmund's wrath by moving noticeably, but she stroked her thumb over the golden skin of Robert's chest with the hand that was allegedly trying to push him away.

His fingers tightened around her hip in response, and the skin tingled pleasantly beneath the satin thrown across her lap.

She had approached Edmund on the second day after her return to Lord Rotherdam's manor, when the sense of waiting for something to happen was threatening to drive her mad.

"I want you to paint me," she'd told him. "And I want you to make it as scandalous as possible."

Edmund had raised an eyebrow and made no attempt to question her motives or talk her out of it. She'd loved him even more in that moment. Robert, by contrast, had taken her shoulders and asked if she wanted this for herself, or if she wanted it as revenge against the people who'd disapproved of her in the past. She'd loved him for that just as much.

When she'd smiled tremulously up at him and told him she wanted it as a way to take control of her own life, he'd nodded and turned to Edmund.

"You'll need a second model if it's to be truly scandalous," he'd said. "You could try to convince Frances, but if you don't want to go the Sapphic route, I volunteer as tribute."

Edmund thought for a moment. "Right. In that case, you're Hades. She's Persephone. Come to the studio after lunch and we'll try out a few poses."

When Edmund had explained that Hades was the god of the underworld, who'd abducted Persephone to rule at his side, Cassandra had immediately adored the idea. As someone whose parents had named her for a Greek prophetess, cursed by Apollo to always utter true predictions but never be believed, it seemed like a definite step up.

Additionally, the thought of playing at being the queen of the underworld while hiding away in a Hellfire Club amused her. The prospect of spending hours with Robert's strong hands clasping her barely clad body was merely an additional boon.

Neither Edmund nor Robert had pursued her for anything sexual since they had all returned safely to Rotherdam's manor, and she was unsure if she was allowed to ask for it. She had a terrible feeling that they were holding back because of her sham of a marriage to Malthorpe. The idea made something cold trickle down her spine, despite the warmth of the sun's golden rays.

This is nonsense, she thought. Wasn't the entire point of the current situation to wrest back control of her life?

Meeting Robert's gaze and holding it, she stroked her thumb over his skin once again, this time stretching a bit further to brush across his flat brown nipple. His hazel eyes darkened in immediate response. A moment later, the fingers grasping her hip curled down and back a couple of inches, until he was practically cupping her backside. Her lips parted on a silent gasp, and the two of them stared at each other in heated challenge. Neither of them so much as blinked.

"Oh!" Edmund called from across the room. "That's *awfully* good. Hold those expressions, both of you."

One corner of Robert's lips curled up, suitably devilish in his normally angelic face. "Scandalous enough for you now, Edmund?" he called back.

"Well," Edmund replied, dabbing feverishly at the canvas with his paintbrush. "We're definitely getting there."

In the next moment, a perfunctory knock sounded at the door. It opened, and before Cassandra could decide whether or not to let out a startled shriek and drag the satin cloth up to cover more of her body, Lord Rotherdam walked in.

"I'm here," he said, his eyes on Edmund. "What was so important that it couldn't wait for—"

Cassandra saw the instant he registered her and Robert's presence, tangled together on the divan. Quite honestly, it would have been difficult to miss; he broke off mid-sentence and froze in place, his mouth still open.

"*Dear God,*" he said, having apparently forgotten that he was an avowed atheist. He took a single, unconscious step backward, his left shoulder impacting the doorframe clumsily.

Cassandra's feeling of mortification fled, replaced by something that felt an awful lot like power. The viscount's gaze flickered between her and Robert as though unsure where to land.

"Oh, hello, Rotherdam," Edmund said conversationally. "Yes, I needed to speak with you rather urgently about finally pulling your head out of your own arse. Do come in and close the door, won't you?"

Cassandra could only imagine how she looked in that moment. She didn't have to imagine how Robert looked. He stared at his master with open longing—distinct from the heated gaze he'd graced her with only moments ago, but equally as heartfelt.

"My lord..." he said hoarsely.

Instantly, Rotherdam slammed the door shut and strode across the room. He caught Robert's loose mane of dark auburn hair in one fist and used the grip to pull his head back, swallowing Robert's breathless gasp as he covered the valet's lips with his own. Cassandra threw Edmund a wide-eyed look, her heart hammering with excitement. She'd promised herself that she would see this day came to pass if it was the last thing she did, but in the end, it looked as though it was Edmund who'd masterminded the plot.

When master and servant broke for air, Rotherdam let his forehead rest against Robert's for a long moment before turning an uncertain expression on her.

"Miss Fenwicke," he began hesitantly, and Cassandra grasped her courage in both hands.

Reaching for him, she cupped his cheek and drew him forward. Warm lips covered hers, and the heat that had been building in her stomach burst into flame. It was everything that the kiss in the park had been, and so very much more besides.

Between them, male hands were tugging and unbuttoning Rotherdam's waistcoat and breeches. Cassandra didn't try to help; she was too busy being kissed. Besides, that sort of thing *was* Robert's job, wasn't it?

Rotherdam dragged his lips to the corner of her jaw and down, kissing and nipping along the column of her throat. She threw her head back with a moan. He didn't stop; his lips pressing over her collarbone and the top of her breast before sliding lower to close around a turgid nipple. A high-pitched cry of pleasure escaped her as the deep pull connected directly to a place low in her belly that clenched, turning hot and liquid.

The viscount's clothing was in complete dishabille thanks to Robert's efforts. He still had one hand tangled in his valet's hair, while the other cupped the weight of Cassandra's bare breast. Trapped as he was between Rotherdam and Cassandra's bodies, Robert made as though to slide off the divan and onto the floor. Before he could, Rotherdam pulled away from Cassandra's bosom with a breathless gasp of, "No!"

"My lord?" Robert asked, sounding suddenly uncertain.

"*No*," Rotherdam repeated hoarsely. "In this room, you never go to your knees for me, Robert." He urged his valet back onto the divan and pulled the blue satin away from Robert's lap.

Cassandra felt a surprised jolt at the sudden reveal of Robert's erect prick, but that was nothing to the shock she experienced when the Right Honorable Lord Rotherdam sank to his knees on the floor, looking up at Robert through sandy lashes.

Another body settled on the seat behind Cassandra. She flinched, taken by surprise — but it was only Edmund, still fully dressed.

"Just me," he said quietly. "Are you all right?"

She craned around and nodded up at him, wide-eyed. He wrapped an arm around her, guiding her to lean back against his body.

"I think you should watch this," he said, for her ears alone. "But take my hand, and give it a squeeze if things start to become too much."

She reached up and clasped his hand where it lay over her heart, having a fairly good idea where this was going and why he wanted her to see it. Rotherdam — or perhaps she should be thinking of him as Frederick now — had thrown Robert's bad leg over his shoulder and was kissing up the inside of his thigh.

Robert looked as though he feared this might be nothing more than a fever dream. "M-my lord," he whispered, right before Frederick's lips closed over the tip of his prick. He arched helplessly and choked on a stifled cry as Frederick kissed and laved at his manhood, taking him deep, only to pull back and tongue at the slit while Robert panted.

Cassandra couldn't look away. The act should have repulsed her. It should have thrown her back to that horrible night when she'd been trapped alone with a monster. But she could not — *could not* — associate what she was seeing now with what had happened to her then.

Robert, far from being in control of his master's actions, appeared helpless with sensation. His expression was almost tortured — St. Sebastian pierced by arrows, his lips parted in martyred ecstasy. Frederick, meanwhile, was the picture of worshipful devotion — a true believer, prostrate at the altar.

It was mesmerizing.

Feeling as helpless before her own need as Robert was before his, Cassandra tugged Edmund's hand down until it rested between her legs. He didn't argue, or ask if she was sure. Placing a tender kiss behind her ear, he slid his fingers through her springy curls, finding her wet and wanting. Sparks sizzled along her skin as he dragged her slickness up and stroked rhythmically along her inner lips — down, up, and around... over and over.

She reached back, fumbling with the fall of his breeches, and he helped open them with his free hand. Between them, they pulled his shirttails out of the way, and Cassandra's fingers closed around his hard length.

Frederick had a hand inside his own breeches, jerking himself frantically as he swallowed Robert's prick to the root, and already, Cassandra could feel that tightening, spiraling sensation that preceded her sexual release.

Of the four of them, Robert broke first, perhaps unsurprisingly. Curling forward with a sound suspiciously like a sob, he twitched and shook through his climax — one hand clutching Frederick's head, and the other gripping the back of the divan as though it was the only thing tethering him to the world.

Frederick made a low, pleased noise like rough purr, not releasing Robert's prick from his mouth as his hand sped up its movements on his own flesh. That male noise of pleasure was Cassandra's undoing. It was so clearly an indication of satisfaction that there could be no question regarding his enjoyment of the act. Edmund's fingers curled *just so*, the tips sliding inside her body. The wonderful feeling of ecstasy pouring over her stole her breath, as her muscles clamped rhythmically around Edmund's welcome intrusion.

When she opened her eyes, it was to find Robert kneeling on the floor after all. His hand joined with Frederick's around Frederick's prick, and the viscount half-fell against him as he spilled over their tangled fingers. The two men collapsed sideways, coming to rest against Cassandra's legs. Robert's hand clutched at her bare thigh in a way that suggested he needed the support to prevent total collapse.

Belatedly, Cassandra remembered Edmund — waiting patiently for her to recover her wits. That lofty goal was still somewhat beyond her ability, but she rolled her head to the side so she could watch her hand moving up and down on his rich, brown skin.

His manhood was a thick and heavy weight in her grip. The same fingers that had so recently stolen her coherence now stroked over her stomach and breasts with luxurious slowness. She varied her grip, sliding a thumb over the bead of wetness on his tip, and he hummed in approval.

"So good, Cassandra," he murmured. "I'm about to spend."

It was probably meant as a warning, but all she felt was anticipation. Unlike Robert, Edmund was silent as he reached his crisis point. He went very still as the member in her hand throbbed and pulsed, pearly liquid spurting from the head in thin ropes. She gentled her grip, not letting go until he began to soften.

Curiosity overcame her, and she couldn't help lifting her hand to lick at the sticky wetness on her fingers.

"*Christ*," Frederick rasped.

She hadn't really thought about having an audience, but it was far more amusing than it should have been that Lord Rotherdam apparently became religious when sexual congress was involved. She laughed aloud, unable to quell the sound.

"If you want her, you'll have to share with both of us," Edmund told him without heat.

Summer-blue eyes continued to hold hers. "So I'd gathered." Frederick made a disgruntled noise. "Damn and blast. I'm a fool. What in the name of insanity have I just done?"

"Well," Edmund replied, "you did say we'd have to organize our own orgies if we wanted them. I only did what you told us to."

"Reprobate," Frederick accused, and Cassandra almost laughed again.

Robert's grip on her thigh tightened, as though he were steeling himself. "You can't take this back, my lord. It happened. I won't pretend it didn't."

Frederick sat back on his haunches and scrubbed a hand down his face. "Oh, *Robert*." The words came on the back of a soft sigh.

Edmund ran a hand over Cassandra's hair, smoothing it away from her face.

"No, I'm with him. You're not backing out after offering him a gamahuching like that, Rotherdam," he said. "I won't watch you pine after these two, and I won't watch you make Robert's life a misery by denying him. Has it never occurred to you to address the problem of Robert's financial security head-on, rather than wallowing in your own self-righteousness about fucking a servant?"

Frederick's brow furrowed in confusion. "What do you mean?"

Edmund huffed a frustrated sigh. "I'm your *man of business*, you idiot. You think I don't have ideas?" He pointed a long finger directly at his employer's face. "We're talking about this tomorrow."

Frederick didn't rebuke him, but he didn't reply directly, either. Instead, he turned his attention to Cassandra. "And what of you, Miss Fenwicke?"

She raised an eyebrow at him, despite her heavy languor. "Well, first—I think that once someone has suckled at your naked breast, you should probably be on a first-name basis with them, *Frederick*."

And beyond that... she had no idea. Everything was in a strange sort of limbo as Malthorpe lingered on his sickbed with blood poisoning from his wound.

"Touché," Frederick allowed, his tone wry.

"We'll need to talk about that, as well," Edmund said. "But not tonight, eh? I went to all the trouble of orgy organization, and I expect an hour or two without this kind of endless nattering. I *swear*, Rotherdam—sometimes I want to thump you on the head."

"I expect you'll need to join some sort of queue," Frederick retorted.

"He does have a point, my lord," Robert offered. "Please come back here and shut up for a bit."

Frederick gave him a look that was equal parts unease and resignation. "Mutiny, Robert?"

The valet reached out and grabbed Frederick by the arm, puling him into their messy tangle of limbs once more. "Absolutely, my lord."

THIRTY-TWO

THE FOLLOWING DAY found Cassandra ensconced in one of the drawing rooms with Edmund, Robert, and one rather disconcerted viscount. From the dark circles under Frederick's eyes, he'd spent most of the night contemplating his actions in the art studio rather than sleeping.

Or perhaps, she mused, he'd merely spent the time regretting being alone in his stately bed. Not that Cassandra had firsthand knowledge of its stateliness—she was only assuming. She, by contrast, had enjoyed a decidedly crowded bed, and had slept like the dead despite the problems still haunting her waking life.

She had also chanced to see Frances sneaking out of Mary's bedroom at a suspiciously early hour, when she'd given Robert a goodbye kiss at the door as he left to begin his morning duties as Frederick's valet. Cassandra was debating whether it would be better to approach Mary or Frances later, in hopes of eliciting the juicy details of whatever was going on between them. Once, she might have been shocked by the idea of her maid dallying with another woman. Now, she only hoped they were both happy with whatever arrangement they were pursuing.

Edmund pulled up a chair next to the low table in front of the settee. Cassandra was the settee's sole occupant, as Frederick and Robert had squared off on opposite sides of the room, and were currently engaged in the act of trying not to appear nervous. In truth, Frederick looked as though he were ready to bolt at a moment's notice. Robert, by contrast, appeared poised to tackle him to the ground should he try—bad leg or no.

"Thank you for joining me, all of you." Edmund began, setting a pile of papers on the table. "Let's start by addressing Robert's situation, shall we? If for no other reason than the pair of you are giving me indigestion."

Cassandra valiantly hid the amused snort that wanted to break free, striving to maintain her ladylike demeanor in the face of the baleful glare Frederick leveled at his man of business.

"I'm still waiting to hear what it is that you believe can be addressed," he said.

"Yes, and that's because you refuse to look past the end of your own nose, Rotherdam," Edmund retorted, turning the top sheet of paper in his employer's direction. "This is a deed outlining the establishment of an irrevocable trust."

Frederick sighed. "In English, if you don't mind, Edmund."

Edmund huffed in irritation. "Did you or did you not go to Cambridge at the same time I did?"

"Yes," Frederick replied. "But as you're well aware, I was drunk for a significant percentage of that time, and pining after one unattainable love interest or another for the rest of it."

"Well, now you have at least one *attainable* love interest, and possibly two. So be quiet and let me explain, *my lord*." The irony behind the title was unmistakable. "You're going to sign this paper with your *Right Honorable* name, and by doing so, you will assign a generous sum of money to be managed by a reliable firm of attorneys of my acquaintance—intended for the benefit of one Robert Barlow, valued servant, for the rest of his natural life."

Frederick's brow furrowed. He drew breath as though to speak, but didn't.

Edmund continued, relentless. "As I mentioned—it's an *irrevocable* trust. You can't change your mind five years from now and take the money back. It's enough to comfortably support a man. It will be sensibly invested to ensure that the principal grows over time. And trust me when I say, you're a rich enough bastard that you won't even miss it."

Robert looked decidedly uncomfortable. "Edmund, this really isn't necessary—"

But Frederick spoke over him. "Yes, it is. It *is*, Robert. Don't you see? This way, I can't possibly destroy your livelihood in a fit of pique. I won't be responsible for you becoming unemployable because some rumor of gross impropriety reaches the ears of a gossipmonger."

Robert stared at him, perplexed. "But you wouldn't do that, regardless, my lord." He straightened his shoulders. "And forgive my impertinence, but I daresay there are plenty of gentlemen in London who would jump at the chance to engage my services as a valet, even if they'd personally walked in on you sucking my cock." He hesitated, then quickly added, "My lord."

Frederick looked pained. "Perhaps there are. And how many of them would expect your sexual services as part of the deal, if they knew?"

"I've no idea," Robert replied. "But they probably wouldn't expect me to plant them a facer before they had a chance to finish speaking."

Edmund let out a soft breath of laughter. "Well, I certainly didn't expect you to be the one digging in your heels on this, Robert. But could you please stop acting like a stubborn arse when I'm trying to fix your problems for you? I worked all night on these bloody papers, you realize."

Robert still appeared frustrated, but after a moment, his expression smoothed. "Fine. In that case, I have a counterproposal. If I am able to comfortably live off this trust, I will accept it — but only as wages in advance, not as a gift."

Cassandra had been watching the exchange with interest. "Oh! That seems fair," she offered. "It's not charity if he was going to earn the money anyway, working as your valet. He's merely getting it as a lump sum, and somewhat earlier than he otherwise would have."

Frederick met his servant's fiery hazel gaze. "That would put your mind at ease?"

Robert hesitated for a beat, and nodded. "Yes, my lord. It would."

The viscount let out a long breath, some of the tension leaching out of his spine. "Then we have a deal."

"Thank all that's right and good for that," Edmund muttered. "Sit down and read this over before you sign it, both of you."

"That's not necessary. I trust you, Edmund," Frederick said, retrieving quill and ink.

"And I won't be able to understand one word in three, if it's the usual legal blather," Robert added.

Edmund looked heavenward as though for strength. "Rotherdam—we've already established that you're an idiot. And Robert—whatever you don't understand, ask for clarification. *Read the blasted papers*, both of you."

Master and man exchanged a glance in reaction to Edmund's caustic tone. Without another word, they both dropped onto the settee next to Cassandra and started reading the papers. Edmund caught her eye and winked. A smile twitched at her lips.

"While they're engaged with that," Edmund said, "you and I need to talk as well."

Cassandra's stomach sank, her earlier good humor draining away as though it had never been. "About the baron? I truly don't wish to discuss it, Edmund."

"Too bad," Edmund told her. "Because there are some decisions you need to start thinking about."

Before Cassandra could reply that there would be no decisions until Malthorpe recovered from his wound—or not—a rapid knock sounded against the locked double doors. All four of them looked up. Edmund scowled, but he rose to see who it was and what they wanted. The door opened to reveal a pageboy, looking slightly harried and more than a little nervous.

"Sorry, sir," he said quickly. "I know you weren't to be disturbed, but earlier his lordship said that we were to deliver any news about Lord Malthorpe urgently—"

Cassandra shot to her feet, her heart rate rabbiting. "The baron? What's the news? Is he—?"

"He passed away last night, Miss. Er... Madam." The lad stumbled over the words.

She fell back on the settee, barely able to draw breath. "He's dead?" she echoed, her voice a hoarse whisper.

Robert scooped up her hand and held it tightly.

"Yes, Miss. I mean... Madam?" The pageboy was flushing scarlet now.

"What are people saying about the death?" Frederick demanded.

"That it was a hunting accident, my lord," the boy said, evidently on firmer footing here.

"Thank you, Charles," said the viscount. "You may go."

The lad dipped into a bow and ducked away. Edmund closed the door behind him.

"He's dead," Cassandra repeated faintly, as though doing so might make it feel more real. A terrible thought occurred to her. "The marriage! Will we still be able to prove it was illegal?"

Edmund pulled his chair closer to her and sat, taking her other hand.

Frederick tapped his chin thoughtfully. "All of the previous evidence still exists, and now you won't have to contend with his denial of the accusation. I don't see that it should make a difference, except possibly to our benefit."

The faintest hint of warmth thawed the ice in her lungs at his use of the word 'our.'

"Agreed," Edmund said. "However, there's another consideration—the very one I wished to speak with you about."

"What other consideration?" she asked, bewildered.

Edmund tightened his grip on her hand. "Cassandra, in the eyes of the world, you've just become the Dowager Lady Malthorpe. As far as society is concerned, you're a baroness... and with the baron's death, you've gained dower rights to one-third of Malthorpe's estate for the rest of your life."

Cassandra's mouth fell open, utter shock robbing her of words.

328

THIRTY-THREE

CASSANDRA STILL FELT as though she were walking through a dream world an hour later. She paced restlessly back and forth inside Mary's bedroom, while her former lady's maid watched her with worried eyes from the comfortable chair on one side of the unlit fireplace.

Frances and little Sadie, the scullery maid, were also there. Frances had shooed the men away earlier, and stood propped against the ornate mantelpiece with her arms crossed over her masculine shirt and waistcoat.

"What do I do here?" Cassandra asked, more than a little desperately. "I have to make a decision before the new baron arrives from London to take control of Malthorpe's estate."

Cecil Pembroke had never sired children, or at least not legitimate ones. Much of the family's estate was entailed. Edmund, who'd been looking into the situation ever since Malthorpe had barged back into Cassandra's life, had informed her that the heir was a seventeen-year-old nephew — the son of Malthorpe's deceased younger brother. As the lad was underage, all of the entailed property would be held in trust for him until he reached the age of majority.

But at seventeen, the new Baron Malthorpe was not a child. He would be taking an active role in matters of the estate, under the guidance of the trust's three guardians. By the time he arrived at Elmlake, Cassandra would have to decide if she were going to approach him as the woman Cecil Pembroke had illegally forced into a fraudulent marriage, or as the Dowager Baroness, with rights to a third of the proceeds of the Malthorpe estate until her death.

Frances had been close-lipped while Cassandra paced and agonized, but Mary leaned forward in her chair with a huff. "Well, I know what I'd do in your shoes, Miss," she said. "I wouldn't even think twice."

Cassandra stopped in the middle of the room. "Oh? What would you do?"

"I'd take the money and run," Mary said. "*My Lady.*"

"Same," Sadie piped up. "I mean, don't it seem like that's the least you're owed, after everything that man put you through?"

For the first time, Cassandra allowed herself to truly contemplate what it would mean to have an independent income sufficient to maintain a comfortable — even lavish — lifestyle. It felt unreal. But if she refuted the marriage, what would her future look like? She would still have nothing except the scraps her aunt and uncle deigned to throw her... along with whatever support Frederick felt compelled to provide her out of pity.

She met Frances' clear gray eyes. "What do you think?"

Frances tilted her head. "I think it's your choice. Disavow the marriage, and you'll be free in some senses — but also penniless. Claim the title of dowager, and you'll be, if not rich, then at least comfortably well off. However, you'll also be constrained by the expectations of society during your so-called period of mourning."

Cassandra's expression soured. "I won't pretend to grieve that man. I'd rather dance on his grave."

Frances shrugged. "I doubt anyone will ask you to weep openly in the streets. Wear black, stay out of the public's view for six months, and I daresay any gossip will burn itself out before too long."

With a sigh, Cassandra began to pace again. A new thought occurred to her. "If I had an independent income, I could hire you back as my lady's maid, Mary."

Her former maid's injury had continued to improve, thank the heavens above. She now had good use of her hand again, though her arm was weak and she still lacked sensation in three of her fingers.

But Mary only smiled and shook her head. "That's very kind of you, Miss — but I'm afraid I've accepted another offer."

Cassandra halted, blinking at her in surprise. "You have?"

A stain of pink darkened Mary's cheeks. "Yes, Miss. I'm to return to London and become a nurse in Miss Hunter's medical practice." Her brown eyes darted to Frances and held, her blush growing deeper.

Frances raised an eyebrow, the corners of her broad mouth twitching as though a grin were trying to break through. Her eyes hid a twinkle when she met Cassandra's startled gaze. "Yes, well... you can't leave such a charming, competent woman unemployed and not expect someone else to snap her up while you're faffing about with baronies."

A startled laugh bubbled up, taking Cassandra by surprise before she could properly suppress it. "Oh, my dears," she said. "That's wonderful. I'm so happy for both of you."

Unable to help herself, she swooped down and wrapped Mary in a hug. After a moment, Mary tentatively reached around and patted her back.

"S'pose that means you'll be in the market for a new lady's maid," Sadie said cheekily, once Cassandra had straightened away from the embrace.

"I suppose it does at that," Cassandra agreed with a helpless smile. "Are you applying for the position, then?"

Sadie gave her a shrewd look. "Depends, Miss. Are you planning on being rich or poor?"

And... that was the question, was it not? Posed in such simple terms, the answer suddenly seemed rather obvious.

"I am planning on being rich, unseemly, and scandalously improper," she said slowly, trying the words out one by one as she spoke them.

Sadie's grin lit the room like the sun. "In that case, I am most definitely applying for the position, Miss."

"You're hired," Cassandra told her. "When can you start? Heaven help me, but it appears I'm going to need a black dress hemmed in the next couple of days."

꜔ ♕ ꜕

"You're certain about this?" Robert asked later, holding both of her hands in his.

"I am," Cassandra told him, feeling more certain about her decision than she'd felt about anything in a very long time. "I will *not* be living at Elmlake, even if that means I have to use some of the dower income to rent a little cottage somewhere. And I *will* be doing everything in my power to drag Cecil Pembroke's name through the mud with my shocking behavior—after a perfunctory period of so-called mourning, anyway." She fluttered her lashes up at him. "In fact, I'm considering joining a Hellfire Club as a way to really drive the point home."

Edmund had been watching the exchange. "I'll ask around and see if there are any openings for membership coming up. Rotherdam, have you heard of any?"

"I believe such an opportunity might arise in six months or so, yes," Frederick said without turning away from the window. He'd been gazing out of it as they spoke, his back to the room. Of the three men, he seemed to be the only one with misgivings, though he was keeping them to himself so far.

"I understand you'll be poaching my scullery maid," he added.

"Yes, I will be," Cassandra agreed. "I can probably send you a couple of girls from Elmlake to make up for it, if you like. Along with the new stablehand I already acquired for you, that seems like adequate compensation." Her voice lowered to a murmur. "Honestly, I wouldn't wish that place on anyone... except maybe the butler and that horrible valet, Johnson."

"Hmm." Frederick sounded skeptical. "You've also domesticated my doctor."

"That wasn't me!" Cassandra huffed at him in irritation, though he still didn't turn to look at her. "I had nothing to do with that matter, as well you know."

Edmund snorted. "Perhaps it's less a case of Miss Stanhope having domesticated Frances than of Frances turning Miss Stanhope feral."

Cassandra chuckled at the image. "Maybe so. Time will tell. They seem happy together, and that's the important thing."

"That it is," Robert agreed.

Silence fell over the room, a hint of awkwardness tainting the atmosphere.

"Well," Cassandra said. "I suppose I'll need transportation to Elmlake in two days. Thankfully, I won't be expected to attend the funeral—even if the assumption that my absence is due to my inability to contain my grief in a public setting rankles. But I *will* need to speak to the new baron." She sighed. "That should be an... *interesting* conversation."

"You'll take Edmund along to act as your man of business." Frederick's tone brooked no opposition. "Consider him on loan for the duration."

Edmund sighed dramatically. "Foisted here and there like a borrowed coat. The things I put up with from you lot."

Cassandra turned and kissed him to shut him up.

"Oh, all right," he said when she released him. "I suppose you've talked me into it."

"I'd offer to act as your coachman," Robert said, "but unfortunately, I've no idea how to drive a team."

Cassandra shivered, sparing a thought for poor, brave Leeds, who'd lost his life trying to protect her and Mary from highwaymen. She kissed Robert as well, to drive the vision from her mind. "Thank you for offering, but you're needed here, I think," she told him, casting a significant glance toward Frederick at the window.

Robert followed her gaze. "Yes, it's true—a valet's work is never done. Nevertheless, we'll make some sort of arrangement once you're settled. I, for one, do not intend to wait six months to see you again, whether you're in widow's weeds or not."

"Agreed," Edmund said.

Frederick was silent for a long moment. Finally, he turned to face them. "Edmund will assist you with whatever you require for your journey, Miss Fenwicke. Or… should I say, Lady Malthorpe."

"I really wish you wouldn't say that," Cassandra told him. "As I believe I've already mentioned, *Cassandra* will do just fine."

"Of course," Frederick replied formally. "Now, I should leave the rest of you to your preparations. Good day."

With that, he stalked out. Cassandra turned a bewildered look toward the others. "What was that about?"

Robert was frowning after his master. "I'm not entirely certain," he said.

"He's always been a moody bastard," Edmund added, though he, too, was looking at the empty doorway with a scowl. He shook it off and returned his attention to her. "Never mind him right now. We need to discuss expectations for the meeting with the nephew and his guardians. Perhaps over a meal?"

"Yes," Cassandra said, still distracted by Frederick's odd behavior. "That sounds lovely."

⚜

Two days later, Malthorpe's odious butler showed Cassandra and Edmund into the drawing room at Elmlake. Parsons ushered them inside with a pale face and a perfectly blank expression.

"My lord," he announced. "The Dowager Baroness Malthorpe and her... man."

Edmund and Parsons eyed each other like a pair of stray cats considering a brawl over territory. Cassandra swept into the room, dressed head to toe in black, and offered a polite curtsey to the slender adolescent lad who'd risen at her approach.

"My lord," she greeted cautiously.

The new Lord Malthorpe was a pale, bookish youth with a beaky nose and narrow shoulders. He appeared visibly nervous, but his features were kind and his blue-eyed gaze soft.

"My Lady," he replied, bowing to her. "My deepest condolences for your recent tragic loss."

Cassandra had wavered over how to approach Cecil Pembroke's nephew, and had eventually decided upon candor. Her possession of the forged marriage lines, combined with the entry in the parish registry, was sufficient to prove her status as the Dowager Baroness Malthorpe. Now that she had decided on her course, her widowhood did not rely on the existence of any sort of sentimentality toward her supposed spouse.

"You are very kind to say so," she said. "But the former baron and I were not close. I no more had feelings for him than he had for me. I wish only to discuss the particulars of the estate and the dower share. After which, I will take myself off somewhere and not trouble you in the slightest."

A crease formed in the new baron's smooth brow. "You don't wish to take up residence here in Elmlake, My Lady?"

"Certainly not." Cassandra gave him a tight smile. "This should be a home for you and your future wife, whomever she may be. The same can be said for the Malthorpe residence in London. Let us simply say—Elmlake holds no good memories for me. I hope that will be different you, once you build a life here."

"I… see," said the lad. "In that case, would you perhaps care to take possession of the lake house instead? The location is rather out of the way, but I have fond memories of the place from childhood visits. It is quite peaceful there, and very beautiful."

Interest piqued, Cassandra glanced at Edmund, who'd been hanging back during the conversation.

"Perhaps," she said. "I would certainly like to know more about it."

"We would also like to discuss the details of the estate and its income," Edmund put in. "If your advisors would care to join us, we could begin right away."

"Yes, of course," the new baron said, all business now despite his young age. He paused, meeting Cassandra's eyes with direct frankness. "And, I do hope this is not out of line—but you say that you and my uncle were not close. I know he was… not a kind man. He and my father were always at odds, and after my father's death, he cut us out completely. I only wish you to know that… I am not my uncle."

Something like fragile hope for the future blossomed in Cassandra's heart, driving away the chill that always settled so heavily there when her thoughts turned to the past. A quavering smile pulled at her mouth.

"No," she said. "I don't believe you are."

THIRTY-FOUR

THE LAKE HOUSE was indeed a rather isolated place, located in Ockley Wood near the shores of Vann Lake, some six miles south of Holmwood. Cassandra's first thought as she stood in the modest back garden, looking out over the water dotted with lily pads, was that she desperately wanted to paint this scene.

"What do you think, Sadie?" she asked.

Sadie turned in a slow circle, taking in the trees, grass, and chirping birds. "It ain't exactly London, innit?"

"Not really, no," Cassandra agreed.

"Could we get a dog?" Sadie asked.

"I think we could, yes," Cassandra replied.

A slow smile lit up Sadie's face. "And chickens?"

"Definitely chickens," Cassandra told her.

The maid's expression turned devilish. "And maybe a couple of horses, too?"

Cassandra narrowed her eyes suspiciously. "Can you even ride?"

"Not yet," Sadie said, completely unrepentant. "But I bet James would teach me."

"James?" Cassandra asked. "Who is James, pray tell?"

"Stable hand from Elmlake," Sadie replied without missing a beat. "He showed up at

Hengewick House and Lord Rotherdam took him on because you asked him to. But his lordship don't actually need any more stablehands. I thought, if we had horses, he could come work here."

"And teach you to... *ride*," Cassandra finished, not sure whether to be amused, vaguely appalled, or both. "I'll mention it to Edmund. I'm afraid I still don't know enough about finances to be able to say if we can afford horses." She glanced at the position of the sun, shading her eyes with one hand. "And speaking of Edmund, we should join him and the others inside."

Sadie nodded, giving the lake a final, long look. "I think I like it here," she blurted.

"I think I do, too," Cassandra said.

⤝ ☙ ⤞

As it turned out, the lake house did, indeed, suit Cassandra right down to the ground. She and Sadie moved in, with the young baron's wholehearted blessing. Somehow, 'maybe we could get a dog' turned into two long-eared spaniel puppies before the first week had passed. Sadie, who had never tended a chicken in her life, quickly grew adept at tossing out scratch grains and slipping fresh eggs from the nest without getting pecked.

Edmund assured Cassandra that maintaining a phaeton, along with a pair of cobs suitable for riding and driving, was an entirely reasonable expense for a dowager baroness living quietly in the country. The much-vaunted James agreed to sign on as Cassandra's groom and man-of-all-work, maintaining the cottage and its modest grounds as well as the small stable and carriage house at the back of the property.

Cassandra paid him well enough to maintain rooms in Ockley, since the lake property didn't include servants' quarters. It was within easy walking distance, allowing him to come out daily to discharge his duties. From what Cassandra had seen so far, Sadie had mostly managed to disconcert the poor lad more than anything else.

It was such an odd feeling to be able to purchase whatever she needed, be it clothing or furnishings or other frivolities. She had a treasure trove of paints, brushes, easels, paper, canvasses, frames, and palettes. Her greatest joy was to stand at her easel on the shore of the lake, looking out over the landscape turning gradually from late summer green to autumn russet and gold.

There was only one thing missing.

Or rather… two things. Possibly three, though she was still uncertain of the third.

Only a few weeks had passed, but she missed her men desperately. She was, as far as the world was concerned, a widow in mourning. Edmund had an excuse to see her, because he was acting as her man of business during this extraordinary transitional period in her life. But there was no acceptable reason for a visit from a notorious viscount—much less from the notorious viscount's valet.

On his third visit to discuss the details of her finances, Edmund sat across from her in the charmingly appointed morning room and met her eyes frankly.

"I think there are other things you'd like to speak with me about," he said.

Cassandra's shoulders sagged in relief, since she'd had no idea how to bring up the subject herself. "Yes. There are. Thank you, Edmund. Sadie, would you mind giving us a few minutes, please?"

Sadie popped up from the chair in the corner, where she'd been studiously practicing her letters. "Of course, My Lady," she said primly. "The dogs seem restless—I should take them for a walk."

The dogs had, in fact, been fast asleep—though they both perked up at Sadie's voice. Sadie gathered them up and left, throwing Cassandra a cheeky wink as she did.

When they were alone, Cassandra turned back to Edmund. "I miss you," she said without preamble. "I miss Robert. Heaven help me, I even miss Frederick. Which reminds me, is he still inexplicably brooding?"

Edmund reached across and gathered her hands in his, lifting them to his lips. "Not inexplicably, no," he replied, somewhat cryptically. "We miss you, too. I've been attempting to look at this period of time as an investment in a happier future for all of us, but I'm beginning to think that's a load of old rot. I've also been restraining myself during our visits, because indulging my desires with you alone wouldn't be fair to the others."

"I don't think any of this is fair to anyone involved," she said, happy to finally have things out in the open. "I know it's barely been any time at all... and it's not that I've been unhappy. I love this place. I love having financial freedom, and finally being my own woman." She paused. "Did you know my aunt and uncle have been sending letters almost daily?"

Edmund blew out a breath. "The gossip about your newly acquired title and wealth is all over London, so I can't say I'm surprised."

"I've thrown every last one of the letters onto the fire without reading them," she said.

"I don't blame you a bit," he told her. "You don't owe them a penny — or a moment of your time. This money is not tied up with a settlement. It's your dower share. *Your* share, mind you... and nobody else's. Don't listen to anyone who says otherwise."

"I know," she assured him. "But I digress. I am happier now than I believe I've ever been since before my parents died. And yet, I'm not certain I'm willing to play the game of societal expectations through six months of full mourning."

"We would wait for you much longer than that. I hope you know that," Edmund said gravely, and Cassandra's throat closed up.

She had to swallow several times before she could speak again. "I believe you, even if I still don't understand precisely what it is that you see in me."

Edmund reached up, taking her chin gently in his long-fingered hand. "We see *you*. I *see* you, Cassandra Fenwicke — and you will have to take my word on it when I say that it's very difficult to look away."

Her breath caught, her heart giving a startled double-thump at his words. A tear spilled over her cheek, and he wiped it away.

"Please kiss me," she whispered.

His thumb brushed her lower lip. "As if I could refuse that request. But do me a favor, and don't tell the others that I cheated?"

"Our secret," she promised, and fell into his kiss.

He kept it admirably chaste, and it was still the most she'd felt in weeks. When they parted, her lips tingled with warmth.

"You're right, though," he said, as though continuing an earlier conversation. "This isn't going to work. Not for six months."

"Agreed," she said.

He thought for a moment. "Hmm. It occurs to me that the equinox is coming up in a week or so."

Her brows drew together in confusion. "The equinox?"

A faint smile tugged at his lips. "Yes, the equinox—a very important day for pagans and other such undesirables. Let me see if I can arrange something. If I'm successful, I'll send a letter with instructions, all right?"

She still had no idea what on earth he had in mind, but she nodded anyway. "All right."

His smile widened. "Excellent. In that case, I should probably take my leave so I can start plotting. Expect to hear from me soon." He leaned in and kissed her again. "Goodbye, Cassandra."

"Goodbye," she said breathlessly.

The following days passed with aching slowness, despite being filled with long walks, good food, and many pleasant hours spent painting. It was two days before the autumn equinox when Sadie came bouncing in with the mail.

"Letters for you, m'lady!" she greeted, handing over two envelopes.

"Thank you, Sadie," Cassandra said, taking them and examining the first. The handwriting was in her uncle's familiar crabbed hand, so she tossed that one in the fireplace, where the edges blackened, curling inward as flames devoured it.

The second one made her catch her breath. She'd seen that neat script often enough in recent weeks, on legal documents and itemized budgets.

"It's from Edmund," she said.

"Ooh, is it an assignation?" Sadie demanded, pronouncing the final word with precise care.

Cassandra looked at her warily. "Do you even know what that word means?"

Sadie shrugged. "It's when people meet someplace in secret to fuck, innit?"

"*Sadie!*" Cassandra chided, her cheeks heating. "Language! I'm fairly certain a baroness' maid isn't supposed to speak like that, you know."

"Right, and we both know you're only a baroness because there's money in it," Sadie said unrepentantly.

"Very, very true," Cassandra admitted. "Fine. I suppose I can't ask you to be proper when I'm contemplating something very improper indeed."

"I knew it!" the girl crowed. "It *is* an assignation!"

Cassandra broke the seal, hoping very much that it would be, but unable to picture how such a thing might work in her current circumstances.

My dearest Lady C, the letter began. *I was so dreadfully sorry to hear about your current illness. I know an excellent doctor from London who will be arriving in the area tomorrow for a visit. I have requested that she and her assistant pay you a visit on Wednesday to check on your health. I assure you, she is a marvel and I've no doubt you'll feel much better if you take her advice. Yours faithfully, E.*

"Well?" Sadie demanded. "What does it say?"

Cassandra blinked. "It's a bit cryptic to be honest. But I believe we may expect a visit from Frances and Mary on Wednesday. And if anyone should ask, I'm apparently unwell enough to warrant a visit from a fancy London doctor."

"Are you?" Sadie asked, deadpan. "So sorry to hear it m'lady. I do hope it's not catching."

Cassandra wrinkled her nose at the girl, who only grinned back at her.

Frances and Mary did, in fact, arrive on Wednesday afternoon. Cassandra, playing the part of the gravely ill, waited until Sadie had shown them inside to greet them with happy embraces.

"It's so good to see you both!" she exclaimed, ushering them into the morning room and sending Sadie out to get refreshments. "Are you down from London to visit Hengewick House, I take it?"

Frances made herself comfortable on the settee, and Mary perched next to her. "We are," Frances said. "Edmund invited us for a bit of cloak and dagger, as it happens."

"How are you faring out here, Miss?" Mary asked. "Or, My Lady, rather."

"Call me Cassandra, please, Mary. You don't work for me any longer, and I hope you'll come to see me as a friend rather than your former mistress."

Mary smiled. "Cassandra, then."

Cassandra sighed. "To answer your question, it's lovely here and I adore it."

"But the fake mourning restrictions rankle," Frances suggested, taking the glass Sadie offered her. Mary did the same — using her previously injured arm, Cassandra was thrilled to see.

"They do," Cassandra admitted. "The more I think about it, the less certain I am why I should give a damn what society thinks about me." She hesitated. "But as much as I'd love to heap shame on Cecil Pembroke's grave... the new baron is a sweet boy. He's been unfailingly kind and thoughtful to me, despite never having met me before. Apparently Malthorpe was horrible to his father, and wouldn't even acknowledge the boy or his mother after the man died."

"Really? Cecil Pembroke, being a flaming arsehole to people he should have protected?"

Frances asked, the words dripping with sarcasm. "*Quelle surprise.*"

Cassandra choked on a huff of inappropriate laughter. "Just so. But in all seriousness, I find myself less willing to do things that might make the new baron's life more difficult."

"That's good of you," Mary told her, with complete sincerity.

"But we can't live our lives based solely on what others would want us to do," Frances added firmly. "And for that reason, it's good that Edmund is a conniving schemer. Which is where Mary and I come in."

Cassandra leaned forward. "Yes... I will admit to being intrigued, not to say a little confused. Is there more to this visit than the visit itself? Because the visit itself is very welcome, I can tell you."

Sadie set her tray aside and sat down as well.

"There is more, if you wish it," Frances said.

"Told you," Sadie murmured, and Cassandra shot her a quelling glance. It bounced off, as it usually seemed to do.

"What's the plan?" Cassandra asked.

"We've come with Lord Rotherdam's driver from Hengewick House," Mary began. "As far as anyone knows, we're here as a favor to a sick woman, since we were in the area anyway."

Frances picked up the thread. "After a suitable amount of time — say, an hour or so — we will leave and return to the house party we originally came to attend. It's a terribly scandalous house party, of course."

"Autumnal equinox at a Hellfire Club," Mary said dryly. "And forgive me for saying so, but I still don't fully know what kind of mess you've pulled me into with this lot of scoundrels."

"They're an acquired taste," Cassandra admitted, amused at the thought of her prim and proper lady's maid ending up as Frances' lover, entangled with a notorious atheist rabble-rouser and his compatriots.

"The point is," Frances said, "in an hour or so, the carriage outside will depart for Hengewick House once more, carrying two women."

"One of whom is rather distinctively dressed," Mary added, tweaking the lapel of Frances' mannish jacket. "It might be us…"

"Or it might be you two," Frances finished. "Then, those same women will return tomorrow, ostensibly to see how your recovery is progressing with the new treatment I'm about to prescribe you."

The puzzle pieces slotted into place. Cassandra smiled. "And what treatment might that be?"

Frances softened. "My prescription is to go see your men. Have a night of scandalous revelry. As you're probably aware, Freddie's club isn't really about bonfires and debauchery. But when the proper motivation strikes, they can put on a decent show, believe it or not."

Cassandra's smile grew tremulous. "You're amazing. All of you. I hope you know that."

Frances smiled back. "We are rather good, aren't we?"

Cassandra turned her attention to Sadie, who was grinning. "What do you think? Would you care to visit your old house for a proper pagan festival?"

"That I would, m'lady," Sadie said, her smile growing even brighter.

THIRTY-FIVE

WEARING MALE clothing felt decidedly odd. Cassandra and Frances were much of a size, so it wasn't that the jacket and breeches were too tight or too loose. They merely seemed very... *confining*.

By contrast, Sadie could have swum in Mary's clothing. Rather than attempt wearing it, she'd merely thrown Mary's cloak across her shoulders and pulled up the hood.

The driver from Hengewick House didn't so much as look sideways at them, only uttering a stoic greeting of, "My Lady," as Cassandra climbed into the cart after her maid. The journey seemed far longer than the five or so miles it actually was, giving Cassandra plenty of time for nerves.

She hadn't seen Robert or Frederick since she'd moved to the lake house. She was confident that falling back in with Robert would be effortless, but Cassandra could never quite be sure of how any given interaction with the mercurial Lord Rotherdam might go. There was also the question of what, exactly, this pagan night of debauchery might entail.

It was dark by the time the cart rattled into the huge circle drive in front of the old manor. The night was unseasonably balmy for September — summer's last gasp, the humid atmosphere lightened somewhat by a faint breeze from the south. Torches had been set up in the driveway to light their way, as footmen hurried out to greet them and convey them inside.

There, they were met by Mr. Fortescue and Mr. Vaughan, much to Cassandra's surprise.

"Hello, my dear," Fortescue greeted. "And hello, Sadie. Cook has missed you since you left, and that's a fact."

Sadie curtsied. "Good evening, Mr. Fortescue, Mr. Vaughan. It's good to see you both!"

"That it is," Cassandra agreed warmly, leaning in for a kiss on the cheek from each of them. "I haven't had a chance to thank you for everything you did to help me in London."

"Oh, it was nothing, my dear—a mere trifle," Fortescue said. "Please, make no mention of it."

"It wasn't a trifle to me," Cassandra told him. "Your assistance during that horrible time means more to me than I can say."

"We're just glad your fortunes appear to have turned," said the normally taciturn Mr. Vaughan. "And we've been tasked with intercepting you here at the door, to give the others time to... er... set the scene?"

"The festivities are taking place outside, as you may have guessed," Fortescue added. "There's a costume waiting in your old room should you wish to exchange male attire for Hellfire Club attire. We'll just go and let the others know you've arrived. Footmen will convey you to the standing stones whenever you're ready. And Sadie? Once you've finished helping your mistress dress for the evening, there are several people below stairs who are looking forward to seeing you."

Sadie's smile lit up.

"What about you two?" Cassandra asked. "Will you be joining the, er, *festivities*?"

Fortescue laughed softly. "No, no, my dear. Prancing around in bracken loses its charm after the first few times. We'll take our pagan rites somewhere private, and allow you and the others to do the same."

With that, he bowed over her hand and kissed her knuckles. "Perhaps we'll see you at breakfast. I'd love to renew our earlier discussion about inheritance law, in light of recent developments."

"I look forward to it," she said, feeling her cheeks dimple. "Goodnight, Mr. Vaughan. Enjoy your celebration."

"Enjoy yours," Vaughan retorted. "Good night, Miss Fenwicke."

Her smile widened at his purposeful misuse of her name. Here, she was more than happy to be Miss Fenwicke rather than the Dowager Baroness. She hurried up the stairs and down the hallway to her old room, with Sadie giggling at her heels. The door was open. On the bed inside lay a sheer white dress, barely more than a chemise. Along with it lay a black lace mask, and also a black velvet cloak lined with red silk.

"Oooh," Sadie said. "You're going to look like a proper virgin sacrifice!"

Cassandra's cheeks flamed. "When I said we should work on your reading, I didn't mean to do it so you could read those kinds of novels!"

"Why not? *You* read those kinds of novels," Sadie pointed out.

The flames heating Cassandra's face licked higher. "I'm a baroness. I'm allowed to read them."

They stared at each other for several seconds. Sadie broke first, descending into cackling laughter. Cassandra followed her into appalled merriment, unable to hold back.

"Oh, heavens. Have I really stumbled into the middle of a Gothic novel?" she asked, once she'd regained a modicum of control.

"One way to find out," Sadie advised. "Come on — try it on! I want to see."

In truth, now that she was here, Cassandra would have done just about anything asked of her, short of parading outside to the others in the nude. Removal of the confining male clothing wasn't the smoothest of processes, neither Sadie nor Cassandra having had much experience with cravats and waistcoats. Putting on the sheer dress was straightforward enough, however.

Cassandra wished for a larger looking glass in the room. But even the small oval mirror was enough to see that she resembled nothing so much as a Greek statue of her namesake, draped in diaphanous fabric belted at the waist, that revealed more than it hid.

"Goodness," Sadie said, taking in the full effect.

"Hair up or down?" Cassandra asked, touching the chignon that had allowed her to pass for the short-haired Frances beneath her borrowed John Bull hat.

"Down," Sadie said with conviction. "Here, turn around."

Deft fingers pulled hairpins and smoothed the blonde mass until it hung down her back and over her shoulders. Cassandra checked the overall effect in the glass, and reached for the mask.

"That's a bit funny, don't you think?" Sadie observed. "It's not like they won't know who you are."

"I'm not certain that's the point," Cassandra told her, lifting the black lace to her face.

Her eyes glittered through the almond-shaped cutouts, catlike. The stylized shape covered the top half of her features, lending her an air of mystery. Sadie reached up and helped her tie the ribbon into place, securing it and rearranging her hair over the band to hide it.

Last came the cloak. Once she shrugged it over her shoulders, it obscured her body shape and the sheer white fabric of the dress. Sadie tweaked the heavy hood up, and she was instantly transformed into an androgynous, vaguely sinister figure. *Hellfire Club, indeed.*

"I think you're ready," Sadie told her. "Do you need me for anything else tonight, m'lady?"

"I don't believe so," Cassandra replied with a smile. "Go have fun, Sadie. Thank you for helping me."

Sadie grinned. "Have fun, yourself. And don't worry. If you end up on your back on a stone altar, surrounded by robed figures standing over you with knives, it's a sure bet that a dashing young rake will show up to rescue you in the nick of time!"

Cassandra wrinkled her nose. "I'm seriously reconsidering what kind of reading material to bring into the house."

Sadie stuck her tongue out, smirked, and ducked out of the room. "She's ready!" the girl called to the waiting footmen as she skipped off, eager to visit with her fellow servants.

With a deep breath, Cassandra straightened her shoulders and exited the room. "Good evening," she greeted. "Please convey me to Lord Rotherdam and his friends."

The footmen bowed. "Right away, My Lady," said the one on her right. "This way, please."

She followed them downstairs, to a small door at the back of the grand old house. Cassandra had spent comparatively little time exploring outside of the manor, since the weather had been disagreeable for much of her first stay. The grounds behind the house were wild and overgrown; it appeared very little effort had been made to tame them.

Here, too, torches provided illumination, defining a path that wound down a gentle hill. Below, she could make out eerie stone ruins, also illuminated by flickering orange light.

"Lord Rotherdam and his companions are waiting for you by the bonfire, My Lady," said the footman, bowing again and indicating that she should proceed.

She did, thanking them. A glance behind her showed that the pair weren't following—merely staying put, presumably to ensure she didn't slip or stumble on the path. Cassandra followed the firelight into the ancient circle of standing stones. Many had toppled, or were leaning drunkenly against their neighbors. The atmosphere of the place was heavy with the passage of time.

Laying a hand against one of the massive megaliths, she was surprised to find it radiating warmth against her palm. She slipped past it, entering the protected area within. As promised, a huge bonfire roared at one end of roughly circular space. It was the other end that drew her gaze, however. Straight out of one of her penny dreadfuls, a low stone altar rose from the trampled grass, with a naked figure bound atop it. Two men in robes identical to hers stood on either side, faces obscured by their hoods as they looked up at her approach.

She walked toward the unholy trio as though in a daze, only distantly surprised to find that it was her beautiful Hermes bound on the stone, his wrists pinioned over his head. His dark hair, russet-tinged in the firelight, fell in a loose halo around his head. Rather than a mask, a black silk blindfold covered his eyes.

Unable to help herself, Cassandra approached to stand next to the taller of the two robed figures. She reached a hand out, sliding fingertips over the bare skin of Robert's damaged leg, up and over his knee to his well-muscled thigh. He shivered, his uncovered prick twitching against his stomach. It was red and engorged, leaking a thin trail of seed into his navel.

"Please," he rasped, and Cassandra's belly tightened almost painfully. That needy place between her legs throbbed, aching. The robed figure across from her reached up and pulled his hood back, revealing sandy blond hair and a mask identical to hers.

"Hello, Cassandra," said the Right Honorable Lord Rotherdam. "So glad you could join us. Welcome to the Rites of Autumn."

THIRTY-SIX

NEXT TO HER, Edmund lowered his hood as well. "We've missed you. Did Will and Lawrence let you know what was going on?"

Cassandra gave a single, embarrassed laugh. "In a manner of speaking. I can't say they quite succeeded in preparing me for the reality."

She brushed her thumb over the soft skin of Robert's thigh again, entirely unable to stop herself from touching him. His breath shuddered out in a sigh.

"Do the festivities meet with your approval so far?" Edmund asked, with all seriousness.

"As if you truly have to ask," Cassandra said. "Tell me though—what, exactly, are the Rites of Autumn?"

"Complete nonsense that Robert made up so that it would sound more impressive," Frederick replied, deadpan.

"Well, we couldn't just call it an excuse to have an orgy, my lord," Robert said from the plinth.

Edmund met Cassandra's eyes, his gaze twinkling with poorly hidden amusement. "Oh, I think we could have," he said. "But really, Rotherdam, she hasn't even been here five minutes and you're already ruining the mood."

"There was a mood, beyond the obvious?" Frederick asked, frowning.

Edmund unsuccessfully swallowed a snort. "To answer your question in the spirit it was intended, Cassandra, we're reaping a bounty tonight. We already have one exceptionally willing sacrifice. You can choose to become a second, or simply join Rotherdam in making sure the first sacrifice is thoroughly devoured, with nothing going to waste."

She swallowed. "And if I were to choose to join Robert on the altar?" Her heart thudded in response to nebulous images of all the things that might befall such a pagan sacrifice.

"Then we would take our pleasure with both of you," Frederick said. "And you will take your pleasure with each other. But we would do nothing that might result in... unwanted complications, shall we say."

"By that, he means pregnancy," Edmund clarified. "Please overcome your genteel upbringing long enough to speak plainly, Rotherdam."

"My apologies." Frederick met her eyes and held them. "Cassandra, all of this is a game, as I'm certain you know perfectly well. You may choose how you wish to play it. You may choose to change roles — or to withdraw completely — at any time."

She chewed on her lower lip, wondering if she truly dared to ask for what she secretly wanted. But... if not now, when? If not here with these men who had protected her and cherished her when she was at her most vulnerable... where else?

"You clearly need a second sacrifice," she said firmly. "We'll wear this one out too quickly."

Gathering all her courage, she trailed her fingers up the last few inches of Robert's thigh and took him in hand, sliding her thumb over the slick wetness at his tip. A low whine was born and died in his throat. His hips bucked into the contact, seeking friction.

Edmund chuckled.

"Eminently practical," Frederick approved, also sounding amused. "Edmund, take our second sacrifice's cloak, while I pour the mead."

Edmund moved behind her and slid her hood down, bending to kiss her temple. "If something becomes too much, say *stop*, or shake your head, or pull away. No one will physically restrain you. And if we see that you've gone unusually still or don't seem to be responding, we may pause and ask if you're well."

His long-fingered hands slipped her cloak off her shoulders, leaving her in the sheer dress. Even as the protective, muffling layer of clothing fell away, a sense of warmth and safety kindled in her chest, spreading outward with a feeling of comforting heat.

"Thank you," she murmured.

"Never thank us for what should be a normal matter of course," Edmund said, and brushed his fingertips up the side of her neck. She shivered.

"Come." Frederick had returned with a metal goblet, and was kneeling on a mossy section of ground at the foot of the altar.

Heart in throat, Cassandra approached and knelt facing him. She felt oddly naked beneath his blue gaze, despite the draped folds of the dress.

"Drink," he said, and raised the goblet to her lips.

It was mead, as he'd said—nothing more. And not very much of it, at that. But there was something so reverent about the act of drinking that it felt like having a sacrament administered. She could pretend, without much difficulty, that the evil viscount was drugging her into submission, removing all of her willpower and inhibitions before commencing his arcane rites upon her body.

Once she finished the mead, she decided, nothing that happened would be her responsibility. She would become another willing victim of Lord Rotherdam's Hellfire Club. She would be as wanton and helpless as Robert, writhing ecstatically in his bonds while hands roamed over him—taking whatever they wanted and giving unbearable pleasure in return.

Cassandra swallowed the dregs, steadying the goblet with her fingers wrapped around Frederick's on the stem. He lowered the cup when she was done, and leaned forward to close his lips over hers in a searing kiss. She was breathless by the time he pulled back and met her gaze with his stunning, sky-colored eyes.

"Each of us will steal a little death from you," he said. "*La petite mort...* I'm certain Satan himself would approve. You and I will also steal one from our other sacrifice. Possibly two, if he's feeling particularly inspired tonight."

"Yes," she breathed.

"Kiss the others," Frederick ordered. "I shouldn't like to think I'm taking advantage of my position and becoming greedy."

Cassandra rose in a daze and practically fell into Edmund's arms. He removed her mask and tossed it aside, kissing her forehead, then her closed eyes, and finally her cheek, before taking her lips every bit as commandingly as the viscount had.

Just as dizziness was threatening to overwhelm her, he pulled away and led her, half-stumbling, to the figure lying on the low stone plinth. Robert returned her kiss as though he was drowning and she was air. When Edmund eased her away from him with a steadying grip on her shoulders, Robert chased her lips until he hit the boundary of his restraint, and fell back with a groan.

Frederick had taken the opportunity to get rid of the goblet and spread a heavy fur on Robert's other side. Robert, too, was lying on decadent fur rather than bare stone, and while the plinth was not precisely spacious, there was enough room next to him for a second person—assuming she was relatively small and slender.

"Lie down, Cassandra," Frederick said.

Her stomach swooped. She crossed to Robert's other side and sat gingerly on the edge of the stone. Like the standing stone she'd touched before, it had absorbed the sun's heat during the day, and was releasing it as gentle warmth during the deepening night. She shuffled onto the fur and lay back, finding that her body fit surprisingly well in the space at her fellow sacrifice's side.

Robert's body was still quivering with anticipation. By contrast, Cassandra felt as though she were melting. Edmund came to stand at her head. She looked up at his upside-down, masked face, feeling lost, and found, and entirely *seen*.

When Frederick untied the sash of her dress with deft fingers, sliding the sheer folds apart to bare her body to their gazes, she didn't feel any more naked than before. His hand came to rest over her heart, his skin like a brand against hers. She gasped, reaching blindly toward Edmund, seeking some kind of anchor.

Edmund eased a hand beneath her neck and lifted her upper body, seating himself on the edge of the altar so she could use his thigh as a support. When she was settled, he took her hand in his, twining their fingers together.

Frederick stroked up and down the length of her torso. The touch was strangely possessive, as though he were mapping the shape of her body with his fingertips, committing it to memory. Cassandra grasped Robert's thigh with her free hand, needing the physical connection to all three of them for reasons she couldn't have explained.

Frederick's exploration dipped lower, brushing through her soaked curls. The touch tingled, spreading fresh heat through her.

"So wet for us," he murmured.

Robert made a faint, desperate noise, jerking fitfully against the ropes binding his wrists in response to his master's voice — or perhaps, the words themselves. Edmund stroked Cassandra's loose hair back from her temples before brushing the pad of his thumb across her lips. She tried to kiss it, but it was already gone.

Frederick's exploratory touch moved to her breasts. Her nipples ached, drawn into taut points and desperate for attention. He didn't disappoint, and she moaned as his deft fingers tugged at the pebbled flesh. When she was squirming against Edmund's body, making small, needy sounds in the back of her throat, Frederick abandoned them in favor of returning to the place between her legs that was dripping for him.

Edmund had touched her there before, and she'd touched herself many times since she'd finally learned about such things. None of it had prepared her for Frederick. Thick, sword-callused fingers delved into the empty, grasping place that Edmund had only teased, filling and stretching her—stroking her from the inside out.

The touch burned with a delicious, bone-deep heat. A primal need to take *more, deeper, faster* propelled her hips in a rolling rhythm that seemed both unfamiliar and as old as time itself. Frederick appeared content to continue teasing this newly discovered part of her until she died of pleasure—*la petite mort,* indeed.

Somewhat unexpectedly, it was Robert who broke first. "Please," he begged. "Please, my lord, I can't take it! I need to see! Dear God in heaven—I can *smell* her…"

But Frederick didn't relent. "You'll have her soon enough, Robert. Patience."

Robert let out a heavy breath, the sound catching in his throat.

Cassandra was only distantly aware of the exchange. Her body was balanced on the edge of something, poised to take flight. Edmund reached down to squeeze her nipple lightly between his fingers, just as Frederick changed his angle of attack in such a way that his thumb brushed over her aching nub with every slow, deliberate thrust in and out of her body. She arched and shrieked, coming apart at the seams, shocked that her body could feel so much at once.

It went on and on—perfect and endless and too much, too *much*—until she was a shuddering, wrung-out mess, her breath rasping in her throat as her chest rose and fell rapidly.

"Oh God," Robert was whispering. "Oh God, oh God, someone *please* touch me... please, *please*—"

"That's an awful lot of blaspheming for someone surrounded by atheists," Edmund observed. "We should probably see to it that he puts his mouth to better use for a bit."

Frederick's snort reached her from somewhere outside of the little bubble of utter serenity surrounding her as she floated back to earth. "If I didn't already know you to be an utter degenerate, I'd be left in no question after this interlude, Edmund."

Robert moaned as though he were in physical pain, twisting against his bonds with more force than before. Strong hands lifted and turned Cassandra's body, arranging her to straddle

Robert's face, with her upper body draped over his torso. In this position, she had an excellent, up-close view of his straining prick. It was an angry red color, growing purple at the tip, every vein standing out. As she watched, it twitched, and another drop of seed dribbled from the tip, joining the growing mess on his taut belly.

He groaned, rooting blindly against her belly. Without a single thought in her head, she scooted forward until her oversensitive folds were positioned directly over his lips. His tongue swiped along her slit, and he began lapping and sucking at her as though she were the first meal he'd had in ages. She jerked and trembled, still shaken by the climax Frederick had wrung from her body mere moments before.

Robert's prick loomed huge in her vision. She grasped it, a vision of Frederick on his knees floating across her memory. She remembered how undone Robert had been, powerless beneath Frederick's lips sliding along the length of his prick. She remembered the salty-bitter taste of Edmund's seed, when she'd licked it curiously from her fingers.

Somehow, it seemed the most natural thing in the world to stretch forward and kiss the tip of her bound Hermes' prick, because she was safe, and drunk on pleasure, and he was one of the men she loved. Breath stuttered against her most sensitive places as she lapped at Robert's slick head, tasting the same faintly astringent flavor that she remembered from Edmund's emissions.

Robert writhed beneath the weight of her body pinning him, his lips and tongue driving her toward the same peak from which she'd so recently leapt. Her limbs felt shaky as her lips stretched around Robert's crown, taking more of him into her mouth.

"So beautiful." Edmund's voice was low. Fingers stroked her long hair aside, draping it over her shoulder.

"He won't last, Cassandra." Frederick had crouched next to the plinth. His chin rested on his forearms as he watched them undoing each other with lips and tongues. "He'll come in your mouth."

She could barely think as her body tightened, on the verge of falling apart once more. She only knew that she didn't care. The flat of Robert's tongue dragged over her nub, sending her senses spinning out of control. She groaned and jerked out her second release, some instinct trying to get more of him inside her as she slid her lips further down his shaft, licking and sucking.

He let out a strangled sound and went rigid, his prick growing impossibly thick in her mouth before pulsing heavy spurts of his release across her tongue. It was a terribly strange sensation, but she was too far gone in her own pleasure to care. She whimpered and swallowed around the shaft in her mouth, both of them twitching weakly with fresh twinges of pleasure every few seconds.

Eventually, Cassandra regained enough control of her own body to let Robert's softening prick slide free of her lips. She rolled sideways, and Edmund caught her in his strong arms. The world shifted, and when it came to rest, she was cradled on Edmund's lap with his heavy velvet cloak enfolding her. Her head rested against his shoulder.

"All right?" he asked, tucking a lock of hair behind her ear.

"Mm-hmm," she hummed, feeling as wrung out as a used washrag. She had a vague notion that he might find what she'd just done extraordinary. Somehow, it didn't *feel* extraordinary. She'd kissed her bound Hermes, and he'd kissed her in return. If they'd been kissing somewhere other than mouths, it hardly mattered, did it? It had been done with love, to give pleasure, and that made it good and beautiful.

She opened her eyes to see Frederick leaning down. His lips pressed against the crown of her head before he straightened.

"You're both exquisite," he observed. "Though, I do believe you've tenderized my valet like a piece of meat. Robert, do you want more? Because I've plenty more to give you."

"Yes, m'lord," Robert slurred. "Give it to me, please. I want it all. Want you…"

"You'll have me," Frederick promised. "I'm yours. You're ours."

Robert gave a low moan of contentment that settled warm and heavy in Cassandra's belly.

"Cassandra," Frederick continued. "I do hope you're not offended by buggery. Because buggery is definitely imminent."

Edmund laughed, low and pleased.

"Whatever you do together, it will be beautiful," Cassandra said, the words traveling straight from her heart to her mouth without any input from her wits along the way. *"You're beautiful."*

"We'll just pretend she said 'dashing and handsome,' shall we?" Frederick asked, with a hint of humor lacing his tone.

"She probably meant Hermes, not you," Edmund consoled, and Cassandra hid a helpless smile against his chest.

She leaned against him to watch, not truly having much idea of what buggery entailed, beyond the very basic and clinical description Frances had included as part of her mission to educate Cassandra in the ways of physical love.

As it turned out, it involved copious amounts of oil, combined with the same long, callused fingers that had reduced her to screams of pleasure earlier. Spending in Cassandra's mouth appeared to have reduced Robert to much the same condition she was currently in. He was pliant and soft beneath Frederick's touch, as the viscount patiently stroked open the only passage a man possessed.

Robert was wearing his *tortured saint* expression, and Cassandra couldn't look away. Agonized and ecstatic at once, it transformed his already beautiful features into something otherworldly.

"I want to paint him like that," she whispered to Edmund, "but I don't think I could capture it."

"Believe it or not, I do know exactly what you mean," he replied. "I suppose if we ever wanted to try, Rotherdam wouldn't balk at keeping him like this for an hour or three."

Somewhat unexpectedly, his words kindled a new wave of heat in her belly.

"You know," she said, "I was promised three little deaths tonight, and yet I've only had two. I still intend to have you, as well."

He glanced down at her with a half-smile. "You're certain? You know me — I'm quite content with voyeurism and my own hand if you're too fatigued."

"Oh, I'm certain," she said. "You don't want to make a liar out of Frederick, do you?"

"Take her Oxford-style," Frederick advised. "I've always found that to be a highly underutilized method, outside of lustful first-year university lads."

"What's Oxford-style?" Cassandra asked.

"Rutting between someone's thighs, basically," Edmund said. "Not one of the most elegant forms of intercourse, but — "

"I want to try it," Cassandra said, intrigued by the idea that she could pretend he was taking her the proper way, while still avoiding the possibility of pregnancy.

He shifted his hips, letting her feel how stiff he was.

Robert chose than moment to let out a low moan of pleasure, and Cassandra saw that he'd grown hard at some point during Frederick's diabolically patient ministrations.

"There we are," Frederick said in satisfaction, he slid his fingers out of Robert's body and wiped them on a rag.

"Here, up you get," Edmund urged. "May I take off the dress?"

Since Frederick had untied the sash and let the front fall open, the sheer dress had been hanging from Cassandra's shoulders like an open dressing gown, doing nothing for her modesty.

"Yes," she said, and allowed him to help her shrug out of it.

"So beautiful," Edmund praised.

"Indeed," Frederick echoed, taking in her naked body with appreciation.

"Would someone *please* take this bloody blindfold off?" Robert asked, his tone growing plaintive.

Frederick whisked the band of black silk away from his eyes, and Robert blinked rapidly in the firelight. His hazel gaze found Cassandra, and a soft smile tugged at his lips. "Yes, that's much better, thank you."

She smiled back helplessly.

"Come on," Edmund urged, folding the extra fur into halves, then quarters. "Hands and knees, right here at the edge. Hermes can kiss your breasts while Rotherdam fucks him."

She shivered at the image, and let Edmund arrange her as he wanted, with her knees padded by the thick fur at the edge of the plinth and her upper body suspended over Robert's face. She yelped as he stretched up and neatly caught a nipple between his teeth. A fresh pulse of wetness dampened the place between her legs.

She'd missed Frederick disrobing—at least in the literal sense of removing his velvet cloak. He wore nothing but a loose shirt, breeches, and boots beneath the dark material. As she watched, he shed the shirt and unbuttoned the fall of his breeches, freeing his straining prick and slathering it generously with oil.

Behind her, the sound of rustling fabric heralded Edmund doing the same. Frederick knelt on the fur between Robert's thighs and lifted his hips, supporting him with an elbow crooked beneath the knee of his good leg.

Robert, who had been sucking and licking at Cassandra's captured breast, cried out as Frederick took him in a long, slow stroke. Edmund nudged Cassandra's legs tight together and slid his prick into the snug, slick place at the apex, his length sliding deliciously against her folds.

Cassandra rocked beneath the steady thrusts, a gentler pleasure building easy and sweet inside her. She fell into Edmund's rhythm, and Robert fell into Frederick's. For a long time, the silence of the night was broken only by the crackling bonfire, the slap of skin against skin, and the men's low murmurs of praise and affection.

Eventually, it was too much for Robert. Cassandra was almost certain no one had touched his prick, but he shuddered and came anyway, his seed splashing against his own stomach and Cassandra's flank. His teeth closed around her nipple sharply, just as Edmund's stiff length slid over her folds and brushed her nub.

She followed Robert into bliss, a deeper and calmer climax than her first two. Edmund and Frederick's movements sped up until they, too, spilled. The four of them ended up in a tangled heap for a few moments, until Cassandra rolled onto a hip so Robert would be able to breathe.

Frederick roused himself to untie Robert's wrists and chafe his hands to restore the blood flow.

Edmund groaned, flopping down to sit on the edge of the plinth next to Cassandra. "Hell's teeth. I'm not entirely certain any of us can make it back to the house right now," he said. "Is it warm enough to sleep out here, do you think?"

"With the furs and the bonfire, I don't see why not," Frederick replied. "Normally I'd order Private Barlow here to make up the camp for us, but..."

"Good luck with that," Robert said faintly.

Between the four of them, they somehow got a usable pile of bedding gathered together near the roaring fire. Without questioning either the wisdom or the propriety of the situation, Cassandra found herself wrapped up between Robert and Edmund, with Frederick curled against Robert's other side beneath the soft furs. In the hazy few moments before sleep took her, a single question floated through her mind.

What do I have to do to have this every night for the rest of my life?

THIRTY-SEVEN

ROBERT SAT PATIENTLY in the corner of the drawing room, watching Edmund and Frederick have a fight. It wasn't the first such quarrel; it wouldn't be the last. However, the circular nature of the argument was becoming a bit tiresome.

"You're an idiot," Edmund said. "We've already established that."

"I am *attempting* to be practical," Frederick shot back, the words enunciated with sharp precision.

They were fast approaching the six-month mark since Lord Malthorpe's untimely but much-celebrated demise. The others were chafing. Of course, Robert was also chafing. However, unlike his companions, he didn't feel the need to strike out at those around him to ease his growing frustration.

It was all down to Cassandra, perhaps unsurprisingly. She was still locked in her socially prescribed period of mourning, and would be for some time to come—even after the official transition into half-mourning. For the last several months, he and the others had turned all of their wiles toward arranging secret trysts that wouldn't risk exposing her to further acrimony, either from locals or the members of the *ton*.

Frances and Mary Stanhope had been complicit in sneaking Cassandra away to

Hengewick House for a night every couple of weeks, under the guise of visiting to administer regular treatments for some vague, unspecified chronic medical condition. Edmund visited as often as seemed proper, allegedly to deal with matters relating to Cassandra's income as a widowed baroness. Robert himself had, on a handful of occasions, snuck into her presence disguised as James, her man of all work.

Even so, Frederick and Edmund were growing increasingly frustrated by the situation. And so, they were fighting about Frederick's potential marriage proposal. *Again.*

"You can't know whether or not she'll accept if you *don't bloody ask her,*" Edmund said.

Frederick ran his hand through his short, sandy hair. "It would be blatantly unfair of me to put her in the position of having to make that choice. It was one thing when I thought she would need financial support through the process of disputing her farce of a marriage to Malthorpe. Knowing she would have the prospect of a decent match at the end of it might have convinced her to accept our bloody help for once."

"And that's the only reason you'd have asked her, is it?" Edmund replied caustically. "So she'd accept your *money*?"

Frederick glared at him. "You know it isn't. But it's moot. Instead, she chose the frankly more sensible option of taking the idiot's dower and living happily ever after on his coin. She has freedom now, probably for the first time in her life.

Shall I ask her to give it up in favor of once more becoming a nobleman's chattel?"

"The dower share of Malthorpe's estate is a *life* estate, Rotherdam," Edmund said. "It's common law. It isn't dependent on whether or not she remarries. Those rights can't be taken away from her, unless the estate falls under mismanagement so incompetent that it goes into debt."

"You are missing the point." Frederick's tone grew frustrated. "It's unlike you to be willfully obtuse, Edmund. If she marries, that money is no longer *her* share of Malthorpe's estate. It becomes *her husband's* share of Malthorpe's estate. Is that, or is it not, the way the law is written?"

Robert raised an eyebrow, waiting for Edmund's response to the well-placed volley.

"Well, I suppose *technically* — " Edmund began, looking uncomfortable.

Frederick cut him off. "There's no '*technically*' about it. You wish me to ask her to hand over her life of freedom, in exchange for making my coffers fatter than they already are?"

Edmund drew breath, only to pause.

Robert cleared his throat. Both men turned to him sharply. As often seemed to be the case these days, he had to catch his breath as Frederick's clear blue eyes landed on him. *Seeing* him. *Knowing* him, in a way Robert had never truly believed would be possible. He swallowed and coughed again, giving himself a moment to regain his composure before he could speak.

"Perhaps you both might agree to let Cassandra make the decisions regarding what proposals she is and isn't willing to entertain?" he asked, purposely keeping his tone mild.

Silence settled over the room for a long beat before Frederick broke it.

"It's not that I object to letting her make her own choices," he said carefully. "My objection is to the pressure such a proposal would place on her. It implies a form of manipulation on my part."

Robert didn't break his gaze. "It *really* doesn't, you know."

Sensing an ally in the wings, Edmund moved in for the kill. "Of course it doesn't. Because unlike certain other filthy toads, *you'll* take no for an answer. And, just as importantly, because we'll talk through all of the legal and financial implications with her before asking her to consider a reply."

"I believe it's mostly a question of how much trust you have in Cassandra's ability to stand up for her own best interests, my lord," Robert added.

Frederick stared at him for a long moment before blinking out of his reverie. "You're implying this is a manifestation of the same behavior I demonstrated with you, Robert?" The words were flat.

"Yes—I was, rather," Robert agreed.

Edmund crossed his arms with the air of a man who was holding back what he wanted to say only with difficulty. Under the circumstances, Robert appreciated his restraint.

Frederick let out a pained sigh. "It's hardly comparable. It's not as though Edmund can draw up a trust or a will for her as he did for you. In the law's eyes, we would become a single individual—

her personhood subsumed into mine from the moment of marriage. Any attempt to sequester money for her independent use would be pointless. Legally, I would be sequestering it for my own use, as her husband."

"Yes," Edmund allowed. "But see, here's the thing. *You* still believe the trust nonsense with Robert was necessary. Whereas we both believe you're a fool."

"I didn't say that," Robert protested, leveling a brief glare at Edmund.

"You were thinking it," Edmund muttered.

"I merely meant this," Robert said, with all the dignity he could muster. "Despite your noble intentions, my lord, you made decisions that affected both of us. And, in general, those effects involved both of us being miserable for years, when we could have been happy instead. The current decision also affects several people—not merely you. And I fear it, too, could result in all of us being, if not miserable, then at least far less happy than we might otherwise be."

"Robert and I won't abandon her," Edmund put in. "And don't think I haven't seen the way you look at her—you're not fooling anyone. We're discussing the difference between a complicated, ongoing affair conducted in secret, versus having the woman we love living safe beneath our roof every day for the rest of our lives."

"And what about children?" Frederick asked, sounding terribly tired. "Have you thought about that?"

Edmund stared at him as though he'd lost his mind. "What *about* children, if she's married to you? In case it's escaped your notice, children inside a marriage are legitimate. It's the children *outside* a marriage that can get complicated."

Frederick rubbed at his eyes. "There's yet another consideration."

Edmund crossed his arms again, scowling. "Of course there is," he grumbled.

Robert had a good idea what that complication might be. "There was a marriage settlement in place with Malthorpe, wasn't there? You implied as much, when you offered her marriage in London."

"There was, yes," Frederick said heavily. "I've no idea why her uncle hasn't already presented it to the new baron. And unlike the dower share, that settlement will almost certainly be dependent on Cassandra remaining unmarried."

"Oh." Edmund appeared taken aback.

But Robert shook his head. "It changes nothing. Cassandra deserves the opportunity to make her own choices. She needs to have all of the information that pertains to her own future, and then she needs us to respect her enough to allow her to manage that future as she sees fit."

"She's young—" Frederick began.

"If you even *think* about calling her naive," Edmund said. "Rotherdam, I swear…"

"No. Perhaps not naive," Frederick admitted. "But will she feel pressured into pursuing a course that may not be what she truly wants?"

"She hit an armed man with a fireplace poker when he tried to abduct her, then took his pistol and used it to steal a horse," Robert pointed out. "I think she's capable of holding her own in civil conversation."

Frederick's shoulders slumped in defeat. "You'll both keep hounding me if I don't do this."

"Well, yes," Edmund said. "Honestly, I see now that I should have set Robert on you right from the start. You can't deny him anything when he uses that soft, reasonable tone on you."

Robert caught Edmund's dark eyes and held them, raising a pointed eyebrow at him. "By the way, Edmund," he said, using the same reasonable tone, "Before I forget, I should inform you that I called in a favor and had a friend of a friend submit *Hermes Lamed* to the Royal Academy."

Edmund went stock-still. "You did *what*?"

"The friend-of-a-friend in question has a connection to the selection committee for the annual exhibition at New Somerset House," Robert explained patiently. "There's a small fee for the submission, which I paid on your behalf. If it's accepted, the painting will be displayed with the rest of this year's selected works."

His friend gaped at him. Frederick's full lips pursed as though he were holding back a comment, or perhaps a smile.

Robert looked briefly ceilingward for patience before meeting Edmund's gaze again. "We all know that if I'd waited for you to do it, I'd still be waiting when I was old and gray. Besides, you *did* give me the painting to do with as I pleased."

Edmund still hadn't found words.

"Well," Frederick said, filling the resulting silence. "As we've both been bullied into taking actions we weren't prepared to take on our own, perhaps we should ready ourselves for Cassandra's visit tonight. I daresay the four of us have much to discuss."

Robert chose to focus on the fact that he and Edmund had won the argument, rather than on Frederick's expression — one akin to that of a man heading to the gallows.

Cassandra was growing, if not *used* to men's clothing, then at least resigned to its utility when it came to hiding her identity. This was the ninth occasion that she and Sadie had disguised themselves as Frances and Mary, in order to steal a night at Hengewick House. It was more contact than she'd feared they would have during this odd purgatory of mourning-that-wasn't-mourning… and yet, it wasn't even close to being enough.

This was not to say that Cassandra spent her days and nights pining for her eccentric little band of rakes. Her life was surprisingly full for a woman essentially living in exile from society. She had Sadie. She had the visits from Mary and Frances, which were often full of merriment as the pair shared London's gossip and described the more outrageous situations that they encountered in the drunken doctor's clinic where they both worked.

She painted; she went on long walks and longer horseback rides. Somewhat surprisingly, she also received regular visits from the young Lord

Malthorpe. Even more surprisingly, she found herself enjoying them. Perhaps it was their shared victimization by the late Cecil Pembroke, but she genuinely liked the young man. The prospect of bringing difficulty or further scandal to his doorstep had grown increasingly uncomfortable as the months passed.

Her desire to dance on her so-called husband's grave was all well and good – but Cecil Pembroke was beyond hurting. She couldn't get meaningful revenge against a dead man. However, she could easily harm the new Lord Malthorpe during her attempt. That knowledge had been weighing heavily on her, these past weeks.

And yet, she would *not* give up her men.

Her clandestine visits to Lord Rotherdam's country manor hadn't all gone the way of her first return – the so-called Autumn Rites. For one thing, it quickly grew too cold for outdoor bacchanalia. For another, she took just as much pleasure in spending time debating art and philosophy with the members of Frederick's Hellfire Club as she did spending time in their beds.

Which... wasn't to say they didn't end up in bed eventually. They did, almost without fail. And that was wonderful, too – even if Cassandra was beginning to ache for more. She found herself wanting things that were dangerous for a woman in her position to want.

Rotherdam's cart pulled up to the huge front doors of the manor house, and Sadie hopped down lightly from the seat. Cassandra followed with more care, not wishing to accidentally rip a seam on Frances' snugly tailored coat or breeches. Tonight, the lord of the manor himself was waiting at the door to greet them.

"Cassandra." He took her hand and raised it to his lips.

She smiled, unable to help it. "Frederick. It's good to see you."

He returned her smile, but she was certain she could detect lines of strain around his eyes in the torchlight.

"And you as well," he said. "Please, come inside. There's quite a chill this evening. Sadie, perhaps you could assist your mistress in changing into something more comfortable for her. We'll be waiting in the blue drawing room whenever you're ready."

He ushered them inside, and again, Cassandra was struck by something ever so slightly odd about his demeanor.

She took herself off to the guest room she'd come to think of as hers, and allowed Sadie to help her change into one of the dresses she'd stored here for use when she visited. Nevertheless, she wasn't able to quite rid herself of the faint tremor of nerves fluttering in her stomach.

Dismissing Sadie to visit with her friends belowstairs, she conducted herself to the blue drawing room. Robert and Edmund rose to greet her, each one pressing a kiss to first her cheek, and then her lips. A fire was roaring in the grate, casting soft light and pleasant warmth throughout the room. She accepted a glass of brandy from

Frederick, who gestured for her to seat herself on the davenport with the others.

She did so, but gave him a small frown. "Forgive me, but I do feel somewhat as though I've inadvertently walked in on a wake. Is everything all right, Frederick? Has something happened?"

"No, no. Nothing like that," he said. "It's merely... well..."

Cassandra was fairly certain she'd never seen the man stumble over his words in the entire time she'd known him. Her eyes flew to Robert's. She sent him a questioning look—but he merely shook his head and smiled.

"Spit it out, Rotherdam," Edmund said, "Before we all die of anticipation."

Frederick huffed. "Yes. Sorry. Cassandra—I have a proposal for you, and I hope you'll hear me out before making your decision on the matter."

THIRTY-EIGHT

CASSANDRA SAT in wide-eyed shock as Frederick spent the next ten minutes laying out the potential risks of entering into a marriage with him. He outlined the financial consequences, the legal consequences, and the social consequences—all in great detail. When he finished, she waited for a few moments to be certain he didn't have more to say.

Then, she blinked a few times in an attempt to gather her thoughts. "That seemed to be a very long speech, given that the only salient point was to tell me it would be a poor decision for me to marry you."

Next to her, Edmund rubbed at the bridge of his nose as though his head pained him. On her other side, Robert let out an audible sigh. Neither of them rode to Frederick's conversational rescue, however.

The viscount frowned. She could practically see him mentally going over the contents of his lecture. "Oh. That wasn't..." He cleared his throat. "It's only that I wish to be entirely certain you don't feel pressured into something that might not be in your best interest, objectively speaking."

She stared at him. "Forgive me, but are you saying that was intended as an actual proposal?"

"Well... yes?" Frederick replied.

"Why?" Cassandra asked.

Edmund let his hand drop to his thigh with a sharp slap. "Stop, both of you. This is becoming physically painful to watch."

"Agreed," Robert murmured.

"Cassandra," Edmund said, "I was a fool six months ago. I should never have offered to make you my mistress. I should have simply asked you to marry me instead. In my defense, at the time I was convinced you didn't know me well enough to understand what you'd be getting into. Marrying the dark-skinned son of Jamaican immigrants comes with its own set of complications."

She digested that. "I... can't say with certainty whether I would have accepted such a proposal or not. But if I'd turned you down, it wouldn't have been because of your parentage, Edmund. It would have been because I assumed you were offering out of pity, or some misplaced sense of guilt."

"If you'd accepted, it would have been an excellent marriage," Frederick said, his tone softer than when he'd been outlining the many pitfalls involved in becoming Lady Rotherdam. "But that was before. Circumstances have changed significantly since then."

"Edmund is no longer an appropriate match for you," Robert said. "Your difference in station is too great. And I'm a servant—lower still, even if my position didn't preclude me from marrying easily."

"But a baroness and a viscount would make an excellent marriage," Edmund concluded. "Especially since neither of you are in a position to tarnish the other's reputation."

"That might be an optimistic assessment," Frederick said. "As it stands, you are in many ways a perfectly respectable widow, Cassandra. I assure you that would not remain the case if you were to marry me."

Cassandra shook her head, trying to understand. "You would really tie yourself to me for the rest of your life, solely so that Edmund, Robert, and I could more easily continue our affair?"

Frederick appeared taken aback. "*No*, of course not. Why would you think—?"

She didn't let him finish. "Well, you clearly don't wish it for yourself." That came out sharper than she'd intended. She consciously softened her tone. "And please, don't misunderstand—I'm well aware that you aren't the marrying kind. I don't hold that against you, Frederick. It's simply who you are."

"Cassandra," Robert said dryly, "he's offered you marriage twice now."

"And he hasn't truly meant it either time," Cassandra retorted.

Frederick folded his lithe frame into a chair and rubbed his hands down his face, stretching the skin.

"I believe you're the one who misunderstands, Cassandra," he said. "I've proposed marriage to someone before, believing her to be in love with me—only to discover that I'd completely misread the situation."

Sudden comprehension flooded her, and she lifted a hand to her mouth as the realization penetrated. "*Christina*," she breathed, the name puffing against her fingertips. "*Oh*. I think I see."

Christina — the woman who'd publicly spurned Frederick, jilting him at the altar so she could run away to the continent with her secret lover. Frederick looked up at her, slumped forward in his chair with his elbows resting on his knees.

"I'm offering what I have the ability to give," he said, and it was as though all of his defensive walls had crumbled, leaving him bare and vulnerable. "My name, reviled though it is. My protection, for whatever that's worth. A home, for the rest of our lives, shared with men who love you. Children — as many as you want. I will claim them as my own to my dying breath, whether they have blond hair or russet, pale skin or dark."

She sucked in a sharp breath, the sound of it catching in her throat.

"And if you accept," he continued, "you will lose your independent income, and doubtless have yet more indignity heaped upon your head by those who despise me. You will become a pariah, as I am. So you see, you have far more reason than Christina ever did to flee into the night rather than appearing with me at the altar."

Still speechless, Cassandra desperately tried to sort through the emotions swirling through her.

Edmund tilted his head. "Actually, there's a thought. Will the vicar in either of your parishes even let you through the door of a church? It would be more than a little embarrassing if we had to travel all the way to Gretna Green."

Frederick gave him an unimpressed look. "The local one would probably attempt to stage an exorcism before he'd agree to stage a wedding. But I'm sure a generous enough donation to St. George's would secure a ceremony there. However, in case you've failed to notice, she hasn't said yes."

Cassandra couldn't help the small shiver that traveled through her at Frederick's mention of bribing a church official in order to secure a wedding. She pushed it away.

"You're both in favor of this?" she asked Edmund and Robert. "Truly?"

"Yes, Cassandra," Edmund said patiently. "We've been badgering him for ages about it, just ask him."

"You must all realize that I can't marry *anyone* for some time yet," she went on.

"We're well aware," Frederick said. "One year. Another ridiculous law—though it does at least mean you'll have ample time to consider things."

"I suppose it does," she said faintly.

⟫⟪ 𑁍 ⟫⟪

She'd been *considering things* for ten days when Frederick showed up at the lake house in the middle of the night, dressed in plain clothing and with a hooded cloak thrown over his head to hide his distinctive blond hair.

Upon seeing who was at her door, Cassandra's heart pounded with alarm, certain that something awful must have happened to bring him here in the small hours after midnight.

"No, it's nothing like that," he assured her. "I merely didn't wish to be seen coming or going, even in disguise. Please—we need to speak plainly... and privately."

Her shoulders relaxed. "Oh, thank goodness. You scared the life out of me. Sadie, you can go back to bed."

Sadie nodded, wide-eyed in the firelight, and retired.

"Let me get a cloak, and we'll speak outside if it's not too cold," Cassandra said, once the maid had gone.

The chill outside was tolerable. The moon was up, providing enough illumination by which to see. She led Frederick toward the lake, where the smell of growing things was just beginning to tease the air with scents of spring.

"I'm glad you came," she said. "Even if you did give me a fright in doing so."

"I do beg your pardon for that. It wasn't my intention." He breathed deeply, taking in the night air as he walked beside her. "There are things I must make clear to you, and I've done a poor job of it so far. I have, shall we say, a certain horror at the idea of misusing my position in such a way that other people are harmed by it."

"So I'd gathered," Cassandra told him, unable to completely strip the words of irony.

He had the good grace to let a huff of laughter slip free. "Quite. It's been brought to my attention on several occasions—I needn't mention by whom. But... I promised you plain speaking. The fact is, you're in love with both my man of business and my valet."

"Your valet... who is also your lover," she pointed out gently. "And your man of business, who is also your dear friend."

"Yes. As you say, my lover and my friend," he conceded, as they strolled along the lake's edge. "They are madly in love with you, as well. But there's absolutely no reason why you should also have feelings for me... and every reason why you shouldn't. I just want to be very clear that my proposal isn't contingent upon your feelings for me. I know I can be... difficult."

"You can, yes," she agreed, without rancor. She reached out and clasped his hand, using it to bring him to a halt, facing her. "I'm not Christina, Frederick. I won't use you and then leave you standing alone at the altar. But I need to know — do you even *want* me as your wife?"

"I want you to do what's best for your future. Whatever that might be."

She lifted her free hand to his chest, resting it over his heart. "No. Stop. Do *you*... want... *me*? That life you described, with the four of us together, our children running and playing around the manor — *do you want that*?"

His head dipped, his chin dropping to his chest as though he had no more strength to hold it up. The moonlight filtering through the trees limned his slumped shoulders in liquid silver. When he lifted his gaze to meet hers, his eyes shimmered in the pale light.

"Of course I do." His voice was a hoarse rasp. "Cassandra, how could I not want that life? It sounds like a perfect, unattainable dream."

Her throat tightened, and the noise that emerged unbidden from her lips sounded suspiciously like a sob. She tipped forward into his arms, completely powerless to do otherwise, and he leaned down so that their foreheads came to rest together.

"Then the answer is yes," she whispered. "I accept your proposal, Lord Rotherdam." Clearing her throat, she continued in a more normal tone. "Since I still have your man of business on loan, I propose we meet with him to draw up a suitable settlement contract. The wedding will take place at St. George's in Hanover Square a year and a day after you very helpfully removed my last husband for me."

He choked on a laugh, even though nothing about it was amusing. "Perfect. Now I suppose I just need to find out how large a bribe will be required to secure a ceremony. Otherwise we may end up journeying to Gretna Green after all."

"If that's what it takes, I'm perfectly fine with it," she said, and tipped her face forward to brush a kiss across his lips in the moonlight.

THIRTY-NINE

WHEN HER AUNT and uncle's coach arrived at the lake house a few weeks later, it was both a surprise and not a surprise. In some ways, the visit felt as inevitable as the tide. In others, it was shocking that they'd left it seven full months before descending on her in person.

"Have you not received our letters, you ungrateful girl?" Aunt Lavinia demanded, almost before they were through the door.

"Yes, Aunt. Of course I received them," Cassandra replied evenly. "They were very... er... *prolific*. Sadie, would you please arrange for refreshments for our guests?"

"Yes, m'lady," Sadie said, and scurried out of the line of fire.

She always had been a clever girl.

Cassandra gestured toward the sitting room. "Please, make yourselves comfortable. My groom will help your driver see to the horses while you say whatever it is you wish to say to me."

Her aunt harrumphed as she sat down on the comfortable davenport, fussing over Uncle Henry as he did the same. Cassandra took in their appearance, and noted that her uncle appeared to have lost weight, his muttonchops drooping against his sunken cheeks.

"You didn't write back," Aunt Lavinia said tightly, biting off the words.

"No," Cassandra agreed. "I didn't. While it appears you have a great deal to say to me, in all honesty, I have very little to say to you."

Lavinia gasped in outrage.

"I will admit to some surprise that it took you this long to darken my doorstep," Cassandra continued. "To what do I owe the visit?"

Her aunt puffed up like an angry cat. "Your uncle was terribly ill over the winter! At death's door, he was!"

Henry cleared his throat. "Now, now— perhaps that's overstating the matter somewhat, Lavinia…"

His wife plowed on, undeterred. "So there I was, with a sickened husband on one side, and a disobedient niece on the other. Surely, I thought, my brother's only child wouldn't leave me alone and without support during my time of need. But, *no*—not a single word from you! Not a single guinea from the *Dowager Baroness Malthorpe!*"

She spat the last few words as though they tasted bad. Cassandra blinked, feeling as though she were watching someone else engage in the conversation, rather than taking part in it herself.

"Support?" she asked. "Like the support you gave me when Cecil Pembroke abducted me at gunpoint and forced me into a sham marriage against my will? That kind of support?"

Color rose in Lavinia's cheeks. She gestured angrily around her, presumably indicating the lake house. "You're happy enough to reap the benefits now that he's dead, girl."

"Well, yes. I am." Cassandra raised an eyebrow. "It seems the least I'm owed after being assaulted, kidnapped, and generally made miserable. What's your point?"

"*You owe us!*" The words were nearly a shout. Lavinia's features, already red, were now turning an alarming shade of purple.

Sadie chose that moment to enter with a tray, only to stop short inside the doorway in the face of the woman's towering rage.

"Leave the tray on the table, please, Sadie," Cassandra said calmly. "I don't believe my aunt and uncle will be staying long."

Sadie nodded wordlessly, her expression clearly asking if she should run and get James. Cassandra gave her a tiny, negative shake of the head. Sadie set the tray down and gave a hurried curtsey before leaving them, though Cassandra would have wagered her entire income that the girl was huddled just outside the door, listening in case she needed help.

She turned back to her relatives. "Cake?" she asked, as though they'd been exchanging pleasant conversation about the weather.

Her aunt looked as though something important inside her skull might burst at any moment.

Henry coughed. "What my wife is trying to say is that we have not received our share of the baron's settlement agreement."

And there it was. Perhaps that declaration should have been cause for alarm. Six months ago, it most definitely would have been. Now, however, Cassandra felt nothing but a sort of distant, vaguely vicious satisfaction.

"Oh? I was unaware of anything related to a settlement, since you did not allow me to be present when you and Cecil discussed the matter," she said blandly. "The new Lord Malthorpe settled a dower share of one-third of the estate's income on me, in accordance with common law."

Here, her uncle appeared to be on firmer ground. "What nonsense! The settlement was legally signed and as such, it takes precedence over common law."

"And this settlement contract included payment to you directly, I assume," Cassandra said, unsurprised.

"Well, of course it did!" Lavinia snapped. "We are your guardians!"

"I'm twenty-three," Cassandra replied in a monotone. "I reached the age of majority two years ago."

"We have paid for every bit of food in your mouth and clothing on your body since your wastrel parents died!" Lavinia said, outraged.

"Yes," Cassandra told her dryly. "You provided me with the bare minimum of a livelihood for an entire two years. It must have been terrible for you." She didn't add that they certainly hadn't paid for the food in her pantry or the dresses currently in her wardrobe. There was no point, since that sort of logic wouldn't sway them.

"We made an investment in you," her uncle said, his voice weaker than she remembered it being. "And a risky one, at that. We *will* have our reward for that act of generosity. I wonder how the new baron will react to discovering that you deceived him into settling a third of his estate on you, when it should have been far less?"

She stared at him. "So you negotiated a marriage settlement that was less than what's normally granted by common law? Oh, well *done*, Uncle. Thank you *so* much."

He sneered. "Common law makes no provision for an ungrateful orphan's relatives. The settlement does. And I intend to visit the new Lord Malthorpe this very afternoon to ensure that it's enforced."

Cassandra sat back in her chair, suddenly tired beyond measure of the conversation. "Yes, please do. What a wonderful idea. In fact, you should leave for Elmlake right now."

Lavinia frowned, her expression growing suspicious. "Aren't you going to ask about the terms of the settlement?"

"No," Cassandra told her. "They hardly matter." She leaned forward and poured herself a cup of chocolate from the tray on the table, then sat back and sipped it. "No doubt the settlement contract is rendered null upon my remarriage, and I shall be remarrying the day after my period of mourning ends."

Lavinia leapt from her chair as though she'd been shot from a cannon. "*What*?"

"You heard me," Cassandra said. "Lord Rotherdam has asked for my hand. We are to be married in August, at which point I will become a very rich viscountess—and in no need of whatever paltry sum dear old Cecil agreed to settle on me as a jointure."

She took another sip of chocolate, watching Uncle Henry splutter and Aunt Lavinia's eyes bulge in impotent rage.

"You… you… *harlot*!" Lavinia exploded. "How *dare* you! What will the new baron say when he finds out you intend to sully his uncle's name with your shameless, wanton behavior?"

"Well, when I told him over luncheon two weeks ago, he congratulated me and offered me continued use of the lake property for holidays and visits." Cassandra set the cup and saucer back on the table and rose to match her aunt. "And now, I really think you should both be going. You'll want to reach Elmlake before dark, after all."

Lavinia rounded on her, fists clenched. "You thankless little trollop!"

Her voice was an angry hiss. She took a step forward, raising one hand as though to deliver a slap. Quick as a flash, Cassandra had the fireplace poker in her hand, holding it poised in clear threat.

"*Enough*." Her voice was iron. "Leave. Now. And if I ever see you on this property again, I will have my man eject you. Enjoy your five months of blood money, while I enjoy a long and happy life that does not contain *either of you*. Good day."

Henry rose, his face as gray as porridge. Again, Cassandra was struck by how very much *reduced* he appeared, compared to the last time she'd seen him. There was a fine tremor in his fingers as he reached out and grabbed his wife's arm, tugging her toward the door. "Come along, Lavinia," he said hoarsely, shooting a brief glare at Cassandra as he did so. "We'll have a word with the baron and see what can be done."

Cassandra waited until she heard the front door open and close before she very deliberately returned the fireplace poker to its stand and reseated herself, returning to her abandoned cup of chocolate. A few minutes later, the sound of hoofbeats and rattling coach wheels clattered away.

Sadie entered, flopping down on the other chair. "Oh, Lor'. That was something. Well done, m'lady—I wanted to stand up and clap at that last part."

"So, you were listening outside the door, then?" Cassandra asked, amused despite herself.

"Course I was," Sadie told her. "Think I'd leave you alone with those carrion crows? I heard what happened at Hengewick House, when they dragged you away to London." She shuddered theatrically.

"Yes, well," Cassandra said philosophically. "A few more months, and they'll have no ties left to me at all. Believe me when I say, that happy event will be worth far more than a dower share."

"Having finally met 'em in person, I can't say I disagree, m'lady," Sadie said, with considerable feeling.

FORTY

THE ONE-YEAR anniversary of Cecil Pembroke's death eventually rolled around, coming none too soon for Cassandra's taste. The day of her wedding dawned stormy. Given the circumstances surrounding her first meeting with Frederick and his Hellfire Club — trapped at his country manor house by storms and flooding — she found the weather to be rather appropriate.

"As long as no bridges wash out between here and London," Frances joked, holding an umbrella over Cassandra's head as they ducked into the coach Frederick had sent for them.

It was only the third time Cassandra had seen Frances dressed in feminine attire. Just as she had in London a year ago, the prickly doctor slipped seamlessly into the role of pleasant and well-bred lady — a role that was more than a little jarring to anyone who knew her well. She was dressed in pink. Cassandra had chosen a lovely gown in pale lavender and white for the ceremony, with long silk gloves covering her arms.

The two of them settled across from Sadie and Mary, already seated on the coach's other bench. They, too, were dressed in their finest. Mary looked particularly radiant. Cassandra had only ever seen her in servant's garb, or in the kind of practical clothing she wore for nursing. Her former maid appeared serenely happy in a sunny yellow frock that accented the highlights in her brown eyes and hair. She was not a young woman, but the faint lines around her eyes and mouth owed more to smiles than frowns these days.

And Sadie — well, Sadie had been something of a revelation. Mary had taken great pains with the girl's dress and hair, calling upon her previous skills as a lady's maid. Sadie's expression retained the cheeky glint that Cassandra suspected could never truly be hidden, but with her hair elegantly braided and her face lightly powdered and rouged, she was revealed as a true beauty.

The four of them stared at each other as the coach rattled into motion... and promptly broke down into giggles.

"Oh, my dears," Cassandra told them, "I certainly never thought we'd be sharing a coach under quite these circumstances. You all look absolutely divine."

Sadie gestured her to lean forward, and reached up to fix an artfully arranged curl that had been whipped out of place by the wind. "I feel like a doll, all dressed up like this," the girl said. "I can hardly wait to get back in an apron!"

Cassandra laughed again. "Enjoy this while you have the chance — you'll get your wish soon enough."

"You'll both be moving into Hengewick House directly after the wedding, then?" Mary asked.

"Yes, that's right," she said. "Most of our things have already been moved there. The rest will be picked up as soon as the weather improves." She sighed. "I shall miss living at the lake house, but the young Lord Malthorpe continues to insist I may use it as I see fit for visits and holidays, even after marrying."

"He seems a pleasant young man," Frances allowed. "A nice change, coming from that family."

"He's been wonderful," Cassandra agreed. "He was terribly apologetic after my uncle presented him with the old settlement contract he and Pembroke had negotiated. He even said something about attending the ceremony today."

"It's reassuring that awful people can still have worthwhile relatives," Frances said.

Mary snorted, tipping her chin at Cassandra. "You've met her aunt and uncle, haven't you?"

"True enough," Frances agreed. "More proof, if any was needed."

Cassandra let the conversation flow around her as the coach rolled toward London. It was the first time she had returned to the city since the events of a year ago. She couldn't deny that her nerves were red-raw whenever she contemplated the idea of entering a church and standing quietly through the same service that she'd experienced once before as a helpless captive.

At this point, it was more the *fear-of-a-fear* than anything else. She worried that her mind would play a trick on her and send her into the sort of panic she used to experience whenever something reminded her too closely of that terrible night at Lady Northcotte's Regatta.

She wondered how Frederick was faring this morning. He had his own reasons to be wary of the marriage altar, along with an unfortunate tendency to turn his fretting inward rather than accepting support from those around him. Happily, he would be surrounded by several people who knew him as well as he knew himself—or perhaps even *better* than he knew himself.

Just as she currently was.

The horses' hooves ate up the miles separating Ockley from London, mud splattering against the sides of the vehicle. Toward the end of their journey, the wind slackened and the rain tapered off to a mere drizzle.

Cassandra tried for the thousandth time to picture in her mind what the future might look like. For the thousandth time, she failed. It was ridiculous—that future lay mere hours away. And yet, even now, she couldn't quite bring herself to trust in it. The part of her that had seen the worst happen over and over again whispered that this was too good to be true... that something could still go wrong.

Cassandra, how could I not want that life? Frederick had said, when she'd finally pushed him to reveal his true feelings about the prospect of marriage and children. *It sounds like a perfect, unattainable dream.*

And that was the crux of the matter, was it not? Living in safety and comfort with three men who loved her—it sounded like a dream. Children. A family. The freedom to think and feel and live as she pleased in a grand old country manor house. How could someone like her possibly have such a life?

She had always been the broken one. The ruined one. The one that no one wanted, unless they could use her for their own ends somehow. Abruptly, emotion overcame her. A choked, gulping sob lodged in her throat. Three pairs of eyes flew to her, looking worried.

She shook her head quickly. "It's all right," she managed. "I'm all right."

"You're panicking," Frances said, seeing right through her pretense. "But there's no time for that. We're almost to the church."

"Don't you dare cry now—you'll smear that rouge I worked so hard on," Sadie said, without a trace of sympathy.

Mary's smile was full of understanding. She reached across the gap between the seats and scooped up Cassandra's hand with fingers that had once been weak and paralyzed by injury. "It's all right," she said. "Sometimes things work out exactly the way they're meant to, you know."

That quiet proclamation didn't help much when it came to the prospect of tears, but Cassandra blinked rapidly for a few moments and managed to keep them at bay.

The coach rolled to a halt. Outside, the sun had found a gap in the clouds, illuminating Hanover Square in all its late-summer glory. St. George's rose above them, Corinthian columns gleaming as brilliant sunlight hit the wet stone. A second coach with Rotherdam's familiar crest stood nearby, as did a handful of other coaches and phaetons.

With a deep breath, she made a concerted effort to tamp down her galloping nervousness.

"Come on," Frances said. "It looks as though the others are already waiting inside."

Cassandra cringed inwardly, wishing they'd been just a bit quicker to leave that morning. The idea of Frederick standing alone at the altar, waiting for her and wondering if she would come at all, had her throwing open the coach door. She leapt down, heedless of the puddles beneath her slippered feet. The others followed.

Frances spoke quietly with the attendant inside the church doors. The man gave Cassandra a wary look, probably wondering if Lord Rotherdam's notorious practice of devil worship had rubbed off on her yet. Nevertheless, he led the four of them deeper into the church, past the vestibule and into the echoing nave.

They walked down the central aisle toward the chancel at the far end. There, a small party awaited them. It included several men in finely tailored clothing, along with a churchman wearing an exceedingly sour expression. Cassandra's heart skipped and stuttered as she recognized the three figures gathered in the middle of the little group. Russet hair on one side, and short black curls over rich, dark skin on the other — both of them flanking a blond head.

Her three men, waiting for her at the altar.

Frederick's shoulders were a tense line, but his posture relaxed fractionally as he looked up and saw her. Instantly, all of her worries over reliving the horrible sham marriage Malthorpe had forced on her drained away. She rushed toward them, leaving her retinue behind. Frederick caught her hands in his sword-callused ones, while Robert caught her gaze with his hazel eyes. She tore her attention away to look at Edmund, who winked at her.

"I'm here," she told Frederick, the words as breathless as they were unnecessary.

The faintest hint of a smile tugged at one corner of his lips. "So you are."

She smiled back helplessly, becoming aware of William Fortescue and Lawrence Vaughan also standing nearby. The young Lord Malthorpe was also present. He dipped his chin to her in acknowledgement, and she smiled tremulously back. There were a few other people in the pews, though they were not faces she recognized.

They hadn't advertised the wedding at all. Frederick had purchased a common license for the marriage, eliminating the necessity of the banns being read. Nonetheless, the presence of Lord Rotherdam's coach at a London church could well have drawn the attention of a few curious people hoping to lay claim to some juicy gossip. If so, they were about to be in luck.

Cassandra wasn't fool enough to believe this marriage would stay secret. On the contrary, it would be all over the broadsheets by the following day. By that time, however, she would be safely ensconced in Hengewick House. London society could titter and speculate all it liked, far removed from her presence.

"Is everything in order?" the clergyman asked, looking as though he'd just swallowed something bitter.

"Indeed it is, Rector," Frederick said, not looking away from Cassandra.

She fell into those blue eyes, feeling exposed in the public venue, yet also protected by the presence of this strange little group she'd come to think of as family. They surrounded her, blocking out the disapproving world beyond.

"In that case, let us begin," said the rector, still sounding less than pleased. "Dearly beloved — we have come together in the presence of God to witness and bless the joining together of this man and this woman in Holy Matrimony…"

The words faded into a meaningless background buzz as Cassandra stared into the eyes of the man who had exercised his money and influence to ensure Cassandra might finally have the kind of life she'd never truly believed could be hers.

Frederick's expression made her think he shared her secret fear that everything might somehow crumble to dust at the eleventh hour. His hands around hers were shaking. She squeezed his fingers tightly and tried to be brave enough for both of them — viscerally aware of Robert and Edmund's supportive presence nearby.

The rector seemed to take an age to get through the form of the thing, until finally he turned his attention to Cassandra. "Lady Cassandra Pembroke, Baroness Malthorpe, will you have this man to be your husband; to live together in the covenant of marriage? Will you love him, comfort him, honor and keep him, in sickness and in health—and, forsaking all others, be faithful to him as long as you both shall live?"

She swallowed the faintly hysterical laugh that wanted to escape. Would she be faithful to him? Yes, she would... but only within the unconventional arrangement that the four of them had already forged.

"I will," she replied solemnly, hoping Frederick would be able to see the mischievous twinkle in her eye.

"Frederick Ashbury, Lord Rotherdam, will you have this woman to be your wife; to live together in the covenant of marriage? Will you love her, comfort her, honor and keep her, in sickness and in health—and, forsaking all others, be faithful to her as long as you both shall live?"

Frederick's expression was wry as he answered in kind. "I will."

The two of them smiled at each other in perfect understanding, sealing the conspiracy without a word being said.

The official turned to address the small gathering. "Will all of you witnessing these promises do all in your power to uphold these two persons in their marriage?"

"We will," the onlookers replied in an uneven chorus.

Edmund's voice was audible over the others, strong and deep. Cassandra couldn't help thinking that the tone he was using sounded as much like a threat as a promise. If either she or Frederick let their many scars and insecurities threaten the family they were building today, both Edmund and

Robert would be ready and waiting to administer a swift kicking as needed.

The rest of the ceremony dragged on. Finally, after numerous prayers were offered up, rings were exchanged, and blessings dispensed with an obvious lack of enthusiasm on the part of the rector, he sighed and concluded, "Now that Frederick and Cassandra have given themselves to each other by solemn vows, with the joining of hands and the giving and receiving of a ring, I pronounce that they are husband and wife, in the Name of the Father, and of the Son, and of the Holy Spirit. Those whom God has joined, together let no one put asunder."

More prayers and exhortations followed, but Cassandra couldn't hear them past the pounding of her heart in her ears. She did vaguely register the lack of an offer of the Eucharist, presumably because the presiding official feared that one or both of them would burst into flames should the bread or wine touch their lips.

Still looking as sour as when he'd begun the ceremony, the rector gestured toward the side of the chancel. "Now, if you would please come this way and sign the registry."

Cassandra walked next to Frederick in a daze, leaning over and signing the book immediately after he did. Next came the marriage lines, and just like that... she was married. Truly married, this time. She looked at the gold band on her finger and felt suddenly rather faint.

A strong hand closed around hers, fingers tangling. Frederick's grip had trembled earlier—

but now that the deed was done, it was firm and reassuring.

"Thank you, Father Andrews," he said. "We'll take ourselves off and trouble you no more."

Father Andrews harrumphed. "I should think that would be for the best, yes. I'll see that your donation is put to good use, Lord Rotherdam. Good day."

Cassandra wondered idly how much it had cost Frederick to arrange the ceremony. Perhaps she would ask him later. For now, she focused on staying upright and accepting the embraces and congratulations from her friends, her stomach fluttering frantically the whole time. Within minutes, the small wedding party exited the massive church, watched by a growing group of whispering onlookers.

Rather than returning to the coach in which she'd arrived, she allowed Frederick to usher her into his coach. He seated himself next to her, looking very nearly as dazed as she felt. Edmund helped Robert in and followed him up, closing the door once they were all settled. He tapped the roof, and a moment later, the coach lurched into motion.

Wide-eyed, Cassandra looked between the three men. "We did it?" she asked hoarsely. "It's really done?"

Robert scooted forward and leaned across the gap, covering her hand where it lay on her lap. "It's done, Cassandra."

With a great, heaving breath, Cassandra fell forward into his arms, reaching out blindly for the others. Instantly, she was surrounded by her lovers, their arms around her, holding her close.

"I believe we've just made a new family... Lady Rotherdam," Frederick murmured against her hair, as the coach rattled toward Hengewick House.

Her home.

Her family... to love, comfort, and honor, in sickness and in health, for as long as they all should live.

FORTY-ONE

A CELEBRATION WAS raging in the great hall when Frederick escorted Cassandra inside Hengewick House. Their driver must have taken his time to ensure the others made it back before them, because the merriment already appeared to be in full swing.

Drink was flowing. A string quartet set up in one corner played a lively tune, and laughter echoed around the huge chamber. Several heads turned as they entered, and a ragged cheer went up.

To say that Cassandra had recovered her composure during the course of the journey would have been overstating matters considerably. She almost certainly looked rumpled and red-eyed after spending much of the trip curled up in the others' arms. Her emotions were still surging to and fro, largely out of her control... and the most glorious part was, *it didn't matter*.

What could anyone here say that would in any way affect her life, going forward? *The new Lady Rotherdam appeared flighty after returning from the wedding ceremony London*? What of it? She was still married. She was still a viscountess. She was still loved by three wonderful men. Let people talk about her messy hair and splotchy cheeks if they wanted to.

Besides, they might not want to. There were people here whom Cassandra didn't recognize, but she doubted they would be present in Hengewick House at all if they hadn't first met with Frederick's direct approval.

"Is your Hellfire Club larger than I've been led to believe?" she asked, glancing up at Frederick.

"It encompasses more than half a dozen people, yes." He frowned thoughtfully. "Most of the group is a bit more loosely knit. Why? Did no one mention that?"

A breath of laughter escaped her throat. "Not as such, no. That's wonderful, though. Introduce me?"

Edmund laughed aloud. "Glutton for punishment, eh? Come on, then. Let's go make the rounds."

In a daze, Cassandra exchanged pleasantries with artists and philosophers, writers and astronomers, composers and adherents of the new sciences. *I am surrounded by extraordinary people*, Frederick had told her once... and it turned out that she hadn't known the half of it. She found the young Lord Malthorpe speaking animatedly with Lawrence Vaughan and an older woman she hadn't met before, who was apparently a vocal advocate for judicial reform.

Lord Malthorpe broke off his conversation when he saw her, waiting until the introductions were made before regarding Cassandra with genuine fondness. "Lord and Lady Rotherdam," he greeted. "Please allow me to once again offer my most heartfelt congratulations on your union."

The evening went on in roughly the same vein, warmth burgeoning in Cassandra's chest as she took in this gathering of passionate, exceptional people who'd come together to celebrate her marriage. Across the hall, Frances Hunter let out an unladylike shout of laughter and draped her arm across Mary's shoulders, leaning into her. There were others who appeared to Cassandra's educated eye to be together—men with women, women with women, men with men... even one trio that included an individual whose gender she couldn't easily determine.

And no one cared.

A few of the people here knew exactly what secret Cassandra's marriage to Frederick concealed. Others didn't, and in the end, it made not a whit of difference. She had at one point expressed a desire to dance on Cecil Pembroke's metaphorical grave. That desire had waned over time... but if Pembroke's sweet and highly intelligent nephew ended up as part of Frederick's heretical gathering of atheistic free thinkers, it would indeed be the sweetest sort of revenge she could imagine.

As the evening progressed, drinking and chatting progressed to dancing. Flushed and giggling, Cassandra engaged in quadrilles and cotillions, country dances, and even a terribly scandalous waltz, once Frederick showed her the steps. After perhaps an hour, she pled exhaustion and escaped the dance floor to regain her breath. A drink appeared in her hand as though by magic, and she turned to smile at Robert, who had approached in his silent servant's manner.

"Where's Edmund?" she asked quietly, after scanning the room and seeing no sign of him.

"Upstairs," he replied in the same low tones. "And if you'd like to feign a swoon or something, perhaps we could join him."

His expression held the devilish glint it sometimes got when they were alone and contemplating bad behavior. That glint had, as time went on, developed a direct connection to the place low in her belly that frequently ached and throbbed for him.

"I'm certain Frederick and I could simply excuse ourselves without the need for drama," she teased. "No doubt everyone here would understand."

"Cassandra," Robert chided, every bit as teasing. "This is a *Hellfire Club*. These people *adore* drama."

She could barely contain the ridiculous smile that wanted to break free. "Oh, well in that case…" Wavering on her feet, she lifted one hand to rest against her forehead with as much dramatic flair as she could muster. "Oh, dear me," she said, too loudly. "I feel so terribly hot all of a sudden!"

Robert took her arm. "My lord?" he called. "I believe Lady Rotherdam is feeling unwell."

Frederick was at her side in seconds. "Cassandra?"

She winked at him, quickly enough that only someone watching very carefully would see it. "Frederick, my dear — forgive me. I fear I have perhaps overindulged tonight. Would you be so kind as to help me upstairs?"

Blue eyes darkened, one corner of his lips twitching into a betraying smile before he controlled the expression. "Of course, my love," he said, before turning to the room at large. "Please continue to enjoy yourselves, my friends. My wife and I must excuse ourselves now. It's been rather a long day."

With that, he swept Cassandra into his arms— holding her bridal style, appropriately enough. She squeaked in surprise and threw her arms around his neck, laughing.

"Barlow, would you go ahead and ensure the room has been readied?" Frederick asked, amusement shining through the words.

"Of course, my lord," Robert replied, demure as ever.

"Good night, everyone," Frederick said, and a round of ribald cheers followed them all the way to the central staircase leading up to the second and third floors.

Cassandra laughed breathlessly and clung, her eyes locked on Robert's hitching gait as he led the way to what she assumed would be the master bedroom.

"I swear, the pair of you are utterly shameless," Frederick murmured, not sounding too put out about it. Cassandra pressed a kiss to the corner of his jaw as giddy happiness flooded her.

The viscount's private chambers were located on the second floor, in the opposite wing from the guest room where Cassandra had previously stayed. The space was decorated with a distinctly masculine flair, the furniture upholstered in dark red leather. Heavy bookcases filled with equally weighty tomes adorned two of the four walls.

Robert held the door open, and Frederick eased Cassandra through sideways, careful not to let her body bump the frame.

"I hope you don't mind spending the night here," he said, as Robert closed and locked the door behind them. "I had thought perhaps we could have one of the spare rooms done up specifically for private orgies. But for now, my suite still boasts the largest bed in the house."

"Yes, it's ridiculously large," confirmed a familiar voice from the next room. "One might almost say ludicrously so. It's also feeling decidedly empty right now, so stop nattering and get your noble arses in here."

Robert chuckled. Frederick snorted and squeezed them through the interior doorway leading to his bedroom. In truth, Cassandra had come to love this room over her year of clandestine visits. It, too, was done up in dark shades and rich oak paneling. The place always smelled of sandalwood and leather, but tonight, a profusion of red roses in vases covered what seemed like every available surface.

She gasped, the sweet scent filling her nostrils. Frederick tossed her gently onto the bed, where Edmund reclined naked except for the coverlet thrown across his lap as a halfhearted nod to modesty.

"Good lord, woman," Edmund said, as she rolled over and rested against his chest. "You look thoroughly debauched already, and we haven't even started yet." He brushed a lock of her hair back, hooking it over her ear. "How are you tonight, Cassandra?"

She gave him a wide-eyed look of innocence, fluttering her lashes at him outrageously. "I swooned during the party."

He stared at her for a blank moment before bursting into deep-throated laughter. "You *did not.*"

"Well, all right," she allowed. "I *pretended* to swoon. It got us all up here, didn't it?"

"That it did," he said, with clear appreciation. "And now that we're here, I assume the wedding-night deflowering is finally ready to commence?"

"God, I hope so," she said, slithering out of his loose embrace and regaining her feet next to the bed. "Robert—*help.* Three of us have too many clothes on. That's your job, isn't it?"

"One aspect of it, certainly," Robert agreed, coming up behind her and starting on the myriad pins holding her complicated hairstyle in place.

"Bloody useless, the lot of you," Edmund teased. "It's as though you don't even know how to sneak away from a party without raising an almighty ruckus about it first."

With his valet otherwise engaged, Frederick started untying his cravat. "Perhaps you'll give us lessons." His tone was wry. "Are we all agreed on what we discussed earlier? Cassandra?"

Cassandra recalled herself from the lovely feeling of Robert's hands in her hair. "Hmm? Oh, yes. Absolutely. And Frances informs me that I probably won't bleed or experience any pain, since we've already, er… *opened the way,* so to speak."

"I shouldn't think so," Edmund said. "But if she's wrong and you feel any discomfort, say something so we know to slow down."

"I will," she promised. "But, Robert? What about you?"

Robert's nimble fingers had succeeded in freeing her hair, which now hung loosely over her right shoulder in a tumbled mass of ringlets. He moved to attack the row of buttons at the back of her dress, and she shivered deliciously at his light touch.

"As long as you're entirely certain you're both all right with this," he said quietly. "I want to make it very clear indeed that I'm happy to refrain from this particular activity until after Cassandra is already pregnant. I would understand if you preferred to ensure that the Rotherdam heir is, in fact, the Rotherdam heir."

Cassandra met Frederick's eyes and held them. He gave a small nod of understanding in return.

"That's not necessary, Robert," he said. "I, for one, don't give a fig for the parentage of the next viscount Rotherdam. I meant what I said. All children conceived within this marriage are legitimate, and will be treated as such as long as I draw breath." He caught Robert's gaze over Cassandra's shoulder. "It would be my greatest honor to raise your child as my own, and see him or her grow up to represent this family." His blue eyes moved to Edmund. "I hope you realize that goes for both of you."

Edmund was silent for long enough that Cassandra turned to him.

"I hear you, Rotherdam," he said, scrubbing a hand over his black curls. "I do, truly. But I need some more time to think about it. I've a supply of lamb's gut quondams, Cassandra, and if you're truly set on having all three of us tonight, I'll happily oblige. I'd like to go last, though — since you know I'm happy to play voyeur and finish myself off, in case you're too tired to go on when these two have finished with you."

Robert slipped Cassandra's dress over her arms. The fabric slid down to pool at her ankles, leaving her in only her corset.

"I don't want you to be uncomfortable with what we're doing, Edmund," she said in concern.

He shook his head. "I'm not, beloved, truly. I just want to think on it more. If you give birth to a russet-haired son, it's just a matter of saying, 'oh, look, he's the spitting image of Great Uncle So-and-So.' Who's to say different? But a dark-skinned infant? That's obvious to anyone with eyes. You may not care, but I need time to think about whether it would be fair to the child."

Cassandra hated it... but she also couldn't refute Edmund's words.

"I understand," she said, unable to keep the sadness from her voice.

"Ah, please don't sound like that, Cassandra," he told her. "Like Robert said, I'll have you often and joyfully, without a quondam in sight — just as soon as you're with child. And in the meantime, a number of unlucky sheep have helpfully donated their intestines to ensure it won't be a problem while I'm deciding."

"I can't help thinking it's a good thing you're a painter and not a poet," Robert observed, making quick work of her remaining laces. "Are dead sheep really an appropriate topic for a wedding night?"

The light pressure around Cassandra's waist and ribcage eased, her loosened corset joining the rest of her clothing on the floor. She turned, naked as the day she'd been born, and kissed Robert on the lips.

"Thank you," she said. "I'd offer to return the favor, but I think I have to go kiss Edmund now."

Robert let out an amused breath and gave her another peck on the lips before turning to the room's other occupant. "I believe we've been temporarily abandoned, my lord," he said. "Perhaps you could assist me?"

Frederick gave him a roguish smile. "I'm sure that between us, we can muddle along somehow."

Cassandra returned to the bed and straddled Edmund's lean waist shamelessly, resting her hands on his shoulders to kiss him. He kissed like he did everything else — deliberately and wholeheartedly. Any attack of nerves she might have been expecting fled beneath the overwhelming flood of rightness at being here, in this room with these men, as she was always meant to be.

Edmund grasped her hips and pushed her back a few inches, so his hard cockstand nestled between her buttocks. It was reminiscent of all the other times over the last few months when she'd had them *so close* to where she really needed them… but not quite there. Even with quondams, they had opted not to risk that sort of intercourse until her mourning period was complete, and Frederick had put a ring on her finger.

Perhaps it had been the right decision, or perhaps it had been an unnecessary precaution. Whatever the case, she was a married woman now, and tonight she would finally have them in the way she wanted them. Edmund's lips plundered hers until she wasn't certain which way was up and which was down. This uncertainty was further compounded when Edmund flipped her neatly onto her back, still kissing her. The mattress dipped twice, signaling the others' arrival on the scene.

Hands slid over her skin. One stroked her breasts. Another clasped her ankle and urged her legs apart. Lips brushed her anklebone… her calf… the inside of her knee. She gasped into Edmund's kiss as whoever was between her legs trailed fingertips and mouth up the length of her inner thigh, not stopping until they found the treasure hidden at the top.

She was wet — already slick for them after only a few moments of kissing and touching. Fingers entered her passage, sliding in without resistance. Edmund swallowed her moan as her anonymous tormenter closed lips around her tender bud, teasing it with light flicks of his tongue.

Cassandra's muscles trembled with strain, pleasure coiling and retreating, coiling and retreating as her three lovers teased her toward a peak. She needed to touch them, her hands reaching out blindly. One landed in long hair, tangling in Robert's silky strands as he lay cradled between her legs. The other encountered someone's fingers and clasped tight.

Robert exhaled harshly against her folds as she tugged at his scalp in silent demand. He nipped lightly at her outer lips and attacked her nub again, licking and sucking as his fingers curled inside her. Someone — *Frederick*? — thumbed her nipple. Edmund licked into her mouth, the slow strokes of his tongue echoing Robert's movements below.

Ecstasy coiled, settling in her belly as though she might stay balanced on the knife-edge of release for the rest of time. The feeling was sinfully addicting, but ultimately unsustainable. The wave inevitably took her, washing her out to sea, and she couldn't stop the muffled cry that escaped into Edmund's kiss. Sensation narrowed down to the points of connection between the four of them as her body shuddered out its first climax.

They eased her through it until she collapsed backward, panting and spent. Robert crawled up the length of her body, the others making room for him as he rested his hands on either side of her shoulders, caging her beneath him. His dark hair fell around her like a curtain, as he leaned down to catch her lips in a kiss flavored with her own essence.

"Now?" he breathed against her lips, his hard prick brushing her oversensitive folds.

"Now," she said with a gasp, needing him inside her body like she needed air.

It was pure instinct to arch her hips, lining him up at her entrance. The blunt tip of his member nudged at her, first gently, and then with more insistence.

"You are beautiful, inside and out," Robert whispered.

Frederick stroked her forehead with the backs of his fingers. "Our Persephone, abducted from the mortal world to rule our underworld."

The stiff prick at her entrance pushed inside, and she moaned at the feel of it.

FORTY-TWO

CASSANDRA PANTED as her body stretched around Robert's girth, accepting him into her. It burned — not in a bad way, precisely, but rather with a sort of aching fullness that made things inside her flutter and grasp.

He remained perfectly still for long moments, poised above her. She didn't even think he was breathing. Only when she wriggled beneath him, trying to get him deeper, did he finally move. His hips rolled in shallow thrusts, advancing and retreating by minute degrees until finally, *finally*, he was fully sheathed inside her.

"Oh," she said, in the tone of a revelation. "*Oh*. Robert, please... please... I need..."

In truth, she wasn't certain *what* she needed. Robert leaned down and kissed her, slowly and thoroughly. When he pulled away, she felt as though the world might spin away from her grasp entirely.

"I know," he said softly. "I won't last long, though. I'm sorry."

"Honestly, Hermes — that may end up being a blessing tonight," Edmund observed, sounding amused. "There are three of us, after all."

Cassandra turned her head to look at him, and found him reclined against the headboard next to her with his hand sliding lazily up and down his prick. She opened her mouth in hopes that something witty would emerge, but Robert chose that moment to start moving in earnest. All that came out was a low, wordless moan.

It felt so... *right*. She wasn't at all certain she'd be able to climax from this full, warm feeling alone—but she also didn't feel as though that was the point. In twenty-three years, Cassandra had never felt this close to another human being. She arched her hips into the steady rocking motion, matching Robert's tempo and listening to his breath stutter. Her legs wrapped around his hips, urging him deeper and faster.

"*Cassandra*," he breathed, burying his face against her neck as his hips snapped into her.

"Yes," she whimpered, as his rhythm faltered, growing ragged. "*Yes.*"

He let out a tortured sound and broke, his muscles jerking as he spent inside her. She wrapped him up tight in her embrace, holding him as he came down, her blood singing in her ears. Eventually, he disengaged from her body, his softening member slipping free as he rolled sideways into the space Edmund had made for him on the wide bed.

His absence left her feeling unpleasantly empty.

Frederick leaned over and stroked sweaty hair from her forehead. "More?" he asked.

She nodded, too breathless for words.

"Let her ride you while she touches herself," Edmund suggested.

"Would you like that?" Frederick asked.

Rather than nod again, she gathered her strength and lifted a hand to his shoulder, pressing him onto his back on the bed as she rolled upright. The movement centered her attention on the feeling of Robert's release inside her passage. A fresh thrum of excitement shivered down her spine at the visceral realization that his *seed* was in her *body*. It might not happen tonight, or this week, or this month — but someday soon, they were going to make the children that she'd feared she'd never be able to have.

Edmund had said *ride*, and that seemed rather self-explanatory. Frederick had rolled onto his back without resistance beneath her touch, and now lay with his head pillowed on his clasped hands. The position showed off the lean lines of his torso in a way she found incredibly pleasing. She climbed astride his hips — despite the shakiness of her thighs — and sat poised above him.

"May I?" she asked, reaching awkwardly beneath herself to take his stand in a light grip and line him up.

Frederick's smile was very nearly feline in its smugness. "Oh, liberty hall, Lady Rotherdam. Liberty hall. I am entirely at your disposal, I assure you."

When she slid carefully down his thick length, however, his smile fell away, replaced by a look of scorching blue-eyed intensity. It felt different in this position than it had with Robert on top of her. Cassandra liked it. There was a sense of control — of *possession* — that spoke to some deep part of her soul. She had become a hunting tigress, and she would have what she desired.

Despite the faintest hint of soreness between her legs, she began to move. It really was like riding astride, and within seconds she'd forgotten all about the slight burn of discomfort. Frederick's hands grasped her hips, suggesting an easy pace. Next to her, Robert had rolled onto his stomach and was watching them with hooded hazel eyes, his chin resting on his hands. On Robert's far side, Edmund watched with heat in his dark eyes, still fisting his stiff length with lazy strokes.

"Lean back, Cassandra," Edmund said. "Touch yourself. Make yourself come."

Lips parted, Cassandra arched her back, changing the angle of the fullness and movement inside her. And, *oh*, that was good. That was very good indeed.

A wordless noise slipped from her throat. She delved two fingers into her folds above the place where she and Frederick were joined, circling the slick, sensitive nub.

"Heavens, that feels *divine*." Her voice didn't sound like her. It was a low purr, throaty with pleasure.

"That it does," Frederick agreed, still lifting and lowering her hips in a steady rhythm. "Touch your breasts, too."

The support of his hands helped maintain her balance, so she hummed and moved her free hand to her left nipple. She squeezed it and rolled the taut bud between her fingers, other hand still teasing between her legs. The sensations grew unbearable within mere moments, and just like that, she was convulsing again. Her passage clenched rhythmically around Frederick's shaft, dragging a groan from him as he followed her into bliss.

When they'd both recovered, he eased her down to lie sprawled across his chest, nuzzling against his neck.

"I sure do like the look of that," Edmund rumbled, and Cassandra almost laughed aloud at the thought of him trying to paint the two of them like this.

"Lovely," Robert agreed, his voice sounding dreamy and half-asleep.

"Perfect," Frederick murmured against her hair.

They lay together for a few minutes until Frederick's softening member slipped out of her. Cassandra could feel his and Robert's combined seed dripping down the inside of her thigh. She wondered idly if there were some way to keep it all inside, so it might make a baby faster.

For now, though, she had another, more important concern.

"Edmund, you're too far away," she said.

"Not so far as all that," he said, amused. "Are you certain you're not too tired? Too sore?"

"Too tired for you?" she asked in disbelief. "*Never*. And I can be sore tomorrow. Tonight, I want you all."

"Tonight, you get whatever you want, Persephone," he told her. "So, apparently I'm not allowed to talk about dead sheep again, but give me a moment here."

She watched sleepily as he reached for the little table next to the bed and retrieved something. He rolled a thin, pale tube down his engorged length and secured it at the base with a bit of ribbon.

"What an odd thing," she said. "I wonder who originally thought of that idea?"

"Someone who really, *really* didn't want to get someone else pregnant," Robert suggested.

"Or who really, really didn't want to get the pox," Edmund retorted.

"If discussion of dead sheep is off the table, perhaps discussion of syphilis should be as well," Frederick suggested. "Good lord, Edmund — and you accuse *me* of a lack of tact."

Cassandra hid her chuckle against his neck, though her shaking shoulders probably gave her away.

"Everyone's a critic," Edmund said. He rose from the bed and circled around, rather than attempting to climb over Robert to get to her. "Here, now. Let's have you, Persephone, before I give into the temptation to thump your husband over the head."

He and Frederick helped her dismount and kneel on the edge of the bed — much as she'd done for Edmund during the so-called Autumnal Rites, when he'd fucked her between her thighs. She hummed as he dragged fingertips over her soaked folds, still dripping with the others' seed.

"Good thing Robert arranged for a bath to be waiting, eh, beautiful?" he asked, a smile audible in his tone.

"He did? Robert, I love you," Cassandra said. "You're my favorite."

Robert chuckled.

"Oh, is he now?" Edmund asked, squaring up behind her and rubbing the tip of his sheathed prick over her entrance. "We'll just have to see about that."

Anything she might have said in reply died in her throat as Edmund pressed inside her with a single, smooth stroke. Her mouth opened soundlessly, her upper body sagging over Frederick's stomach. He reached down and ran his fingers through her tangled mass of hair, smoothing the sweaty strands.

"Still want to be sore tomorrow?" Edmund asked, running his artist's fingers over her buttock teasingly.

"*Yes*," she gasped, and grabbed fistfuls of the coverlet as Edmund pulled back and snapped his hips forward, filling her aching passage with a slap of flesh against flesh.

In no time, he was setting a pace just this side of brutal, wringing sharp little cries of encouragement from her with every thrust.

"Look at you," he said, leaning over her back to get a better angle. "And to think, you thought you were already ruined when you first met us."

"Didn't... know... any... better!" she managed between gasps, feeling something huge and bottomless opening up inside her.

With each stroke, he pounded against the place on the front of her passage that Frederick's cock had only teased earlier, and it was unraveling her piece by piece.

"Oh God... don't stop... don't stop..." she begged.

"I have no intention of stopping, my beautiful Greek goddess," he said, as he continued to dismantle her from the inside out. "Not until I feel you come around me so hard you forget your own name."

He wasn't going to stop... wasn't going to ease off, and she was *losing her mind*. Time was meaningless; she had no idea how long he'd been at it when the bottom dropped out of her awareness, dumping her into the endless depths of her pleasure. It shook her from the roots of her hair to the tips of her toes. A piercing shriek echoed around the room, and... oh, dear... that had probably come from her, hadn't it?

She was gushing. Spurting. Drowning.

And she never wanted it to end.

But of course, nothing that good could last forever. Her body was a distant and heavy thing. Around her, the others were moving. She was being kissed and stroked, lifted and carried. Strong arms deposited her in a generously sized tub of warm water, turning her already limp muscles into useless liquid. Hands ran a washrag over her skin, soaping and rinsing her. Water poured over her sweaty hair. Fingers massaged lather into her scalp, followed by more water sluicing over her.

She was only halfway aware by the time she was dried with towels and returned to the huge bed. Sleep took her for some time. When she woke, she lay sheltered among warm, naked bodies. The fire had burned low, its orange glow casting flickering shadows. Quiet voices conversed in relaxed tones, soothing in their familiarity.

She stretched, yawning widely.

"What are we talking about?" she asked, still mostly asleep.

"Edmund and Robert are debating whether to submit *Hermes Lamed* to the Royal Academy again next year, or try with a different painting," Frederick said.

"I'm not certain why you want me to submit *anything* next year," Edmund grumbled, "since they've already turned me down."

"It's competitive," Robert said. "Just because the judges this year were idiots doesn't mean they won't see sense next year, or the year after that."

"What he said," Cassandra mumbled against Frederick's chest, as her sole contribution to the debate.

She let their words flow over her, enjoying the utter relaxation of lying in bed with them, sated, warm, and safe. Her mind drifted, sifting through the past... idly examining the many events that had led her to this point.

Time passed in pleasant lassitude. She wasn't sleeping, but she clearly hadn't been listening, either, because Edmund's "... Cassandra?" sounded like it wasn't the first time he'd said her name.

"Hmm?" she asked.

"You're miles away," Frederick said. "Is everything all right?"

She blinked the room into focus, lifting her head to look at them. "Oh, yes... merely woolgathering, sorry." She laced her fingers together on Frederick's chest and rested her chin on them. "Honestly? I was thinking about my Tom. In reality, I'm sure he'd be shocked beyond all speech if he could somehow see me now. And yet, a part of me can't help thinking that he would have liked you all immensely."

Robert lay stretched out on Frederick's other side. He rolled onto an elbow, resting his head on his hand so he could meet her eyes. "Who's Tom?"

"Her first sweetheart," Edmund explained, saving her the trouble. "They were to be married — it was a love match."

Robert's brows drew together. "Oh? What happened?" He paused. "Or should I not ask?"

"No, it's all right," she told him, smiling. "It was years ago."

"Thomas Jacoby," Frederick said. "That was his name, wasn't it? He perished in the war."

Robert sat bolt upright. "*What*?"

Startled, Cassandra pushed into a sitting position as well. "Robert? What is it? What's wrong?"

"*Thomas Jacoby*? From Warnham?" he demanded. "Dark hair, gray eyes, about my height? You were *Thomas Jacoby's sweetheart*?"

Cassandra stared at him in shock. "Wait. You knew Tom?"

"We were in the same training regiment," Robert said faintly. "We bunked in the same barracks for months. He was always going on about the girl he was going to marry as soon as the war was over."

Her hand flew to her mouth.

"Good heavens," Edmund said. "What are the odds of that? Robert, please tell us you two got on. He didn't hate the sight of you or anything, did he?"

"No." Robert's tone was blank. "We used to play cards and talk about all the things we'd do when we got out of the army."

Frederick helped Cassandra slither over the top of him so she could fall into Robert's arms and cling.

"You know... there are times when being the head of a Hellfire Club is rather inconvenient," Frederick said. "For one thing, it means I'm not supposed to believe in fate."

Robert held Cassandra close, cradling her to his chest. "Maybe not, but perhaps one might make the occasional exception for extraordinary circumstances."

"Seconded," Edmund said.

"In this case," Frederick replied, "I'm not inclined to disagree."

His hand came to rest on her shoulder, and Edmund's covered her hip. Cassandra pressed her face into the crook of Robert's neck, and tried to decide if it was possible to laugh and cry at the same time.

EPILOGUE

Five years later

"EMMA! STOP chasing your brother at once!" Cassandra called, shooting a nasty look at Edmund when she caught him laughing silently from the corner of her eye.

"He started it!" Emma stamped her foot, sending her golden curls bouncing as the family's pair of spaniels yapped excitedly around her.

"Did not!" Brilliant sun illuminated the reddish highlights in four-year-old Thomas's dark hair as he lifted his chin stubbornly.

"*Children.*" Caroline, the governess, bustled out of the front door, cradling baby Richard in her arms. The tiny boy had managed to free one light brown fist from his swaddling and was waving it wildly to and fro. "Come inside, both of you. Your parents need to leave for their engagement, and it's time for lessons."

Thomas groaned theatrically, even as Emma's expression brightened.

"When we get back, we'll all go to the studio and paint for an hour," Edmund said. "*If* you're good while we're gone."

"Preferably not using the walls as a canvas this time," Frederick murmured, for Cassandra's ears alone. She choked, attempting with limited success to turn a laugh into a cough.

Edmund's promise of time in the art studio was enough to brighten Thomas's expression to match his younger sister's. The little boy darted in for a kiss on the cheek from his mother. "Hurry back, Mama!" he said, and dutifully followed Caroline into the manor house with his sister and baby brother.

Edmund watched them go, before turning an expression rife with uncertainty toward the waiting carriage. "I still don't see why we have to make such a fuss over this."

Robert, who had been stowing a basket of sandwiches for the trip, gave a long-suffering sigh. "Because it's the opening day of the Royal Academy's annual exhibition, and one of your paintings will finally be hanging on the wall, you clod."

It wasn't just any painting, either. After five years of trying, *Persephone's Abduction* had been the work that finally caught the Academy's eye. Five years ago, perhaps Cassandra would have had misgivings about traveling to a large gathering of the great and the good of London to view a painting that featured her naked breasts. Now, should anyone dare to say anything—which was frankly unlikely—Cassandra would merely raise an eyebrow and point out that the female subject of the painting had red hair, not blonde, and therefore it couldn't possibly be her, could it?

If there was one thing that years of marriage to a notorious rake had taught her, it was how to turn society's unwritten rules of politeness against them. It was rather a pity no one had thought to teach her that skill when she was a girl. Possessing it might have headed off all manner of unpleasantness.

Still, she couldn't bring herself to regret the unfortunate events of her youth. Those events had, after all, paved the road that ultimately led to this lovely spring day spent with her scandalously unconventional family.

"I don't believe I've ever been a patron of the arts before," Frederick mused, as he handed her into the carriage.

"You still aren't," Edmund said dryly, settling across from them. "*Patron* implies you paid for it."

"Well, I paid your salary, didn't I?" Frederick retorted, only the glint in his eye betraying the teasing. "Same thing, surely."

"Arse," Edmund muttered.

"I think it's wonderful," Robert said. "Edmund—you *will* go to this exhibition. You *will* mingle. And you *will* make professional connections with the other artists and collectors there."

The words '*or else*' went unsaid, but Cassandra heard them all the same.

"Yes, yes," Edmund said. "I shall be the picture of professional behavior and amiability."

In truth, he was as nervous as Cassandra had ever seen him—and tempting though it was, she knew any attempt on her part to reassure him would only put him even more on edge. Once they were all settled, the driver whipped up the team.

The carriage rolled off, heading down the winding drive toward the main road.

The four of them passed the journey in light conversation, letting Edmund slump in the corner of the seat unremarked. Cassandra had attended a few smaller exhibitions in the years since her marriage, but never at the Royal Academy. She was very much looking forward to seeing what the foremost authority on English art considered *avant garde* this year.

Among other pursuits, Cassandra had begun to branch out into oils under Edmund's tuition; though she suspected watercolors would always remain her first love. Cassandra had been thrilled to find a handful of other female artists among Frederick's extended circle of radicals, and had forged a number of new friendships.

"Did Frances write back to say if she and Mary could make it today?" she asked.

Frederick shook his head. "I received a terse note that included the sentence *'Some of us work for a living,'* along with a suggestion that we meet for dinner afterward so they can give Edmund their congratulations in person. I believe Will and Lawrence are planning on attending, though."

"They're just on the prowl for politicians and nobles to satirize in their pamphlets," Edmund said.

"Well, yes. Obviously," Frederick agreed, and Cassandra hid a smile.

"I'm certain they'll come up with something nice to say about your painting if you fish for compliments overtly enough," Robert offered, all innocence.

"They'd better, or next year I'll submit the one with the grapes and the homoerotic subtext," Edmund said.

It was a lovely day for a country drive, but eventually they entered the bustle of the city. The carriage made its way through increasingly heavy traffic to New Somerset House, joining a line of other carriages waiting to drop off or pick up people attending the exhibition. Cassandra, who had never had cause to visit the place before, took in the sprawling Neoclassical architecture situated on the south side of the Strand.

Eventually, their carriage pulled up to the entrance and they alighted, leaving instructions with the driver to pick them up at five o'clock sharp. They followed the crowd inside, going through to the main exhibition hall. As they entered echoing space, Cassandra caught her breath, unprepared for the sheer scale of it. The hall was huge, and every square inch of the walls had been hung with paintings of all sizes—right up to the carved frescoes beneath the domed ceiling. Natural light entered through glass windows set around the base of the dome, illuminating art of all description.

She wasn't the only one gaping at the display, but Frederick gently nudged her forward so they wouldn't be blocking the people behind them.

"My goodness," she said, the words wholly inadequate.

"Where's *Persephone* hanging?" Robert asked. "Do you know?"

"No idea," Edmund replied, so they started a slow circuit of the room with the other viewers.

"There," Frederick said when they'd turned to view the second wall. "Third row from the bottom, fourth from the right."

Cassandra followed his gaze and saw the painting, familiar and yet seen in a new light in this open, airy place full of art.

"That's a good location," she said. "Not too high up, and the light should reach it for most of the afternoon."

Indeed, Edmund's work seemed to be garnering a fair amount of attention from the other onlookers, with a knot of people in discussion over it.

"Go mingle," Robert said in a tone that brooked no argument. "We're not leaving until you have at least one paid commission, just so you know."

Edmund grumbled something, but he went to join the small group of men discussing his work. Frederick offered Cassandra his arm, and they continued their slow perambulation through the crowd.

As promised, Mr. Fortescue and Mr. Vaughan made an appearance about an hour into their visit — the pair easily identified from a distance by Mr. Fortescue's outrageous gold and apricot-striped waistcoat. The five of them chatted amiably for some time, shooting occasional glances at Edmund to make sure he didn't need rescuing.

Happily, now that he'd settled into talking about art with other art enthusiasts, his earlier discomfort seemed to have evaporated. Cassandra smiled as she saw him gesturing animatedly to make some point to the men he was with.

She and the others were making a second pass around the hall to return for closer inspection of the handful of paintings that had caught Cassandra's eye the first time around. She was examining the brushwork on a rather extraordinary still life when an unexpected — and unwelcome — female voice cut shrilly through the murmur of conversation.

"*Cassandra Fenwicke!*"

With a sinking feeling in her stomach, Cassandra turned slowly, just in time to see Aunt Lavinia dragging Uncle Henry through the crowd, heading straight for them.

"Oh, dear," said Mr. Fortescue. "That looks like trouble."

"My aunt and uncle," Cassandra said through clenched teeth. "I haven't seen them in years — nor would I wish to."

"I see. And is there any reason you need to acknowledge such rudeness?" Fortescue asked.

"No," Frederick answered for her. "No, there most certainly is not."

The truth of it hit her like a blow. "Good heavens. I suppose there really isn't, is there?" she said.

Several people had already turned to watch the prospect of gossip-worthy entertainment. Lavinia marched toward them with her husband in tow. Cassandra noted that he at least appeared to have fully recovered from whatever ailment had sickened him during the winter before her marriage, five years ago.

"Cassandra Fenwicke," Lavinia repeated sternly, "how dare you show your face in society with *that man*? As if you haven't brought shame enough on our family already!"

Beside her, Frederick eyed the pair with a frosty expression before very deliberately turning away and resuming his conversation with the others—delivering the cut direct. "My," he said to Fortescue, "it does seem to have become rather noisy in here, has it not?"

Lavinia's jaw dropped open. Cassandra continued to watch her, but did not reply to the open slight on her reputation.

Robert cleared his throat. "Forgive me," he said, with his usual mild and deferential manner. "Perhaps you've made a mistake. There's no one by that name here. Unless you are perhaps referring to the Viscountess Rotherdam?"

Lavinia looked between Cassandra, Robert, and Frederick in outrage. "Well, I never!" she snapped. "I didn't come here to be slighted in public! Come along, Henry!"

Red-faced, she turned and stormed off, once more dragging her husband behind her like an awkward valise, leaving muttered conversations in her wake.

"How terribly rude," Robert mused, as though to himself. "And to a peeress, no less."

"One wonders at the gall of some people," Lawrence Vaughan said blandly.

Several onlookers spoke up in agreement, and just like that, interest in the little drama waned as people returned to looking at the art. A few moments later, Edmund appeared at Cassandra's elbow.

"Everything all right?" he asked. "And was that who I think it was?"

"Yes and yes," Cassandra said, surprised to find that it was true. "I'm sorry—I hope my family drama didn't interrupt anything important."

"No, don't worry," he said. "As it happens, I've already received two offers for portrait commissions."

"That's wonderful!" Robert said.

Edmund looked faintly dazed. "It is, rather, isn't it?"

Fortescue slapped him on the shoulder. "It *definitely* is. Congratulations, old chap."

"Yes—congratulations, Edmund," Frederick echoed. "Does this mean I can finally start looking for a new private secretary who doesn't hate the job?"

Cassandra let out a soft snort.

"I suppose it does," Edmund said slowly. "At least, it does as long as you're resigned to also having a live-in artist in residence."

"Of course I am," Frederick replied. "I told you earlier—I'm a patron of the arts now."

Edmund's lips twitched. "And I told you that you're an arse. Are we still meeting Frances and Miss Stanhope for dinner?"

"We are indeed," Cassandra told him firmly. "Congratulations, Edmund. Though I hope you'll still have time for a family portrait as well."

His eyes crinkled at the corners. "Oh, I imagine I'll be able to squeeze you in somehow. Shall we go? We're going to lose the light soon anyway, and the driver should be back for us shortly."

Cassandra shared a brilliant smile equally between her three men, looking from dark eyes, to hazel, to summer blue. "Yes, let's go," she said. "Mr. Fortescue? Mr. Vaughan? Would you care to join us for a meal? We've got friends to see and good news to share."

"My dear Lady Rotherdam," Fortescue said, "that sounds absolutely divine. By all means, lead the way."

finis

For more books by this author, visit
www.rasteffan.com